IF TENDERNESS BE GOLD

by Eleanor Albanese

Library and Archives Canada Cataloguing in Publication

Title: If tenderness be gold / Eleanor Albanese.
Names: Albanese, Eleanor, 1957- author.
Identifiers: Canadiana 20200160109 | ISBN 9781988989174 (softcover)
Classification: LCC PS8551.L3765 I4 2020 | DDC C813/.54—dc23

Printed and bound in Canada on 100% recycled paper.

Cover Design: Kasandra Diane Henry
Author photo: Alan Dickson

Published by:
Latitude 46 Publishing
info@latitude46publishing.com
Latitude46publishing.com

We acknowledge the support of the Ontario Arts Council.

ONTARIO ARTS COUNCIL
CONSEIL DES ARTS DE L'ONTARIO
an Ontario government agency
un organisme du gouvernement de l'Ontario

IF TENDERNESS BE GOLD

by Eleanor Albanese

This novel is dedicated to my grandmother Lillian Morrow, my sister Monica Storozuk, and to all mothers who have lost a child.

CHAPTER ONE

Fiorella's Promise—Aspen Bluff, Manitoba, 1897

Mary:

When I first saw her, though she was across a field and barely a speck on the horizon, sure I knew she was one of my kind. As she made her way toward me, a rush of warm wind moved across the tips of the wild grasses. It was so quick; on another day, I might've missed it altogether. But that day, I noticed everything. As I held my young lad's hand, she glided across the field, and when she was a stone's throw away, she shouted, "You come for Fiorella?"

I smiled but didn't answer straight away. My mind was buzzing with the many warnings the townspeople had filled my ears with since my move to Aspen Bluff. I'd no sooner stepped on Canadian soil when I felt the air droning with gossip. The women pulled me aside in the general store to tell me Fiorella had been under suspicion of murder, warning me to stay away from "the Italian witch". But this smiling woman was no more a witch than I was a leprechaun. I'd told my husband that the Italian woman's well had run dry. This was a lie, but everyone—even a woman scorned by all—needed water, and no one could argue otherwise.

Dowsing was also the one thing that allowed me an afternoon to myself, or almost to myself as I'd brought along my youngest.

"I've come to see you, indeed," I said. Fiorella swept us into her house—if you could call it a house as it was more of a shack—where a simple table sat in the middle of the room with two rickety chairs on either end that looked as if they could barely hold the weight of a turnip apiece. There was a counter for chopping vegetables, shelves from floor to ceiling to hold foodstuffs, and a woven rug to soften the steps of the few who graced her tiny home.

My lad and I settled into her *bockety* chairs while Fiorella busied herself in the kitchen. A clothesline was stretched alongside the length of the woebegone house with dried herbs, flowers, and branches with berries dangling from it. While Fiorella reached up to snip off a bit of this and that, we quietly took in our surroundings. Within our reach, a jar of pink clover, devil's paintbrush, and goldenrod brightened up the faded blue tablecloth. Yellow pollen from the field flowers had drifted down, and with the mid-afternoon sun finding its way through the windowpane, for a second, I thought fool's gold had been sprinkled onto her tabletop. Fiorella's calico cat was curled up by the stove on a stuffed chair, keeping the home free of mice, although the creature didn't seem to put a dent in the numbers of spiders spinning webs underneath the table. Holy cards of the Blessed Virgin were tacked in every corner and alcove. 'Twas the picture of sweetness and, in an instant, I was glad we'd made our way up to the bluffs to discover Fiorella's tumbledown farm, her wild fields, and her cozy four walls.

Fiorella shooed the cat to the floor and, pushing the chair up close to the table, she sat with us. As she spoke in broken English, I could hardly keep myself from floating up to the roof. It was all in her eyes—chocolate brown with crow's feet from too many tears of sadness or laughter, and dark pupils that reflected an ocean of might back to me. No matter what others thought of her, that day, she found a friend in me. Fiorella told me that I was carrying a baby, but that wasn't news to me. She offered her help when the time came. If only she knew that time hardly existed for me anymore. Sure, the seasons marked time, as well as the ten lunar months I'd be with child. I wanted to explain to her how, in my three children, I saw the stamp of time as clear as the moon on a winter's night. I felt as if I'd left variation behind, though, somehow left it in my childhood where change was a fact of everyday life.

To be sure, life is not perfect for anyone. I married a man who has a great love of the bottle. James turns to whiskey for comfort as he can't find his way to soothing his wounds. And yes, he has wounds. As do I. As do I. The difference is, I am willing to put my hand to the plow, no matter the odds. And I take comfort wherever I can find it: a pipe under the stars, singing songs my mammy taught me, or slipping away to visit my Italian friend. Though Fiorella has the aging face of a crone, I now know she's not much more than a decade older than me—a burdensome decade of hardship, no doubt—a widow with her children grown and moved away. On first meeting, it didn't matter a pinch to me how weathered her face was, or how broken her English happened to be. I was as happy as a clam at high water.

"These are for you," I said, handing Fiorella three blue-tinged mother-of-pearl buttons that I'd slipped into my coat pocket before leaving home. She smiled. The buttons sang out *ting, ting, ting* as they found their way to the bottom of her teacup.

"You have long time, I think," she said.

"Since I was a girl. They were my mother's so."

As a young lass, I'd stolen a pair of scissors from an old man's shaving kit to get at the buttons. He'd already passed over so it wasn't quite stealing, but neither could you say I borrowed the scissors as you can't borrow what can't be returned. I began snipping buttons from coats and sweaters—mother-of-pearl, black glass, metal, leather, wood, and bone—even as my family lay sick and dying on the ship from Ireland. I kept one button for every person I lost, but from my mother, I kept all five, as I couldn't part with a single mother-of-pearl. Even though it was as dark as coal in the bowels of the ship, I held up one of her buttons, turning it this way and that until it caught a bit of light from somewhere, God only knows where. To my delight, it gleamed purple and blue and silvery white.

'Twas a coffin ship that carried us over to the new land. All ten siblings, as well as Mammy and Da and grandparents alike, made their graves of the salt water seas, overcome with typhus. I suppose taking their buttons was my way of fastening their souls to mine. With so many people dying from the fever, the boat was surely haunted. Once a poor soul died, if you wanted a button, you had to work fast. My mother's were the easiest. The round little buttons on her dress just popped off, hanging on by a thread. Her buttons were loose from my brother Frankie tugging on them trying to get milk. But if Frankie did get any milk, 'twas sour from all the tears she'd cried. Too many tears spoil the mother's milk. Everyone knows that. Now Da, he was a different story—dark steel buttons they were. Must've been sewn on with thread from the devil because there was no getting them off, not even with my stolen scissors. I had to use a blade from my father's shaving kit.

They promised us an hour of fresh air each day, but when the disease began to spread, we were to breathe the salt water air only when the priest blessed the body, just before it was tossed into the sea. I was worried that if the priest himself died, there'd be no holy water. And then the dead would be forever chained to the bottom of the sea, imprisoned in a watery purgatory.

The journey lasted nearly four weeks, and to survive a single day was a miracle. The air below was so foul, it's little wonder the rats didn't throw themselves overboard. I remember well the stench of it, and how we were half-starved. The dried biscuit bread could only be endured by dipping it in tea—tea that was steeped two, three, and four times, bitter and dark as rust. Once on the journey, I had the glory of tasting cheese. An old woman with black lace wrapped around her head called me over with a wave of her hand, pitying me as I'd only just lost my mother that morning. From her pocket she pulled out a small bit of linen, unwrapped it, all the while darting her eyes here and there to make sure not a soul was watching. Before I could ask her what it was, she popped it into my mouth, a sweet and creamy delight such as I've never tasted before or since.

Once we arrived, the ship docked at the East River pier in New York. Most of the crew and a handful of cabin passengers passed through American customs as easy as turning apples into sauce, but the rest of us waited on the ship another two days. The authorities were hemming and hawing about delivering us to customs at Ellis Island, afraid of the diseases we might carry. Before we disembarked, we were instructed to leave all of our possessions behind. Most of us had nothing but the clothes on our backs, but I did have my buttons, which I hid inside a square of cotton and fastened with a pin to my petticoat.

Finally, we were brought out into daylight. With women and children in one line, and men in the other, they filed us down a wooden plank and onto dry land. Children clung to whoever they could find, as some were orphaned. I was lucky to have a relation to claim me, my great auntie Helen. She was as crusty as week-old toast, but she was family. After being trapped in the bowels of the boat for weeks, I felt as if I'd stepped into a world of sparkling light. My legs felt wobbly, as if they might crumble beneath me. Holding onto Auntie Helen's firm hand, we were herded onto a barge and hauled over to Ellis Island as if we were nothing more than a pile of logs making our way to a lumber mill.

I felt a sudden urge to turn my face back to the sea, to where my family lived under the dark ocean. I pictured their sweaters and socks unraveling, with all of those coloured yarns twisting and turning, knotting up. Then I saw the yarn weaving them all together; first Mammy and Da, then Caleb, then Emma and Molly, after that Jacob, and the twins Georgina and George, and on and on, Grannie and Granddad too, all of them woven together as if they were fish caught in a grand net. *At least they're together. I'm all on me own.* No matter if I lived to 101, the yarns in my sweater would never knot up with theirs. Yes, I had their buttons, but buttons were only useful when they fastened one thing to another. Who was I fastened to? No one. Nothing. Auntie Helen, I suppose.

"Mary Quilligan," my aunt said, tugging at my arm, "don't be looking back at the sea! Have you never heard of Lot's wife? Turned to a pillar of salt, she was. Do you want that to happen to you?"

"Lot was a mean sort of man," I said, "to let his wife turn to salt and not turn his head an inch to wave goodbye."

"Then he'd be salt as well. Better to have one pillar than two."

Though we were crammed shoulder to shoulder on the flatboat, my aunt took a notion to put a comb through my hair. "You've the look of a stray cat. One glance at you and they'll be after shipping us back to Ireland."

"I can't help it, Auntie. I'm all in flitters."

"Flitters or no, stand up straight. And not another word out of you!" When she wanted to, my Aunt Helen could bite the head off a nail.

I craned my neck to see above everyone's heads, and there I saw a round building with flags reaching up into the clouds. I felt suddenly glad I'd taken Auntie Helen's advice and turned away from the sea. Maybe once we reached this castle, as it had to be a castle of sorts, maybe we'd be greeted by the Queen of America. Maybe she'd be seated at the head of a table and serve us cakes and tea from a shiny silver pot. Did this new land have a queen? It was on the tip of my tongue to ask, when I stopped myself. Ireland cursed the crown of England, so I knew better than to mention such a thing to Auntie Helen.

As we drew closer, I began to imagine what I'd say or do, once I met the Queen of America. Surely, she'd take one look at me and turn away in disgust. I hadn't bathed since I'd left Ireland, and smelled like a pissy old cat, to be sure. And worse, if the queen discovered my buttons, she'd look down at me, her eyes sharp as razors, and say, "You, child, are a thief and a dirty thing. You are not welcome here."

Once inside "Castle Garden"—as the sign said above the entrance—I could see there was no chance of tea from a silver pot. Though it was grand, there was no place to rest our legs, let alone have tea. I looked up in amazement at the dozens of pillars reaching up to the ceiling, like long tree trunks with umbrella leaves and flowers spreading outward at the top. At the centre of the hall, a circle of light poured in from above, almost as if the Holy Spirit was shining down on the poor souls below. We lined up along with hundreds of others, all of us bedraggled and worn, waiting our turn to speak to the customs man.

"Well now, young lady," the customs officer said, "are you glad to be off that big boat?"

"I am. But I'm not to look back to the sea, that's what me auntie says."

"Shoosh now," said Auntie Helen.

"And why is that?" the man asked.

"We'll be turned into—" My aunt gripped my fingers, sending a shot of pain around my knuckles.

The man removed his spectacles and stared into Auntie Helen's sea green eyes. "Where's the girl's mother?" he asked.

"Must we speak in front of the poor girl?"

"Mammy died from the fever on the boat," I piped up. "And Da too. Seven sisters as well. And four brothers. They're all under the salty seas."

"Is this true?" the officer asked my aunt.

"As true as the sky above."

"Are you the next of kin?"

"I am."

"You intend to provide for this girl?"

"Indeed, I do."

"Papers!" the man commanded. As Auntie Helen produced the papers, her lips were pinched tighter than fiddle strings. "And the girl's?" the man asked.

"She hasn't any."

"And why is that?"

"The family moved about and never had a parish to call their own."

"You realize we could send you back to Ireland, both you and the child."

"We paid our fare. Hardly made it out alive. You might as well clap us inside a jail cell as send us back."

"Who's to say what kind of family she comes from? We don't welcome illiterates."

"Look at her! A mere slip of a thing. Surely to God you wouldn't be so cruel as to send an orphan back over the waters."

"We'll do what's best for the United States of America. I'll remind you, you're foreigners."

My Auntie Helen was having the effect of a burr on the man's neck. I decided to try my luck at charming him. "Mister, is it too late?" I asked.

"Too late for what, young lady?" he asked.

"For the circus. Me granddad told me all about the circus in America."

"Mary, must you put words to every twitch of a thought?" my aunt chided.

"And what did your granddad tell you?" the customs man asked, ignoring my aunt.

"That the night sky fills up with lights, like a thousand fireflies of every colour. And there's dancing bears." I knew I was asking for a severe scolding from Auntie Helen, but once my lips came unbuttoned, I couldn't help what flew out of my mouth.

"He told me America's got so many bears, once you piled them up on top of each other, they'd reach the moon. We haven't any bears in Ireland. Only old bones in caves, and sometimes the bones rattle and shake like ghosts—"

"For goodness sake, girl. Listen to your runaway tongue." My aunt squinted her one good eye at me, like a taunt arrow. Her other eye tended to wander off to the side.

My so-called nonsense was having an effect on the man. His scowl had given way to a grand smile, after all. "What did you say your name was?" the man asked.

"Mary."

"Well, Mary, it's too late for the circus this year. But if you take a trip up to Canada, you might find a bear in the wild." I wanted to ask him more about this Canada, but I knew I'd asked enough questions if I wanted to escape Auntie Helen's wrath. One glance at her cross face was enough to finally put the plug in.

The man turned to my aunt and said, "All passengers will be in quarantine for seven to ten days."

"Dear Mother of God. Why so long?"

"We can't take a chance with you Irish infecting the rest of the country. You're lucky I'm not sending you back. Next."

"But sir—"

"Next!" the customs man cried again.

As we turned away, my aunt said under her breath, "Who stitched him together?"

With my eyes wide as seashells, we were shuffled into an empty room where four women in white uniforms gave us orders to strip down naked. My aunt insisted on covering my eyes, but I peeked between my fingers. Never before had I seen so many women, from girls to old crones, naked as the day they were born. We were told to make a pile of our clothes in the centre of the room. They took our clothes for burning. But before I added my shabby slip and dress to the pile, I stole the tiny bundle of buttons into my hand as if it were the Pope's own diamond ring.

The women in charge then marched us into another room where strange fixtures on the walls spurted out fountains of water, like indoor waterfalls. We scrubbed ourselves with soap that burned my skin. By now, Aunt Helen had little hope of shielding my eyes from the naked shapes all around me. "Naked as Eve, every last one of us," I heard her mumble. Once we dried off, they handed us horrid smocks, more like potato sacks than dresses. To my dismay, there wasn't a single pocket to hide my bundle of buttons.

After waiting for hours, I was seen by a doctor and a nurse who checked my teeth and throat, and listened to my breath with a strange contraption. It didn't take long for the doctor to discover my treasure, and when he did, he pried the bundle from my stubborn fingers. He untied the knot to see what I'd smuggled into the country, then handed it over to the nurse saying, "For disposal." Naturally, I took to weeping. The nurse winked, as if to say that we had a secret, the two of us. Later, she slipped me the bundle, bringing her finger up to her mouth as if to say, *Don't say a word about it.* From that day onward, I kept the buttons in safekeeping, not parting with a single keepsake—until the day I gave Fiorella three buttons from my mother's own dress.

Looking back, I wonder now what possessed me to give Fiorella buttons in the first place. You couldn't make a meal out of buttons. And what exactly did I expect Fiorella to do for me? Certainly, she knew a great many things: how to relieve the kind of toothache that can drive a person mad, how to procure or prevent a miscarriage, how to turn around a lackluster life. But even so, what drove me to her door? I hardly knew myself.

"*T'alla camomilla?*" Fiorella offered, on that first day.

To be polite, I answered, "That would be lovely," though she could've been offering me spider's legs and I wouldn't have known the difference.

"Why you come see me?" she asked, as she fussed about the kitchen, rinsing out jars for cups for Faolan and me. Her own teacup had as many chips in it as her front teeth.

"There's a change in the air," I said. "I feel it, as sure as the sun on my face."

"I no can change what God bring you," she said, adding water to the kettle.

"Sure, I know that."

Wanting to say whatever words came to my lips, I thought I should send Faolan outdoors.

Now take any three Irish children: a McGarrigle, an O'Reilly, and a McDonald, and their characters will be more like each other than my own Thomas, Patrick, and Faolan. The eldest, Thomas, takes life as it's served up to him. If it's a king's breakfast one day and pauper's groats the next, you won't hear a complaint. The only trouble is his scorn for school, and in particular, arithmetic. If he be figuring how many acres it takes to yield so much grain, taking into account the variables of weather and prices, he'll come up with a number in his head with no trouble at all. When I point out he's doing arithmetic, he'll say, "That's not arithmetic, Ma. That's farming."

Patrick is my second eldest. He takes after me with his wide face and pale, narrow lips, but in every other way, the lad is his father. And like his father, he has a double dose of original sin, always getting into scrapes and scruffs. The one thing saving the bold lad from calamity is how he worships his older brother. As a young lad, he was Thomas's shadow on a fair day as well as a gloomy one. Back in North Dakota, the two of them fished all summer in the nearby brook. In the winter, they broke five miles of trail until a long band of white ribbon circled in and around the shelterbelt of trees. To this day, Thomas and Patrick are as close as brothers can be.

When Thomas finished the seventh form, and the time came for him to help run the farm, it was a fight to keep Patrick in school. He begged us, on both knees, to give him a chance on the farm. Lord knows, we needed the help, but I didn't want my boys ignorant of reading and writing like my own Da. We told Patrick to stick with his lessons until summer. By June, he could recite "The Raven" by Edgar Allan Poe. It was a dark poem, well suited to his gloomy ways, but the fact that he'd learned every word, from top to bottom, suited me fine.

We christened our third one, James Faolan, after his father, but Thomas was after calling him by his middle name, and it stuck. Faolan is as different as salt to pepper from the others. He's never been prone to shenanigans, poking pins into dragonflies, or hunting toads. He prefers to play with sticks and stones at the creek, and climb trees where he can be close enough to talk with the birds. He sees what others don't: a frosted spider's web in the early winter, or coyote tracks in the snow, or a garter snake sliding across a pebbled path. My husband accuses the lad of lollygagging, but I was much the same as a girl. Not to say I didn't work hard, because in a family of twelve, everyone needed to do their part.

"Out you go to play, Faolan," I said, wanting time alone with my new friend, Fiorella.

"But when are you looking for water?" Faolan asked.

"There's plenty time for dowsing. I'll call you when I'm ready." I didn't want to tell Faolan that I had no plans to douse, and that it was only an excuse to see Fiorella.

Faolan scuttled outdoors, glad to be free of our chatter. Fiorella set a cast iron stew pot on the table and filled it with boiling water from the kettle. She then dropped flowers and herbs into the steaming pot. Minutes later, she dipped our jars into the hot tea, wiping the drips with her apron. The two of us fell into conversation, like two old friends. Even during the silences, and there were many as her English was poor, even then, our words lingered in the air like the scent of wild roses floating through an open window.

"When come springtime, *bambino* come," Fiorella said.

I thought about my recent dream where I'd opened a cupboard filled with linens that were white as snow and pressed flat. When I tried to pull the top sheet from the pile, it stuck fast. I noticed that a tiny tree sapling had put down roots through the layers of sheets. *So, I'm with child*, was my thought as I awoke.

"Is no why you come?"

"I'm happy to carry this child, if that's what you're asking. But fearful all the same, and I wish I knew what to make of it."

"When you have new *bimba*, big change," she said, slurping up her tea like a thirsty cat.

"This is different. I can't explain. Only that it's left me unsettled," I said, taking a first sip of tea. It was a light yellowy colour, and tasted like wild flowers and sage.

"When you first get feeling?" Fiorella asked.

"Early springtime. Our cow was calving out. She was having a hard time of it and my husband wasn't sure if she'd come through the ordeal."

"Tell more."

"My husband got it into his head that our Faolan should watch. I didn't like it, but he didn't care a twitch how I felt. A terrible dread came over me, worse than the day..." Here I paused before continuing, "...worse than the day my own mother sang to me, just before her passing. She hadn't the strength to finish the song."

"But you Mamma's song, it go inside you."

"I suppose so."

"Mamma's song go Mamma to daughter. Some time, it go Mamma to son." Fiorella rose and reached up to a high shelf, pulling from it a tiny jar of treasured honey. Her strong hands wrenched open the sticky lid. She dipped the handle of a knife into the jar, twirling it around until it was dripping with sweetness, then stirred the knife into my cup, letting the honey dissolve before pulling it out.

"Tell me about day with cow. Maybe something you no think *importante*, you tell too."

"The cow was on the ground when it came out lopsided, the calf, that is. James, my husband, pushed the one foot back in, and was preparing to use rope, but before he could force his hands up, the feet came out together. With the hind feet presented, as you know, nature takes care of the rest. The calf was fine, but our cow, Cattail, wouldn't come to standing. My husband thought *paralysis*."

"What this?"

"Nerve damage. Best to get the cow on her feet once she's calved out."

"Same like goat."

"It was March the 9th, just another day on the farm, just another animal giving birth, an ordinary day. But here's the strange thing. My baby will come roundabout March 9th, one year later. Why should it matter? But I keep asking myself if this is a blessing or a blight."

At mention of the word *blight*, Fiorella clutched both my hands in hers and cried, *"Mal occhio!"*

"What?"

"Evil eye! Maybe you have."

"I've never heard of this."

"It make you sick, sick in heart or body."

"How do you catch it?"

"Maybe it come from animal, or someone jealous of you, bad spirit. We have to see. Wait, I tell you." Fiorella flitted around, filling a bowl half way with water and setting a bottle of oil on the table.

"You lie down," she said, pointing to the floor. When I hesitated, she took off her apron and rolled it up into a pillow to make things more comfortable. To this day, I've no idea why I followed her instructions, and once on the floor, it did occur to me that she was half mad. She set the bowl on my forehead and asked me to hold it in place, which I did. She then added a few drops of oil to the water and, leaning forward, she looked into the bowl as if it were a crystal ball. "Is good," she said, lifting the bowl from my forehead. "No evil eye. Other problem maybe. But no evil eye!"

"Well, that's a relief, isn't it? It doesn't sound like something I should be after having," I said, coming to my feet.

"Talka more."

"About the cow?" I asked. She nodded so I continued with my strange tale. "The eveningbefore, James had told me the cow was ready. When he said this, my hands felt as if they'd been plunged into ice water. They went cold and numb as the grave."

By now, we'd returned to our chairs, as if our little interlude with water and olive oil was as normal as blueberry pie. "You have this before? With hands?" Fiorella asked.

"I do. Sometimes it's a warm tingling in my fingers, but that's a welcome sign. Sure when a death is near, my hands turn stone cold. Mammy always said I had *the gift*, even as a wee girl. Before she crossed over a field, or cut brush for a fire, she always asked me first if my hands had the tingling. If so, she went roundabout, so as to not disturb the *raths*, the faerie forts, that is."

"You see that?" Fiorella swept her arm up toward a shelf of dark bottles. They were all shapes and sizes; some small and fat with corked lids, others the length of a finger with rubber droppers, and others still with metal screw tops. "All the thing, depend how you use," Fiorella went on to say, "maybe medicine or poison." Then touching her heart, she said, "*Pero sempre, la scelta devrebbe essere fatta col cuore.*" I don't think she realized she'd switched to her mother tongue, but those foreign words seemed to hurl me toward the true reason for my visit.

"I've had miscarriages before. More than my share and can bear another. But what if something happens to me? Women die in childbirth. It's common enough."

"We have contract with God," Fiorella said, slowly, as if I were a child, with a child's view of the world. "Two thing on contract—the day you born, the day you die. In between, we pray for this thing, that thing. Birth day and end day, I no argue with God."

"So, you think it's possible? That I might see my last day soon?"

"No, no, no, I no say that. Lot of nice thing we can do, for to make healthy, yes? But not all the thing we know."

"Sure we'd crumble into dust if we knew it all."

Fiorella got up from her chair to toss the water-oil mixture down her sink. Though she had a sink, taps weren't connected to it. With her head bowed down, she made the sign of the cross, then turned to ask, "You husband, he love you?"

"He works hard, takes care of us, me and the boys. If that's love, then yes, I suppose he does." Fiorella didn't look convinced. "We always have food on the table," I went on to say, "and he doesn't take his troubles out on the children, unless they've crossed him. But listen to me, filling your ears."

"We have nice visit. Nobody come see me. They say *crazy witch*. But you come."

"And I'm glad I did." I happened to glance out the window, and was shocked to see that the trees had begun to darken against a sapphire blue sky. "What's become of Faolan?" I said, leaping from my chair. Dashing outdoors, I called, "Faolan! Faolan!"

As Fiorella rushed up behind me, I asked, "Where's he taken himself?"

"He maybe find shed."

As sure as ice melts in the spring, we found my curious boy in the shed. The poor lad had fallen through the roof where he'd left a gaping hole. We bandaged him up with a strip Fiorella tore from her own skirt, as she hadn't a rag handy. Truth be told, her skirt was headed for the rag pile, threadbare as it was. I hurriedly carried Faolan across Fiorella's garden and into her house, as the sunset was now upon us with the tips of trees singed in red. Fiorella thought it best to give the boy time to recover from his fall, and I agreed. She warmed goat's milk, flavoured it with cloves, and gave my boy a cup full. As he sipped, Fiorella told me something of her country.

"In Italy, *il dieci agosto*, we sit on hill and make fire for *Santo Lorenzo. Notte delle stelle cadenti.* Beautiful star fall on feast of Santo Lorenzo."

"That sounds lovely."

"When we come to Canada, we take children up hill and make fire, me and Salvatore. We see lot of star, one thousand star, but never see falling star. After, we pick up ash from fire."

"We have a day like that, as well. The Feast of St. Brigid. We make a bonfire for her and leave out oat cakes all buttered up on the windowsills."

Fiorella reached up to the wall, and from a nail, she unloosed a small bundle. Handing it to me, she said, "Ash from *notte delle stelle.* You take."

"Are you sure?"

"*Si.* Put in little bowl, beside Madonna picture. You can do, okay?"

"Mammy, we should go." Faolan had been quiet all along, gazing off into the distance, and it was a good sign to see him liven up. "Da gets mad when we're late."

"Don't worry about your father, lad. I'll see to it he doesn't punish you." When I said the word *punish*, a look of concern flashed across Fiorella's brow.

"Wait, wait," Fiorella said as I gathered up our things. "This for you," she said, pressing a paper bag into my hand. It was her chamomile tea mix, though I didn't know it until I had my first cup a few days later. As well, Fiorella loaned me a goat cart for the journey as Faolan had little strength to manage on foot. The foot path was barely wide enough for the cart, and it was all I could do to not toss it away, and carry Faolan in my own arms, rather than face another bulbous tree root or wicked rock. But finally, we reached the road and I was glad of it.

Soon night overtook the sky and we had only the moon as

our lantern. To keep my spirits up, I sang a lullaby song. *My child, the new moon is a cradle/ Soft winds rock each baby star/ That peaceful murmur is their sleep song/ coming from afar/ Sleep, sleep, my babe.* When one song ended, I began another, and in this way, kept myself calm. I thought of Fiorella's words, that songs go from mother to child, and how yes indeed, I sang the songs my mother once sang to me. As we drew nearer to home, the cart grew heavier, and I sensed trouble was waiting. My Mammy used to say, "However long the day, the night must come." But what if the night is worse still than the day?

I summoned up whatever *misneach* I had, and with Faolan at my side, we entered our small stone house. Though James kept his face to the fire, I saw the overgrown hairs on the back of his neck, and imagined they were standing up on end, like a wild dog's. Without turning his head a single inch, he fumbled to remove his belt. "You made a promise, lad. And I'll teach you to keep your promise."

Faolan crouched behind me. "No need to strap the boy," I said. "He's had punishment enough for one night."

"What's that supposed to mean?" James said, turning to face me. I smelled the liquor on his

breath, though I had little need for proof.

"If you weren't so taken with the drink, you'd see. He's bandaged up. Got a nasty wound falling from a tree."

"What kind of stupidity makes a boy fall from a tree? I should strap him for being the *eejit* that he is."

"Off you go to bed," I said quietly to my boy. "*Oíche mhaith.*" In that moment, I felt my mother's voice coming through me. How many times growing up did she say those very words to me, wishing me a goodnight?

The minute Faolan left the room, James tightened the grip on his belt. I needed to speak and fast, before the strap came down on my own shoulders. "I've something to tell you!" I said. James threw the belt against the wall and drew nearer to me. Grabbing my wrist while scooping up the lantern from the mantle, he pulled me outdoors. He then pushed me in the direction of the barn, as though I were a troublesome plow on uneven ground. All the while, I fought to free myself from his grasp, while suppressing my own screams. I was loathed to frighten my Faolan.

"I'm carrying a child. Your child. For the love of God, will you—"

"Shut your gob," he shouted, opening the barn doors with one hand, and throwing me down onto the dirt floor with the other. "How am I to know it's my child?" he said, glowering over me like a ghastly creature.

"Who else's could it be? Of course, it's yours!"

"I see how you look at men," he said, now casting the lantern-light over my face. "You don't think I see. I'm not blind." Whenever James took to the drink, jealousy gummed up his brain, like dark molasses. I'm plain and ordinary, that's a fact. And a strong cup of coffee or a pipe of tobacco is more tempting to me than any man. One is trouble enough. Why would I torment myself with another?

"I swear to God. I swear over the ocean graves of my own mother and father."

"Shut up. Shite hawk. Whore!"

The sheep were all worked up by now, bleating and crying, as though they didn't like the state of things any more than I. A madness took over James's face, his features as distorted as storm waves on a dark ocean. I was afraid he'd set the barn ablaze by dropping the lantern—flames devouring us all, animals and humans alike. But he snuffed out the lantern, leaving us both in darkness. "Don't think Thomas is going to save you because I've sent him to the city," he said. "On the train, him and Patrick both. It's just you and me and that coddled boy in the house." James's face was now so close to mine that his spit skittered on my face, and his liquored breath turned my stomach. Just as I was about to retch up my tea, he growled, "You wait here. Don't move an inch." I nodded in agreement as he disappeared into the shadows of the barn.

I felt pinned to the ground, though it was only fear that held me there. If I cried out for help, it would enrage him all the more. There was no telling what he would do next. I thought about leaving James, but how could I with Faolan alone in the house? I wondered if I had time to wake Faolan so the two of us could flee together. But where would we go? I couldn't imagine dragging an injured boy into the night for a second time. Out of the corner of my eye, I spotted the glint of sheep shears up on the barn wall. Not knowing exactly where James had taken himself, I reached for them. I had no plan, other than defending my life, once it came to that.

The moment my fingers touched the shears, James threw his hand over mine and pried them away from me. With his free arm, he pinned me to the wall. "Didn't I say, 'don't move an inch'?" he asked through his teeth. *One thrust and I'm as good as dead.* After a struggle of sorts, I ended up on the ground with James stooped over me, the shears glinting from the small bit of light finding its way in through the slats in the walls. He laughed like a lunatic and began hacking off my long hair. As it fell in clumps on the floor, I chanted ever so quietly, "It's only hair; it's only hair." Sure it was more than hair. He took pieces of me and flung them away, never to be recovered. When you harvest rosehips or wild flowers, you're to take a pod here and a flower there. If you take too much, the meadow will never return to its charm. The same was true for me that night.

Morning came. I rose with the sun, taking care to cover my head with a scarf as I didn't want to shock my Faolan. I slipped out to the barn where I saw clumps of hair strewn on the dirt floor like burnt chaff. I collected it up and, going out to the far field, I dug a hole and buried it. Back in the house, I remembered the bundle of ash and packet of tea from Fiorella, both still in my coat pocket. I wondered where to safely put the ash, as James was apt to spit on anything that I called my own. I climbed a chair and set it on top of my pantry cupboard, beside my Immaculate Heart of Mary holy card.

I was about to sit with a cup of tea when, through the window, I noticed James heading in from the field. He was all for walking with his head down. Once inside, he poured himself tea and sat across the table from me. I got to my feet to tidy up.

"It won't happen again, Mary. What happened last night," he said, as I sliced up a loaf of bread. It was a loaf from the day before, baked while I still had hair to twist into a braid atop my head. I wondered if my bread would lose flavour now that I'd lost my hair, like Samson losing his strength.

"And me with child," I said.

"I'm telling you now, I won't browbeat you again. You've seen enough of the back side of my hand. Your hair will be down to your knees, and you'll have no complaint between now and then," James claimed. He was all prunes and prisms with me, but I didn't believe a word of it. He'd made promises before and not kept them. Either way, I thought, *I'll return to the herb woman. I'll soak up her tenderness, as the earth draws in the rain.*

It was nine weeks before I could slip away. Faolan was off to school, and James and the lads were headed to town to pick up feed. As soon as they disappeared from sight, I collected up a jar of jam and a bit of cheese from my larder, then wrapped a loaf of fresh bread into a remnant of cotton. I don't care to ride while in a delicate condition, but feeling rushed, I bridled up a horse and set off to Fiorella's cabin, all the while carrying my basket.

It was now autumn and her little home was surrounded by a half dozen trembling aspen, adorned with golden leaves. It was like an archway into a chapel. A single black poplar grew up the side of her tattered house, leaning into the window as if to invite itself in. I tied up my faithful horse, then adjusted my headscarf so Fiorella wouldn't notice how catty-cornered I looked. Though time had passed, and I'd done my best to coax my chopped hair into something pleasant, it always fell whichever way the wind blew last.

I called out, "Hello, it's me," as I stepped in through Fiorella's canvas door. The place hadn't changed much since my last visit, other than the autumn light washing in through the windows. The table still stood proud at the centre of the room, the curtained alcove in the corner still housed Fiorella's bed, along with a wooden rocker. The rocker doubled as a potty pot, a clever invention of a round hole cut out from the seat with a pee pot below. The stuffed chair was now a few inches away from the wood stove, sinking into the floor, almost as if the weight of human worry had been absorbed into the straw seat over the years.

Fiorella emerged from the shadows, and kissed me on both cheeks. She took my coat and let out a cheerful sigh in response to my growing belly. She then placed her hands on me, giving her blessing to the unborn child. It crossed my mind that my husband hadn't once bothered to ask when the baby was expected to arrive, and had shown as much interest in my condition as a complete stranger. Fiorella wasted no time in unwrapping the lunch I'd brought. As she sliced up the bread and cheese, I said, "No need. Save it for yourself."

"Food better with friend, no?" she said, setting out the bread, cheese, and my juneberry jam.

"I've been drinking your chamomile tea in the morning. It's lovely. And warm milk at night to help me sleep."

"And pray to Madonna?"

"Every time I reach for the tea, the Sacred Heart of Mary is there. And the bundle of ash."

"But still you have worry, no?"

"There's not a holy card in the world that can cure worry."

Fiorella pulled a shawl from a wooden peg by her door. 'Twas the colours of the Bible's own coat of Joseph. She held it up to the wood stove, and then placed it over my shoulders as gently as a sparrow's landing. Comfort was the medicine I'd come for, and she had it to spare. "Something happen to you," she whispered.

"Fiorella, I feel my strength dripping out of me, like a slow leak. When my time comes, I won't have strength left in me."

"I give something for you body to get strong. *Ma* you soul need strong too. *Forze vitale.*" I don't know what came over me at the mention of those two foreign words, but straightaway, I threw myself into Fiorella's arms. A wail rose up in me. Sure it was my own voice, though it sounded as if it came from a wild banshee. As Fiorella held me in her thick arms, I told her that, until this pregnancy, James had never laid a finger on me while I was with child, no matter how much drink he'd taken. I told her of the three miscarriages I'd endured, one after the other, and though they were a trial to me, pregnancy also kept me safe from his blows. I told her how he'd promised not to harm me again and that, so far, he'd kept that promise.

With my tears falling, Fiorella said, "Still he hurt you, no?"

"He does. In so many ways."

"I think, he no change, you husband. *Cattiva è quella lana che non si puo tingere.*"

With my head on Fiorella's lap, she gently untied my scarf and ran her fingers through my hair. "I'm ugly," I whispered. "He's made me ugly."

"No! Is no true."

"It's not just the hair, is it? It's the light in my eyes, gone, snuffed out. Maybe I have, what do you call it? The evil eye? Maybe I caught it, after all."

"You no say this."

"Whatever it is, it's as terrible as a curse, isn't it?"

"Poison come in bottle some time, but it come too in

word. *La lingua non ha ossa ma fa rompere il dosso.* You husband, he make poison with word."

"I could endure it better if…the thing is, every time he touches me in that way, and to think I once enjoyed his touch, now I dread it—not so much the act itself, but how I feel afterward—cold and empty as a well run dry."

Fiorella pulled me up to sitting, locked her eyes with mine, and said, "Is something we can do."

"I'd like to keep him from touching me, at least. I'd happily sleep in a chair if I thought it would help. But there's no way to control that man's urges."

"Maybe is a way."

"If you know of something, 'tis worth an ounce of leprechaun's gold."

"I give oil with smell in it," she said, motioning as if she were dabbing perfume on her neck.

"Perfume?"

"*Si. Profumo.* When you husband, he come close, he smell. But how you say? Is quiet smell. He no take you to bed. Why he change his mind, he confuse."

"The scent takes away his desire?"

"True."

"How?"

"Is like medicine. No promise, but we can try, yes?"

"I'll try anything. If you told me to dance naked in the snow, I'd do it."

"Is no winter yet. No rush for snow. Please!"

I watched as my dear friend concocted up her potion, first running her hands along the length of the shelf, lightly touching each bottle as if she were strumming guitar strings. I knew her hands were making the decision, rather than her mind. *Hands never lie. Hands are fastened by invisible twine to past generations, to our grandmothers and great-grandmothers who have much to tell us.*

Fiorella warmed oil in a small skillet, then poured it through a funnel propped up inside a bottle. With a dropper, she added this and that, taking whiffs between drops. Screwing on a tiny metal lid, she shook the bottle so vigorously that it seemed her hand might fly off her wrist. She then pressed it firmly into my hand, as though it were Our Lord's own chalice. "Husband afraid of you," she said.

"I don't think so."

"He act big, but really is small. Wait four day. Put like this. One drop, two drop, maybe three. No more than three."

On the way home, rather than mount my horse, I meandered along the path by foot. Fiorella lived in the lower part of the tree bluffs, where fields stretched in one direction and forest in the other. I thought of the trees as belonging personally to Fiorella, as if the prairie could go for a thousand miles in every direction, but would never encroach on her doorstop. As I walked, the whispering aspen leaves glistened with silver dust. Each tree had a story, as did I; each pebble along the pathway had a secret, as did I; each bird fluttering from branch to branch had a plan, as did I. When I took air into my lungs, so did all living beings around me. My hands began to tingle, as if a hundred dragonflies had alighted on my fingers. All the while, I led my horse on, lightly holding the worn leather reins slack. The horse was too old to pull a plow, but agile enough to step along the rough path until we reached the road.

When I stepped inside, I found my Faolan sitting by the stove, reading a school book. "Mammy! You look like Lady Mary from Robin Hood," he cried. Faolan pointed to the yellow leaves and black crow-berries I'd picked along the way and tucked into my head scarf. I suppose, in his eyes, I looked like a fey spirit, that had sprung from the roots of a faerie tree.

"When the little one comes, we'll name her Mary. Would you like that?" I asked my son.

"But what if it's a boy?"

"Sure, it's not a boy."

"How do you know?"

"My skin's been dry and splotchy. Sure sign of a girl."

"Your face looks soft as ever."

I touched my face. The splotches had indeed disappeared. "Must be Fiorella's tea cleared it up. Just think, Faolan. You'll have a little sister before the snow melts away."

"Snow hasn't come yet."

"True enough. It needs to come before it can go. But a sister you'll have. And we'll name her
Mary so."

"Like you Mam. You're a Mary."

"I am. I was once Mary Quilligan. Now I'm Mary Moore."

"Mammy? Why'd you name me Faolan?"

"You don't care for your name?" For an answer, Faolan shrugged. "You have the name of a wolf. And if ever the day comes when you need the heart of a wolf, you'll be glad of it. Now run along, and I'll make us up *colcannon* for supper."

"I don't like cabbage," Faolan said, making a sour face.

"If you knew what we ate on the boat from Ireland, you wouldn't be so fussy. It's potatoes and cabbage tonight, and that's that."

"Alright, Mammy."

"It's more than alright. It's the next thing to wonderful."

⁓

Just as Fiorella promised, my husband's interest in me dwindled. Whether it was the oily perfume, which carried the scent of clove, wood of the oak, and lemon, or whether it was my growing belly that turned him the other way, I can't be sure. Either way, I was determined to spend as little time as possible in his company.

Every day, once Faolan arrived home from school, the two

of us set off on our walk, making our way to the wind break, weaving pathways in and around the trees. Along the way, we took notice of the open prairie sky always in flux, the fields of grasses for miles around, and the odd flake of November snow, disappearing before it touched the ground. Every now and then, we'd break into song or chatter.

"Faolan, tell us that poem, the one about winter frost," I said, as we made our way through the wild grasses.

"Our teacher taught it last year. I forget it mostly."

"Just the last verse, the one with fairies so."

"I'll try. 'He went to the windows of those who slept/ And over each pane, like a fairy, crept/ Wherever he breathed, wherever he stept.'" Faolan paused, trying to conjure up the next line. "I forget what comes next," he said, giving up altogether.

"'By the light of the moon were seen,'" I said, helping him along. "Begin again, why don't you? This time, say it with feeling, like you're on a stage with lights all around and velvety red curtains. Everyone's come to hear the poem. Pretend those crows up in the tree are your audience," I said, pointing off in the distance.

"'He went to the windows of those who slept/ And over each pane, like a fairy, crept,'" Faolan said, this time with a tad more enthusiasm. "'Wherever he breathed, wherever he stepped/ By the light of the moon were seen/ Most beautiful things.'"

I saw Faolan hesitating and helped him along. "'There were flowers and trees/ There were birds and bees/ There were cities with temples and towers/ and these'" I said, pausing, before together we said the last line, "'All pictured in silver sheen!'"

"Every time it snows, you'll recite it to me, and I'll never grow tired of it!"

"But it hasn't snowed yet. Just little specks."

"Winter has a way of coming when you least expect it."

Faolan sprinted ahead of me, like he had grasshoppers in his shoes. The boy kept my spirits from sinking too low. Always curious, my Faolan. Once we've lost our curiosity, we may as well hammer together a coffin and put ourselves in it. Just as I was thinking these thoughts, Faolan beckoned me to catch up with him. He was standing near the tree where the crows had taken up residence. They were carrying on, like they were holding a meeting of high importance.

"Mammy, see that?" Faolan whispered.

"See what?"

"A pigeon." Faolan pointed up where, to be sure, a white pigeon sat with the crows.

"Well now, isn't that strange," I said. "I never saw a pigeon with a murder of crows."

"Why do they call it a murder?"

"'Tis a charm of finches, a gaggle of geese, and a murder of crows. Who's to say why."

"What's your favourite?"

"A charm of finches. I'll always take a charm, once it's for the taking."

Together, we drew nearer to the foot of the tree, our footsteps light so as to not frighten off the birds. Looking up, we noticed that the white bird wasn't a pigeon at all. Its pointed beak, the shape of its body, and its clawed toes were all in the shape of a crow.

"It's like a ghost crow," Faolan whispered.

"Our Good Lord must've forgotten to paint the poor thing black." At the sound of the

word *black*, the birds flew off, cawing as they took to the sky, the white crow along with them.

Once they were out of sight, Faolan said, "I counted seven. What's seven for?"

"I don't know."

"You do. You're always singing that counting rhyme, when

you see birds."

"Oh, well now. It's 'One for sorrow, Two for joy, Three for a girl, Four for a boy, Five for
silver, Six for gold—'"

"So, if I see six crows all in a bunch, I'll get rich?"

"Getting rich is for those born with a silver spoon in their mouths."

"Doesn't matter. I counted seven, not six."

"Seven for a secret, never to be told."

"Do you have a secret, Mammy?"

"Sure we all have a secret or two, stored in our hearts for safe-keeping."

"I don't have a secret, except for something I hid. I guess that's a kind of secret," Faolan said.

"It's not good to have too many," I warned, "as they end up burdens on our backs."

Without another word, my lad and I turned to make our way home, stepping over the tree roots that crawled along the ground like fingers in search of hands from neighbouring trees.

Just as the house came into view, Faolan asked, "What does it mean, the white crow?"

"I don't have a rhyme for white crows."

"But it means something. Doesn't it?"

"It's whatever meaning we're after giving it," I answered. *Black crows are a sign of battle and strife, and I know enough of both to not want more. But what of an albino crow? Is it ominous or good fortune?*

"Maybe it means we'll have an early snow and a long winter," Faolan said.

"Could be, my lad, could be."

～

Faolan was right. The snow fell early, clinging to the ground like a miser clings to gold. I was anxious to see Fiorella again before the full force of the season came with all its teeth and bluster. I looked for the first opportunity to slip away, and thankfully it came before the snow made it impossible to travel. With James' reputation with treating horses, he was called away to lend a hand to a neighbour with an injured horse. As James set off, I took myself to the barn.

"Where are you going with Blanket?" Patrick asked, as I saddled up the horse.

"I told Mrs. McLeod I'd have tea with her," I lied.

"I'll take you there, Ma. Especially in your condition."

"I'm fine on my own."

"Da won't like it."

"Can't I visit a neighbour without a fuss?"

"I'm just saying, you know how Da is. He says things, when he's drunk."

"What things?"

"Just don't give him reason to think the worst," my son said.

"Am I to be held captive then? Is that it? I'm sorry, Patrick, but this is how it's going to be.

I'm having tea up the road, and I'll hear no more of it."

The path to Fiorella's place is no more than a half mile from the main road, but that day, the ground was covered in a fresh layer of snow, making it more difficult. I let go of the reins and Blanket picked her way through the trees at her own pace, though I had to keep my head forward or tree branches would've knocked me flat.

I took up singing one of the dandling songs my Mammy once sang to me—songs to make a baby smile. *Cuirfimid deandaí, Cuirfimid deandaír Mháire, Cuirfimid deandaí, Bróga ⊠s stocaí bána.* My voice seemed to have the ill effect of slowing my horse down, so by the time I reached Fiorella's, it was near middle of the afternoon. I tied Blanket by a creek no wider than a row of *taties* and, finding a sturdy stick, I took the last few yards by foot.

When I stepped inside Fiorella's snug but drafty house, I promised myself that I would send my boys over to build Fiorella a proper door. The door, as she called it, was a canvas tarpaulin hung from nails above, with two heavy stones at its base. Each time she came or went, she rolled the stones aside with her foot. It had worked a deep groove into the plank wood floor. On a summer day, she tied back the canvas, inviting the mosquitoes and black flies to come and go as they pleased, but how she managed through the winter was a mystery beyond telling. I knew the odd kind soul from town brought her up a sack of feed or a bag of sugar in exchange for her advice. They came in secret and only when every other remedy was exhausted. It was desperation only that kept the path between the road and her canvas door traveled at all.

As Fiorella was nowhere in sight, I banked up the shrinking embers in her stove and added a fresh log before collapsing into her soft chair. The long walk and warmth of the wood stove had the effect of sending me off to sleep.

I woke up to the sound of Fiorella slurping up a bowl of soup. "Where's the day gone? I must be off home," I cried.

"Is too late. You stay."

"Why did I let myself doze? Better not to have come at all."

"First soup. You need food." I followed Fiorella's orders, dutifully eating in silence. The plain ingredients of grouse with carrot, onion, and Jerusalem artichoke made for a flavourful broth. I ate quickly, distracted with worry. How would I explain this to James? Would I be able to find the path home in the darkness?

"Is there any chance of me making it home?" I asked my Italian friend.

She looked out the window and said, "More snow come

tonight."

"So, it's impossible."

"I make bed for you."

"I won't sleep. Not a wink."

Fiorella pulled an old rug from the entry-way and dragged it near the wood stove. Apart from the dust shaken up, there on the naked floor was a painted scene, so faded that it was barely visible in the evening light. I made out a tree with branches stretching off in all directions. At the tip of each branch burst an object: a moon, a key, a fish, a frog, a heart, on it went with the tips blossoming into one thing or another. I wanted to ask Fiorella about the strange pictures, but something in her mood halted me from saying anything. Instead, I thanked her for the perfume she'd made me on my last visit.

"Is good?"

"Not every time does it keep him away, but often enough. As I hoped."

"You hope? Is no good to hope. Better to pray." Fiorella said as she stormed around her little house, pulling out blankets as if from thin air and heaping them onto a chair. "All the time people hope for tomorrow," she muttered. "What is tomorrow? An idea in you head." I didn't know what to say. She was talking in riddles, just as the painted floor was also a riddle. I began folding the blankets, not knowing what else to do when Fiorella said, "No, no! Is to make bed for you. On rug." Together we built a nest of blankets on the floor. As a final flourish, Fiorella tossed a ratty old pillow onto the newly arranged bed. It crossed my mind that she'd given me the cat's bed. Fiorella then straightened her back, exhausted with the flurry of work, and asked, "You weave?"

"I did once. The sisters at the convent had a loom. 'Twas a contraption with heddles and harnesses and God knows what else. I never figured it out, though they tried like the dickens to teach me."

"For you, *non è difficile*. Very easy."

"You wouldn't say that if you saw this thing. It was like the insides of a piano, but strung with threads. A mystery for a girl of seven."

Fiorella was suddenly full of questions, and the more I chattered, the more it seemed to cheer her. "You go to school with nuns?" she asked. As I prattled on, she cleared the table, then picked up her broom to sweep the hearth, sending soot swirling through the air.

"For a spell," I said, "when my mammy took sick. The nuns opened their doors to me and my sisters and brothers, as there was no one to look after us. My da took the older boys with him on the road. He was a horse trader. The day my mammy was back on her feet, she told my father, 'That's it. We're moving to America. I won't have our family broken apart again.'"

I knelt down beside Fiorella and together we cleaned her hearth with a damp rag. "The nuns offered to keep my baby brother, adopt him. Imagine that. A boy raised by nuns! They wouldn't have it, my parents."

"You sisters and brothers in America now? You talka to them?"

"I'm the only one left. They all died."

"Justa like me. Alone in world. I have daughter, but I can no write letter to her. You go to school to read? To write?"

"Truth be told, here and there, but I mostly taught myself."

Fiorella motioned for me to sit at the table, her face brightening. I felt encouraged to share more about my girlhood years. "I was in America only a short time when my aunt pulled me from school to work on a farm. Besides all the housework, the Mister had me help the youngsters with their lessons. I thought, why not learn from their books? With my first bit of savings, I bought a dictionary. Even though I had the look of a waif with my coat in tatters, and boot soles as thin as paper, sure it was that grand book I was after. Maybe it would put a bit of polish on me. If you want elegance, an Irish farm isn't the place to find it. The minute I opened my mouth out in the world, I was called a 'dirty mick' or worse."

"Me too. The people, they no call *Fiorella*. They call *The Italian*."

"To me, you're Fiorella."

"Lot of people coming here. *L'inglese, il portoghese, i russo, gli svendesi, il francese, il polacco. Ma*, before ship come, people live already here."

Fiorella reached under her tablecloth, which was an old cotton sheet cut to size, and pulled out a few pennies. She waved me over to the window and, pressing a penny into each of my hands, she pointed up to a sliver of a moon. Taking my cue from her, we bowed our heads as she chanted, "*Benvenuta Luna che mi porti fortuna*." Fiorella repeated her chant thirteen times. I don't care for the number thirteen, so I gave one an extra bow, to even it up. Fiorella collected the pennies and put them back where she'd found them.

Fiorella picked up talking where we'd left off, as if she'd only just paused for a sneeze. "When you aunt make you to go away and work, you sad?" Fiorella asked, turning her head to look out the window again.

"To be fair, she was as old as Methuselah, and it was a strain, taking on a *cailin*. She lied and told the farmer I was fourteen, though I was barely a day over thirteen. She thought it a fair bargain. I would care for the children and, in return, I'd have a roof over my head. It served me well enough, but the poor woman had more children than beds to put them in. It's little wonder she was drowning in a sea of melancholy."

As if bit by a wasp, Fiorella leapt up from her chair. "Over there," she said snappishly. "You see?" Fiorella pointed to a dark corner where a loom sat on a tabletop. "You try. I go to bed now." In a flicker, Fiorella turned in for the night, pulling the makeshift curtain around her bed, leaving me with the cat—who eyed me suspiciously—as my only company. I wondered if Fiorella had grown tired of my visits. I could hardly blame her. What right did I have showing up at her doorstep, hungry for a crumb of her wisdom, or an ounce of her potions?

Though my heart was oh-so-tired, my mind was wound tighter than a spool of thread. I reached inside my coat pocket for my tobacco and pipe. Using the pipe as a scoop, I stuffed the bowl, packing it with my thumb. I tossed on my coat and stepped outdoors. I expected the sky to be as black as coal, but no, it was a soft, greyish blue, even at that late hour. A light snow had begun to fall, just as Fiorella predicted. My pipe didn't catch right away, but when it did, I felt bathed by the sweet flavours, and—for a few breaths—not a single thought entered my head. As I stood sucking on my pipe, I found myself thinking, *I don't give a shiny shoe what James thinks. I'll stay here one night, two nights, ten nights if that's what it takes to get my strength back.*

Once inside, I quietly rolled Fiorella's door stones back to their spots. I'd been careless on the way out, and snow had found its way in. I lit the flat-wick oil lamp and watched as it flickered and danced, lighting up the china plates and jars on her open shelves. I adjusted the flame to a small, steady glint, and sat down by the fire in the stuffed chair—now robbed of its cushioned seat. Fiorella's cat had reclaimed her pillow and was purring away. A mouse skittered across the roof boards, startling me. Now wide awake, there was nothing to do but bring myself to the loom. The simple gadget amounted to a row of nails tapped along the frame. A piece of wood tipped it forward, so the weaver wasn't forced to hunch over. It was a makeshift loom, to be sure, but judging from the colourful rug near the wood stove, Fiorella managed to make lovely things from it. She must've raised sheep long ago, as there were baskets of grease wool crammed under the table, not yet scoured or carded.

Along the wall were hanks of wool the colours of forest: the green of pine tips in the spring, the deep pink of a wild rose, the blue of a winter's sky. I couldn't see a spinning wheel in sight, but by the thickness of the yarn, and the number of snarls and loop knots, Fiorella had likely used a drop spindle. I noticed a large glass bottle filled with discoloured water with two rusty spikes at the bottom. It came back in a flash that oxidized water was used to fix the colour, something I'd long ago forgotten.

I settled in and chose three colours that took my fancy. As Fiorella had already strung the warp, my hands began weaving the filling yarn in and over the warped threads. With no mechanism to create a shed, it was a slow undertaking. As I worked, I quietly sang, beginning with one of my favourites, *Three Brave Blacksmiths*. 'Tis a true story of three brave fellows, and how they refused to make shoes for the rich. As punishment, they spent a night in jail for every nail they would've used to make shoes for the *grabber*.

One song melded into the next as rows and rows took shape on the loom. What did the pattern remind me of—meadowlarks against a field of spear grass? The design wasn't fixed, and my fingers seemed to dance all on their own. A deep red circle against a violet sky found its way into the arrangement. The colours in the weave grew more intense as the night wore on, though it may have been only to do with the lamp burning down its wick. I worked on, giving no more thought to my neglected family than an owl gives to the coming of daybreak. For the first time in a long while, a warm tingling spread into my fingers. At some point, I became sleepy and made my way over to the pile of blankets on the floor. I woke up to the sound of Fiorella humming.

"My horse!" I cried, sitting up, straight as a broom pole. Mischief was on Fiorella's face as she pointed out the window.

There was my Blanket, nose up to the glass, a rug thrown over her to keep her dry from the lightly falling snow. Feeling at ease, I sat at the table where a cup of dark coffee and a slice of bread sat waiting. The coffee tasted bitter, then changed into a sweet elixir as it trickled down my throat. The irritation in Fiorella's voice had vanished with the dawn. "You make rush home?" she asked.

"I'd like to stay, if it's all the same to you," I said. I knew I needed to face James, but did it have to be any time soon? He would already be in a knot. What difference would another night make?

"Stay all winter. Is no problem," Fiorella said, shaking her hands dramatically. "Come, put coat."

We stepped outdoors where the whole world slept under a fine sheet of snow. Blanket, still standing under Fiorella's roof overhang, looked no worse for wear.

"You watered and fed her?" I asked.

"Oh, that horse, she like me. You no worry, we good friend now."

"Such a pretty day, isn't it?" I asked, feeling at peace for the first time in weeks.

"This make day better," Fiorella said, pulling a jar of coffee from her pocket. She opened the lid and poured it onto the snow, swirling her hands, as if she were a magician transforming one thing into another. As if from thin air, she handed me a spoon, and motioned for me to taste the darkened snow. I'd often made pudding, and ice cream once or twice, but before that day, I'd never tasted anything like it. The mixture of coffee and sugar, fluffed up with snow was a sweet fit for a queen. I told Fiorella just that. She laughed and said how she'd rather be a peasant than a queen; queens had to live by rules, whereas she had only one rule to live by—the Golden Rule. She didn't say it quite like that, given her broken English, but I understood her meaning all the same.

"I was thinking of naming the baby *Mary*," I said, as we enjoyed our winter treat. "But it could get confusing, with two Marys in the house."

"Give more name too."

"Mary Grace or Mary Rose? It's not so easy naming a baby, is it?"

"When you see *bambina*, you know."

"I'll help out today," I said, suddenly feeling like I could tackle the world. "What would you like done?"

"We go to shed."

On the way, I noticed that Fiorella had patched the roof with straw where my son had fallen through. How she'd managed to climb up to the roof was a mystery. It was my second visit to her garden shed, though the first time I was too preoccupied with my injured lad to take notice of much. As I stepped inside the dim room, I half closed my eyes and breathed in the scent of mint, musty earth, and roses.

Together, we filled a basket with dried leaves and roots, and then trundled back to the house. We tied bundles of prairie sage, mint, and butterfly pea flower and hung them on Fiorella's clothesline. She then showed me how to scrub twisty roots with a dry brush. I sliced and laid the bits onto stretched gauze, hung by the window to be dried by the sun. As I worked, Fiorella roasted up a small pan of those same roots, and gave me my first taste of dandelion coffee.

That afternoon, when I considered making my way home, my heart sank like a stone to the bottom of a well. I felt torn. We'd moved Blanket into Fiorella's small barn, but I felt guilty using up Fiorella's small bit of feed. With winter nipping at our heels, her goat would have no more grasses and weeds and shrubs to nibble on. All the same, I shook off my guilt, and stayed on.

The day passed quickly and, in the evening, I felt myself pulled to the loom. When Fiorella saw what I'd woven, she laughed and said, "You weave funny story."

"I didn't know it to be a story."

"Girla have bird friend. See? Then bird fly away and girla sit on sun. Her come all around big world." I studied my patterns of shapes and colours and wondered if Fiorella was pulling my leg, or if she actually saw images. "Wait, wait! Something missing from story," Fiorella said with the devil's wink in her eye.

"To be sure, it's not finished."

"You husband."

"What about my husband?" I asked.

"Maybe put mouse in corner. Husband little mouse." Again, she laughed, and this time, I joined in her merriment.

"Wasn't there a saint, one of the martyrs who covered herself in hair to keep the men from looking at her?" I said. "Maybe that's the trick!"

"I love one man and he go to heaven."

"I'm sorry. Do you miss him so?"

"I miss. *Ma*, I see again. He is with *i santi*. I no care what bad thing people say about my Salvatore."

I wondered what Fiorella meant. Did he have a gambling itch, or a love of the bottle? Whatever it was, Fiorella loved him. That was clear as day.

The fifth morning, I woke up feeling homesick for my children, and Faolan most of all. I wondered if James had been out looking for me. What would my husband do with me—a wayward wife who'd stolen his horse? I'd have to face him sooner or later, there was no avoiding it. All this had me feeling plucked, pulled, and coiled. At Fiorella's gate, I blurted, "Once the worst happens, what will become of my baby?"

"Why you talka like this?"

"He doesn't believe the baby is his. How will he treat the little one if I'm dead and buried? He'll neglect the child, and worse. If I die, the baby can't stay with her father."

"But you feel better, yes? More strong?"

"Sometimes—I know this is a terrible thought that could send me into the fires of hell, but sometimes I wonder if it's better for a child not to be born at all than to be at the mercy of a loveless parent. Fiorella, if I die—"

"You no talk about die. Is no good for *bambina* when you talka like this."

"I'll never bring it up again. Just this one time. If something happens to me, will you do whatever it takes to keep the baby from being raised by my husband?"

"No, no, no. Better to ask farm lady for this. No ask me."

"You're the only one I can trust. Please. For my peace of mind. If it comes to that."

"I help on the day you have *bambina*. Everything come out good."

"Then you won't mind making a promise, if you're so sure things will go well."

Fiorella looked at her hands. She turned them one way, then the other, as if examining every

crooked joint and callous. At long last, she said, "Okay. I say okay. But you keep to pray to Madonna. *Ogni giorno*. Every day!"

By the time I arrived home, not a soul was there to greet me. Maybe they hadn't noticed Blanket clomping up the road, or pretended they hadn't. Other than scads of dirty dishes and a floor littered with crumbs, our house was in order. The thought crossed my mind that a strange magic had stopped time. Perhaps, as far as my husband was concerned, I hadn't disappeared at all, and the calendar was stuck on four days past. The idea was as fanciful as the man in the moon, but it helped my nerves.

I tended to Blanket in the stables before returning to the house to tidy up, glad of the work to keep my hands busy. The first to welcome me back was Faolan, bursting through the front door. "Mammy!" he said, "I saw Blanket and knew you were back."

"Well then, here I am," I said, opening my arms, but my lad stood back, refusing the embrace.

"Are we so terrible? That you had to go away from us?" Faolan asked.

"Didn't you know? When a woman goes off, she comes back wearing a crown."

"You don't have a crown. You're not a queen."

"Oh, but I am. The queen of the Moore farm. My crown is my children all around me."

"You talk like I'm a baby," Faolan said, pulling his hat from his head and flinging it to the

floor. "I'm not a baby! I can do almost everything Thomas and Patrick can do."

"Now pick up your hat, and don't be carrying on so," I said. As Faolan reached down, he said quietly, "You were seeing *The Italian* again, and she put a spell on you."

"If it be a spell, 'tis a grand spell, one that gives me the pluck to carry on," I said, the words leaping from my mouth.

"And Da says you're keeping secrets."

"Oh, he does, does he? And you believe everything your da says?"

"You said it too. You said we all have secrets in our hearts. I heard you say it. The day we saw seven crows!"

"Faolan, calm yourself. You're getting worked up over nothing."

"But where were you?"

"I'm sorry I left without a word. I was visiting Fiorella, just as you said. The thing is, she's my only friend," I said, opening up my arms again. This time Faolan fell into them.

"Da says *The Italian* is too old to be your friend," Faolan said, trying his best to hold back tears.

"Your father cares more for a bucket of warped nails than he does for her. And she's not that old. It's fending for herself winter after winter that's carved wrinkles into her face."

Obviously while I was away, my husband had done his mightiest to drive a wedge between Faolan and me. I asked Faolan if he knew the whereabouts of his father. Then I filled a small basin with soapy water and went out to face my moody husband. I wasn't sure what I would say to him, if I was to say anything at all.

I found James in the stables, grooming Blanket, even though I'd done so already. We avoided each other's eyes, though we were close enough to spit. I picked up the milk pail and turned my attention to our cow. As Nettie can be fussier than a granny's knitting circle, I made sure she had water and mineral licks close by. I plunked myself down on the stool, cleaned Nettie's teats, then slid the pail between my knees and began milking her.

Out of the corner of my eye, I noticed my husband's face, his wide nose and ruddy skin softened by the barn light. On first glance, he seemed calm, but his clenched jaw betrayed him. As he groomed Blanket, my body trembled like a mouse cornered by a cat, but I carried on squeezing and pulling, filling the pail quicker than usual. It was James who broke the silence. "I suppose you ran out of tobacco. Is that why you came back?"

"You never had a problem with my pipe before."

"Just trying to figure out why a wife would lie to her own son about her whereabouts. Tea with Mrs. McLeod, was it? A lie if there ever was. And it was hard on old Blanket."

"No harm's come to her."

"Her coat's lost its shine and there's a hairline crack in the left hoof. If you call that *no harm*."

"It's nothing that can't be fixed."

"I'm glad you're so damn sure of yourself. And what were you doing, going out in the snow in your condition?" We continued our chores in silence. Once again, he spoke. "The boys thought you'd gone for good. Gone to live with that crazy woman in the tree bluffs. You know what folks say."

"It's no concern of mine what people say."

"Now you've associated yourself with her. It damn well should concern you."

"People say the sky's green and the clouds are moss pudding. People say a lot of things, don't they?"

I felt a crumb of satisfaction hearing his complaints. He'd had a fright. He thought I'd gone for good, even though he knew where to find me. There were enough nosy parkers in the village to fill a church. I was sure someone had seen me coming or going, and it was enough to get their tongues wagging. It didn't matter who said what as I now had a friend, a true friend who changed my outlook from bleak to buoyant.

That evening, as I smoked my pipe in our porch, my mother's words came back to me. "Joy and woe are cut from the same cloth." Since I'd landed on this new continent, I'd clung to the notion that it had to be one or the other. Fiorella opened a door, though, where I could now peer into my life as a girl: crouching inside a holy well with the Blessed Virgin's trinkets and rosaries all around me, or standing under the mantle of the sky where stars pierced the blackness with pinholes of brilliance, or my sisters and I wading in the water in the early morning, with our nightgowns hoisted to our knees. We girls felt the power of the river as it ran its robes of cool silk over our bare skin. We knew we weren't separate from all the other creatures. We knew what we saw with our eyes was only a tiny fraction of what surrounded us. Everything was different then. Time was a wild thing that raced against the wind one minute, and shrank itself into a buttonhole the next. Time could not be tamed into minutes and seconds, neither could it be captured on a ticking box perched on the mantle.

For better or for worse, I couldn't live by the clock any more, dividing my life into seconds, minutes, days, weeks, months, years. The pane of glass over the clock had shattered and winter winds had come rushing in, carrying with it the wreckage of my marriage. Things had changed. I now had somewhere to go, safe with Fiorella. But it wasn't so simple as that, was it? What of Patrick and Thomas? Would they take their father's side? And Faolan—my boy who sees white crows, my window-frost boy—what of him? And what of this child to come?

CHAPTER TWO

The Mother, the Midwife & the Crone—Aspen Bluff, Manitoba,
1898

Fiorella:

"Is no good what she want for me to do. First when she visit, I think, is no problem. Her have no problem to bring *bambina* into world. Look, she is strong, healthy. What go wrong? Nothing. But last time *Maria* come, I wake up in night and look down at her sleep. Her lip is no colour, like ghost. I make sign of cross and go back to bed, but I no sleep. If she die when baby come, what she ask for me to do maybe put me to jail. One time before, police try put me to jail. They say I kill my husband. 'Why I do that?' I ask. 'My husband bring me all the way from Italy, now I'm going to kill?' Justa because I make the medicine, they see the herb all around, that is why they want put me to jail. No because my husband die. They no care if he die.

"Every day, I talka to you, Carmela, but you far away. Before, when you justa girla, you no want to talka Italian. Now maybe you forget. So, I talka *Inglese* to you. Maybe wind come, and pick up the word and push to you window. I think wind can blow far, all the way to you house. Is faraway place, yes? Ontario. Only one time, when we come from Italy, we go on train and see Ontario. Is big, big. I start one day on train, go all night, is new day and still Ontario. More and more tree all the time, I think, *When come Winnipeg?* Then it go flat, and some tree yes, but no like before. Then we go off train to Winnipeg. Sound funny to me when I hear that word, *Winnipeg*. Sound to me like name for cow or pig, not for big city.

"After you Papà die, I want to tell all the thing to you and you brother. But you go away to Salvatore's family. To Ontario. You think is good to go to city with *Zio* and *Zia*. You think, 'Mamma have nothing, why I stay with her?' Sometime I think you no care about you Mamma. If you care, why you no come visit? Still, every day, I sit in chair and talka to you. I no talka to you brother. The men, they no have *intuizione*. What you call in English? I think maybe is *six cents*.

"But now I tell you true story what happen to you Papà. Why he die. If I tell you, maybe you think different thing about you Mamma. You Papà come all the way on the boat for the job. Then, after six month, I come. We have good place to live, close to village. He work on railway. Is no perfect but it give money for food, for clothe. When you justa little girl, you Papà, he get sick and go to bed for maybe one day, two day. One time every month, he get sick. I make medicine, help for him to feel *tranquillo*. I make tea with the herb: *la lavanda, il luppolo, i fiori di calendula, l'angelica*. It work good, my tea. He get up, go back to job. But always he have sick again. Summer come, I grow special plant. I learn about plant in Canada because everything have different name in Italy. Even dandelion different name in Italy. Some plant no grow here but still I learn all the thing. I try. I grow. I try more.

"I get book from lady who come on the train. She have train car full of the book, so I ask if she have book about plant in Canada. She say *no*. One year after, her come and give for me the book. I no can read but I see the picture and word in *latino*. I think that funny to see word in *latino*. Only time I hear when I go to church. Now I see in book for the plant! That lady, she help for me to order the seed. After I grow and keep seed.

"Then you Papà, he lose job. We have to leave house. We go far away, where people no bother us. Salvatore, he make small house, this one, the house you grow up, you and you brother. We have the sheep, the goat, no horse, but lot of chicken for the egg. I make big garden and you help in garden. Salvatore help some time too, but other time he sleep in bed, because he is, how you call? Triste. You know this word. If you forget lot of Italian word, you remember this one, I think.

"We live okay. Is good day, bad day, but sometime is good. Then something go bad for us, like mold growing on old cabbage, worse, worse than mold, maybe like big basket of rotten tomato with worm in it. On that day, you Papà, he look *terribile*. His hair no wash, his hand shake bad, his eye full of tear. His heart broke but nothing come to break. He look like bad wind come to blow him away. He tell me he no sleep for two day. I make tea to help sleep, but he no want my tea. I make prayer for evil eye. I think maybe he have. After, he go out. All day, I feel the nerve. You and you brother just little. No baby, but *bambini piccoli*. I wait all day, look out window. Why he sick all the day? Why sad? Why *triste*?

"Next day, I find out where you Papà go. He take train to see doctor. He no pay ticket for train. He jump in box car. When he go to city, doctor give medicine. Is strong. Laudanum. It come in red bottle, like blood. When he show to me, I know what this is, come from poppy plant—*oppiacei*. When you get from doctor, colour like rust in fry pan, and is strong, very strong. Ten time more strong.

"Before lot of people, they ask for me to make the medicine, but now only one time in a big long year, they come. In secret they come. All the time, they look this way, that way, nervous. They no want anyone to see how they visit Fiorella. One time, a lady, she come. She bring little baby and she is cry when she come. I say, 'Come in, come in.' She open dress and she have red cyst on breast where baby suckle. On nipple! *Madre di Dio*! Breast come full with milk, and the mamma have to put baby there to take off the pressure. That mamma, she scream for pain, dig finger in my arm.

"Poor lady. First, I give *liquore*, sweet drink from wild *prugne*. Is good for pain. Then I take loaf of bread, fresh loaf, and slice thick. I warm goat milk on stove and putting slice of bread in milk. Then I'm putting bread on cyst, cover with cloth, and tell her to hold. Her hold for one hour. I cut bread and she hold again. I make little bed for Maria Violetta. She sleep on sheep wool. Baby wake only one time and feed on good breast. All night that lady, she cry like puppy. I'm putting that bread until bread is gone.

"Early in morning, I see hundred pinhole come where cyst was. Pinhole that go down, down, down into body. Infection coming out through all the little hole. When light come better in window, I show her. Eyes big wide in shock. Her never see like this before. I say, 'Is good. Now you get better.' I go to garden, dig hole and put sick bread in ground. After, maybe two day, three day, her husband come and give salt for animal and big bag of oat. He give me present, wrap with paper and string. I open. *Pagnotta di pane*, bread that lady make for me. This give for me smile.

"Carmela, when you girla, you listen to all the people and think you Mamma is witch. But is no true. I make the good medicine for to help. And I no kill you Papà. The medicine from doctor kill you Papà! You Papà put rope on neck, and hang from barn. But is no rope that kill, is strong doctor medicine. Why? Because all you Papà think about is doctor medicine. All he care about is doctor medicine. Before he have some good day, some bad day. Now he have all the time bad day. I watch how he get more sick, but I can do nothing. One day, *terribile giorno*, I find him in barn and I cut down right away. I have to do so you Papà go up to God. Hanging on rope is no good for soul. He half way this world, half way next.

"You know you Papà is big man, no tall but thick body. So I push wheelbarrow under to where he hang. I put in barrel lot of blanket from the bed in the house. Then I cut rope and he fall on blanket. Is no easy to take in house, *ma* I put wood on step so I can push wheel barrel over step. I see you Papà do this one time when he bring stove in house. I put one blanket on floor and roll you Papà onto blanket. Right away, I put salt under you Papà's head to keep spirit from coming back. Spirit need to go to next place, to heaven. How I can put salt under head if he hang from rope?

"When I look at you papà, I ask, *'Perché hai messo fine alla tua vita in quel modo?'* Okay, I understand why he do this, but why with rope? Is violent. All the year, I worry this happen. He go out some time in night and walk under dark sky. All the time I worry, but never I think he do this thing with rope.

"After he die, I make for him *unguento* for neck. I use for him *olio di rosa* and *fiori di calendula* and rub on neck wound. I wait for you and you brother to come home from school. I hear when you come, laugh like two birds, and I think, *This day take away smile from my children*. When you come in house, Carmela, you try shake you Papà for him to wake up. I tell you, 'Carmela, you Papà gone. With God now.' You brother, he no make word. He just look and his heart go hard, like stone. I tell him, 'Go to village for help.' He go and you go, too. I want for you to stay, for putting the clean clothe on you Papà and to wash you Papà's face. But you go with you brother.

"Then I wait. Before one star in sky, the police, they come to house and push down door. Door have no lock. They can justa open like everybody open but no, they break door like soldier coming. I no put back up the door. I leave broke all the year. I cut tent and nail all around. Keep out rain, keep out snow. But I no put back up door because it make me think of the day when you Papà die and the police come.

"The police, they ask lot of question. 'Why you take body down? Why you no wait for police? What you hide?' I try to make answer but they talka fast and not all the thing I understand. They walka circle around me, like wolf make circle around deer with disease. 'How I can do this?' I say to police, 'Me, no big. I have to get chair to pick up sugar from shelf. How I can put rope on high board in barn? Okay, I have strong arm, but no strong to lift big man like Salvatore.' They say, 'You strong to take husband down. Maybe you put husband up on rope too.' All the time they push guilty on me.

"The police make all the people think I do this, that I kill you Papà. At funeral, the police stand close. *Zio* and *Zia* think I'm guilty for this. *Zio Franco* and *Zia Alessandra* take you far away to city. But something you don't know. I open you Papà's tobacco tin, you know the one he keep by the stove. I want put little bit tobacco in coffin for him, before they put in ground, so I open tin box. I find letter. You Papà write how he love me, how he love you and you brother, how he feel sorry to do this. He ask for me to forgive. I wish he pick easy way to die. I wish he drink doctor medicine. If he drink doctor medicine, it put to sleep easy.

"I put little bit tobacco in coffin. I do other thing too. I put *camomilla* for *mia mamma*. She like to drink *tè* and when she die, I can no go to funeral in Italy. I tell my cousin in the telegram, I tell her to put *tè di camomilla* in *la bara*, in coffin, but she forget. My cousin, she spend all the time to fix hair, make pretty and she no care for other people. Is okay. Next time somebody die, I put *camomilla* in coffin and they give to Mamma in heaven. We do like this in Italy.

"You remember you Papà's coffin? Is no fancy, justa from

old board. *Ma*, you Papà look nice in clean clothe and I make shave too. That morning they bury you Papà, the police come too. They take *camomilla* out and sniff, like maybe is bad. I say to them, 'Put back. This is for Mamma. She wait ten year for this.' They think is funny, but they put back. All the thing, no time to tell you, because you go away after funeral. I never see again. I wish I can show you the note, but the police, they never give back, even though note like this *molto importante*.

"When I give note to police on day of funeral, no one read Italian, so I have to wait. I wait one week, two week, and all the time, *giovanotto*, young police come to house every day. When I see him, I give insult in Italian. I tell him he have *faccia di culo*. He ask, 'What that mean?' I tell him lie. That police in garden, in shed, looking in window, always with gun in hand, mean face. If I go to milk the goat, police watch. If I go to hang the clothe, police watch. He want for me to feel scared. I wear horn around neck, under dress, to protect from bad police. After two week, they get translator for note and now police know all the word you Papà write to me. They tell me, 'No press charge, but we watch you close.'

"I ask police if they help to find my daughter and son, because I no have address for you. They say to me, 'If you are my mother, I stay far away from you.' Carmela, I don't tell you this to make you feel the guilty. Okay, maybe little bit guilty is good, but not too much, because I want to see you again. I want to talka to you, about this lady, Maria.

"Maria, she nice lady; she make friend for me. For too many year, I have no friend. Maria, when she visit, we laugh, we make tea. Is nice. But now she want for me to do something. If I do this thing, police maybe come get me again. Maria, she think when baby come, maybe she die. And she no want baby to stay with father. He drink too much. Maybe he hurt baby. If she die, what she want for me to do? Steal baby? Poison baby? How I can do that? If I do that, I go to jail.

"Carmela, I want for you to be in chair beside me. Maybe you tell me what I can do. You maybe tell me, "No make friend with this Maria lady. She make trouble for you." I ask question, then listen for you answer. I talka close to fire, because voice travel lot of mile through chimney, like spirit voice. Every day, I listen for you to give answer for me. But I no hear you.

"All the time, I pray to Santa Filomena. I try everything to help Maria. I give tea, some night I keep her to stay when her husband drink. I have little bit food only, not enough for one person, but I share with Maria. All night, all day, I think about promise to Maria and what I should do. Always before, I keep my promise. I make promise to my husband, I keep. I make promise to Madonna, I keep. I make promise to Maria too. But I no like this promise. This promise have one part with angel, one part with devil."

Mary:

As my belly grows, my irritation with James grows as well. No matter how late he staggers through the door, he always wakes with the dawn. The other morning, while he pulled up his trousers, I feigned sleep until his shadow disappeared from the room. In that early morning hour, I imagined myself back at Fiorella's house hidden in the trees. I saw myself by her wood stove as she wove a crown of silver sage to ease my headache, then rubbed my temples with her lavender oil. I knew it was selfish of me to indulge in such childish daydreams. Still, I found I better managed the day because of it.

"No breakfast yet?" my husband asked, coming in from the barn.

"Are you wanting some soup? It's hot on the stove," I offered.

"I'll wait for eggs. It's colder than a witch's tit out there."

"Don't be talking so," I said, as I rinsed a few eggs and dropped lard into the skillet. "I don't
like gutter talk around the children."

"What children? Two are almost grown and the third is in school."

"True enough."

"Didn't I tell you it would be a long, cold winter?"

"You did. As did Faolan." North Dakota was cold enough when we lived there, but it was here in Aspen Bluff that I came to know the true meaning of winter. The wind was the worst, stinging through our layers of woolens like juggling swords. It was the Dominion Act that had us moving from North Dakota. At the time, I had little desire to uproot our family, but James was fixed on that quarter section of land we could claim for ten dollars. James talked as if, in Canada, pure cream flowed from the cow's udder, and corn grew as golden as Midas' touch. After the move, the truth came out about why we'd left home and hearth in a flurry. There were horse races to be had at River Park, seven times a day, seven days a week. Lucky seven, I suppose. Though James knew that it was a fair journey from Aspen Bluff to the track, it was still the horse racing he was after more than that quarter section of land.

I took a step away from the stove to avoid the spitting grease, but not soon enough. As James waxed on about the weather, I cleaned the grease spot with baking soda.

"The birds built their nests up high," James said. "Always a sign of cold weather to come. What about you? Have you had breakfast?"

"Not yet."

"Got the morning sickness, do you?"

"Not anymore, no. I'm like a dog with two tails," I said. I didn't enjoy his chattiness and wished he'd get on with his day.

Most mornings, James will barely string three words together. In fact, most days, once his chores are done, he goes to the neighbours to tip the bottle. But when he comes home with the smell of whiskey thick on his breath, that's when his tongue loosens. He starts to question me as to whose child I'm carrying. I refuse to answer when he's making as much sense as square wheels. Sometimes I imagine him frozen stiff in a snow drift. I picture his funeral too and, if that's not morbid, I don't know what is. It's a sin to think of such things, and I pray for God's forgiveness, but if my thoughts are the only thing keeping me from heaven, I'll choose purgatory. The Italian women attend Mass on the first Friday of every month, praying us all out of purgatory. Fiorella told me so. I'll get in line and wait for the next Italian lady to send me up to the pearly gate so.

"Here you go," I said, sliding eggs onto a plate. "Yolks are hard, as you like them. I'm off for a ski."

"What for?"

"I'm after a sprig of cedar for my linens."

"You sure you have time for that?"

"Peeling a pot of potatoes takes more time than a ski."

"Get one of the boys to break trail before you go. You'll enjoy it more," James said.

Underneath his false words, I sensed his hidden rage. He talks like a fancy dancer, but it's a thin layer of veneer covering his true nature. "There's been some snow," he added.

"It's only a dusting. I'll be fine."

Once outdoors, I felt a bite in the air, but I was glad to be away from James. After adjusting to the cold, I found myself in a faerie tale land: spindled aspen trees in the distance against a silvery sky, a lone bur oak, shadows cast from the distant trees like graceful dancers. As I skied across the field, with the shelterbelt drawing closer with each glide, something told me to turn my head. There was James watching from the window. He was likely watching to see if I might disappear again. If I did it once, I could do it again. But he had nothing to worry about, did he? How could I foist myself on Fiorella when she had so little? The next time I took a notion to see her, I'd fill up a sled with food from my larder. We'd sit together by the fire, drinking tea and eating apple cake. But these thoughts were only fancies, because, in my condition, there was no way to get to Fiorella's doorstep until spring.

To keep myself from thinking of James and his beady eyes at the window, I began to sing to the growing child inside of me, as I've done since the day that I found out I was with child. Most would say the tiny creature can't hear me, but I know she hears every note. And the times I cry, she hears that as well.

Returning home, James was gone from the window, and I felt my spirits lifted. Faolan met me at the front door saying, "Mammy, do you still have those buttons? The ones from your brothers and sisters and your Gran?"

"I do, but in the spring, I'm to give them to the church tea. They're after raising money for the missions in Africa."

"But they're special."

"Lately, they only make me somber," I said, tapping the snow from my *brógs* and setting

them by the stove to dry.

"Then give them to me."

"And what's a lad to do with buttons? You can't sew."

"I always watch you sew."

"Watching and doing are not the same thing. If it was, we'd all be cleverer than we are."

"I'm good at threading needles, and I'd sew if Patrick didn't laugh and call me a girl."

"He's no business calling you a girl. He mends his own sweaters and socks. If that isn't sewing, I don't know what is." I set the cedar I'd picked that morning onto the kitchen table, noticing how it filled the room with a hint of evergreen.

"So, will you? Give them to me?"

"So long as you put them out of my sight." When Faolan skipped off, I almost called after him to say I'd changed my mind, but the urge passed. And, I thought, if anything happened to me, God forbid, at least the buttons would be in good hands. As I came closer to the birth, I found myself tormented with worry.

Now that we're deep in winter's cold, one single thought calms me as I await the day—Fiorella's offer to be at my side. I've been waiting all this time to tell James, to warn him that she'll be here. I know the mention of her name is enough to curl his toenails, so I haven't mentioned it yet. But time is running out, to be sure.

⁘

Ten lunar months meant the baby would arrive in the middle of March, not the best time to be giving birth with the snow drifts piled up, and the mercury stuck below zero. But my biggest worry was that the birth might land on March 19th. 'Twas a queer feeling I'd had on that ominous day, and it didn't leave me, even when my husband told me that the cow and the calf were out of distress. All that evening, my hands stayed numb and cold, and it wasn't until morning that I felt myself again. So, I couldn't be faulted for dreading March the 19th. And I couldn't be faulted for wanting protection from Fiorella or the saints, or wherever else I might find it.

On the eve of St. Brigid's Day, I put oak cakes on the windowsills and hung ribbons in the bushes and trees near the house. They weren't fancy ribbons, more like thin strips of rags. Though they were tattered, the colour—the red of a crossbill—looked pretty against the white of the snow as they danced in the wind. The next morning, February 1st, I unfastened the ribbons and brought them inside to be hung above the doorways and tied around our bedposts. With the few that were left, I climbed up into the garret and fastened them to Patrick, Faolan and Thomas's bedposts. I didn't think the boys would notice and, if they did, they'd likely chalk it up to a mother's whim.

When March 19th came and went, I breathed a sigh of relief. On the eve of the equinox, mild cramping woke me up in the night, which I took to be false labour. At the first sign of daylight, and still in my nightgown, I pulled on my coat and boots and stepped outdoors. The stillness of winter's long night lingered, with not a single bird to announce the new day. Hardly a whisper of wind touched my skin. During the week, the sun had melted and refrozen the top layer of snow, and now a heavy crust sat atop the surface, gleaming like diamonds. It was a pleasant change to leave my skis behind and walk willy-nilly toward our tree shelter. Once or twice I almost broke through the snow's surface, but it held my weight well enough.

I circled back toward home when fresh snow began to fall, like feathers shaken from a worn quilt. I was reminded of my mammy. Whenever she saw a speck of snow, she'd point up to the sky and say, "See that, girls? The swans have lost their feathers." I wondered, what would she say to a Canadian winter? There weren't enough feathers in the world to account for all the snow in this land.

I'd only just stepped back inside, and tossed my coat over a chair when my waters broke. My only thought was that I needed Fiorella at my side, no matter that her presence was like a poison ivy rash on my husband's skin. I shouted at Faolan, who sat at the table with sleepy eyes, "Go fetch your brother!"

"Thomas or Patrick?" he asked.

"Either one. Go quick!"

Thomas arrived moments later, flushed and out of breath. "What is it, Mam?"

"The baby's coming. With this weather—"

"I'll hitch up the sleigh. Mrs. Watts is a solid hour."

"No, lad. Not there!"

"But you'll need the midwife!"

"Thomas, listen to me. It's Fiorella I need."

"Not her. Da won't stand for it."

"Is it your father giving birth? Now do as I say and bring my friend to this house. I won't move from the window until she's at my side."

Thomas would rather have flung himself at a pack of wolves. "But Ma," he groaned, "what does she know about birthing?"

"It's what she did in the old country."

"Her backwards country."

"No more backwards than Ireland. I beg you, Thomas. Go and get Mrs. Watts if you must, but first stop at Fiorella's—"

"They're in opposite directions," he argued. A contraction began. I gripped the back of the nearest chair, and that was enough to send Thomas flying out the door.

None of my children came dancing into the world with a wink and a nod. They all avoided the entrance as if it were lined with thorns. Knowing it could be a long labour, I thought it wise to keep myself busy. I first climbed down to the root cellar to scavenge for vegetables. My choices were slim: shrivelled turnips, a few carrots stored in a bin of sand, some pale-looking squash. The *taties* were as soft as tomatoes, and the onions were long gone, though I'd saved up a basket of onion skins for a tasty broth.

Once the soup was on simmer, I sat by the window praying the snow would let up. I began to rummage through my mending basket, pulling out a corner of this and that: a half-done embroidered doily, a blouse in need of a button, a shirt with a torn pocket. By now James knew of my situation and tapped at the window to see if I needed anything. I shook my head *no* and pretended to be busy mending. At long last, I found the white bonnet I'd crocheted for my new baby girl. My nimble fingers took to the needle as I added blue ribbon to tie it up with. My labour pains continued to rise and fall, yet I kept the rhythm of the needle without interruption.

After a time, the front door swung open, bringing with it a gust of frigid air. The silhouette of a body claimed the better part of the opening. I expected to see the face of Fiorella but no, it was Mrs. Watts, looking as tough as old boots. Before I could speak, the woman blurted out, "Now what's this I hear of you bringing a foreigner to the house? We'll have none of that. I've been midwife in these parts for close to forty years."

"Where's my son?"

"Tending to the horses, while I tend to you."

I stood up, reaching for my coat. "Mrs. Moore, have you lost your senses?" Mrs. Watts asked. "You're not in any shape to be traipsing about in the snow."

"I need to talk to Thomas."

"Who's Thomas?"

"My son! The one who brought you here!" "It was your Patrick who came for me. Mr. Moore, sensible man that he is, sent him to get me. Now if everything is in order, I'll ask after Thomas, but not until I've examined you."

I followed the midwife into the bedroom. What would be the point in arguing with her? She was like a great rock holding back the sea. The waves would crash all day and night, but she would not budge. She had me roll onto my side, and did her check by going between my buttocks and up inside me. It was anything but pleasant, and I didn't pretend otherwise. A woman goes through it all the same, as it tells us how close the baby is to coming. The midwife finally said, "We will certainly need to be prepared. But it's nothing I can't handle."

"Tell me it's not feet first."

"No. The baby's facing forward. I'm not worried and neither should you be. We'll get him turned around, if it comes to that."

"You'll ask after Thomas now?"

"Not until we move you upstairs."

"My sons sleep up there!"

"You're a stone's throw from the kitchen. You'll need a ceiling between yourself and the rest of the family. So up we go."

"Once I talk to Thomas, I'll move to the moon if you say so. But I'll not shift an inch until then," I said.

Mrs. Watts frowned, which was little effort, given that her mouth rarely turned its corners up to the sun. But to my surprise, she turned to let herself out.

"And the youngest, Faolan," I called after her, "when the time is close, send him outside to play."

"I've brought over fifty babies into this world. I can manage your Faolan perfectly well,"

Mrs. Watts said, as she firmly shut the bedroom door behind her.

I crawled to the end of the bed. When the labour pains came, I took hold of the baseboard and leaned into it. Shooting pains now gripped my hard belly and circled around to my lower back. I called to mind the walk I'd taken that morning, and the magic of winter's light at dawn. The sky had taken on a dull bluish colour, while the white fields glowed like a crystal ball, almost as if heaven and earth were reversed. I thought how, to be sure, beings of light hide in the world—in fresh fallen snow, in the breasts of chickadees, in the wind—eager and waiting to offer glimpses of joy to us all. I would bring this radiant snow into my body, and allow its glow to fill me up. I would invite it in, not only for my own sake, but for the sake of my unborn child.

I was suddenly reminded of how my Aunt Helen took me north to a lake. 'Twas my first springtime in North America, and I noticed how the snow clung to the ground in all the shady places, as if the snow loathed the idea of melting. We found a flat rock along the shore and sat a while, but my auntie began to complain of the damp, so we took a stroll in a wooded area.

Sprinkled here and there, tiny blue violets poked their blooms up through the snow. I would name the baby Mary Violet. She would be a wild flower in this cold world—as fragile as a new petal, yet tough enough to break through the snow.

I was sorry to have my thoughts interrupted by Mrs. Watts barging back into the bedroom. "Your other son, Thomas, has arrived. And I'm sorry to say he has that foreign woman with him."

"Thank God!"

"I told her straight away, I won't have her poking her nose in—"

Just then, Fiorella swooped into the room. Mrs. Watts didn't waste any time speaking her mind. "My dear woman," she said to Fiorella, "we agreed you'll wait in the kitchen with the men."

"No understand. My English no good," Fiorella said.

"You understand perfectly well when it suits you."

Fiorella slid her soft arms around my waist as I leaned into her, groaning through another birth pain. They were coming now, a minute apart. Fiorella then faced Mrs. Watts square on, and said, "If Maria want me to stay, I stay. Her want me to go, I go."

"Stay, I need you here!" I shouted.

"Fine, but this is how it's going to be," Mrs. Watts said, facing Fiorella. "First, we move Mary, and her name is Mary, not Maria. We'll move Mary upstairs where we won't be tripping over each other like two great oafs. You can hold her hand, wipe her brow, but don't meddle with me!"

Another birth pain began on the heels of the one before. I imagined my body as the ocean, and the cramps as waves, carrying my child to shore.

"Good God," said the midwife, "things are progressing quickly!"

"Baby come fast now. No good to move," Fiorella said.

"Where on earth is that boy?" Mrs. Watts snapped. Just then, I heard a hesitant tap at the door and Patrick's voice, saying, "Mrs. Watts? Do you have everything you need?"

"As of yet, I've only one basin of water."

"We put the other one upstairs, like you told us. And clean sheets. We warmed up a brick too, for the bed."

"We'll manage from here. And don't keep your ear to the door. This is woman's work," she said sternly.

If we'd taken the stairs a minute later, I couldn't have managed it. As it was, Fiorella held me up on one side while Mrs. Watts supported from behind. I was no sooner in the room that I felt the urge to push. The midwife insisted I climb up onto the bed first. Once I was on the bed with pillows stuffed behind me, Mrs. Watts held my knees apart. Maybe she expected the infant to pop into her receiving hands, as easily as catching a ball. She quickly examined me, and said, "We're almost there, Mary, but you're not quite ready. Breathe. Breathe slowly. Never mind the urge to push."

"I can't!" I shrieked. I felt as if it would've been easier to hold back the tide, but I did as she asked.

"I'll breathe with you. We'll do it together. That's it. Good girl."

Just when I thought it impossible to take another deep breath, Mrs. Watts commanded, "It's time, Mary. Time to push. And don't hold back."

I pushed. I pushed hard. Then I pushed again. And again. It felt like an eternity. "Oh God oh God oh God! Dear mother in heaven, how much longer?" I wailed.

"Something no good," I heard Fiorella say. "Look, her face white. *Come la neve.*"

"I've reached my limit with your broken English. If you can't say something in English, don't say anything at all!" Mrs. Watts said, laying down the law. She took a gentler tone with me and said, "Come along, Mary, you can do this. It's close."

I pushed again and this time, Mrs. Watts declared, "That's it! The wee one is crowning. Now, the next time you feel the urge, breathe through it. We don't want you to tear."

Sure, a terrible weariness had taken hold of me, and I drifted into a dream. 'Twas more like a nightmare with a fog that filled the room, thick as pea soup. I felt like a drowning woman with a hundred stones pressed down upon my breast. *Where is my baby? Is she all alone? Is she on a boat at sea? Have the winds changed course?* I tried to climb out of the bed, but fell back into the murky waters of my mind. All around me, I saw St. Brigid's red ribbons moving chaotically, as if a terrible wind had ripped them from the bedposts. I fought to tear off my heavy clothes, but my cotton gown clung to me like tangled seaweed. My legs felt numb from the cold and icy waters. *Where is she? Where is the boat to take Mary Violet to safe shores?*

As I fought for life, I called to mind Fiorella's promise that, if anything should happen, she would not allow the child to be raised by my husband's hand, raised by the drink and all its offshoots of turmoil. Eventually, I had no choice but to give over to the ocean waves, or whatever force I was battling. The minute I let go, the fog cleared, and I fell back into the room. I saw Mrs. Watts at my side. I tried to ask her if my baby had been born, but she didn't seem to hear me. She just kept shouting, her voice as shrill as a whiskeyjack, "Mrs. Moore! Mrs. Moore! Come back to us!"

I answered, "I'm here, safe," to put every one's mind at ease. The midwife pulled the bloodied sheets out from under me, and tossed them in a basin. After that, I heard Mrs. Watts, but her voice was muffled, as if she stood behind a closed door. The voices of the two women came together and then separated into two voices, only to blend again into one. A word here and there found its way into my ears—*unconscious, pulse, we could lose them both.*

A while later—though I can't say exactly when—I saw my

tiny baby in Fiorella's arms in a shadowy corner of the room. Mary Violet's eyelids were like the gossamer wings of a dragonfly, her brow soft as a fawn's, and her face the moon in a wintery sky. Her tiny fingers were like the delicate ghost plant shooting up from the bluffs in the spring. I watched as Fiorella pulled something from her pocket, a glass vial, and dabbed it on my baby's tongue. What was she doing? And then my own words came back to haunt me, "Do *whatever it takes* to keep the baby from being raised by my husband."

A familiar tingling began, first in the tips of my fingers, then my hands and finally rushing through my body. Was this my charm of finches? They were birds of the air, carrying years of struggle, carrying grief as snowflakes on their wings, carrying it far away where it would sadden me no more.

Fiorella:

"I am surprise to get letter from you! I no understand word, but I see picture of you in wedding dress. *Sei bellissima.* I like to write letter, too, but I can no write for the English. Carmela, I hope that man you marry is good husband. Remember what I tell you; two things to run away from husband—if husband hit you, or husband drink too much. If husband smell bad some time, or maybe you no like how he complain for nothing, or if he want same food all the time, is okay. But if he do bad thing, pack suitcase and come home to me. Okay? Is better to have poor, than live with man who make prison for you.

"I tell you now about trouble with Maria. Maria, she have three boy. One justa young, and two almost grow to man. When baby starting to come, one boy get me and one boy get midwife. Midwife is big lady who speak good English. Everybody is listen to her, and she no like me. She look at me funny eyes all the time. She tell me, 'You no talka. Just sit.' She want for me to go. I stay, hold Maria hand and pray. She shout all the time this thing, that thing—no Maria, but the midwife. I look in Maria eyes and tell her, 'You no worry, Maria. I no leave you side.'

"All the time, I pray to Madonna Maria, *ma*, never I see like this before. Maria pushing baby. Baby little bit coming. We see head. We need Maria to push out baby but she go in sleep world. Midwife put hand inside and pull baby out. She yell for me to cut cord. I no see, what you call—*le forbici*. I no see, so I take ribbon from bed, and tie strong. After midwife, she give me cutting thing, so now I cut cord. Then wrap *bambina* in blanket. Midwife lady, she stay with Maria. Maria have big problem. I think maybe she die. I think so many thing, like marionette go fast dance.

"I remember all the thing Maria tell me, what to do if she die. I have heavy rock in heart. I have to keep promise. I have to do all the thing in secret. Midwife, she have eyes like crow, but she busy, talking all the time. After I say to midwife, 'Baby is dead.' She no believe, but then she look. No breathe, the baby. Doctor in house. Midwife tell me doctor have to make paper for baby. All the time, I think about when you Papà die, how the police make the paper, how they say is my fault. I'm scared, but keep strong for Maria. Keep strong for the promise.

"The Papà of baby, he coming up the stair. Heavy boot on step. Midwife tell him baby is dead. Hard man, face like ice. He no want to see baby. He say, 'This baby no my baby.' I want to tell big man, *You give for me to bury baby. I do good prayer for baby. No pieno di rabbia,* full of hate. He hate baby and he hate me. I have to make lip shut, say nothing, or maybe he do something bad. I don't know what, but maybe throw baby or hit me hard with stick. So I say nothing and pray nobody come to take me to jail."

CHAPTER THREE

The War to End All Wars—Autrecourt-et-Pourron, France 1918
- twenty years later

Faolan:

I opened my eyes to a strange bedroom, not knowing which end was up. A water jug sat two feet away, but I was too weak to reach over and pour myself a glass, which was a disappointment because my throat was so dry that it felt as if someone had scraped off a layer of my vocal cords. I was weighted down by what felt like ten blankets. Lifting my neck a few inches, I could see the bed's wrought iron foot board and a dresser behind it. A simple chair with an embroidered cushion sat next to the bed. The room was decorated with blue linen curtains, a plain wooden cross above the door, and a dresser with a lacy tablecloth draped over it. *Either heaven is not what I thought, or I've just landed inside the prettiest hospital room this side of the ocean.*

My head was pounding and I felt groggy, confused. I drifted back to sleep, and when I woke up a second time, I saw a woman, who I guessed to be thirty years of age, staring down at me. I noticed fine-lined crow's feet at the corners of her eyes, hair blonder than any girl from Canada, and a thin figure. It was her face that put me at ease. It was a face that erased any sign of fragility—strong cheekbones, serious eyes, and teeth lined up like a row of dancers. She wore a plain, grey, button-up dress with a small bit of embroidery around the collar. I watched her pull back the bed sheets and point to my leg, explaining something to me in French. Looking down at my legs, I didn't notice anything too serious: no dressings, no lesions to the skin, no bullet wounds or burns. My one leg was ballooned right up and reddish in colour, but that was all.

Bustling out the door, the woman returned a few minutes later with a basin filled with what looked to be steaming milk. She set it on top of the dresser, then pushed a woolen blanket into the liquid, stirring it around with the help of a wooden spoon. Once the blanket was completely immersed, she plunged her hands into the basin and wrung out the fabric. She placed a couple of wooden blocks under my right leg, and then wrapped my leg in that hot, woolen blanket. This lady was no stranger to hard work.

The woman, whose name I later discovered to be Simone, left the room with my leg all cocooned up, and me no wiser as to how I'd landed there. I knew my own name, thank God for that, and that I was a soldier. I could see my service coat hung over the bedpost and that was proof enough. But what was I doing in this place? Why wasn't I in a medical facility? The American army had nursing stations and hospitals spotted all through France. I had a lot of questions that day, but didn't see anyone lining up to answer them.

When Simone returned to do the unwrapping, I asked, "What am I doing here?" Her only answer was a shake of the head. "I need to know. You got to find someone who talks English," I pleaded. She held a cup of water to my lips, but I brushed it away, spilling it all over her and the bed covers. It wasn't the most polite way to treat my nurse, but I wasn't my-self during those first few days. It occurred to me that while I was knocked out, she must've changed the sheets and given me fresh underwear, which was downright embarrassing. It wouldn't be so bad if she were an old lady, or a nun.

At one point, maybe a few days later, the bedroom door opened a crack and two serious little faces peered in at me, a boy and a girl. The girl stared at me with eyes clear as glass. I winked at her—the first sign of my humour returning—but my wink only scared her off. It took a while before those two sprouts advanced to the front lines, that is, crossed the thresh-old of my bedroom door. Once the ice was broken, they made a regular habit of peeking in. The first time the boy ventured to talk, he had me write down my name on a scrap of paper. The two of them went scurrying downstairs, shouting to their mother, "*Maman, Maman! Le nom du soldat!*"

The kids taught me a few words in French and I taught them English words, mostly objects around the room: picture, window, door, that sort of thing. Pierre and Marguerite were their names, just like storybook children. They always had a look of hunger on their faces, so whatever bit of supper was brought up to me, once I graduated from liquids to solids, I made a habit of saving some for them. For most of the day, I was left on my own, other than Simone who continued to wrap my leg twice daily and refresh my water jug around the clock.

Eventually, I could recall my division, my roll-call num-ber, every member of my squad, but when it came to how I'd landed on Simone's doorstep, only vague impressions came to mind. It's funny to think that, when I enlisted, I was flattered because they assigned me to 2nd Engineers. I thought it was some kind of compliment on my intelligence, but I soon found out that engineering duties meant building barges and bridges to get across rivers, repairing roads, and digging trenches. By the time we arrived, hundreds of miles of trenches had already been dug, zigzagged lines severed deep into the earth. Since the war began, the allied forces had been trying to push back enemy lines and, in the end, they'd moved only a few miles forward or backward, like a deadly chess board game.

Me and seven others made up a squad and we were subordinate to an infantry platoon. On first arrival, they kept us busy building accommodations for the incoming flux of soldiers from the US. After training, we were meant to support the infantry by performing engineer duties. Repairing roads was one of our mains—some of the roads so torn up from years of fighting, they'd all but vanished—but we also went into battle as wire cutters when necessary. Going out in teams of four, two of us cut the heavy gauge barbed wire, one carried an axe to chop down posts, and a fourth man cleared the way. Safe to say, casualties were high in the 2nd Engineers. On account of that, we were close to each other, as close as brothers.

Little things make a big difference when you're stuck with the same guys day in and day out. If Frank offered me a bit of tobacco, that made my day. Everyone had their good luck charms. Frank had a picture of his girl, Charlie had a cloth doll his kid sister had given him, and Pat refused to shave on odd days of the month. I sewed two small buttons into the lining of my service coat, buttons that were my mother's and before that were her mother's. Like I say, we all had our charms, but it would take more than charms to save us from the perils of war.

Some days I wonder what possessed me to enlist. I had it good up in Northern Ontario, working on the railway. I boarded in a hole-in-the-wall place called Hurkett where most days, the train slowed down enough to toss the sack of mail, some dried goods, and the all-important newspaper. Everyone waited for the daily *Port Arthur News Chronicle* the way a kid waits for candy and oranges at Christmas time. The war was all anyone talked about, but loyalty to the King wasn't a given. Most families were from Russia, Poland, Finland, Bulgaria, and the

Ukraine. Still, quite a few of the Hurkett boys went off to war—Richard Kohler, Oziase Dumas, and others—whether or not they had a drop of English blood in them.

The men sat outside the train station every morning, scanning the paper for reports on casualties. "Do ya think you Americans will jump in now? With the Germans getting cozy with Mexico?" asked Old Freddy, who wasn't nearly as old as he made himself out to be. I had showed up early for my shift, and was chatting it up with the locals.

"The Americans, they've been sitting on that picket fence so long, it's worked holes into their arses," said Budic Kwasnuski, spitting out his chew at little too close to where I was standing.

"What do you think, Faolan? About them Americans taking a neutral stand while our boys are over there fighting?" asked Freddy.

"I got no opinion on that."

"Well, you're American, aren't ya?" Everyone, including the station master's cat, knew I carried an American passport. Consequently, the men looked to me for the American point of view.

"I was born there, but that doesn't mean anything," I said, pulling out my steaming thermos of coffee.

"Never be ashamed of who you are," said Budic.

"I'm not ashamed. I just don't remember much about it. I was only a little gaffer when we moved up to Canada, all of seven years old."

"Old enough to milk a cow and learn your numbers," said Budic. Somehow, I couldn't picture Budic learning arithmetic at the age of seven, but I didn't argue.

"When I was no bigger 'n a peanut, I was helping out my mother on the farm while my old man disappeared for months at a time," said Freddy. "Worked the bushcamps, eh. Camp one."

"Talk to my brothers; they'll remember North Dakota better than me," I said. "When we moved north, they had to travel in the cattle car."

"Well, sure. You got to keep your livestock watered and fed. Them railway men aren't trained for that," said Old Freddy.

"Every chance they get, my brothers remind me how I had the soft passenger seat while they were crowded up in the stock car."

"Momma's boy, were ya?"

"I've never seen a seven-year-old in a cattle car. Have you?" I asked the two men.

"Maybe if you got Calamity Jane as a mother," Old Freddy said with a chuckle.

I was convinced I was as Canadian as the rest of them, but not long after, I discovered I was more American than I realized. Again, we were at the station, discussing politics, when this older bushworker, who didn't usually talk much, turned to me and said, "I lost my son overseas. It'll be a year tomorrow. My only...my only son. Five daughters and one son." By God, I felt bad for him, the way he had trouble finishing his sentence, his eyes glossing over. Even in this tiny hamlet, the tollkeeper of war had extracted a price. Why had this man chosen to tell me about his son? Maybe he thought I could sympathize, being that I was more or less the age of his boy. Or maybe it was because there, on the front page of the paper that day, the headlines read *United States of America Declares War on Germany*. Not too often did the newspaper print with red ink, but on that morning, the headlines were beetroot red.

After that, the war was never far from my thoughts. Then one Saturday, I took the passenger train into Port Arthur to get my watch fixed. I spent a night in a rooming house, which had the unpleasant odour of fried garlic and urine. First thing in the morning, after attending Mass, I headed back to the station, but instead of taking the *Canadian Pacific* line back to

Hurkett, I switched to the *Intercontinental* going west to Fort Frances. Then I hitchhiked across the border and landed in International Falls where I enlisted. The whole trip took me less than two days, including the overnight in Port Arthur. I felt bad that I hadn't said goodbye to my Aunt Kate, but when I left, I earnestly thought my main purpose was to fix my watch. There's an irony there, especially considering the watchmaker did a poor job and my watch never did get fixed properly.

For my basic training, I was sent to Camp Baker, Texas. I was confident I'd pass the height requirements for the military, but wasn't sure about the chest measurement. It turned out there was a minimum thirty-four-inch requirement and I easily measured thirty-eight inches. I passed the medical without a problem, too. I was twenty-eight years of age and it was my first time ever seeing a doctor. I was full of something, though I'm not sure what. Was it patriotism, or loyalty to all those soldiers who'd lost their lives?

After training, we crossed the ocean in real style on *The Carpathia*. I thought of my mother often, and how she'd crossed the ocean in the belly of a whale like Jonah, or something worse considering Jonah didn't get infected with typhus the way my mother's family did. *The Carpathia* was a fine luxury liner, until it picked up speed. Then it shook and rattled and wheezed like an old piano with loosened keys. They told us it was seaworthy, but it didn't sound like it was. I guess it got worn out when it went full speed to save those poor souls from the wreckage of *The Titanic*. After landing in Glasgow, then Southampton, England, we took another boat to Havre, France, and finally a train brought us to Uruffe. In Havre, everyone came out to cheer for the Americans, but we were about as ready for war as a mouse facing a lion. Still, it was nice to get a warm welcome because, before we knew it, they were preparing us for trench warfare.

How in the heck do you describe war to your loved ones

back home? How do you describe the threat of machine gun nests, or the shrill sound of the whistle sending us into battle, or having to work under the barrage of striking shells? Of course, we weren't always on the edge of things. Plenty of times we puttered around, and even mixed it up a bit with the French folks, depending on whether we were at the base or in a town. To this day, odd images stay with me: a soldier sitting with a French family and he was kidding around, pretending a potato was a shoe, and trying to fit up a barefoot girl with the potato, like in that Cinderella story. Or going to a restaurant and the waiter was making a big fuss, coming out with a silver tray, lifting the lid to reveal a fish so small that it would barely feed a cat. We laughed over that, me and Pat, who happened to be with me. Here we thought we'd be getting the best of French cuisine, and all we got was an oversized sardine. Course, it was winter, and it was wartime, so you can't fault the restaurant for not having basic ingredients.

I guess it's those flashes, almost like photographs, that helped give me the one-up on letter writing. Off the start, my comrades would hand me their letters before mailing them and I'd mess around with the words. Before I knew it, I was inventing and reciting love letters for the fellows to send to their girls. I'd compose some phrase about the mist in the early morning or stars in a midnight sky, giving the idea that we were all in the pink—not a thing to worry about. The boys said it was the Irish in me, but I think it came from reading the Psalms. The Psalms are full of poetry. My mother always liked a good poem, too.

"It wouldn't hurt to throw some humour in there, eh? Keep your girl from worrying too much," I told Charlie one day.

"Let her worry. Might keep her mind off other men," Charlie said.

"You mean those old-timers walking with canes and forgetting to trim their whiskers? The rest of us are over here fighting a war," I reminded Charlie.

"I'm no good at letter writing, and you better think twice with them censors reading every word."

"I'm sure you could come up with something entertaining for the censors. Or for your girl," I said.

"Anything we get a kick out of? Too crude for my Cathy's tender ears," said Charlie.

"What about the sawed-off brooms?" I suggested.

"Ah yeah. But I'd make a mess of that story. You write it for me."

"I'll recite it. That's as far as I'm going. I talk. You write."

After scrambling for a scrap of paper, Charlie said, "I'm ready. Shoot."

"Two soldiers, Pete and Johnny, refused to bathe. This is back in Texas, during training," I began.

"We don't need to say where. That's a lifetime ago," said Charlie.

"Leave it in, take it out, who cares?" said Frank, listening in on the sidelines.

"Pete and Johnny were starting to stink really bad and it caught the attention of our superiors," I continued. "The Major told us, 'Find two brooms. Cut them off where they're sewed. Take the men back to the showers, give them five minutes to bathe.'"

"Slow down, slow down. This ain't a race, is it?"

I waited a minute and launched back in. "'Give them five minutes to bathe, and if they don't cooperate, scrub them with the brooms. And scrub them good.' When Pete and Johnny saw those sawed-off brooms, the soap bubbles flew!"

The boys in our squad sent the broom story to their girl-friends or to their folks. It got around.

"I hope those girls don't know each other," I mentioned a few weeks later. We were sitting at the back of a Liberty truck, rattling along some dirt road in France. "They're going to smell something fishy if they talk to each other."

"Nah. My girl's in upstate New York," said Charlie. "But Adam here, he's got a girlfriend in every State, don't ya Casanova?"

"Wish I did. Wish I did," said Adam. "Only three states with girls waiting for me."

"No more love poems for you, my friend. You've got an unfair advantage," I said.

"How do you manage it?" Charlie asked. "That's what I'd like to know."

"Must be this good-looking mug of mine," said Adam, cocking his head to the side.

"If one girl finds a new beau, you've got two others in the wings. Definitely unfair," said Frank.

"Hey Adam, you got a little sister?" I asked.

"As a matter of fact, I got two little sisters."

"Maybe you should be sending them letters until you make up your mind which girl you're going with," I said.

"Jealousy is so obvious, it's written across your goddamn forehead."

"Nah," I claimed. "I'm just waiting for the right one to come along." This was my stock answer whenever anyone asked me if I had a girlfriend. Part of me knew it was crazy to be thinking about finding a wife, especially since the chance of any of us making it out alive wasn't exactly encouraging. In wartime, everything can change in a single heartbeat. As it turned out, a heartbeat did change everything. I ended up confined to a bed in the village of Autrecourt-et-Pourron, and I couldn't even say what brought me there. With each passing day, I tried to clear my brain of cobwebs. I felt like a piece of my reasoning was on leave, and it caused me great aggravation.

❧

During those weeks in that bedroom infirmary, I found myself remembering my childhood days, almost as if my soul wanted to reach back before the war in an effort to tie the two pieces of my life together. With my eyes closed, I saw miles of prairie corn fields, barn swallows dipping into the wind with the tips of their wings tinged in golden light, and the sun hanging low in the horizon. I saw my mother, Mary Moore, kneading bread with stray black hairs floating across her brow, and singing lullaby songs long after the stars first lit up the sky.

Some women are beautiful, but my mother was handsome. Her skin was pale and soft, her face wide, and her features arranged nicely, like the man in the moon. She had dark eyes, darker than most Irish women, and set wide apart. When my da was in a good mood, he called her *my lovely doe*. Her mouth was small and her lips didn't have much colour. Her hair was what folks noticed—thick and dark, and long enough to be braided around her head like a black crown of rope. I never understood why she cut off her hair, but it was one of those things a boy knows not to ask.

Sometimes, on a good day, my mother would tuck a daisy or black-eyed Susan in her hair, but only if my father was in town picking up supplies. As soon as she heard the horses clopping up the road, or the *boreen* as my mother called it, she'd pluck those flowers out. She'd open her hands wide to let the wind or gravity take the flowers, almost as if the blossoms were creatures and she didn't want to hurt their feelings by abruptly tossing them away.

If a neighbour needed a well dug, they always headed over to the Moore farm to fetch my mother. My father made noises about that because he didn't like her getting attention from anyone. If the crows came around for her kitchen scraps, that was too much attention for my Da. Of course, his grumbling disappeared when a laying hen appeared at our doorstep, or a cut of beef come killing time, wrapped in butcher paper and set in a crate of ice. The neighbours thought Ma was strange, but when she marked the spot to dig a well, they always struck water as sure as lightning strikes the highest tree, and they had to show their gratitude somehow.

"Your mother's going out to do her water witching. You'll be taking the day off school," my father said when I was just a little fella. I hadn't yet gone dousing with my mother, but a day off school always promised to fun. Out on the land, the farmer handed my mother a branch. She frowned and shook her head. Then she went off wandering, looking for the perfect switch to do the job, like a carpenter who'd rather use his own tools. She kept her eye out for something both tough and bendable. Pulling a knife out from her bag, she cut a willow bough to the precise measurement. As she held out her forked divining rod, I skipped a few paces behind, feeling like an explorer's sidekick. All of my mother's attention was focused on that stick in the shape of a Y and she held it out in front of her like it was Moses's staff parting the Red Sea.

While my mother dowsed, she didn't look up or down or sideways, and kept her gaze fixed directly in front of her with wisps of hair blowing lightly across her face. I even saw a hornet land on the end of her nose, but she didn't flinch. When she found the spot, her arms began to tremble and, though she resisted, I witnessed that stick being pulled down by an invisible force. While I jumped up and down like we'd struck gold, my mother waved to the farmer who stood in the distance. He made a run for it, marking the spot with a stake. As we headed back to the road, the farmer's wife came out to thank my mother, but we never got an invite for tea and cake. Maybe they were jealous of her special talent, or maybe they didn't like that she was odd and kept to herself. Either way, we didn't get tea.

Once home, my father tormented me with questions: how long did it take for my mother to find the spot? Who did she talk to? Was the farmer's wife around? Did the farmer talk to my mother, and if he did, what did he say? Even though I said nothing to incriminate my mother, I still felt like I was betraying her. She was serious about doing her job; finding the right place to dig was her only focus, so why did Da insist on asking so many questions?

After that, my father always sent me along as the spy. Can a kid love and dread something at the same time? Because that's how it was with me. My mother went dousing for water only once in a blue moon. After all, how many times in a person's life do they need a well dug? Even still, word got around and during the summer months, she'd have two or three properties to visit.

"I'll be heading down the *boreen* tomorrow," she announced to my father one August day.

"What for?" my father asked, shooting his head up from the kitchen table where he sat rolling tobacco.

"The Italian woman. She's been hauling water from the creek. It's time she had a proper well," Ma said, continuing to stir up a simmering pot of blueberries. She seemed to deliberately take her time locating a funnel to pour the hot jam into the jars, which were lined up along the counter. "I'm after helping her find a spot," she said.

"You can find it, but no damn fool from any place will help her dig it. Unless you're planning to dig it too."

"She has a son so."

"That boy moved away ages ago."

"Surely he'll come back to help."

"Why would he do that? The woman's not right in the head. Besides, I heard he's a priest, her son. And we all know, they hate to get dirt under their fingernails."

"I'll help in my own small way," my mother snapped back. Then, sauntering out of the kitchen, she added, "And I'll bring Faolan along, if that suits you."

"None of it suits me," Da called after her. "But you'll go anyway, if I know you." Now alone with my father at the table, he leaned in toward me and said, "You make sure your ma gets back before dark. If you come in late, I'll have you strapped."

"Yes, Da."

Early the next morning, my mother and I made the journey by foot. It was about four miles to the Italian lady's place, and the last leg was up through the tree bluffs. In autumn, the trail disappeared under the leaves, but it was a summer day, and easy to see the twists and turns of the path. When the Italian woman met us, she hugged me like I was her own grandson. Inside her elf sized house, we ate biscuits that were so hard, we had to dip them in tea or we'd end up with chipped teeth. Fiorella and my mother had an awful lot to say to each other. Every few minutes the Italian lady let out a cackle that would scare away the crows.

"Mammy, should we be getting back?" I said, after we'd been there for what felt like hours.

"Soon," she promised.

"You give him to play outside. Day nice today, yes?" the Italian woman said. Whenever she spoke, she said all the right words, but seemed to jumble up the order.

"Faolan, take yourself outdoors. Keep away from trouble," my mother said.

The little farm didn't have much on it: a field enclosed by a rotted fence, a small barn, a hen house—not exactly Sherwood Forest. I wandered around, coming across a garden with stone pathways winding here, there, and everywhere. The garden didn't have rows, more like round clusters of weeds that needed thinning. In the middle of the garden was a stone grotto with a statue of Mother Mary poised up on a ledge. Though the statue had some protection from the elements, the paint was worn and faded. Mary's plaster nose was partially chipped off, though to a boy's eyes, it still looked pretty enough for a church. Behind the grotto, I spotted a shed concealed by gooseberry bushes. Now if there's one thing that attracts a boy's attention, it's something that's half hidden.

Circling the shed two or three times, I searched for a way to get inside. A metal bar securely bolted the door closed, and the window shutters were nailed shut. The roof was carpeted in moss, and I wondered if I might find a rotten board or two that I could peel off to peek inside. I found a pile of punk wood and, tilting one log vertically, I stepped onto the flat end. It brought me up high enough to put one foot on the window ledge and, from there, I hoisted myself up onto the roof. Taking small steps on my hands and knees, I herring-boned myself over to a section of the roof that looked like it could hold my weight. Then I got reckless. I reached out as far as I could, lifting up a corner of a mossy shingle, and a split second later, I was down with the breath knocked out of me.

Once I got my wind back, I felt something wet and warm running down my right temple. Up above me, a shaft of light from the hole in the roof lit up a patch of dirt on the floor. The floor was spotted with my blood, though the colour looked more purple than red. Dust particles were dancing like specks of diamonds in and out of light, and it had my imagination going overtime. *Have I fallen into faerie land? But no. Faeries are a myth from Ireland. Here in North America, the only spirits are the Father, Son, and Holy Ghost. Even saints live in far-away places, like Italy and France. There aren't any saints in Manitoba.*

It was mighty eerie in there, smelling of mold and mint and damp earth, reminding me of my mother's cough syrup. As my eyes adjusted, I saw—hanging from the rafters—hundreds of bundles of dried herbs. I recognized the sage and goldenrod, but not much else. In the hazy corner sat a work bench, and up above it rows of shelves littered with dark bottles. I wondered what was inside those glass vessels, but felt too woozy to start exploring.

The right side of my head began to pound, and that's when I got worried. What if no one found me, and I was left to bleed to death? But my worst fear was facing my father if we arrived home after dark. I tried getting to my feet, but felt dizzy and decided against it. After that, I heard the voices of women talking in that hushed kind of way that women talk when they're both excited and worried. But I couldn't open my eyes. It was as if there were lead weights on my eyelids. When I did finally open them, I was sitting inside with a bowl of hot milk on my lap.

"Drink up, Faolan. You'll want to get your strength back," my mother said, lifting the cup to my lips. The next thing I remember, I was laying in a cart looking up into the starry sky, lightly bouncing down a dirt road. My throbbing head was wrapped in some kind of cloth—an apron or towel—and tied snugly under my chin.

Just inside our gate, my mother stopped. I thought I'd get a scolding for the mischief I'd gotten into, but instead she said quietly, "You know what happened, don't you? You fell from a tree."

"I did?"

"Fell onto a piece of old lumber, you did. Gave yourself a nasty gash to the head."

"But—"

"A tree it was," she repeated. "Remember, when your father asks, it was a tree."

"Yes," I said. "A tree. A box elder, was it?"

"It was. Faolan, you'll have to walk from here. I can't be pulling you an inch further," she said. As my mother helped me out of a wooden cart, I noticed a lantern dangling from a wire strung across the bottom end of it. I didn't see a horse or goat hitched up to the rickety contraption. My mother looked completely chin-strapped with her hair matted, and a sheen of sweat across her brow lit by the lantern light. We walked the last hundred yards, the two of us leaning into each other. She took a minute to dab the moisture from her face with a handkerchief before opening the door.

"There's been an accident. He's all bandaged up. No cause for alarm," she announced to my father. "Got a nasty wound falling from a tree, he did."

"He was to have you home before dark," my father said, pulling at his belt.

"No need to punish the boy. He's had punishment enough for one day," she said. I could hear a waver creep into her voice, and wondered if my father could hear it too.

"I'll be the judge of that," my father said, turning around to face me. I was afraid to look at him but if I turned away, he'd accuse me of showing disrespect. The fire from the wood stove lit up his whiskers in red. From an eight-year-old boy's eyes, my father was a big, stout man with broad shoulders and thick hands. His face, ruddy and tanned, had the look of a man who'd spent most of his life out in the weather. The shadows from the coal oil lamp on the tabletop exaggerated his facial scars—a white line across his nose and another scar slicing one of his eyebrows in half. I wondered if the lack of kindness in his steel grey eyes was something he'd always had, or if it had come over him slowly, like a hidden tumour.

"The boy's never going to learn, with all your mollycoddling," he said.

"You can't discipline him now, can you? The boy's lost blood. He can barely walk." Shuffling me into the kitchen, my mother said, "Come along, Faolan. We'll soak your clothes in salt water. They'll be no use to you with blood stains, will they?"

"You stay away from that foreign woman!" my father bellowed after us. "My boy comes home bloody, both of you after dark. She must be some kind of pagan witch."

"She's Catholic, same as you and me," my mother answered from the adjoining kitchen. "She's got a statue of the Blessed

Virgin Mary in her garden so."

"She may have a statue, but that doesn't make her any more a Catholic than putting antlers on a horse makes it a moose."

There hadn't been any shouting or things being thrown around, which was the usual way of things when my father got bladdered. But later that night, I woke to the sound of the front door opening and my mother's soft footsteps. Even as a young fellow, I knew by the way she walked—like a person in pain—that she'd paid a price that night. As I clutched my blankets to my face, I swore that I'd never grow up to be like my father.

After that incident, my mother stayed close to home. That's what expectant women did. Some didn't even go to church once they started showing, so that made it even more shocking when my mother up and disappeared for a week. My brothers told me if anyone asked, I was to say she went back to North Dakota to do some visiting. *But what kind of mother vanishes and doesn't say where she's going?*

These and all kinds of boyhood memories came back to me in that French woman's home, with no regard for night or day. Then, my musings got disrupted by a burly man who came bursting into the room and proceeded to plunk himself down on the chair beside the bed. He had a face that could compete with a circus barker's, and the look of one too; the only thing missing was a striped jacket and straw hat. *This fella is either going to murder me or entertain me with a soft shoe dance.* I made the sign of the cross and he broke out into a belly laugh, his moustache bouncing up and down like a bush in the wind.

The Frenchman uncorked a bottle of *plonc* and thrust the entire thing in my hands. I didn't refuse. He also tossed a pack of cigarettes onto the bed, gesturing that they were for me. For three days, Simone and the two children were nowhere to be seen, but this hearty fellow, Oncle Bernard as he introduced himself, took her place. Whatever he lacked in social graces, he made up for in good cheer. We spent the afternoons laughing, though if you asked me what was so funny, I couldn't tell you. If he found something funny, I found it funny too, and I guess the wine helped.

It was Oncle Bernard who first got me out of bed, helping me over to the open window. Propped up on the sill, I lit up a smoke while he sucked on his pipe, and the two of us kept an eye on the town. I enjoyed the view: a quiet street with vestiges of what once was a cobblestone street. It crossed my mind that the street may have been destroyed by artillery fire. In a glance, I could see row houses in stone and brick, tile roofs, and wooden fences surrounding the enclosures in the back. A few of the windows were shuttered, and, on the second floor, where the windows didn't have shutters, a robust looking woman stepped out onto a tiny balcony. Though she was a few doors down, I noticed her squinting her eyes to get a better glimpse of me, or maybe it was Bernard she was interested in. Sheds spotted the landscape, as well as gardens here and there. From my window, I could easily see the plants and trees that would've been bursting with life only a few months previous. The trees were trimmed just so and, even with the season change, some of the heartier vegetables like kale and cabbage remained in the gardens.

Across the street stood a town hall where men with woolen scarves and caps sat on the steps or leaned up against the bannister, smoking and talking. There was an obvious lack of young men in the town. A dusting of snow covered the scene, which gave it the look of a photograph. Women wrapped in shawls came and went, knocking on doors or hanging laundry. The snow seemed to have a cheerful effect on the townspeople, almost as if they welcomed it. Occasionally, someone would notice us at the window and offer a friendly wave. It occurred to me that this was not a town under the weight of war. Had the war ended? Had the world so completely changed in a matter of weeks?

After a few hours of jolly chatter at the window, understandable by neither of us, Oncle Bernard disappeared downstairs. I felt an urge to open my kit and shave. Looking into the mirror above the dresser, I saw someone I hardly recognized. I thought, *I just need to take off the grizzle and I'll be back to normal.* Even clean shaven, though, my looks didn't improve by much. The lids of my eyes weighed heavy, my jaw drooped, and my hair looked only slightly better than a rat's nest. My shoulders seemed too wide for my sunken rib cage. War had left its mark without my asking it to. If I could see my own breath, I wondered, what would it show me? Would it hold the shape of death and despair that weighs heavily on every soldier, or would it appear with acts of goodness that also exist in times of war?

Thomas's letter came to mind, the one I'd reread a hundred times and committed to memory. "Don't worry about us," Thomas wrote. "You just keep yourself in one piece." I was in one piece. I had all my limbs, but what my brother didn't realize is that war can break you into fragments you can't see. Those pieces may as well be shards of glass, rattling around inside a person's bodily frame.

After a few days of drinking too much wine, Simone returned home with the kids. Suddenly, it was coffee twice a day and enough cigarettes to last a month. Every day I paced up and down the hallway, but didn't want to risk the stairs. The kids found me a stick that served as a cane. Pierre had stripped the bark and lacquered it up, and a darned good walking stick it was too, made from a lilac bush. I could tell by the purplish rings at its base.

With my strength slowly returning, I became all the more curious to know what had landed me in the village in the first place. From the very first day, my boots had been polished and set at the foot of the bed. My uniform, with its brass 'doughboy' buttons, had been cleaned and neatly folded on the dresser top. After Oncle Bernard's departure, I shook open the layers of stacked items, and dug through all the pockets looking for clues, but found none. I couldn't shake this feeling that something had been stolen from me, but I also couldn't pinpoint what it was.

During those weeks, the only thing I had left to hang onto was my soldier's pocketbook New Testament and Psalms. I made a habit out of flipping it open to a random page to see where it would land. I searched the Holy Book for coincidences, personal meaning, prophetic signs. It fell on Psalm 91 more often than any other page. "Whoever dwells in the shelter of the Most High will rest in the shadow of the Almighty. I will say of the Lord, He is my refuge and my fortress, my God, in whom I trust." It gave me some comfort, but there's only so many hours a man can sit by the window reading the Good Book and thinking of things that needed to be buried along with the war.

Then, as if in answer to my prayers, a fellow by the name of Paul Greer came by to see me. I recognized the chaplain straight off. He was an American I'd met when we first landed in France. At the time, the allied soldiers were worn out; we arrived fresh and eager to help. As we went through our training, Paul did his best to guide our souls and he also organized sports activities. The soldiers took to calling him "Devil Dodger" behind his back, but I never did. He was always Chaplain Greer or Paul Greer to me. Boy, was I glad to see him when he stepped into my sickroom; a long-lost friend wouldn't have received a heartier welcome. From him, I got all the news. "Germany's agreed to end all hostilities," he said.

"You sure it's not a stalling tactic? I mean, how many times have we heard rumours of Germans negotiating peace?"

"It's a done deal. Armistice papers are signed. In a railway car in the Forest of Compiègne. 11:11:11. It's over, soldier. Next step is a peace treaty."

I couldn't believe my ears. I should've felt like a million

bucks. I should've thrown my cane out the window and danced. Instead, I pulled myself upright, and almost blurted out, *What the hell was it all for?* As I tried to absorb the news, Paul began wandering around my room, examining every detail as if he were thinking of renting the place. "No one knew where you were," he said. "This French woman just showed up at the base one day with your name scribbled on a piece of paper."

"Simone?"

"That's right; the woman who's been looking after you."

"Why'd she take me in? I can't figure that one out."

"Just doing her bit for the war."

"But that's going above and beyond, taking in a stranger," I said, throwing my legs over the side of the bed. I grabbed my cane and got myself to standing.

"Not only that, she made her way to the Damremont Barracks. And that's no walk around the block. Must've had relatives in the area, or something."

"Showed up with her kids?"

"Yup. Seemed like she was looking to collect your rations, but her English was so bad that no one could make out what she was saying," Chaplain Greer said, moving to the chair to sit. "Then the Lieutenant got the idea to find a Canadian Frenchie to translate. But you try and find a Canadian roaming around American Headquarters and you got your work cut out for you. In the end, they found a priest who knew some English."

"And what did Simone say?"

"Just reported that you were alive, and she was looking after you. Like I say, she was hoping to collect your rations."

"She went to the wrong place for that."

"Ah, yeah. But to keep her happy, they sent her back with some coffee, cigarettes. Speaking of smokes, you got one?"

"Didn't know you smoked."

"I do now."

I hobbled over to the window and pushed it open with my

cane. I lit a cigarette, offered it to the chaplain, and then lit up one up for myself. With both of us now leaning out the window, Chaplain Greer said, "They're not fussy about you being here. We prefer to look after our own, us Americans."

"If you can get me down the stairs, I'm all set to go with you."

"You can't make it down on your own?"

"Maybe in a few days."

Paul dragged on his cigarette with more intensity than it deserved. "So, what happened to you?" he asked. "How did you end up here?"

"I was hoping you could tell me. I guess I picked up an infection. Looks like I'm not out of the woods yet."

"You got to watch for gangrene."

"You don't have to tell me," I said. "How do you figure she got me up the stairs?"

"Who? Simone? I guess she had help. They'll send up a car, Friday at the latest, and get you transferred to a medical station. Maybe they'll take you up to Nevers. There's twenty-two camps in that area," Paul said, looking for somewhere to butt his cigarette. I motioned to a tin can under my bed.

"Like I say, get me down those stairs, and I'll go wherever I'm ordered."

"You'll have to get checked out. Once they find you to be of sound mind...you are of sound mind, I hope."

"As sound as a man can be after living in this madness. Any chance I'll get discharged?"

"I doubt it. Those Canadian boys 've been here since the start. Same with the British. From where I'm standing, it makes sense they'll keep us a while longer. We'll be marching into Germany is my guess."

"Yeah, you're probably right." I still couldn't fathom that the war was at an end. It seemed downright strange that we'd be freely entering the country we'd been in battle with only weeks previous.

"But, Faolan, there's one other thing." Chaplain Greer gazed up at the wooden cross above the door. Without taking his eyes off of it, he said, "I hate to talk about this, but it's got to get cleared up."

"What's that?" I asked reluctantly. Something in his voice made me not want to know.

"When Simone went to the headquarters, she turned something in."

"Oh yeah?"

"Identification tags and some odds and ends, letters, photographs."

"Belonging to who?"

Paul Greer turned around to say, "Two soldiers—Patrick O'Donnell and Charles Granfield."

I felt my body jerk at the mention of their names. "Where the hell are they?"

"I was expecting you to tell me."

"I hope they weren't captured!"

"Germans have begun to release American POWs and so far, Patrick and Charlie haven't been accounted for. Mind you, it's going to be chaos for a while."

"That's no good. They got to get found," I said, lighting up a fresh smoke.

Paul fixed his eyes on mine and said, "Faolan, why do you think you had their identification tags?"

"What do you mean?"

"In the pocket of your service coat, ID tags for both of them."

"What was I doing with their tags?" I couldn't believe what Paul Greer was saying to me. "You sure about this?"

"Listen, they wouldn't have sent me all this way to talk about the weather. Simone turned them in, like I told you."

"She went through my pockets?"

"You can't blame her. It's a war. Hard to know who to trust."

"It doesn't look promising, does it?" I said, my hands suddenly shaking so severely I had trouble bringing my smoke to my lips. "Dog tags aren't to be removed unless the soldier dies."

"That's right," he answered, setting his hat onto the chest of drawers.

"And you're sure I had them?" Paul nodded his head.

"I don't know what to say."

"When did you last see them?" Paul asked, with kindness in his voice. "Do you recall that much?"

My brain scanned the times we'd spent in the trenches dealing with the nerve-shattering sounds of shells screeching across the skies, and repairing roads that were buried under a foot of mud. But other than vague impressions, I couldn't conjure up a single thing to tell the chaplain. "Darn it, Paul, you've got to help. Stay here another day, will you? See if my brain starts remembering. Can you do that?"

"Sorry, Faolan, I've got to get back."

"You can't stay one day?"

"I'm just following orders, same as every other soldier. Give it time. It'll come back to you."

I regretted the chaplain's visit. I regretted this new information because it changed everything. Here I'd been thinking that my main problem was recovering from an infection. "Would you give me a blessing?" I asked, not knowing what else to say.

"I'm not a priest, Faolan. Look, the Catholic church is right out your window. Just stick your head out and wave up a priest." Seeing my disappointment, the chaplain said, "How about we recite the Lord's Prayer?"

We said the Our Father, and as Paul Greer made his way out the door, I asked, "Do you think it was worth it? This war?"

"I think it was God's will to stop Germany from stealing

our freedom."

"So, you're saying God takes sides."

"God is always on the side of justice."

"There's one thing I can't understand. I don't mean to be disrespectful, but those German soldiers, they read the same Bible same as us, don't they? Do you really think God wants to crush those men any more than he wants us crushed? Don't we believe in one God, the God of all?"

"We have a duty to protect what is right and good, and that's what we've been doing," Paul said emphatically.

I knew I was getting under the chaplain's skin, but I couldn't stop myself from asking, "At what cost?"

"War is always costly."

"Germany had to be stopped. I'm not arguing with you there. I just wonder if there was some other way to do it."

"If there was another way, it would've been done."

After Paul's visit, a terrible exhaustion fell over me for a few days. I could do nothing more than look out the window, waiting for my ride to pull up. It was a good thing I sat there for hours on end, otherwise I never would've taken notice of a horse making its way toward the village, cart in tow. Something was familiar about the horse, but in an unsettling kind of way. That's when it all came flooding back to me: finding myself alone and feverish in the woods, unable to walk, and afraid for my life. Eventually, I remembered it in a natural progression from one event to the next, like a history book. But that's not the way it first came back. It came in waves, but in reverse, first the horse, then the time in the woods, then the night with Pat and Charlie. With each wave, I found myself retching in the bathroom. *I've got to put the pieces together so I can report back to my commanding officer. Once I've laid it out from start to finish, I*

can put it away, like an heirloom that gets wrapped in paper and stored for decades.

It started with Pat, myself, and Charlie. We were missing Adam, as he'd come down with a fever at the last minute. With the numbers dwindling in our platoon, the officer gave the three of us the go-ahead. Late in the day, we were dropped off at the side of a road just north of Haraucourt, handed a map, and sent out to troubleshoot along the Meuse. They brought us as close as they could to our destination, given the rough condition of the roads. In fair weather, we could've made it to the river in less than three hours—by the way the crow flies, that is.

After walking east until sunset, we needed to take some rest before pushing on to the river, so we camped out in a wooded area. The plan was to sleep for a few hours, then continue the last leg of the journey before first light. We found a perfect spot, concealed by spruce and pine and one linden tree, a type of tree I'd never seen before coming to Europe. Most of the leaves had fallen, but it still looked grand.

We were all worn to the bone, and hadn't had a good night's sleep in ages. For a group of soldiers meant for pick and shovel, we'd seen a lot of action—too much. Only weeks before, the Marines had struck difficult wires and needed us. We went over the top as wire cutters, crawling on our bellies in the hazy light of dusk, cutting through the massive coils of barbed wire. Then, for three days, we fought alongside the marines, escaping exploding shells and gunfire all around us. The whole world was ablaze and I honestly didn't know if we were the ones making progress, or the enemy. Then we went from the front lines to repairing roads under the cover of darkness, always under fire, and always in the rain and the mud. It had to be done. Without roads and bridges, there was no way to transport supplies to the front lines. In spite of all this, we did our best to keep in good humour.

This night, when Pat unrolled his pack, he discovered he'd lost his shelter half. "What the hell? I'm sure I packed up my roll last night," Pat said.

"That's too bad, eh," I said. "It's going to be awful wet out there on the ground."

"You could always sleep in the tree branches," Charlie said. "Nice and dry up there. You got your blanket, don't you?"

After teasing Pat, Charlie and I put together our shelter halves—designed to house two men—and the three of us crammed into the tent.

"You never know. They could show up late," Charlie said. Another squad had been sent out as trap hunters, and we expected them to camp out in the same general area that we were in.

"I don't give a damn if they show up a week from Tuesday, so long as nothing happened to them," said Pat.

"No need to jump to conclusions," I said.

"What do ya think they're planning next?" Charlie asked.

"Who?"

"Who do you ya think? The Division Commander. Surprise attacks along the Meuse, that's what I say. Why else are we troubleshooting if there ain't any trouble?" Charlie asked with a sarcastic chuckle. Charlie was probably right. Only days before, we'd built raft foot bridges in sections—twelve feet by six feet—and, as far as we knew, they'd brought them up to the village of Yoncq in wagons. They were likely transporting those bridges as close to the Meuse as possible.

"It's not my job to be tactical. I'll leave that to our superiors," Pat said.

"The war's almost over. It's so close I can smell it," I said.

"It ain't over till it's over, that's what I say," said Charlie.

"Don't forget those German sailors in Kiel, how they mutinied. That's significant, if you ask me." I wanted to believe the end was near, but it was a forced hope.

"How many days are we now without relief? I lost count but it's gotta be over a month,"said Charlie.

"How about that night of high comfort in Sommerance?" I asked. "Showers. Clean sheets. Heck, I even had a pillow, and as far as I could tell, it wasn't even crawling with lice."

"Yeah, that's all a chap needs. One night in a bed every three weeks. What the hell am I complaining about?"

"I'll tell you one thing, them Germans aren't going to give up easy. As soon as we start lashing those foot bridges together, we'll come under fire. Let's just hope for fog when that day comes, and lots of it." Pat's remark halted the conversation. Though we were quiet, none of us were ready for sleep. "Hey Faolan, you go to Catholic school?" asked Pat, breaking the silence.

"Catholic church, yeah. Not Catholic school."

"You never had the pleasure of nuns cracking your fingers with a pointer stick?"

"I grew up on a farm. Convents are in the city."

"They used to line up the boys on one side and the girls on the other. You know, after recess?" "All teachers do that."

"Do all teachers tell you to leave room for your guardian angel?"

"Don't remember that."

"To keep the boys from pushing in line, we had to leave a twelve-inch gap for our angels. I never saw anyone's angel. I'm not doubting they were there. I'm sure they were, or none of us would've made it through grade school."

"What are you trying to say, Pat?" asked Charlie.

"I don't know about you guys, but so long as we're in this tent together, I need at least twelve inches on all sides of me. You got that?"

"Bunk outside, why don't you? You can have a whole team of angels," Charlie said.

"Can I not make a comment here? I'm just saying, we're

grown men, not scrawny waifs," said Pat.

"I wish I had a waif with me right now. Like that Mary Miles Minter from the moving pictures. Doesn't that just roll off the tongue—Mary Miles Minter? She's one sweet waif," said Charlie. "And if she was here, I'd know just what to say to her."

"Oh yeah? What? 'If you're real sweet," Pat said, "I'll catch some rats and roast them tender. And if you're extra sweet, I'll share my cigarette with you.' Come to think of it, I could use a smoke right now. You boys got any?" We all rummaged through our pockets, with no luck. "You're telling me, between the three of us, we haven't got one single coffin nail?" Pat said. "That's just dandy. Finally, we're someplace quiet, where we can enjoy a smoke under the stars."

"What stars? It's a damn cycle of rain that never ends," said Charlie. We stopped to listen, and sure enough, we heard the patter of rain against the tent canvas. After a dry summer, the autumn rains had taken us by surprise. We started to wear our uniforms to bed, discovering that it's a whole lot easier to sleep in damp clothes than putting on wet, cold clothes come morning. That night was no different; we were sleeping in our uniform minus our socks, tunics and puttees.

"We got tea," I said.

"I'm not boiling up water in the dark," said Pat. "What do you take me for, some kind of Brit who can't go without *me cup of tea*?"

Charlie propped himself up and said, loud enough for Pat to hear. "Pat's new here. He doesn't know the benefits of smoking tea."

"I've been overseas as long as you," argued Pat.

"Face facts, Patrick. I was cutting barbed wire before you were cutting your milk teeth."

"Oh yeah? What kind of soldier—"

"Hey, hey boys. How about this," I said, pulling out a few

shreds of tobacco from my pouch along with rolling papers. "Enough tobacco for one anyways."

"Thank God, cause I'm not desperate enough to smoke tea. You got a Lucifer?" asked Pat.

"That's one thing I never run short of," I said.

It was against the rules to smoke in the tent but we did it all the same, passing the roll-your-own back and forth. As I was in the middle, it crossed over me twice as often, so I took more drags than the both of them. We had a good laugh about that. Other than our own voices, it was quiet, too quiet. It gave us a false sense of security.

In the early morning, before I opened my eyes, I heard the wind. Usually if a man hears the wind, he'll also hear the canvas walls rippling like a flag, but no, the tent itself was still. In my half-sleep, with the distant sounds of snapping twigs and stirred up leaves, I wondered if maybe a thunderstorm was close to erupting. I felt groggy and my body ached, head to toe. Then it hit me—we'd slept too long, and bungled up our orders. Opening up my eyes to the early light of day, nothing looked right. One side of the tent was ripped wide open while the other side remained propped up by tent poles.

My friends lay on either side of me. Blood was leaking out from their ears and noses, and I knew they were gone. Flying out and away from the scene, I fell face down and vomited. I'd seen much worse on the battlefield, but this time it was my closest friends. And maybe it was an accumulation of everything I'd experienced up until that point. It wasn't a straw that broke the camel's back; it was a weapon of war that broke our souls. I screamed, but didn't recognize my own voice; it seemed to come from far away, like a wounded animal in the distance. I wondered if I was alive, or dead and gone to hell. I kept screaming, sending the terror I felt into the ground, but no place was deep enough for me. I screamed until I sounded like a wheezing, raspy-voiced old man.

I hated myself for not waking up. It's crazy. During the war, I had trouble sleeping most

nights. Why the hell did I sleep like a log that night? It made me think of how the Good Lord asked the apostles to "Stay here and keep watch with me," and they couldn't do it. It was His last night on this earth and they just kept drifting back to sleep, like it was a regular old night. Finally, Our Lord came up with those famous words, "The spirit is willing but the flesh is weak." Who wouldn't sleep through some horrible trial, rather than face it? Either way, Our Lord was dying on the cross, with or without Peter and James and John dropping off to sleep. And either way, we were getting bombed that night. But why was I alive? Weeks later, it was explained to me by the doctor, but at the time, I couldn't understand why their lives were taken, and not mine.

With my face planted on the cold ground, I felt my heart seeping out of my body. It was as if my sternum had split open, and all my life force was draining out of me. I knew I had to *do* something, *say* something, before my heart stopped altogether. Sure, my heart was ticking the same as always, but it felt mechanical, no different from my pocket watch. *Why did my life get spared? It doesn't make sense. None of it makes sense. Let me go with them. For all the good I'm doing, I'm better off dead. I don't belong here. Don't make me face another day of this war. Don't ask me to return to duty. I couldn't, not even if I wanted to. I'm dead too. Didn't Jesus once say, 'Let the dead bury the dead'? That's what I am now, alive and breathing, but dead all the same.*

I felt like a bird that had flown head first into a pane of glass and fallen to the ground, limp and lifeless with not a single muscle flinching. The only sound was the creaking of the tall, thin spruce trees as they reached for sunlight. I waited for something to rouse me, but for a long time, nothing did. And then a warm breeze brushed up against my face. Beyond where I lay, leaves swirled up in circles and touched down again, only

to be tossed up once more. The sound of the wind was lay-
ered, like harmonies in a piece of music by one of the musi-
cal greats and it was a small comfort to me. I found myself
whispering, "Lord, if you need me, I'll stay, even if this isn't
home. I'll give whatever days I've got left, one day, one hundred, makes no different to me. I belong to You now. I don't
belong here anymore."

The wind died down, but not before leaving a fresh carpet of leaves on the forest floor. I finally got to my feet and
wandered around, looking for I don't know what. I half expected to see a shell crater nearby and, I'm sure if I'd looked,
I would've found one. I wasn't sure what I should do, stay put
or make my way back with the hopes of meeting up with the
other squad. We'd been moving east. Should I reverse direction and return to our starting point? But before I could go
anywhere, I felt the urge to revisit the tent as I had to do what
I couldn't the first time.

I walked back to the place where I'd slept the night, the
same place I'd shared a cigarette and kidded around with my
friends less than eight hours previous. To this day, I've no
memory of taking their ID tags, but I must've. I do remember
locating Pat's haversack and fumbling to find his roll as I knew
it would contain his personal effects, things that would mean
something to his loved ones. I did the same for Charlie. I had to
use my pocketknife to cut open Charlie's haversack on account
of my hands shaking so badly. I grabbed my own pack, and
started to move away from the scene when I heard a dull rat-
a-tat-tat, rat-a-tat-tat. My head jerked toward the sound as my
body tensed up, ready to bolt. And then I saw a black-feathered
bird near the top of a tree, driving its beak into the bark and
I realized it was only a woodpecker. *Woodpeckers go after dying
trees. Death all around. Song birds clear right out of fighting zones.
They're a lot smarter than us, those birds.*

Predicting a long walk ahead of me, I took my time wrapping my puttees around my calves, getting them on just right. By now, I felt a dull ache in my chest, like someone had punched me hard. I figured I needed to get myself to a medical treatment station, so I held out my compass and headed west, hoping to backtrack to the road. I walked slowly, but without breaks, and rested only to take a swig of water. It was a clear, dry day and I was glad of it because my trench boots were still damp.

One thing I'm grateful for is that I was never ordered to fire a cannon or take direct aim to shoot at the enemy. I'm not excusing my part in the war; I am a soldier and I follow orders. Even so, that day alone in the woods, I hugged my thirty-caliber rifle close to my side, keeping my ears open for snapping twigs or footsteps, ready to defend my life, if necessary. By evening, I noticed a cluster of trees surrounded by a sea of withered ferns—a clue a stream ran nearby. It was dusk, and too late to go on a hunt for water, but I found a good spot to bivy up for the night. Without anyone to pair up with, my shelter half didn't offer much protection. All I could do was wait for morning.

The morning wasn't kind to me. I woke up with shooting pains in my head, not to mention that my legs were in real bad shape. At first, I thought it was from all the walking I'd done, but when I took a closer look, I could see how my one leg was badly swollen. Then there was the shock of not being able to get up onto my feet. The only thing I could think to do was crawl around on the ground, looking for a stick or something sturdy to pull myself to a standing position. Then it occurred to me to use my gun to hoist myself up. Even with me leaning on it for support, it was hell trying to pack up my gear and, in the end, I decided to leave the dog-tent sitting where it was. I also ditched my gas mask and hoped to God I would never find myself in need of it. I'd heard of the silent killer; how during those first chemical attacks, the soldiers didn't know enough to run from the vapour, but stood watching as the cloud floated toward them, resulting in excruciating pain and blindness, sometimes death. At the very least, my comrades hadn't endured this.

Before moving in any direction, I needed to locate water and, thankfully, I found a trickle of a creek nearby, just as I'd hoped. As I filled up my canteen, I thought of a soldier who I'd seen give his last drop of water to a dying man. It was during battle and that soldier had no idea when his canteen would be filled again, yet he didn't hesitate. War has a strange way of bringing out the worst and best in us. As I limped through the woods, using my rifle as a cane, I kept my eye out for some kind of road or cow path or farmer's lane—anything to make my walking easier. I reflected on my life before the war. I'd felt restless, moving away from the farm and heading off to Northern Ontario, searching for work. Now, not knowing if I'd live or die put the farmer's life in a whole different light. If I survived, I told myself, I'd remember glory is possible with the most ordinary life: a farmer seeding a field, a fisherman putting out nets, a small child calling for its mother in the night. It's not the same as a decorated officer or soldier, but it's *glory* all the same.

In spite of the situation I was in, the woods were enchanting in the morning hours. A rabbit hopped off through the trees, the odd wildflower remained stubbornly alive, and the mist slowly lifted as the morning light found its way through the trees. Yet the forest was also tinged with the darkness of a folk tale, as if a troll or grotesque giant might make its appearance at any point. As I walked, carefully avoiding tripping over tree roots or stones, I went through my options, but none of them were worth pinning my hopes on. Either I could stay put, knowing I was within range of enemy fire, or I could continue to limp along, only to find myself lost. My brain wasn't working right. Even though I glanced at my compass on a regular basis, I couldn't manage to stay on course. I kept looping back this way or that way to correct my course. For all I knew, I was walking in circles.

By midday, I was exhausted and my legs ached badly, although the right leg was much worse than the left. I collapsed against the trunk of a tree. To keep myself from going down a tunnel of fear, I pictured my life before the madness of war. On the farm, I'd be up and out of bed before dawn, hearing the farm animals stretch their vocal cords, and the crisp air of winter biting my skin. If I was lucky, I'd see the dance of the Northern Lights in the prairie sky. Conjuring up the sights and sounds of the farm took all of my concentration until I began to wonder if my boyhood adventures on the prairie were nothing but a made-up story. The only reality was this war. Bone weary from the effort it took to stave off panic, I drifted off to sleep.

Waking up clammy and feverish, I fumbled for my canteen and downed the last few gulps of water. Through a flock of trees, I detected a wild field, the late afternoon sun lighting up the tips of the yellowed stems and dried stubble. I wondered why I hadn't noticed the field earlier, but then again, when everything's out of the ordinary, nothing's out of the ordinary. Something moved in the distance, and I instinctively placed a hand on my gun. Stretching my neck, I saw it was only a horse hitched to an open cart, likely a farmer's cart. It was obvious the horse didn't belong to the military, but a lone horse in a lone field got me wondering. *What's a horse doing here? Was it stolen by the Germans?* Horses were a sought-after commodity on both sides of the war. An hour passed with no movement other than the horse occasionally flicking its tail, which didn't make sense since it was too late in the season for flies or mosquitoes.

With my right leg throbbing and my throat parched, I

struggled to think through the fog of the fever when it suddenly hit me—I needed to get myself up onto that cart. Going anywhere, forward, backwards, or sideways could be suicide. But staying put was equally dangerous. The horse would make its way back to a town or village or farm, I told myself. Even with the use of my rifle, though, I couldn't bring myself to a standing position. My legs kept buckling under me. Finally, I made progress by driving my fists into the ground and shimmying a few inches forward. It took all my strength to nudge close enough to get a clear picture of things. The horse was a typical workhorse, heavy set and about fifteen hands high. It had nice colouring, beige with some cream coloured spots. The cart, worn by rain and sun, held a bushel of apples, a grain sac, and a milk churn. I wondered if the churn happened to catch a bit of rain water on its rim. If it did have milk in it, it was likely to be sour.

Making clicking sounds, I tried out my best horse-talking voice. "Hey, there girl. What chu doing out here? Lost like me, eh? Maybe we can help each other out. Come closer. Come on, girl. Don't you play shy with me. You're friendly, I can see that. What's your name? How about Millie? That's what I'll call you—Millie. Come on closer and I'll feed you apples." Eventually, the horse turned her ears to hear what I had to say. I knew Millie wouldn't understand a single word of English, but I coaxed her all the same. "That's a good girl. There's apples on the back of the cart and you know it too, don't ya?"

The horse finally took one hesitant step forward, but that was it. She wasn't going to move another inch toward me, no matter if I promised her the moon. Using my gun for balance, I made my way over, dragging my right foot while hopping on my left. When I got close to one of the wheels, I took hold of it, shuffled around to the back of the cart, and hoisted myself up. The milk container, which I discovered was empty, had an inch of rain water trapped around its rim, and I slurped that up like it was ice cream.

I tossed a few apples to Millie like I was sending birdies over a badminton net, but the last thing I wanted to do was spook her, so I laid off for a bit, and tried rolling a few apples forward. One came close enough that Millie nudged it with her nose before gobbling it up. I gave a flutter to the reins, calling *walk-on*, and Millie was roused to move forward. I didn't attempt to direct her one way or the other; she moved forward along that field road all on her own. At the back of that cart, I must've passed out and didn't gain consciousness until waking up in Simone's house. This was the true story I prepared myself to tell the doc, or my commanding officer, or anyone else who had the authority to decide my fate.

Now here I was, with my memory more or less intact, standing by the bedroom window watching for my ride. By now, I was a familiar face to the townspeople, and many of them made a point to call up *Bonjour* or *Salut*. It was the third day of waiting when, once again, I saw Millie making her way through the village. This time, I didn't feel that vice grip around my heart, that sense of confusion and nausea I'd felt the first time. I called the kids into the room, and put on a real charade for Pierre and Marguerite, pantomiming climbing up onto Millie's cart, throwing apples, and taking the reins. The children laughed like I was a regular entertainer. Pierre disappeared and, minutes later, returned with a toy horse no bigger than my thumb, wanting to make a gift of it. I refused to take it, but his face looked so glum that in the end I had to, or it would've broken his heart.

When my ride finally arrived, I looked around for Simone and the kids, but the house was empty. As I departed, I knew for certain that Simone had saved my life by wrapping my legs in those wet, milky blankets. Why, though, had she taken me in and looked after me? Maybe her own husband was a soldier; maybe even a fallen soldier, and she felt some debt toward those of us who crossed the ocean.

I told the doctor at Nevers everything. Once it was out of me, I hoped I'd never have to talk about it again. The doc explained to me that the impact of the exploding shell had knocked me out, given me a concussion, but had done much worse to my friends. He said that their bodies probably protected me from the shock, since I was between the two of them. He told me they still don't understand much about the invisible effects of an exploding shell, but they know it's enough to kill you, even if not one fragment of shrapnel comes close. It's terrifying to think what we men have created with our hands. What will happen if we don't stop now, if we keep on creating these kill machines?

I thought the doctor might consider me too damaged to be of use to the military, and wondered if they'd ship me off home. Part of me wished they would do just that, but when I considered what other soldiers had endured, my tale wasn't so different from anyone else's. In the end, they kept me. I joined up with my regiment during their one-week rest in Luxemberg. I'd missed the march into Belgium, but heard all about it. I guess young and old came out to greet the troops, waving flags and setting out a banquet. Groups of singing children marched with the troops from one town to the other, waving home made flags of all colours: Belgium, British, French, and American. Some of the soldiers kept the flags as souvenirs. The Belgium people had a general idea that the American flag had stars and stripes but as to how many stars and how many stripes, that varied greatly.

On December 14th, we finally crossed the Rhine into Germany to occupy Koblenz and the surrounding area. When we marched into the German towns, folks came out to silently stare at us. In the small villages, we slept in their hay lofts and the floors of their homes. We were now all marked—from babies in their mother's arms, to us soldiers, to old folks hobbling through the streets—none of us were spared the brushstrokes of war. As we began to occupy their country, stationed in a small town called Engers-on-the-Rhine, I had to wonder if the mothers and sweethearts and children in Germany weren't so different from the mothers and sweethearts and children back home. Maybe not, but as long as there's war, we'll keep believing we're drastically different.

CHAPTER FOUR

*A Crescent Moon, Keys & Horns—Aspen Bluff, Manitoba,*1921
- two years and one month later

Faolan:

Since my return home, I mostly feel like a visitor, other than in the early mornings when me and my brother Thomas sit drinking coffee and catching up on things.

"Oh yeah, I almost forgot," Thomas said, after I'd been back a week or two. "Remember that crazy widow living in the bush?"

"You mean Fiorella?"

"That's the one."

"What about her?" I asked.

"She came by here one day, a couple of years back now, looking as haggard as an old fishwife."

"What did she want?"

"She was looking for you."

"What for?"

"She didn't say."

"And you weren't curious?"

"Nope."

"I guess I'll wander over there," I said, getting up from my seat to refill my coffee. I usually felt satisfied after one cup, but not that day.

"She's gone," Thomas said.

"She died?"

"That's right."

I sat back down, not sure how I felt. "Where'd they bury her?"

"Not a clue."

I looked over at Thomas and, for the first time, I noticed how he'd changed. Thomas was always the brother who kept his beard trimmed, and his clothes clean and mended. Looking at him now, his bushy eyebrows emphasized his scraggly beard, and his suspenders were worn right out. I wondered if maybe he'd gained weight, because even though it didn't show on his tall frame, his face seemed to have swelled. Still, it was more than just his looks. He was always quick to tease or joke around, and that mischievous grin was no longer there.

"I guess I'll ask around town."

"I wouldn't tell Da that you're sniffing around, asking about *The Italian*. You know how he feels."

"Yeah, I do."

"No, I don't think you do. It's been how many years, and still, whenever he gets going on the whiskey, you should hear him. *The Italian* put a curse on him. He should get out of farming before she ruins him. When he found out she died, you know what he said? 'That doesn't mean I'm free from her devil's curse.'"

"When did Da ever make sense when he's bladdered?"

"And to this day... nah, no use bringing that up," Thomas said.

"Bringing what up? You can't just leave a sentence hanging."

Thomas got up from where he sat, pulled his chair over by the floor mat, sat down, and picked up his boots. He loosened the boot laces as he said, "You probably don't remember. You were pretty young, but Ma didn't want the midwife delivering that baby. She wanted *The Italian*."

"Well, sure, they were friends."

"I was the one sent to bring her to the house. Da's never forgiven me for that."

"You only did what Mammy asked."

"Some folks say she put Ma in her grave," Thomas said, slipping his foot into a boot.

"Fiorella? Come on. We all know she died in childbirth."

"I've always loved these things," Thomas said, referring to the boots. "See how the leather's shaped to my foot? I've had these, going on five years. They were Da's before they got passed on to me."

I felt like Thomas was making some kind of point about how he took on the responsibility of running the farm, fitting into my father's shoes, while I ran off. But doing what? Fighting a war, that was what I was doing. "What are you trying to say Thomas?"

"Nothing at all. And about *The Italian*? I'm just repeating what I heard. But I'd be lying if I told you I didn't wonder about it myself. Ma wasn't happy those last few years."

It had never crossed my mind that my mother had given up on life. She was doleful sometimes, but I didn't think of her as a person with a gaping hole in her heart. "So…what? She gave Mammy something to hurry her death? You can't go around saying things like that unless you've got some kind of proof."

"I'm not saying *The Italian* did anything deliberate. I just wonder if there was something she could've done, *should've* done, and didn't."

"What about the doctor? And the midwife? How come they don't get blamed?" I said, coming to my feet. "They were here, too. I remember a lot more than you think about that day." I was glad no one was around to hear our conversation.

"It's something to consider. That's all I'm saying," Thomas said, tightening his laces to get a snug fit.

"I know one thing for sure," I said, "Our mother's in heaven. And something else too. Ma was happy the day she met Fiorella, happier than most other days. I was with her, don't forget."

"Yeah, well. I guess you've got to take them town gossips with a grain of salt," Thomas said, reaching to get his coat and hat from the wooden pegs.

"A pound of salt is more like it. You'll manage alright without my help today?" I asked, getting up from the table.

"Never had your help for years. One day won't break the farm," he said, stepping through the door and shutting it firmly behind him.

Minutes later, I bridled up Chester, the one gelding my father owns, and headed off to Fiorella's, taking with me a snow shovel and snowshoes. After I tied off the horse to a tree, I trudged through the bush breaking trail. Along the way, I thought about how I couldn't expect my father to feed me and put a roof over my head while I tinkered around with this or that. What had I accomplished since my arrival home? Not much. I'd managed to rig up a wooden box and fasten a set of skis to it in order to haul deadwood from the tree belt, but I was still no closer to getting the job done. My mother used to say, "You'll never plow a field by turning it over in your mind." Maybe I shouldn't've come home in the first place, but by the time I got my discharge papers, the parades were over, and so were the jobs—snapped up by returning soldiers.

In some ways, it seemed near miraculous that the war had come and gone and I was back in Aspen Bluff. I was home, yes, but the farm didn't feel all that familiar. A new barn stood where the old one was, and new stables had been constructed.

The house was pretty much the same, but the smells were different. My father had hired a cook while I was away, a Polish woman, and now the place smelled like onions and cabbage around the clock; not a bad smell, but not what I was used to either.

Who would think that a cook would have sway over the house, but Mrs. Wojciechowski was as tough as most army generals I'd met overseas? She stood firm that we smoked in the sitting room. No one dared light up in her kitchen, and a spotless clean kitchen it remained, with a white cooking range scrubbed shinier than a new penny. Since my return, I'd been eating Mrs. Wojciechowski's meals—provided for by my father—and this didn't sit well with me. The food was delicious enough, but I wasn't accustomed to someone paying my way in the world.

Upon my arrival at the blanketed field by Fiorella's house, my mind returned to the task at hand. Approaching the grotto, I noticed how half of the Blessed Virgin's face had crumbled, giving the overall effect of an aging, sorrowful Madonna. I also found the cabin in ruins, with all the windows cracked or shattered. From the looks of things, it had been a few years since the one-room house had seen human occupants. Just as snow had found its way into Fiorella's ramshackle place through the windows and makeshift door, the frozen moisture from my brother's words had also crept into the corners of my mind. I was more disturbed by his comments than I cared to admit.

Looking around the cabin, I wondered what would give way first, the arched ceiling or the rickety floor. There wasn't a single medicine bottle that wasn't broken and scattered on her tabletop and floor. I began to pick up the glass pieces and, as I crouched down, floor patterns caught my attention. Taking a closer look, I saw that someone had painted a scene. What a puzzling thing to do, to paint something by the entranceway, where footsteps and wet boots would be sure to ruin it. At first,

I hoped it was a picture from the Bible, maybe Noah's Ark or Jacob's Ladder, but the more I studied it, the more I decided it wasn't a scene at all, but random objects: a ring of keys, a fish, a branch of a tree, a crescent moon and strangest of all, a set of horns. I won't say the images spooked me, but I did find myself making the sign of the cross and quickly vacating the place. I knew now that my brother's suspicions had definitely wormed their way into my head. *Did* the Italian woman play a role in the death of my mother? Or in the death of the infant?

I asked around town, but no one wanted to talk about Fiorella, other than to tell me she'd passed away a few years back. I could try to make contact with her children, as I remembered my mother telling me she had a son and a daughter. But where to begin when I didn't even know their names. I thought about traveling to the nearest Catholic Church—as there were none in Aspen Bluff—to check baptismal papers under her surname, but even then, I had no guarantee of finding anything. On a whim, I visited the local Episcopalian church to talk with the minister, thinking that he at least wouldn't stir up gossip. He was busy shoveling the walkway, and I didn't have to convince him to hand me the shovel.

"That's right, she passed on," he said. "But there wasn't a Christian burial for her."

"Why not?" I asked.

"She didn't attend church."

"There's a statue of the Blessed Virgin in her yard."

"Well, maybe she was Catholic, but you can't give a Catholic a Protestant burial."

"How did she live here all these years, and somehow no one knows a thing about her?"

"She wasn't interested in mixing. But I do know this, a couple of Indian trappers found her. She was frozen in her bed."

"It's a miracle the coyotes didn't get to her first. She had no front door to speak of."

"The next day, some local men got together and buried her on the land."

"Not the cemetery?"

"The Justice of the Peace was notified, but by then they'd already laid her in the ground and no one was keen on moving the body." As I scooped up snow and tossed it, the minister elaborated. "The men took grub hoes to the frozen earth, but it was an impossible task. Worst time of year. So, they put together a box and covered the whole thing up with field stones, which they had to drag up with a horse and sleigh."

"Too bad she picked such an inconvenient time of year to die," I said sarcastically, tossing another shovel full onto my growing mound of snow.

The pastor sighed. "It wasn't an easy task, but I'm sure the Lord blessed their efforts."

"Who were they?" I asked, stopping to catch my breath.

"I believe it was Tom. You know Tom? And his Uncle Walt. But Walt is gone now. He died last year. A good Christian man, buried just behind the Church if you want to pay your respects. Of course, it's all under snow now, but I could show you where."

"First I'd like to pay my respects to Fiorella. Is the spot marked? Where they laid her?"

"Just a hill of stones, as far as I know. I doubt you'll find it."

"If it's there, I'll find it," I said, driving the shovel into the nearest snow bank.

"Did you know that's Crown Land where she lived? They didn't legally own one inch of soil. Squatters. And that goat of hers made quite a mess of things too," the pastor said.

"If you really think about it, we're all squatters."

"I don't get your drift."

"We took it all away from the Indians, didn't we? Every last bit of land from sea to sea.

Basically, stolen land, all of it." I was thinking of my Aunt Kate's point-of-view and how she always prodded people to think differently about things. Not that she was always right, but at least she used her good common sense to figure things out.

"Well now, that's a misguided viewpoint. The government bought the land, fair and square."

"I'm just saying, it's all in the way you look at it. But thanks for your help all the same." As I wandered away, the preacher called after me, "I know you're Catholic, but if you ever want to hear the Good Book read aloud, service is at 10:00 on Sunday morning."

"I appreciate the offer," I called back.

I returned to my father's farm, found a scrap of barn board and painted it up. Something drove me forward as I collected a few tools, and made my way to Fiorella's for the second time that day. As I walked, with the mercury dropping by the minute, I recollected the day my mother died: me spying through the attic door, looking in as Fiorella rocked a baby in her arms, my mother lying lifeless in the bed. When my brothers told me the baby died, I never asked any questions, even though their story didn't match up with mine. Why would someone rock and sing to a stillborn baby? Then again, Italians have strange customs. Not only that, a boy's imagination is bound to be overactive on such a troubling day.

In the field behind Fiorella's shed, I jabbed here and there through in the snow with the handle of my shovel, and it didn't take long to locate a mound. Once I removed as much snow as I could, I discovered the hill of stones. The stones were partially hiding a wooden box. It looked as if a wild animal had gotten at it, but I didn't have the stomach to investigate further. The last thing I needed was the unearthing of human bones. A few feet away I noticed something poking out from the snow. It turned out it was a cross made of two sticks and haywire. I put the cross back in its place, and found a spot to mount my grave marker. Guessing at the birth year, I'd written, "Fiorella. Born 1870. Died 1919. A true friend to Mary Moore."

As I removed my hat to say a prayer, a thought took hold of me. What if my infant sister is buried here on Fiorella's land, or should it say, on Crown Land? It's possible, as nothing on my mother's tombstone mentions the infant. She could be here, under that mound of stones. But no, that isn't logical. Fiorella was buried long after my sister. I'm getting carried away with my imagination. As the cold air bit at my ears, I tried to direct my mind back to prayer, but I couldn't shake this feeling that something about the friendship between my mother and Fiorella was veiled in secrecy.

Back at the house, I felt even more unsettled about things. Not only was the house tinged with hostility toward Fiorella, but I also had so little to contribute. While I was active in the war, my father had taken up horse breeding, but he didn't trust me to go near the horses. I didn't dare breathe on them, let alone exercise or groom them, other than filing down Knox's hooves. Knox was old and tired; he'd trot down the road a few miles and back on a good day. The sad truth was, I'd rather be puttering around in the freezing cold than listening to my father's opinions on the weather, horse racing, and war. The war was the last thing I wanted to discuss. There was a time that wasn't true. There was a time when I was as eager as the next fellow to offer my opinion.

"The war to end all wars," was what the upper ranks told us. I guess the phrase was coined by H.G. Wells, even though President Wilson gets the credit for it. I hope he was right, but I now have my doubts. During the Occupation, the kids in Germany were half starved, little kids begging daily. I came around to seeing that the everyday German people never were our enemies. And it's sad to say, ordinary Germans are getting punished for the mistakes of their leaders. Sooner or later,

Germany's going to get her strength back. Then, what's going to happen? All I know is, I don't want to live to see another war; one was enough for my lifetime.

When I enlisted, I wanted to do my part. But was it worth it, for all we sacrificed? And that's all of us, including our so-called enemies. Because those German soldiers, they're just a product of the lie-factory coming from their own government. And when you think about it, none of us soldiers are trained to think for ourselves, whether we're Russian or American or German or whoever we are. We take orders. We trust those orders are for the best and we face whatever we're asked to face. And, in the end, we all have our stories. A soldier might never tell his story but it's there, just under his skin. If he gets a sliver on a finger and pulls it out, a piece of that story comes with it, because every drop of blood in his body has that memory branded into it. It's the reason we soldiers sleep with shadows, and it's also the reason I wake up and throw water on my face, giving thanks to God each and every morning of my life.

At supper time, on that same day of my visit to Fiorella's cabin, my father was excited to give me news about the pregnant mare. "She's close to foaling," he said. "Her buttock muscles are practically sagging. It won't be long now, son." As my father talked, bits of potato mash flicked here and there from the cavity of his mouth. I noticed the cook glancing over at him with a look of disdain. "I'm just waiting for her to break into a sweat and, when she does, there's no turning back," my father said. "I'll be getting up during the night to check every hour. If you want, I'll wake you. There's nothing like a newborn foal to make your day."

Thanks to my father, the day I stopped being a kid was the day he dragged me into the barn to watch our cow calving out. For hours, I was held prisoner while the cow groaned, her big eyes begging for relief. A few times, I tried to sneak off. "You're not going anywhere until Cattail's done her job!"

my father said. One thing in his favour, my father never drank when there was an important job to be done. On that day, he had steady hands and an unpolluted mind, and it was a good thing too because things got dicey. The calf presented one leg and my father had to drive his hands up inside the cow to pull out the other leg.

After the birth, Cattail lay on the ground, unresponsive to everything including my father's barking orders. "Come on, girl. Get on your feet. Don't just lie there. Get up! You want to turn into chicken feed before your time? Cause that's what it's going to be, if you don't get up." When his yelling didn't have the desired effect, he changed his tune, "Look at your calf. How's it to get on without you? Even more helpless than you."

My mother knew there'd be trouble with the birth. She'd said to my father the night before, while we were sitting around the table eating stew and dumplings, "It's not going to go well. Every time I go out to the barn, it's like someone's plunged my hands into a bucket of ice."

"You and your superstitions," my father said. I'm sure he half believed my mother, which added to his aggravation.

"Was it superstition when I predicted the wind storm?"

"I'll leave you to your job. You leave me to mine!" he shouted. My mother gave him a look that could turn back the tide. She refused to talk to him for the rest of the evening and into the next morning too when the cow went into labour. After breakfast, my mother pulled me aside and said, "Remember, you don't have to watch. Close your eyes if you don't like what you see. That's why God gave us shutters on our eyes."

But I did watch. When things got difficult, my father said to me, "If you're squeamish about birthing, you've no business being a farmer." Even though it was touch and go, my father did manage to coax Cattail onto her feet. We lumbered back into the house to report that the cow and calf were safe. Only then did my mother break her silence. "I'm glad to hear it," was all she said. But a ghostly shadow flashed across her face. For the rest of my growing up years, I made myself scarce during births. I made deals with my brothers that, if they took my shift in the barn, I'd repay them by getting up at night to feed the fire, or whatever it took to avoid attending a birth.

"There's nothing like a newborn foal to make your day," my father repeated, bringing me back to the present moment. He lifted a corner of the tablecloth and used it to wipe the bits of potato from his half-grown beard. "Well?" he asked.

"That's okay, Da. If you don't need my help, I'll stay out of your way. But maybe I can get things ready?"

"I don't see what. The stable's all cleaned out, isn't it, Patrick?"

"All lined with fresh hay. Not much to do," Patrick mumbled.

As predicted, the mare did go into labour during the night and Patrick was only too eager to help out. It went off without a hitch.

"See that? She got latched on, it couldn't've been more than an hour after she was born. Hungry little thing," my father said, proudly the next day, showing off the newborn foal. "I just stood back and let nature do her work."

"Well, Da, I'd say you're a natural at breeding."

"When I sell a horse, the coat is smooth as a polished piano lid, and that horse is going to be damned strong too. As long as they find the right jockey, it's going to be a winning horse. Doesn't matter if it's a race on Tuesday or the Sabbath, the horse they get from me is going to perform."

"You're telling me they race on Sundays?"

"Seven days a week, son."

"They take bets on Sundays?"

"Well sure. What if Sunday is your lucky day?" my father said.

"There's no such thing as a lucky day," I said.

"I wouldn't say that. Plenty of races have been won on luck. Plenty."

"Can't you breed horses for some other race track? One that closes Sundays?" I asked. *Gambling on Sundays can't lead to any good. In the Book of Genesis, the word holy is written only once, and that's in reference to keeping the Sabbath holy.*

"Look, if you want in on the business, you got a say on how things are run. Until then, I do things my way."

"Sure, Da."

"I don't know what happened to you over there in France, but you're starting to sound like a holy roller and I don't like it."

"I can think of worse things than being a holy roller," I mumbled.

"I won't be criticized under my own roof, that's for damn sure!"

Since our little spat, I've come around to seeing my father's viewpoint. This is his farm and

I've no right to judge him. I guess none of us would decide anything if it weren't for a hot poker jammed into our ribs. It's time to head on down the road, even though the army hasn't coughed up my wages, and I can't rely on Aunt Kate to get work for me. She's a good soul, my Aunt Kate, giving shelter to hundreds of people over the years, mostly trappers and families traveling to and from the reservation. She doesn't give one wink about what people say, and from where I'm standing, she knows something the rest of us don't. Still, I can't expect her to solve my work problems. Either way, it's time to pack my bags and head north. Hopefully, the wind will blow at my back.

CHAPTER FIVE

Blueberries and Babies—Hurkett, Ontario, 1923
-two years later

Primrose:

A few weeks ago, my mother hitched a ride from Dorion to spend the day with me, bringing along my little brother, Jacob. When I went to meet her at the road, I got an earful. "A tent's fine in the summer," she said. "Well, it's *nae* good any time of year, but what will you do if October rolls around and you've still no house? *Thoo cannae* move in with us again. We're bursting at the seams *noo*, and me with another on the way."

"Don't worry, Mum. We'll make out fine."

"It's a mother's job to worry. *Thoo* should know that, *noo* that you've a *bairn* of your own." We suddenly noticed my brother racing off, his chubby legs taking him away from us. Scooping him up, I said, "Look, Jacob. See over there?" By now, we were back at the property.

"What Pimooz?" he asked. I get a hoot out of how Jacob says my name.

As Jacob tried to squirm out of my arms, I said, "See? Blue

water. Through the trees."

"Oh, dear me," my mother said, "why would Faolan build so close to the lake?"

For a prairie man, Faolan sure loves the water. The first time I noticed, we were taking a picnic up at Hurkett Cove. He sat on the beach staring out at the waves with a far-off look in his eyes. "Faolan loves the water," I told my mother.

"Can he swim?"

"No better 'n me."

"So, he *cannae* swim. Tell him to stay on dry land, *whar* he belongs."

From the tent came the squawking of my baby. If it's not a wet diaper, it's gas, and if it's not gas, it's teething or hunger. "Caroline's up," I said, heading in to check on her. My mother took Jacob by the hand and followed. While I got busy changing Caroline, I said to Mum, "When I was in school, the teacher told us a story about mermaids. No, not mermaids—sirens. Anyways, these sirens sang to sailors, and the next thing you knew, the boat got shipwrecked."

"I wish the teachers *wouldn'y* read stories like that. They should stick to the Old Testament. It's full of good reading."

"Bible stories can be scary, too," I said, remembering the passage about Ezekiel and the Valley of Dry Bones. In the story, the bones came to life as dancing skeletons, and, as a little girl, it was enough to give me nightmares.

"At least Bible stories are true," my mother said. "Not this nonsense of mermaids."

"Mum, do you still want to go picking?"

"Let's head *oot* before the sun gets hot. It'll be hours before Mr. Kelly *taks* me home."

I brought us to a nice spot with birch trees and jack pine for shade. We spread out a blanket next to a patch of star flowers, and I got myself settled on the blanket to nurse Caroline. Jacob kept wanting to touch her face and uncurl her fingers, but my mother put a stop to that. "Let her be. She's having a feeding," Mum scolded. After that, Jacob began stomping through the star flowers until he found a caterpillar, and that kept him busy. After the baby was fed, I laid her down on her back so's she could kick up her legs, then joined my mother.

"Primrose, do you remember berry picking when you were a wee *gairl?*" my mother asked.

"You gave us pots with handles so's we wouldn't spill the berries."

"Aye. You and your sisters had great competitions over who was picking the most. Once I heard Rose calling *oot*, 'Primrose, is your bottom covered?' 'No. Is yours?' 'My bottom's almost covered.' It was the bottom of your *pots* you were talking about. But for any folk overhearing, you'd think you were both bare bummed. *Ach*."

I'd heard the story many times and every time, it's a different sister I'm berry picking with. Me and Mum always have a good laugh over it.

"Mum, it's slim pickings. Do you want to hunt for another patch?"

"I'm fine to stay put. So long as your *gairl's* settled."

"Fast asleep."

"Until Jacob starts pestering her. He's found the biscuits you *packid*. There won't be a single
one left for our tea."

"I'll mix up another batch. It only takes a minute."

"*Hoo* you cook your meals on an *ootdoor* stove is a lesson in patience. And bread, no less. *Hoo*
did you manage the biscuits?"

"I just dug a hole and got a good fire going."
"You *cannae* bake bread in a fire."

"Well no, I have to wait for the hot coals."

"You'll be turning into Paul Bunyan before long. I just hope you're settled before winter comes. You *dinnae* want to go back to that shanty you were in last winter." The *shanty* was a shack that'd half sunk into the ground. We were only married a few months when Faolan lost his job at the sawmill. Even if we could pay rent, which we couldn't, there was no other place to live. The windows didn't have glass, so Faolan nailed oil skins over the openings. It was like a bear's den in there, dark and smelling like rotting wood. After a heavy snow, we had to dig our way in and out of the front door. The only good thing was how the snow gave us insulation from the cold. Sometimes at night I heard wolves howling, and they were close. Real close.

"There's nothing left of the place now," I said to my mother. "The roof gave way in the spring."

"You're lucky it didn't cave in while you were there. And to think you had your first *bairn* in that place." *It's true. Caroline was born in a shack. But what do babies know, so long as they're dry and fed and warm?*

"It'll be two winter babies in a row for you," my mother said. "You won't last to the middle of February, especially since this is your second."

My mother's a midwife, and does all the birth calls for Pearl, Hurkett, Dorion, and Mackenzie. Sometimes, she makes her way to Red Rock. From the age of nine, my mother took me out of school whenever she got called to a birth, so's I could stay home and look after the kids. Or, if the new mother wasn't up on her feet, I'd go to help out. My teacher wasn't happy about me missing school. One day, the teacher marched right up to our door to talk it over with my parents. I remember my mother saying, "Learning about birthing is an education, too, just like reading and writing."

Before my mother came over from Scotland, I guess the husbands took on the job. Being that most folks from around here are farmers, they know a thing or two about animals and birthing, but once you add in human emotion, it's a different cup of tea. Not that birthing is ever a cup of tea. It's more like a cup of our Swedish neighbour's *bäsk*—hard and bitter.

"I just hope there's no storm when your time comes," my mother said.

"Mum, you'll have another baby yourself soon."

"Never mind that. I'll leave the baby with your sisters. Haven't I *gan oot* in every kind of weather to deliver a baby? Never heard a word of complaint from your father either."

"Maybe he takes his complaints to the bottle," I said. The words just popped out of my mouth, and once something's said, there's no taking it back.

"Primrose!"

"I'm sorry, Mum. I don't know why I said that." *Why did I go and sour the mood?* Maybe it still bothered me that my father agreed to the marriage, but didn't give his honest-to-goodness blessing. How many times did I listen to my father complain about the Irish, or how the Catholics did things backwards? Catholics didn't know their Bible, and you couldn't get a rousing hymn out of a Catholic even if you filled them up with the Holy Spirit. And how twirling a prayer necklace around your fingers didn't give you a one-up with God. Our Lord looked into the heart of a man, and not how many times a prayer was said to the Holy Mother. My father tended to say these things about Catholics only after a few drinks. He probably thinks he's teasing me, but I'm thin-skinned when it comes to Faolan.

"Who put a roof over your head last winter, when you and your baby were close to freezing?" my mother asked. "I *dinnae ken hoo* your husband expected you to live in that shack."

"We had no other place to go after Faolan lost his job."

"You build something, you find something, you *dinnae tak* up lodgings in an abandoned *laroch*."

By now, my berry patch was stripped bare. I started rooting under the leaves to find some silvery berries. "He's building something for us now," I said. I didn't want to set my mother off again, but I didn't want her to think badly of Faolan either.

"He'll have to *give it laldy*, if he wants it done. And then there's the problem with fresh cut logs. You should give them six months to dry. You'll be knee deep in snow by then."

"We can't wait for logs to dry."

"When they shrink, you'll have cracks and drafts the size of cucumbers."

"He's not using dove tail joints. It's some kind of frame so's the logs can settle."

"Settle? Well, I just hope he knows what he's doing."

I set my bowl of berries down to check on Caroline. She was still asleep, but my little brother was getting antsy, pulling at the blueberry plants and throwing clumps of leaves into the air. "Should we be getting back?" I asked my mother.

"Did we pick enough for a pie?"

"Maybe a tart," I said, looking at my bowl. "We'll eat them fresh, with cream."

We walked back, me carrying my brother, squirmier than a worm, and my mother holding the baby. Little Caroline was turning her head this way and that, excited to see the speckles of sunlight along the path. As soon as we stepped onto our bit of land, my mother said, "I'm sure it'll all work *oot*. If you want the truth, your father's still steaming over the mill shutting down. *Nae* a speck of decency in that boss. He should've seen to the men and their families, at least until spring."

"We got through it."

"You were brave then, and you're brave now. I'm proud of you, Primrose, living in a tent *withoot* complaint."

Faolan had borrowed the huge tent from one of the timber camps. He'd also scrounged up some free blankets, thick with dirt and pine needles and sap, probably laced with bugs and whatnot. I boiled them for hours, rinsed them, boiled them again, and a third time before they were fit for human use. One blanket I cut into strips, and wove into a rug. With the rug, our table and folding chairs, a big curtain to separate the beds, it was easy to forget that it was a tent at all. Still, it did me good to hear my mother call me brave.

Once we stepped inside our canvas home, I saw how bone-tired my mother was. With a two-year-old to run after, and seven months along, I figured she'd need a rest. While she napped, I held Caroline and gave my brother a pile of wooden blocks to keep him amused. I also opened the tent flaps to get a nice cross breeze. Tent living suits me all right, but not Faolan. The night before my mother's visit, he had one of his dreams. He woke up shouting, "We've got to keep our legs moving! We've got to move! Now!" In the dark, his eyes lit up like sparks.

"Faolan. Faolan." I said, trying to sound calm.

"Give me your pack. Now lean into me, lean into me. That's it. Don't stop, whatever you do, don't stop!" He looked at me, but wasn't talking to me. He was talking to a fellow soldier.

I fumbled around in the dark to light the lantern, then held it up to my face. "It's me. Prim," I said calmly. "No one else is here."

Once Faolan realized who I was, he settled down. "Sorry. I don't know what came over me."

"It was a bad dream," I said. "People have them." But I never knew a single person to have dreams like Faolan.

I was thinking about all this when Jacob started kicking up a fuss. He wouldn't take the apple sauce and biscuits I offered him. Instead he kept going for the curtains, trying to crawl underneath to find his mother. I thought about nursing him, but I figured he'd want his mother's milk, not his sister's. Before I could catch hold of the little rascal, he'd made it through to the bed and began tugging at my mother's arm. She unbuttoned her dress, and gave Jacob a warning, "When the new *bairn* comes, there won't be milk for the two of you." It got me thinking of my own condition.

"I guess I'll be nursing two at once," I said.

"You'll have Caroline pulling at your buttons out of pure

envy. Wean the lassie first, that's what I say."

While my mother nursed Jacob, I opened up the folding chairs and cleared a spot on my jerry-rigged table. I filled two bowls with fresh berries and cream. "Do you want to sit inside or out?" I asked my mother.

"I'd rather stay put. My ankles are swollen from the heat."

I got Jacob interested in the blocks again, and put Caroline in her little floor hammock. By the time we sat down for a cup of tea—as much as two mothers with babies can ever sit—we were laughing at how few berries we'd picked. I said if we made a pie, it'd be the size of a lily pad. Then Mum said it'd be no bigger than a Scottish tam, then I said a silver dollar. We kept getting sillier, until my mother told me to stop, or she might go into early labour from laughing so hard.

At home, my mother tends to be on the quiet side, but once she steps out the door, she goes from being a round lady with a soft voice to a take charge lady you don't want to argue with. Her blouse is starched, and her voice gets pointy. She doesn't mind a good laugh either. I've seen her use humour to get out of a pickle more than once.

While Caroline bounced in her hammock, we ate up our berries in a jiffy. On our second cup of tea, a look of mischief came over Mum's face. "Look at this, Primrose. A perfect ledge for my *wee cuppa*." she said, balancing her cup and saucer on her belly.

"Watch you don't spill it!" I said.

"The way my belly pushes out like Sumburgh Head, you'd think I was having twins."

"Are you?" I asked.

"With number thirteen on the way, God wouldn't play such a mean trick."

As I cleared off the table, I brought up something I'd been wanting to mention all afternoon. "Mum," I said, "I was picking up sugar at the general store and I heard some women talk."

"That's always a bad beginning to a story…women talking."

"They said I was having *Irish twins*. What did they mean?"

"Sounds to me like two gossiping *nebbies*. What business is it of theirs when this baby comes?

Or the one after that? You've nothing to be ashamed of Primrose Moore. You're a married woman."

"But what's an Irish twin, anyways?"

"Before your lassie reaches her first birthday, you'll have another. For one month of the year, they'll be the same age."

"So, it's not a compliment."

"Nothing much said about the Irish is a compliment."

Whenever Mum mentions anything like this, I find myself wishing that my parents would see that Faolan is more American than he is Irish. But he's as Catholic as any Irishman. With my parents being Presbyterian, Catholicism doesn't sit well with them. If you wanted to marry a Presbyterian in Dorion, though, you'd have to choose between Mr. Guinne, who has his own whiskey stall back in the bush, or Mr. MacFarlane, who's been widowed twice. Mr. MacFarlane tells every girl within a hundred miles, "Three times is the charm," which seems more of an Irish thing to say than Scottish. So maybe there's a reason my father didn't put up a fuss about me marrying Faolan, not at first anyways.

Funny thing, it was my father who introduced Faolan to me. "Here's a soldier just come back from overseas, fighting for our freedom," my father said. "Be sure you give him a dance." Faolan didn't seem the dancing type. He stood with his feet wide apart, hands crossed, staring out at the dance floor like it was a boat full of holes. I took that as him not being interested in me. I figured he'd seen the world. I hadn't. Other than crossing the ocean as an infant, which counted for beans, the furthest I'd been to was to Port Arthur.

I knew I'd be an old woman before Faolan opened his

mouth so, even though I'm not the outgoing type, I asked, "Are you related to Kate Moore?" Kate's famous around here. She carries a pistol and does a man's job of being station agent up at Mackenzie.

"She's my aunt," Faolan said. "She got me a job during the war, before I enlisted. Spent a spring and summer here. Boarded in a box car."

"From Mrs. Keating?"

"That's right."

I wondered why I'd never met him before, but as a girl of thirteen years old, I wouldn't've been in the mood to notice a grown man. "You can't say you've lived here until you've seen a winter," I said.

"Just put on an extra pair of long-johns, I'm all set for anything," Faolan said, tapping his feet to the music. "Would you like a glass of punch?" he asked, turning to look down at me. Some fellas bend their knees to talk to me, like they're half way to squatting. I'm short, but I don't need reminding. While Faolan talked, I took notice of his face—a square jaw, a bit of a hook nose, and lake blue eyes. His wavy hair was messy, but it suited him.

"No thanks. I'm looking after my sisters." Me and my sisters weren't allowed anything stronger than tea. Mum's plum pudding with rum sauce was the closest we came to having a drink.

"How many are there of youse?" Faolan asked.

"Twelve. I'm second oldest."

"Is that right? I don't envy your father, with twelve girls to worry about."

"Only eleven. The youngest is a boy."

"Only eleven, eh?" he said, chuckling.

He was beginning to warm on me, this giant of a man. I wanted to keep talking, but me and my sister, Violet, were taking shifts with the kids. "I better get downstairs. They'll wonder where I got to," I said.

At the start of the night, we had a handful of babies to look after. By the time the moon came out, dozens of youngsters were sleeping on coats and blankets, and whatever else soft we could find. The floor looked like a checkerboard of blankets. The dancers were making a big racket, but it didn't seem to bother the little ones. The whole time, I couldn't stop thinking of Faolan. I was almost seventeen and hoping to have a family of my own, like most girls my age. I wanted to go upstairs something awful and wondered if Faolan was dancing with other girls. I hoped not. Finally, Mum said, "Primrose, go back up to the dance. I can manage on my own."

"But you haven't heard the band."

"I hear them just fine through the floorboards."

"Are you sure?"

"Never mind me. You're young. Go up and have some fun."

My sister, Violet, gave me a sour look, but I ignored her and shot up the stairs. By the time I got up, the dance floor was cleared, and the musicians were taking refreshments. Faolan hadn't moved an inch, and from across the room, he winked at me. A couple of the local men were with him, but I felt shy about joining them. I inched my way through the crowd just to be in earshot. Mr. Papp, who everyone calls *Pappy*, was entertaining them with a story. "Simore got talking to some fancy city guy, eh? That city slicker was doing everything short of magic tricks to convince Simore to buy insurance on his house. You know his place, eh? No bigger than a shoebox. The kids are all crowded in there like matchsticks. Skinny too, the whole lot of them. And furniture? They got nothing to speak of. Just a stack of butter boxes in the kitchen and some old chairs stuffed with straw. So Simore says to me, 'I'm thinking of buying insurance on my house. If the house burns down, I'll build another. But it's the *furniture* I'm worried about.'"

Pappy laughed so hard at his own story, it's a surprise his teeth didn't fall out.

A man I didn't recognize said, "It's gonna be hard to replace all them butter boxes and sawhorses. And what about the sugar sack curtains, eh?"

Next, a fellow from Dorion jumped in. "You know Bobcat, eh? Mean SOB. Took his boys out splitting wood. You know how he's got that glass eye, eh? Pulled it out and set it down on a tree stump. 'Boys,' he says, 'don't stop for nothing. See this eye here? I'll be watching your every move.' Then the bastard went back inside to sit by the fire, while his boys worked liked dogs. The damned coldest day of the year too. Minus thirty-six."

Mr. Toivonen said, "Too bad that glass eye didn't crack in half from the cold. That would've taught him a lesson."

I'd heard all the stories before, maybe fifty times, because when there's no chance of going to the moving pictures, you embroider your own stories. I didn't want Faolan to think I was spying, so I slipped into the kitchen to help the ladies. As I scooted back and forth filling up sandwich trays, I kept an eye on Faolan. I saw him with the same glass of beer for hours on end. By the end of the night, it must've been as flat as creek water, which surprised me since most men like to take a drink or two. Or six.

A few weeks after the dance, Faolan came by the house. It was a Sunday, so he had to sit through two hours of Bible reading. Afterward, my father poured them both *a short one*, while me and my sisters got supper on. My father wanted to talk about the war, but Faolan didn't have much to say other than, "If anyone thinks hell doesn't exist, he's never seen war."

Faolan kept visiting, Sunday after Sunday, and I don't think he was coming to hear another chapter of the Bible, even if he is religious. Every week, by Wednesday, I'd start wondering if maybe he wasn't coming back. Finally, after a few months, I figured he had his eye on me. He laughed at all my stories, and got in the habit of winking at me whenever my father turned his head.

One Sunday in May, Faolan asked my mother if he could take me for a walk. My father was napping in his chair, after drinking too many *short ones*. My mother said, "You'll need to keep an eye out for bears, especially the yearlings. Stay on the main path."

I explained to Faolan, "There weren't any bears where my mother grew up."

Mum piped in to say, "*Whar* my father moved us to live, it's as far north as you can go. A godforsaken island called Sanday. Not *Sunday*, but *Sanday*. When you met up with a friend, you'd tell them to meet you at the tree. *Thar* was only one tree, so *thar* was no chance of a mix up. So no, *thar* were no bears. The only good thing you could say about the place."

"The winters here weren't too much of a shock?" Faolan asked my mother.

"At least you can find a tree to hide behind," she said with a laugh. "Go on, enjoy your walk."

We walked holding hands, Faolan and me. When the house was out of sight, I turned off the main path and headed into the bush, against my mother's wishes. Faolan followed, reminding me about my mother's warning.

"This time of year, bears are rooting around for new green shoots. Open meadows. We're safest here in the bush," I said.

"Is that right? Well, if we do come across one, you can protect me," Faolan said, laughing.

We walked over the wet spongy ground, skipping from one gnarled tree root to another. Our feet got wet, at least mine did, but that didn't faze me. The tree branches hung low to the ground, as if they were tired out from a hard, long winter. The woods were drenched and dark, and if you looked closely, you might see patches of snow hiding in nooks where the sun never shines—behind a stone, or under a tree root. The sun found its way through the trees in streams of light, like that picture in my father's Bible of the Holy Spirit coming down to baptize Jesus. The new growth on the tips of the evergreens was bright, like someone'd come along with a paint brush and painted the ends. The leaves and sky and moss and stones were all soaked in colour, and we were in the middle of it, but not really the middle. It was more like we were a part of it, not separate.

I hoped Faolan would kiss me. His fingers, folded between mine, told me everything I needed to know. His hands were meaty and strong. I felt like those hands could plow a thousand acres, do a thousand days of labour without a complaint, hold me up for a lifetime. When Faolan ran out of things to tease me about, he pulled me close to him. Up against his chest, I could smell the woodsmoke and tobacco in his clothes. *Whatever might happen to me in this life, good or bad, I know I can face it with this man at my side.*

Faolan leaned down and, after kissing me, he whispered, "Let's get married. What do you say?"

"Sounds good to me," I said, "so long as you don't mind inheriting ten sisters." *This is everything I need, right here.*

Faolan wanted a Catholic wedding. I thought my father would hit the roof, but all's he said was, "As far as I know, they read the Bible. And he's got a job. A man needs a job if he's to marry one of my daughters."

Faolan and me didn't waste any time taking our vows. I moved in with him, as he was renting a spot from the owner of the sawmill. Five months into our marriage, Faolan came home looking awfully glum. I waited until we were almost done eating, then said, "Faolan, if that shadow across your face gets any longer, I'm going have to trim it up with my scissors."

"Ah, sorry. The thing is Primrose, I got some news."

"I got some news too," I said. I was three weeks late for my monthlies so I figured I was

carrying.

"I'm pretty sure yours is better than mine."

"What happened?" I asked.

Faolan twirled his coffee cup around in his hands. Finally, he downed the last drop and said,

"Since Mr. Caldwell died... how long's that been now?"

"Can't be a month."

"I didn't want to worry you, but now I got no choice. The mill went to Caldwell's brother and he's got no interest in keeping it running. Looks like he's folding up shop."

"But it's busy season."

"It doesn't matter what season it is. At four o'clock today, we were dismissed, every last one of us."

"How'll we pay rent?" I asked. Faolan looked at me sheepishly. I began cleaning the table and getting the kettle heated for dishwater. It crossed my mind that maybe Faolan couldn't fix everything. We needed to face things together. "Is there any other work?" I asked.

"Maybe cutting pulp."

"Finlanders've been doing bush work all their lives, and some of them are having trouble making ends meet."

"I heard they'll need someone to drive the log stamp. It won't take skill. Just strength," he said. Faolan explained that, every year, timber gets loose from the booms. And with the logs stamped with the company's initials, they can eventually identify what's theirs.

Faolan scraped the last bit of food from his plate and asked, "Prim, what's your news?"

"It can wait. It's nothing we need to talk about tonight." Those words stung me. It was the first time I'd held something back from Faolan.

The next day, Faolan went out first thing, and didn't come home until dark. The morning after that, just as I was opening my eyes, Faolan said, "One of the fellas owns property with some outbuildings."

"What kind of buildings?" I asked, barely awake.

"He used to put up lumberjacks, kind of a guest house. I went to see it yesterday."

"And?"

"It's in bad repair, but he said we could stay there until we find something else."

"Does it have a kitchen?" I asked, sitting up and throwing my legs over the side of the bed.

"No."

"Sink?"

"No."

"A roof?"

"After a fashion. Listen, it's a tumbledown room with a wood stove and a couple of bunks."

What've we gotten ourselves into? "Beats sleeping in a snowbank," I said.

Faolan draped his arm over me, and said, "You still never told me your news." Even with everything going wrong, I still looked forward to carrying our child. After seeing dozens of babies come into the world at my mother's side, it was finally my turn.

In the outbuilding we moved into, I opened up my hope chest only once. It's not a fancy chest, just a wooden box with rope handles that my father built for me. Before getting married, I sprinkled cedar chips inside the chest to keep my treasures from getting the moth. Everything in that chest meant something: eight skeins of wool I'd spun myself to be knitted into a sweater for my husband, an embroidered bluebird tablecloth to make the kitchen feel homey, a wedding photograph of my mother and father to remind me they weren't so far away, a few yards of cotton print to sew a maternity frock. I cherished it all, even a tan wool blanket meant to keep us warm during our first winter together. In the end, though, I couldn't turn that shack into a home, and the only thing I made use of was the blanket.

My firstborn, Caroline, came in early March. Winter was so cold in that drafty shack that my parents took me and the baby in for a month. But my mother's hands were tied with a house full of kids, and I didn't feel right about imposing on her any more than I had to. So, I moved back in with Faolan as soon as things warmed up a tad. All that winter, Faolan worked at driving a hammer the length of his leg onto the ends of logs, branding the company's initials. Some nights, Faolan came home and fell into bed without eating supper, he was that tired.

After a few months, I came up with an idea. I waited for a Sunday to bring it up, as Faolan is always more agreeable to things on the Lord's day. Caroline was asleep in her cradle, and we were sitting by the wood stove. "If only you didn't have to snowshoe there and back, on top of a long shift," I said.

"There's no other way. Unless I learn to fly."

"You could do it with a team of dogs."

"We just have enough to feed ourselves. And we're going to keep dogs?"

"My Uncle Freddy's got that fishing outfit, and the fish heads just get thrown to the gulls. Also, if the fish don't come up to standards, they sometimes give them away. They wouldn't mind passing them along to me."

"I don't like taking charity," Faolan said, getting up to feed the fire.

"It's not charity. Except the herring gulls might not be happy with us."

"Dogs can't live on fish, can they?" he said, adding too many logs to the embers, and smoking out the fire.

"You don't know Hurkett dogs. They'll eat anything you throw at them."

"I don't see how to make it work," he said. I wasn't sure if he was talking about the dogs or the fire.

"You can get us a deer or moose again, can't you? I'll dry out the tougher parts of the animal. I got no problem making dog biscuits either."

"How many do you think we'll need?"

"Dogs or biscuits?" I asked, teasing him. But he wasn't in a joking mood. "Three dogs to start," I said. "They're only hauling one man. No supplies, no other weight."

"The sled weighs something," Faolan said, fussing with the damper until the logs caught fire.

"Our neighbour had the most ragtag group of mutts you ever saw, but get them hitched up, and they'd go like lightening."

"I scooped out too much ash. Good to leave a four-inch bed," Faolan said, happy his fire was finally going strong.

I didn't bring up the dogs again, but not long after, Faolan came home with three mutts, all male. Then my mother told me about a St. Bernard abandoned by its owner in Dorion. The neighbours were taking turns feeding her, but no one wanted to take her on. Faolan took a chance and brought her home. Maggie, that's her name, turned out to be the strongest of the bunch. Faolan built every dog a shelter to keep them from quarreling with each other, but that's just what you do with working dogs.

Things were looking up. Here we were, racing with time to build our house so's we'd have a warm spot for the winter. With me carrying again, a log house was just what we needed, even if we did end up with cracks in the walls the size of cucumbers.

When we first got married, I thought that Faolan was unbreakable. I figured if he could survive the war, he could handle anything. But now I wonder if his devotions and prayers are the one thing keeping him from unraveling. Some nights, when Caroline's asleep and Faolan pulls me into his arms, I feel like it's me protecting him. I know that's not logical being that I'm half his size, but I can't help feeling the way I do.

CHAPTER SIX

The Wild Rose—Hurkett, Ontario, 1924
- eight months later

Faolan:

During spring breakup, the timber bosses hire local fishermen to shuttle workers across the bay. This year, there were some early layoffs long before the lake opened up, so they needed me and my dog sled. I was sure the workers were organizing a strike, the company got a whiff of it, and decided to send the ringleaders home. This bush camp is down Wolf River way and the quickest route in winter is to cross the cove at the narrowest point. The crossing is no more than 800 or 900 feet. With a long enough stride, you could almost jump from one side to the other. Black Bay is first to freeze and last to thaw, so I knew the ice would be at least three feet thick, plenty safe for my dog sled. I could be there and back in a few hours.

We sent word to Dorion, and by supper, my mother-in-law was at the door, ready to take charge. She assured me that Primrose still had a way to go before the birth. I harnessed up the dogs and headed out, hoping to make it there and back in swift time. We'd had a wet snowfall the night before, and when I got to the bay, the tree limbs were heavily coated with ice. A breeze knocked the icy branches into each other setting off an eerie tinkling sound, like fine china cups in a haunted house. I gave the dogs their signal and carried on across.

When I arrived at the camp, I could see the men had hit the sauce, which gave me an unsettled feeling, but I had a job to do, so I dove into it. I led the tipsy bush workers, Eino and Teppo, down to the sled where I got Eino—the fella who was the most inebriated—to sit in the basket. If I'd had a belt handy, I would've buckled him in. I was planning to shuttle them over one at a time, but neither one of them were giants, so I decided the dogs could handle it. The wiry one, Teppo, took his place standing at the back of the sled, while I weaseled my way in beside him and took hold of the handlebar. With one foot ready to use the break, and the other on the floor boards, I called *hike* and we were off.

About half way across the cove, the dogs slowed down. It's not in their nature to slow their speed once they get rolling, but there they were, crouched low to the ice until they came to an all-out halt. They were sensing danger, so I drove my pick into the ice, and *shoom*, it went right through. I turned the sled around and headed back to the camp. By now, it was getting to be dusk.

I tied up the dogs, and begged the cook for kitchen scraps to hold the dogs over until morning. The company managed to find a spare bed for me, but between worrying about Primrose and trying to figure out a safer route home, I tossed and turned most of the night. I should've listened to Henri and Old Freddy. They'd warned me about Lake Superior's tides, influenced by the position of the sun and moon. When you considered the push and pull motion of tidewater under the ice at the mouth of a cove, you could easily end up with areas of danger, yet every time they mentioned it, I argued with them.

"You can't have tides on a lake," I said. "Tides are for oceans. Sure, if the wind gets too strong at one end of the lake, it only makes sense it raises levels somewhere else, but you can't call that a tide."

At the first light of day, I got the dogs watered and harnessed up, preparing to head out a second time. "We'll take a different route," I told the men. "It's roundabout, but there's no risk of thin ice."

"Nothing would make them happier than a couple of dead communists at the bottom of that lake," the taller fellow, Teppo, said to his friend.

"Teppo, don't talk like that. The man here said he'd get us to the train station."

"You can come or you can stay. It won't make a difference to me," I said, "but I'm not waiting around." All I could think about was Primrose and whether our newest child had come into the world. Guilt was beginning to gnaw at me for taking the shuttling job in the first place.

The men followed me out to the sled. Eino, who was still half pickled from the night before, ran alongside the sled. I told him the sled was the safest place to be, but he wouldn't listen. Teppo took his place beside me, and I noticed he hung on with a tighter grip than the day before, even though I circled around the entire cove, turning a 15-minute route into well over an hour.

I wasn't in the house a half minute when my mother-in-law stepped into the kitchen from the bedroom. "How's Prim?" I asked.

"She'll be fine. But Faolan? The infant didn't *mak* it." I gripped the edge of the table. "Sit down, Faolan," Prim's mother said, pulling out a chair for me.

"I need to see Prim," I said, darting toward the bedroom door. Mrs. Logan put up a hand to stop me. "She's sleeping. You don't want to wake her."

"What happened?" I instantly regretted my tone of voice. It wasn't Mrs. Logan's fault.

Mrs. Logan insisted I take a seat. "He *cam* out alright," she said, "and gave us a good, healthy cry, too. I bundled the *bairn* and set him in the Moses basket, but I had to turn my attention to Primrose. She hemorrhaged."

"You're sure she's okay?" I asked.

"It wouldn't surprise me if she's laid up for a few weeks, but she'll get her strength back. Faolan? I've birthed dozens of *bairns* and he *lookid* healthy. Once Primrose was out of danger, I went to pick him up, but he was gone. Cot death is the only thing I can think of, but that's rare for a newborn. Or a heart defect."

Birthing was dangerous business. It was a lot like the crossing I'd just made where there's thin ice and no way of knowing it. If it weren't for the dogs sensing danger, Primrose would've lost both her newborn and her husband in the course of twenty-four hours. "You did your best, Mrs. Logan."

"*What's fur ye'll no go by ye,*" she said quietly, then added, "Only God knows why."

"What time was he born?" I asked, staring at the closed door of our bedroom.

"Three in the morning. Not a minute before or after."

I'd been up during those hours saying prayers. "And where's Caroline?"

"The McDonalds have her. They'll keep her another day, if need be." I wasn't keen on leaving our little girl with the McDonalds. The wife is nice enough, but the husband's a crotchety Scotsman who's known to take a slash of whiskey every chance he can. The problem with those hard-drinking types is that when they're not down-and-out, they're celebrating.

"Don't worry, Faolan. Mr. McDonald is a good Presbyterian and doesn't touch a drop on Sundays. Mrs. McDonald assured me of that."

"I'll be fetching Caroline before noon on Monday. I'll take care of things from here. Thanks for all your help," I said.

"And I put out some tea in a jar, to get her strength back. I'll come back around in a few days."

"How're you getting home?"

"Same way I got here. Mr. Kelly's horse and wagon. And Mr. Kelly himself."

After seeing Mrs. Logan out, I opened the door to our bedroom. It let out an awful creak and I kicked myself for not oiling the hinges. In the twenty-four hours since I'd seen Prim, the life had drained right out of her face. She half opened her eyes. "Don't try and talk. Just rest. You've been through an ordeal," I said. As her eyes fluttered shut, I turned to see our tiny infant boy in the bassinet, cocooned inside a flannel square. He was the colour of ash, but his skin was perfectly smooth, with not a single blemish. His eyelids were glued shut. I wondered; Had those eyes opened at all? What had he sensed in those few hours he lived? He had the life span of a wild rose, blooming and fading in the same day. I lifted him, tucking that child—smaller than a doll—into the crook of my arm, and I whispered, "I baptize thee, Joseph, in the name of the Father, and the Son, and the Holy Ghost." Joseph was the name we'd already picked out: Joseph for a boy, or Constance if it was a girl.

I spent the next few hours hammering up a little box to serve as a casket. We had a couple of rabbit pelts hanging in the porch, so I used one of them to line the bottom of the box. I wanted to bury the baby right away, but Prim insisted I wait a day. Early the next morning, I scouted out a place past the railway tracks, along the path and into the bush. I chose a place with trees all around: white pine, some birch and a high-bush cranberry. I wanted our Joseph close to where the birds make their nests, and wherever there are berry bushes, there are song birds. For the remaining winter months, the sounds of chickadees would cheer his resting place.

It was a big job as I had to shovel away a spot, then build a fire and let it burn down. The hot coals thawed eight inches or so of frozen earth. I dug that out and started all over again with a new fire. Thank God I'd hauled enough firewood to the site as it took three fires to get below the frost line. While the final bed of coals cooled, I went back to collect the baby. Prim was in a deep sleep and I wondered if I should disturb her. It saddened me to see how she'd organized all the baby things on the dresser top, washed and folded and full of hope. I lightly touched her arm and it was enough to wake her. Placing the baby in her arms, I left the room to give her a chance to say goodbye. When I lifted the infant into my arms twenty minutes later, Primrose turned to face the wall. It occurred to me that sleep would be the only chance to escape the grief she must've felt, and I was relieved to see her drift off again.

With Primrose asleep, I switched up Joseph's blanket, as the one he was swaddled in seemed too lightweight for a winter's resting place. I slipped out of the room, placed the infant in the box I'd made, and returned to the site. Once there, I lowered the doll sized box, then covered it all up with four feet of charred wood and ash. By the time I was done, it didn't look too pretty, and I looked forward to a snowfall to cover up the mess. On the way home, I collected Caroline from00 the McDonalds.

A few days later, I went back to Joseph's resting place. Since Primrose was still laid up in bed, I took Caroline along with me, pulling her in the sleigh. She cooed and talked to the wind the whole way there. My pockets were full of grey and white stones from Lake Superior's shore, and I carefully set them in a circle to mark the spot. Each stone would represent family: me, his mother, his sister, his grandmother and grandfather.

As I arranged the stones, I found myself again thinking of my own sister, the infant that died the day my mother died.

Why had I never asked anyone where she was laid to rest? Maybe the infant was buried along with my mother, as that was the usual order of things when a woman died in childbirth. Why then didn't my mother's epitaph read *Mother and Child* or something to acknowledge the infant? I did have a recollection of the wake, seeing my mother laid out in our living room, and there was no baby in her arms. The more I considered it, the more it seemed clear they weren't buried together. When I was growing up, my mother's death was something you didn't bring up. Whenever my father got drunk, he'd start raving about *the bastard child*. As a kid, I didn't even know what the word *bastard* meant. I thought maybe it had to do with the baby being born without fingers or toes, or some other infirmity. It's no wonder I didn't ask questions.

When I marked Fiorella's grave just after the war, I was overcome with an impulse to look around the property to see if I might find a cross or picket fence to indicate a child's grave. But I stopped myself, realizing that my line of thinking was illogical. No one, not even my father, would've agreed to Fiorella burying the infant on government land. And thinking about it just led me around in circles.

It took Primrose close to three weeks before she could get out of bed. As soon as she was up and around, we went into town to get her checked out by a doctor, and get the paperwork taken care of. The doctor told Prim, "There's nothing wrong with you that time can't heal." He also asked what type of cooking pots we used in the kitchen, which I thought was a strange question. But Primrose explained that when you cook with cast iron, the metal leeches into the food, which is a good thing for someone anemic.

On the train ride back to Hurkett, Primrose opened her purse and handed me the copy of the death certificate, saying "I don't know why the doctor wrote *stillborn* on the papers. That baby breathed. I heard him cry with my own ears. And he latched on, too."

"I heard you tell that to the doc."

"But did he listen to me?"

"Maybe an infant that's born and gone in a few hours is considered stillborn."

"Not to me," she said.

It struck me that they'd used that same word when my baby sister died—*stillborn*. "Ma's gone. And the baby didn't make it. Stillborn," Thomas said flatly on that sad morning.

"Was it a boy or a girl?" I asked my brothers, once inside the house, as I'd spent the night in the barn.

"No matter, is it?" said Patrick.

"What's its name? The baby?" I asked. "Cause Mammy wanted to name—"

"—Doesn't have a name," Patrick answered.

"Why not?"

"You can't baptize a baby already gone, can you? Baby Moore, that's what the death certificate says. Just Baby Moore."

"But I saw—"

"What did you see?" said my father.

"Nothing. I didn't see nothing," I answered. But I *did* see something. I saw a living creature in the crook of Fiorella's arms.

"Because you were out of the house the whole damn time. Weren't you?"

"Yes, Da."

"Got us worrying about you, too, as if we don't have enough to think about."

The train chugged along with Primrose and I side by side, but I wasn't in the train anymore. I was back in my father's kitchen, as a nine-year-old boy.

As the scenery slowly gave way to darkness. Primrose quietly called my name.

"Yes, Prim," I answered.

"Our baby—Joseph—his face was perfectly formed."

"He was a handsome boy." I said. But what I wanted to say was, "At least we know where Joseph's buried. We can visit him whenever we want to. Not like my infant sister. She could be buried anywhere—with my mother, out in a cornfield, or even next to Fiorella's cottage. Who knows?" Instead of saying these things, though, I took Prim's hand, and we finished the journey in silence.

Since Joseph's death, now six weeks passed, I feel a need to confront my father and settle the question about my baby sister's death. But how can I justify a trip to Manitoba when we have our own loss pressing down on us? I suppose I could write a letter to my brothers, but what good would come of that? Maybe I'm just trying to satisfy my curiosity, and that's not a good enough reason to disturb the ghosts of the past.

Chapter Seven

Secrets and Storms—Hurkett, Ontario, 1936
- twelve years later

Primrose:

I stripped the beds and gave everything a good scrubbing including the rugs, curtains, and wool blankets. Every year, the blankets get a little thinner and I get a little rounder. Not too many women keep a trim waistline after going through seven births. When I opened up the chest to put away the blankets, something caught my eye—a parcel wrapped in brown paper and string. I snipped the string, and pulled out a blue muslin square. I wondered how it got there, and why it was wrapped so neatly, almost like it was a gift that never got opened.

Sitting on the edge of the bed, I pulled the pins from my bun and let my hair droop over my shoulders. I looked at my hands. How did my fingernails get so dented and cracked, and my knuckles all wrinkled up? Coreen, my three-year-old, climbed up beside me and asked, "Can I play with your buttons, Mommy?"

"So long as you don't drop any. Agnes might think it's candy and put it in her mouth."

"I won't drop any."

"I know. You're a good big sister."

"Where are they, Mommy?" Coreen asked.

"Where's what?"

"Your buttons. You said I could play with them."

While I was stepping up onto a chair to grab the jar of buttons, Coreen folded the quilt and put it near the top of the bed. She pulled the wrinkles out of the sheets just like she's seen me do a hundred times. When everything was just so, she dumped the buttons onto the bed.

"It'll be hard to see white buttons on a white sheet," I said.

"Most of them are coloured, Mommy."

"Most of them are."

I meant to catch up on housework while Agnes was having her nap. Instead, I sat on the edge of the bed and watched Coreen make a game of sorting the buttons into piles of metal, wood, leather, mother-of-pearl, and glass. I was surprised Coreen knew the difference between glass and mother-of-pearl. If she wasn't sure, she'd rub the button between her fingers, scrunch up her nose like she had a big problem to solve, then plunk it down where it belonged. A long time ago, I taught her that glass feels smooth, while mother-of-pearl has a chalky feel to it. Once the piles were done, she jumbled it all up and started again, this time sorting by colour.

When we were first married, Faolan'd made me buttons from deer antler. I thought Coreen might like to see them, so I wandered off to dig them up. When I walked back into the room, the sun was trickling through the window, and Coreen's face was lit up with dapples of light. Her cheeks were round and rosy, and her eyes bright as a pixie's. She was wearing the blue corduroy jumper I'd made her, and her woolen stockings sagged at the ankles. I watched her pick up a button and put it in the blue pile. It was the most beautiful sight in the world.

Coreen looked up at me and asked, "Mommy, are you sad?"

"Look at these, made from deer antler," I said, showing her the buttons.

"But why are you crying?"

It had something to do with the baby blanket. I didn't remember where it came from, and I wondered if it was meant for the infant we lost. When Joseph died, Faolan'd built him a box and buried him in the woods. I was too sick to help out or go with him. Was Joseph wrapped up in a blanket, or just a diaper? I expect Faolan'd wrapped him in *something*. But maybe the swaddling blanket, the one in the brown paper package, was meant for our Joseph.

"I'm not crying," I said, using my sleeve to dab my tears, "just a bit of dust in my eyes." I glanced up at my bundles of lavender, all hung in a neat row above the bed, with twelve bundles in all. It put me in mind to check on my seasonal garden. "How about we go for a walk?"

"If you want to, Mommy." Coreen's plump fingers reached out to gently pat my hand.

Just as we got the buttons put away, Agnes woke up. I bundled up the two girls and we set out together, first stopping at the garden. Everything was just starting to shoot up—mint, chives, sage, peonies, Bee Balm—all the heartier varieties, and scads of weeds. Rooting through the twigs and dried leaves, I thought I'd lost my lavender. A hard winter will kill it off, so most folks won't bother with it. But there it was, a bit of green. Every fall, I pick it, tie it up with ribbon, and hang it with the other bundles. It was now coming on fourteen years since we'd lost Joseph.

I wondered if losing Joseph was the thing that brought on Faolan's interest in the big lake. Because it wasn't long after our baby's death that he took up fishing. I found myself remembering the first time I laid eyes on *Lucy*. Faolan came home with a smile stretched so wide, he could've had fish hooks on either side of that grin.

"See that?" Faolan said, shuffling me out the front door.

"I've got supper to cook," I said.

"Not until you tell me what's out there," he said, pointing into the bush.

"Trees."

"What else?"

"I don't know. A fox? A crow? What am I even looking for?"

"What's out there," Faolan said, turning me to face him, "is Black Bay. A proud bay sitting in the largest lake in the world. And I'm going to be out there, because I just picked up a fishing boat."

I shouldn't've been surprised, but I was all the same. "A fishing boat?"

"You heard me, my darling wife, a fishing boat."

"But what do you know about fishing?"

"I guess I'm about to learn. I'm naming her Lucy, after St. Lucy. What do you think?"

"I have to see it before I think anything."

We all headed down to the lake. I was holding Malcolm, who was only a little gaffer, while Faolan scooped up Caroline and jogged ahead. When we got to the bay, there sat a twelve-footer wooden boat, all beat up and beached on shore. *Not this old thing, I hope.*

"It's seen a bit of weather, I'll admit," Faolan said, "but you just wait until we get her fixed up and out on the clear, blue waters."

"That's where your pension went?" I blurted out. Faolan'd just gotten a pension for his service overseas. It wasn't much, but after years of scrimping, it felt like a pot of gold.

"Not gone. Think of it like a bag of seed. It'll grow in no time. If the Kirkpatricks' can float a stone boat, I can float this." Faolan was trying to get a smile out of me.

"The only floating you'll get out of a stone boat is dragging it through muskeg," I said.

"I promise you, Prim, before long, I'll be catching whitefish, lake herring, you name it."

"And what about my cook stove?" I asked.

"We'll get you a new stove," he said, losing his smile. "If anyone deserves one, it's you. Give me a year and you'll have it."

"What's another year?" I said. But I wasn't too happy. My oven was so rusted out, I had to cook everything on the stove-top.

"There's nothing left of that stove. It's good for scrap," Faolan said, showing he was on my side.

"I've waited this long," I said, "I can wait another year."

Maybe this was what Faolan wanted all along, to be out on the lake. The lake was calling him, the same way those sirens called the sailors. I only hoped he wouldn't end up shipwrecked.

"I talked to Henri," Faolan said, "and he'll help me get up and running. He puts the fish on a train to Port Arthur. Some go to Montreal, twenty crates at a time. Alonzo—you know him, eh? Alonzo Nuttel? He fills an entire box car. Can you picture that? A hundred crates of fish at a hundred pounds a crate. Course, they've got a huge fishing boat, but that's one heck of a lot of walleye."

"You mean pickerel?"

"Pickerel, walleye, same thing."

"You'll have to catch them before you can sell them."

"Don't you worry. I still have a bit of Irish luck. I haven't used it all up."

"If you want something, you have to work for it. Don't wait for luck. Anyways, it's here now," I said, "let's make the most of it."

"The Lord is on our side, Prim. Don't you worry." Faolan puts all his confidence in the Lord above, to the point where it rules out common sense. One thing my father taught me— you can't avoid misfortune just because you pray. Maybe you handle it better, but Our Lord's not going to stop the rain. You better put on a raincoat if you want to stay dry.

Coreen lightly tugged on my arm, pulling me from my thoughts. "Mommy, you said we were going for a walk." Off we went, taking the narrow path between our house and the railway station. Along the way, I snapped off a sprig of cedar, rubbed it between my fingers and put it up to my nose. Without thinking, I stuffed it inside my pocket. As we wandered, we stopped to look at this and that—fiddlehead ferns, which Coreen said looked like little dragons, and Wood Nymph wildflowers with their wispy petals.

Everything I saw brought Joseph back to me. When I lost him, I put on a brave face, not just for Caroline, who was still a baby herself, but for Faolan too. When I was a new bride, I didn't know how tender the job of raising children can be, and how one angry word can break a child's heart. I didn't know that tea, left to sit in the pot all day, turns bitter. Words not spoken, left to sit for days or weeks, can turn bitter, too. I didn't know I'd sometimes feel so alone, little ones clinging to my apron ties and me watching out the window, waiting for my husband to step through the door.

When Faolan does come home after toiling from sunup to sundown, I'm not about to fill his ears with complaints, or worse, come unraveled at the seams. I see his eyes getting older with each passing season, and I refuse to add to the burden he's already carrying. What would be the good in that? I guess I have Scottish marrow in my bones, after all. Why wouldn't I, being that I was born with the North Sea a stone's throw away from the cradle I slept in? Or the cradle I cried in?

So far, I've filled my pockets with juniper berries, feathers from blue jay and grouse, seed pods, a dormant wasp nest, and a rare find—a piece of turtle shell. Not all in one day. I take Agnes and Coreen for a walk in the bush every morning. It wouldn't be so bad if I grubbed up some wild radish or picked clover for tea—something useful—but I don't seem to care a pinch about practical things. I store everything inside a round toffee tin with a picture of a ship sailing into an orange sky. When the toffee first came in the mail as a present from my cousin in Winnipeg, we were living in that shack. Every time I popped one of those dandies in my mouth, I told myself, *things will get better*. And things did get better. So why am I neglecting my housework, my mending, my laundry, just so's I can spend another hour scavenging? Maybe because the forest whisks my worries away, like a broom for my thoughts.

Yesterday afternoon, I left the two little ones with Caroline so's I could wander over to Joseph's resting place. Whenever I'm there, I don't like to meddle with anything. Nature's done a fine job of keeping the place charming, so why interfere? But along the way, I picked a bouquet of Twin Sisters pink blossoms. They looked like the softest breeze might blow them away, so next I picked a bit of greenery and wrapped it around the half dozen stems.

When I got to Joseph's resting place, I noticed one of the stones'd up and disappeared. I looked around for it in the woods thinking maybe a squirrel or fox dragged it away, but couldn't find it. Giving up, I opened my coat and spread it out on the forest floor to have a sit. In a funny way, I felt like I'd arrived home—a different kind of home, but home all the same with trees all around me, Joseph's stones at my feet, birds flitting from branch to branch. It was as if my bottom was sewn to the ground below me, and even if I wanted to, I couldn't get up. For once I understood the Scots and their fear of the *sidhe*—faeries. Because if faeries'd tried to lure me away, I would've followed them into their hidden-away places. The whole thing gave me a fright, and I scooped up my coat and bolted home, tripping on a stone and not even stopping to see if I was bleeding before getting back up on my feet.

By the time I got home, the kids were back from school and Faolan was there too. He was playing horsey ride with the little ones, and Caroline was practicing her violin amidst the shrieks. No one seemed to notice that my wool stockings were torn open at the knees, and blood was trickling down my leg, or that the house was in shambles with dirty dishes climbing a ladder to the ceiling.

I wasn't raised to stand idle. My mother would be shocked to know I'm roaming the bush for hours with no purpose. When I was a girl, my mother filled a jar with beans and asked me, "Is the jar full?" I said, "Yes, Mum." Then she poured a cup of salt into the jar until the salt took up all the spaces between the beans. She asked again, "Is the jar full?" I said *yes* again. "Are you sure there's nothing else I can *mak* fit into this jar?" "No, Mum," I answered. Then she said, "Primrose, it's *nae* full and I'm going to tell you why. I could pour a cup of water into the jar, *couldn'y*? Then it would be full. That's the way time works. You think you're filling your time with some-thing useful, but maybe it's just beans. Maybe you could fill it with salt. And water too!"

I washed the scrapes on my knees, and then soaked my torn stockings in salt water. Bare-legged, I began tackling the kitchen. Caroline and Coreen offered to help, but I sent them away saying I just needed an hour to myself. Faolan asked the kids, "Who wants a wagon ride?" The two little ones jumped with glee and Brigid ran downstairs, wanting to be part of the fun. "I'll harness up the dog, but we'll have to take turns,"

Faolan said. "You come too, Caroline. I might need you to coax Maggie. She gets tuckered out these days." It didn't take two winks for the girls to pile out the door.

I finally had the house to myself, which is as rare as a January thaw. I dug into the dishes, but after twenty minutes, I abandoned the job. I marched over to my cupboard and fished out the tin full of bits and bobs. When I opened the lid, a whiff of rotten odour breezed into the room. Walking twenty feet from our back door, I flung it all away. My treasures looked out of place, some of them hanging off tree branches and the rest scattered on the ground. Something about the robin's egg, how small it was, and the colour of it too made me want to keep it. So, I picked it back up. Inside, I scrubbed the tin with soap and boiling water three times, made biscuits, and filled it to overflowing. When the kids and Faolan came back inside, we had warm biscuits and tea. Faolan said that if anyone came around, we should close the curtains as he didn't want to share the tea biscuits, they were that good.

Once the kids were settled for the night, I wrapped the eggshell up inside the same muslin square I'd found during spring cleaning. *Will I ever get up the gumption to ask Faolan about that blanket, whether or not it belonged to Joseph? I remember hearing Faolan rustle around just before he left the room that day. I couldn't watch, as I was heartsick. But now I'm left wondering—was our baby buried swaddled or naked?* When I went into labour with Joseph, Faolan told me he'd be back before dark. He was gone overnight. He said a couple of drunks held him up, but what did he mean by that? My mother was all alone, with no one to help her, and things got dicey with me losing so much blood. I can't help wonder if the baby might've lived if Faolan'd been here to hold him. Still, it's not fair to put the blame on Faolan, either.

A few times, the words've been on my lips to talk about that day, but there's a long way to go from the heart to the lips, and that distance can't be traveled in a sentence. Besides, it's been too many years. Yet how many times have I gone out to visit that circle of stones marking the spot where Joseph sleeps? Maybe it's not an official cemetery, but to me it's as holy a place as any church. Maybe I don't have Faolan's faith, but I have my own kind of faith—the kind that puts family first, and takes care of the little ones. It'd be an awfully mean God to not see that as a kind of prayer.

⤧

"Are you worried the sun won't rise if you're not up and dressed and waiting for it?" I asked

Faolan:

"There's only so many hours of daylight. You can't work in the dark," he answered. Faolan's

been working Sundays to keep up, but when he does, he takes his Sunday wage and gives it away to the Jesuits or to a needy family around here. Faolan's especially busy since a boom—three thousand cord of pulpwood—broke open on its way to Port Arthur. Most of it's floating in Thunder Bay out of reach, but some of it ended up here in Black Bay. It's a little gold mine for Hurkett. All up and down the shoreline, you can see log piles, waiting for the government scaler to come up from the city to measure. They let Faolan do his own measuring, but I wish he'd leave it for the government man because, if anything, he cheats himself.

As soon as this windfall happened, Faolan started making noises about buying another fishing boat, probably another vessel needing twenty-seven coats of varnish like *Lucy*. The first boat did us kind, so why wouldn't a second? And as it turns out, Black Bay is a special place. The bay is shallow, only

100 feet at its deepest, so we get a real variety of fish, like the little present Faolan surprised us with yesterday. When I saw Faolan pushing the wheelbarrow up the path with something wrapped in an old blanket, I had a pretty good idea what it was.

"The last one you brought home was still alive," I called. Sturgeons can breathe out of water longer than any other fish, sometimes for over an hour. I don't like to see a living creature struggle, even if it is only a fish.

"You got to see this, Prim. I'll bet it's bigger 'n you. It put an awful big hole in my gill net."

Just then, the kids piled out the door like it was Christmas morning. Faolan flipped open the covering so's we could see the sturgeon in all its glory. The girls had eyes as round as silver dollars, other than Coreen who hid behind Brigid. Sturgeon are a queer looking fish with a wide mouth and pointy nose, and whiskers as thick as haywire.

"Dad," said Malcolm, "I thought it couldn't be no bigger than thirty inches to be legal."

"Thirty inches tip to tail. But that's the minimum. Any smaller, you got to release it," Faolan explained.

"There's no maximum?"

"If you can drag it in, you can keep it."

"It's got old man whiskers. How old is it, Dad?" Brigid asked.

"Older than you and me put together," Faolan said. "What do you think, Prim? Sell it or keep it?" I was torn. Lately, the smell of fish doesn't agree with me, but I'm married to a fisherman, so that's like a bird being allergic to the sky.

"There's lots of good meat there. Come winter, we'll need it," I said. I knew my evening and all the next day would be taken up with canning. I'd already put up 500 jars of jam, string beans, moose meat, and of course, fish. My usual method is to half-cook the fish so I can press more into the jars. With pickerel, I preserve it bones and all, boiling up the jars for two hours just to be on the safe side. With a splash of vinegar, the bones get as soft as potato skins.

"Who do you think weighs more, this fish or your mother?" Faolan asked the kids.

"The fish!" said Coreen.

"How about I lift your mother up in one arm and the fish in the other? I'll tell you who weighs more."

"The only thing you'll be lifting is my spirits," I said.

"And how will I do that, Mrs. Moore?" Faolan said, picking me up.

"By putting me down!" I said.

"Not until I get you weighed along with the fish."

Faolan likes to tease me, but I get him back. I'll put a few dried beans in his boots, or knit him a pair of mitts, both right-handed. One time, I hid his favourite wrench inside a cake I baked. He always knows it's me, but I blame everyone else—the kids, the trolls, the chipmunks. Sometimes I think he gets more entertainment out of my antics than I get from dreaming them up.

Faolan finally decided that I weighed more than the fish, but only by a few ounces. Faolan and Malcolm then carried the monstrous fish over to our boat house, setting it down on the fish cleaning table. The girls skipped along to watch. I wiped the surface and began cleaning the fish just as naturally as planting a row of potatoes or milking a cow.

"Take a good look, Coreen, Agnes, and Brigid," Faolan said, "because you're looking back in time. This noble creature's been around since Adam and Eve. That's why I don't catch many. And your mother wouldn't be too happy with me neither."

"Can I catch a sturgeon with you, Dad?" asked Brigid.

"What do you think, Mrs. Moore? Is Brigid old enough to go fishing?"

"I want to go, too!" said Coreen.

I wasn't keen on the idea. There were life preservers in the boat, but what good is that going to do if the boat tips and the passengers end up falling into frigid waters?

"Let's catch a fish with a berry. Remember, Dad? The poem you told us about Agnes?"

asked Brigid.

"Me, Agnes!" said our youngest.

"I don't remember a poem about Agnes. Unless you mean 'The Wandering Aengus,'"

Faolan said.

"Will you tell it to us, Daddy?" said Brigid.

"If anyone can recite a poem, it's your father," I said, sharpening my fish knife on the rim of a clay bowl. It took me a year and a day to figure out how to fillet a sturgeon, but I got wise.

"Please, Daddy?" begged Coreen.

"Alright, but no promises. 'I went out to the hazel wood/ because a fire was in my head/ And cut and peeled a hazel wand/ and hooked a berry to a thread/ And when'... something, something about moths. Do you know this one, Prim?"

"The only poem I know is 'To a Mouse' by Robbie Burns," I answered, not looking up from the job at hand. Faolan usually helps with filleting the fish, but the kids were enjoying his poem and I didn't want to spoil their fun. Malcolm was hovering close to me, watching as I cut off the *scutes*—small, bony hooks on the sides of the fish. I left the guts in tact and carefully guided my knife along both sides of the fish, so as to not break into the stomach. The fish was male, so I didn't have to remove eggs. As I was peeling off the skin with pliers, I felt my stomach turn. "Run and get me some cold water, so's I can clean the table," I told Malcolm. Why did I think a clean table would help my nausea?

"Try it again!" Coreen said.

"Sing, Daddy! Sing!" said Agnes, not knowing the difference between a song and a poem.

"Well, I'll have to start over. Can't jump in half way." Faolan cleared his throat, and gave it another try. "'I went out to the hazel wood/ because a fire was in my head/ And cut and peeled a hazel wand/ And hooked a berry to a thread/ And'... oh I know. 'And when moth-like stars were flickering out/ I dropped the berry in a stream/ and caught a little silver trout!'"

With Faolan giving his all to the poem, I abandoned the fish station, wandering behind the boathouse to gather my thoughts. Was it possible? I was only five weeks late on my monthlies, and I didn't need to go into a panic just yet. From my hiding spot, I heard the kids. The wind carried their cheery voices toward the bay, and I had an odd feeling that the lake was pulling them away from me, away from our log house, away from our berry picking patches.

"Did you ever catch a silver trout?" I heard Brigid ask.

"I've seen quite a few speckled trout," Faolan said. "They can't be too different from silver trout. We should start out catching little fish and working our way up to the big ones. We'll have to clear it with the boss, though. Where'd your mother get to?"

"I'm right here," I answered, heading back to where all the fun was.

"What do you say to taking the girls fishing?"

"If it's a calm day, and the bay is clear of ice. But stay close to shore."

"Hear that kids? We'll have to tell the fish to stay close to shore." The girls squeezed each other's hands, excited for this adventure.

"But you'll need more 'n a little berry to catch a fish," I added.

I always knew Faolan would make a good father, even though he says peanuts about his own upbringing. All's I know is that he's got two older brothers, his parents are Irish, and when he was a youngster, his mother died in childbirth. One man has it tough growing up, and he takes it out on his own kids. The next man has it tough, and it gives him a tender side. That's my Faolan.

"Go ahead, Faolan. Get yourself a second boat," I said, cleaning up the fish station.

"You're sure?"

"When else are we going to have a boom break wide open? If you want that boat, now's the time."

The kids all let out a big cheer, like they'd just won the New Year's Day hockey game. I saw Faolan give Malcolm a look, and I knew what it meant. It meant, *Son, in a year or two, you'll take over Lucy. You'll be a true fisherman, just like your Dad.*

When I went out to hang laundry, the birds were chattering away. Not long after, a hush came. A warm wind picked up, and then the clouds started rolling in so fast, you'd think someone was blowing them across the sky—dark, sinister clouds too, the kind that make you scoot inside, not bothering to take down the clothes you just hung. Just as I shut the door, I heard thunder, and the rain coming down in sheets, first hitting the house from one direction, then the other.

The worst place to be in a thunderstorm is out on the water. Without so much as a how-do-you-do, it can go from clear calm waters to choppy and dangerous. I stood by the front window, my mind going like a racing team of dogs. *Malcolm's not a swimmer, and neither is Faolan. What if something happens to them? I should've told Faolan about the pregnancy. Why didn't I tell him?* For weeks, every time I opened my mouth to give Faolan the news, I choked on my words. It would've been easier to juggle eggs than tell him. And now, here he was, him and Malcolm both, out in a storm and me not knowing what might happen to them.

To take my mind off things, I put supper out for the kids. When I glanced out the window, the tops of the trees were dancing, bending one way, then the other. The kids ate, laughing and carrying on like any other day, but for me, it was the longest hour of my life. I finally heard Faolan's voice in our porch, and I shushed the kids. "That lake shows no mercy in a storm," I heard Faolan say. "You go down, you go down for good. Superior doesn't give up her dead. When you get eight-foot waves, you maneuver the boat to appease the lake, not the other way around. But if we're respectful of the lake, she'll repay us the favour." Faolan lowered his voice and I couldn't make out anything else.

"Sorry we're late," Faolan said, as he and Malcolm stepped inside.

"Everything alright?"

"Everything's just dandy," Faolan answered. I could see neither one of them were dandy. Both were drenched to the bone, and poor Malcolm looked like he'd seen a ghost. "Good as gold, aren't we, son?"

"Change into dry clothes. I kept your supper warm," I said.

Later that night, when Faolan shuffled down the hall to our bedroom, I was all set to tell him. But something about the way he pulled his suspenders down with stooped shoulders, and me knowing he'd be up and gone before the sun rose, made me put it off again. *Soon I'll be letting the seams out of my dresses, and surely, he'll notice at that point. Already my clothes are pinching me at the waistline.*

A sliver of light cut through the crack in the curtains and sliced across our bed covers, with me on one side and Faolan asleep on the other. My mind was wound tighter than a corkscrew thinking about how we should've been more careful. Maybe I should've taken Mrs. Oivo up on her offer. After Agnes was born, she had me over for a cup of tea. As she was pouring, she said, "I know your husband's Catholic, but there's something you can do. And he won't notice, if you're sly about it."

"What do you mean?" I asked.

"This is what I mean," she said, as she fished a round, rubber cap out of a jar. "It's a womb veil. I've been using it for years, and if you count how many children I have—three—you'll believe me it works."

Everyone knows there's rubber coverings for the man, but I'd never heard about something for the woman. "Where'd you get it?" I asked.

"From this catalogue," she said, pointing to the tabletop. "Go ahead, take a look."

I glanced at the catalogue put out by "Dr. R. F. Young and Company." Flipping through the pages, I asked, "So, what about picking it up from the general store? Isn't that embarrassing?"

"The catalogue sells everything. Face cream, shoulder braces, ointment for warts. Unless Mr.

Keating opens up the parcel, he's not going to know what's in it." I was quiet, taking it all in, then Mrs. Oivo asked, "How many do you have now?"

"Six. But I lost one as an infant, so that'd be seven."

"Now you know it doesn't have to be eight, or nine or ten. And with him being Catholic, you might want to keep it to yourself."

I knew what I was getting into marrying a Catholic. Anyways, it's not just the Catholics who are strict. What about Presbyterians? I'm sure my mother never used anything. The proof is in the pudding, thirteen puddings in all. "I don't like the idea of slinking around like a weasel. And I don't know ahead of time when we're going to, you know. I'd have to put it on every night, just in case."

"Then tell him to sleep on the sofa. That's what I told my husband, and he came around quick."

"It's not like that. I want us in the same bed." What I meant was, we have so little time together, Faolan and me. Where'd we be without our half hour before sleep? Mrs. Oivo, though, thought I was talking about intercourse with my husband.

"Yes, I like it, too. But not enough to push out a baby every year," she said.

I wasn't offended by my neighbour's advice. I knew she meant well. I also knew the Catholic church came first, so I don't know why I bothered to bring it up with Faolan. He said, in good conscience, he couldn't use fertility control. For the next few weeks, Faolan made himself a place to sleep on the floor. I wasn't happy about that, especially after he picked up a bad cold from the draft. I told him, "No more sleeping on the floor."

After that, Faolan ordered in a book called *The Rhythm of Sterility and Fertility in Women*. Faolan told me the church wasn't outright against the book, but it didn't have the Vatican's blessing either. All the same, I saw him reading it at night, after the kids'd gone to bed. He must've talked to a priest because all of a sudden, he was all for using this *rhythm method*.

Now that I was with child again, I had to wonder if the only true rhythm was the heartbeat of another baby. I didn't fault Faolan for being a Catholic as I went into the marriage with my eyes open. But why hadn't I told him yet that I was carrying another child? Was there some kind of riff between us? The more I lay in bed thinking about it, the more that line of light cutting across our quilt just seemed to exaggerate my thoughts. When you can't sleep, anything can be bothersome.

I crawled out from the covers, put a sweater on, and opened the curtains up. A half moon hung low in the sky. *Soon the moon will wax to full. And hopefully, it'll send light into my world; my world of pianos and mandolins; my world of house dresses, cotton diapers, tea towels, curtains, spun wool, spinning thoughts; my world of Lake Superior storms and dangers; my world of flour up to*

my elbows, kneading bread, baking bread; my world of seven chil-
dren, one asleep under the ground, and another arriving around
the time the ice begins to melt and the lake heaves and groans like
a woman in labour. Feeling chilled, I crawled back into bed,
scooching up close to my husband. It's no wonder we get in
a family way so often, with the two of us trying to keep each
other warm ten months of the year.

⤳

It was after school and something got into the two girls. It all
started with a doll. Coreen accidentally dropped Brigid's doll
into manure, and, just to be spiteful, she used a stick to roll it
around in the cow dung. I gave her a scolding, then told her to
spend her supper hour scrubbing the doll clean.

"What did you go and do that for?" Faolan shouted, when
he got home from work.

"I was just playing," said Coreen.

"How do you call that *playing*, making your sister cry? And
where'd the doll get those eyes?"

"They're only buttons. They're not real eyes." By now,
Coreen was whimpering. She wasn't used to her dad losing his
temper.

I piped up to say, "I took them from the lining of your
army coat. Not sure what use they had in the first place."

Faolan sat in a chair and stared at his shoes, like they were
the most curious thing he'd come across since the *Flying
Dutchman* sank in Lake Superior. I picked up some mending.
I darned one red sock and was picking out yarn for another
when Faolan said, "You should've asked. Before you took the
buttons from my coat."

"I didn't think they were anything special. I got a jar full
just like them." I could see

Faolan's ears turning red as he rolled himself a cigarette.

The kids will always be getting into scrapes, we'll always be up to our armpits in work, some accident or
other will crop up daily. There's never going to be a good time to tell Faolan. And it's not like before. Back when I was slim, Faolan always knew right away. But now that I'm rounder, he has no idea. No more excuses. Before the sun sets, he's going to find out we've got another one on the way.

I pulled my sweater from the back of the chair and headed in the direction of the door. "Caroline, I'm going for a walk," I called out, "so keep an eye on things."

Faolan still had his face glued to the floor. "You coming?" I asked. He lit his smoke, and in three long steps was out the door. We crossed the tracks and headed up the path. As we sloshed through the fallen leaves, we kept our thoughts hidden. I waited for Faolan to light a second roll-up before I said, "It's only natural, them getting into quarrels every once in a while. They're good kids."

"I don't doubt it for a minute."

"And they got long days too, eh. Maybe they're tuckered out."

"Not too tuckered out to get into squabbles."

I wanted to remind Faolan how, every morning, the children do their chores. Brigid loves milking the cow, but she never properly empties the bag. I have to go out and finish the job, otherwise there won't be a second milking from Winifred. The younger ones collect the eggs, and bring scraps to the coop while the older kids feed and water the barn animals. The walk to school takes them an hour in the winter and forty minutes this time of year, if they don't dawdle. They walk the way the crow flies through farmers' fields, taking the old corduroy roads—logs laid across the swampy areas—then along the packed trail. There's one farmer who's always cross and has a mean dog. I don't know who's worse, the dog or Mr. McDonald, but it doesn't matter because Jari Toivonen makes up for them both.

Years ago, Jari had a bush camp accident and lost four fingers. After that, the company tossed him away like an old shoe. But he took up farming and manages not too badly with the help of his boys. Anyways, in the winter, Jari meets our kids with his team of horses and sled. A shack sits on top of the sled where a little wood stove chucks out heat. With the kids all crammed together, it's like a small army in a toasty warm box, gliding across his property.

"You're right," Faolan said. "They work hard. I shouldn't've lost my temper."

"You never took pride in that coat," I said. "It's been hiding at the back of the closet for
years. Moths've gotten at it."

"Eighteen years I've had that coat."

"If the buttons mean something to you, I'll sew them back on."

"They were my mother's."

"I didn't know. I'm sorry," I said.

"Don't be. You put them to good use. Just like you put everything to good use. I got no complaints." Faolan's voice was warm again. One thing about Faolan, he may be as Catholic as the Pope, but he's kind. I'm not saying the Pope isn't kind. Maybe he is and maybe he isn't. I'm just saying, kindness is the only thing worth salt in this life, that and a good laugh. And Faolan has both.

Thirty or forty yards off the walking path is the place where our infant is buried. When I walk alone, I pick my way through the underbrush to visit Joseph's resting place, but whenever I'm with Faolan, we don't stray from the path. For some reason that day, Faolan stopped in his tracks, then veered toward the spot, almost like a big wind took him there. I followed, as there was no point in hanging back.

When Faolan got close, he stopped and half-closed his

eyes. Even though his lips weren't moving, I knew he was saying a prayer. A white-winged crossbill chirped and trilled. Standing there with Faolan brought it all back to me—how as soon as the umbilical cord was cut, my mother laid the baby on my chest. At first, little Joseph didn't make a sound. My mother picked him up and rubbed his teeny back and limbs until he let out his first cry. It was a good strong cry, and I was glad to hear him say hello to the world. Then my mother helped him find my nipple and he latched on, tasting his first drops of colostrum. By then, I'd delivered the placenta. That's when the problems started.

Fragments of the afterbirth were still attached to my uterus, and I was bleeding hard. My mother bundled up little Joseph, and put him in the cradle. She tried to contract my uterus by massaging my abdomen. Finally, she went up inside me with her hand, pulling out what was left behind. I remember feeling pain, then I got hot and chilled. I must've fainted. When I woke up and saw my mother's face, I knew, without her saying a word, I knew. Her eyes were wet with tears, and she said, "I thought I'd lost you both."

My confinement lasted three weeks. All the while, I was haunted. Did a wild animal get at Joseph's grave? Was a wood box enough to keep away the wolves? Did Faolan have the strength to dig below the frost line? Did he use a pick axe to chip at the ice? As soon as I could get out of bed, I asked Faolan to show me where he'd buried our infant. When we got there, Faolan brushed away the fresh fallen snow to show me how he'd marked the spot with stones.

For months after the birth, my mother had me drinking stinging nettle tea to build up my iron. Later, I switched to cinder conk tea. Every spring when we were girls, after the sap started to run, my mother took us out harvesting. If we cut too deep into the fungus, it would kill the birch tree, but if it was done right, the black growth would come back year after year. It was a Russian lady who taught my mother about it. As a girl, I didn't always remember the names of herbs but that one stuck with me, cinder because of the black colour and conk because it conked out illness.

When my mother first moved to Canada, there was nobody to help with birthing for miles around. She looked up this and that in a thick medical book, but always told me, "You *cannae* learn to swim by standing on shore." My mother learned a lot of things about birthing from an older Ojibwe woman—Kokum, they called her. The old woman lived in the bush with her granddaughter, and assisted births for her people. My mother told me how, after the baby was born, Kokum would bundle the infant in rabbit fur, and wash the face clean. After that, the afterbirth would get wrapped up and buried. Mum didn't do all the same things, but she always said that, if it weren't for Kokum, she wouldn't know how to help a chicken lay an egg, let alone a human person. And before Joseph's birth, my mother took pride in never losing a single newborn.

All this was running through my head as Faolan and me stood near Joseph's resting place. Even with the bright sky, leaves the colour of goldenrod, bunches of berries—all these things as gay as a country dance—I didn't want to linger. I swung around and hurried to the pathway, as this was no place to share my announcement. "Did you see the crossbill?" I asked my husband. "Just back there a ways."

"Rose colour?"

"No. It was female."

"The females are as plain as a burlap sack."

"But they sing a sweet song."

"Maybe there's something to that. God gives us all gifts, even a small, plain creature."

"Faolan? I've something to tell you." There it was, out of my mouth.

He straightened his back and said, "That can only mean one thing."

"In seven months, well no, six, we'll have a baby," I said. "I wanted to tell you sooner. Every time, something got in the way. Like that night you and Malcolm came home in a storm."

"What about all the other nights?" He was hurt that I hadn't told him sooner.

"You always go to bed looking dog-tired," I said.

"I'm never too tired to hear something like that," he said. Then he asked, "How're you feeling?"

I couldn't just put a candy in my mouth and expect sweetness to pop out. "I could be better," I said.

"Maybe we should've been more careful. We can sleep in separate beds, once the baby's born."

"We haven't got two square feet to put another bed. And you're not going back to sleeping on the floor."

"Then we'll build beds into the walls, like they do in Holland."

"I'm sure in Holland, they don't build log houses. Anyways, I don't want to sleep in another bed. When would you read to me?"

"Good to know my reading's not a trial for you."

"The poetry, I can take it or leave it, except for Emily Dickinson. It's like she writes hymns for us ordinary people. And that novel, *Woman in White*. That had me hooked."

"And all these years, I thought you were spellbound by my Clark Gable voice."

"How'd I know anything about Clark Gable? I never get out to the moving pictures."

We walked without saying a word until our house came in sight. Finally, Faolan said, "So what's your mother's prediction? I know she's always first to know."

"She thinks it's a boy."

"A boy, eh? After three girls in a row."

I wasn't ready for picking out names, and I was worried he'd bring it up. "We should beat the sunset," I said, picking up the pace.

"We should, my dear, we should." Suddenly, everything, even the air around us, felt lighter. After so many weeks of holding everything in, the steam was finally out of the kettle. It's funny how things you *don't* talk about take up more room in your head than things you *do* talk about.

As we walked, I thought about my mother, how when she found me crying, she let me blurt it all out—how I wasn't up to it, that I could barely keep up, let alone adding another one. She waited until my tears waned, then said, "Now that five of your sisters are married, we're not so crowded. I'll raise the little one. We've always had a wee *bairn* in the house and, if you want the truth, part of me misses it." She gave me a way out. Still, could I hand my baby to be raised by someone else, even if that someone was my own mother?

"I couldn't hamper you with another little one," I said.

"Once you're up to number thirteen like me, raising a *bairn* is no harder than facing one more Canadian winter."

I wondered if my mother was trying to make up for the day we lost Joseph, but it wasn't her fault. She didn't have anything to feel badly about. "Mum, you don't have to fix everything. And anyways, what would Dad say?"

"You leave him to me. He's got a soft spot, and I know just where to find it."

I couldn't bring myself to tell this to Faolan, and anyways, my mother raising the baby didn't seem a likelihood at her age. Just before we stepped in the door, Faolan asked, "When do you want to tell the kids?"

"Not tonight," I answered. "Not on bath night."

It takes ten kettles to warm up the bath water, sometimes more. Then, one at a time, starting with Agnes and working up to the boys, we take turns. After everyone's bathed, I use that same water to mop up the floors. On bath night, I also do up the girls' hair. Bath night was full enough, without adding to the excitement. And besides, I knew the children would find out soon enough without us saying a word.

⤚

Two weeks passed, and it was bath night again. Faolan and me were sitting at the table with our cups of barley coffee. The girls—with their hair all up in rag curlers and their faces shinier than scrubbed eggs—said their goodnights. The boys were outside laughing and probably sneaking a smoke, so Faolan and me were more or less alone. Faolan leaned across the table and said, "Maybe it's your turn to name this one, but if you haven't got anything picked out, I was thinking of Jerome."

It was the first time Faolan'd mentioned anything about the new baby. "So long as it doesn't get shortened to Jerry," I said. "I'm not fussy about Jerry. And if it's a girl, I'm naming her Emily, after my mother."

"Fair enough. But can I tell you about Saint Jerome?" Without waiting for an answer, Faolan went on to say, "He helped out a lion, took a sliver out of its foot. From that day on, the story goes, the lion was found wandering around the monastery, devoted to St. Jerome."

"I wouldn't want a lion as a pet. It was crazy enough that Mr. Nieminen harnessed up that moose to pull his sleigh last winter."

"Better 'n sitting down to eat the moose for dinner."

"I don't know about that. You'd have to ask the moose."

Later that night, in the darkness, Faolan stretched his arm over my pillow and ran his fingers through my loose hair. "I can't believe your mother didn't run out of flower names," he said. "If she kept having girls, she'd have to name the next one

Dandelion."

"Or Bellwort," I said.

"Or Toadflax."

"Nothing wrong with naming boys after flowers, too. Remember that old man, used to come through every summer? Hyacinth. I thought it suited him fine."

"I'll tell you what suits me fine. Being married to you, Primrose."

We'd come back to our old selves, Faolan and me, but he didn't know the full story. I figured there was no use in putting only half of my cards on the table. "Faolan, can I tell you something?"

"Are you having a hard time of it?"

As soon as Faolan said those words, my throat tightened. He reached over to me, and said, "It'll get better."

"My mother said she'd take the baby," I said. It wasn't my plan to sound so frank.

"Did you ask her to?" he asked, pulling his arm away.

"No. She just offered."

"You're feeling that low?"

"We're not giving up the baby. With your help, and Caroline's, I'll be okay. I just thought you should know."

"Primrose, you just tell me what you need. Will you do that for me?"

"I just need some time to adjust." *Some things only a woman can understand, like carrying a child and birthing.*

"Whatever you say, Primrose. You just point the way."

I didn't know what Faolan meant by 'point the way' since the way was already pointed in a certain direction. For the time being, though, I resolved to be tough, like my mother. "Can you believe my mum? She was having babies at the same time as me."

"You mean our Caroline and Malcolm?"

"They have uncles younger than they are."

"More like cousins, I guess. We never had cousins where I grew up."

"Just your two brothers, eh?"

"Not only my brothers, no. There's the baby who died in childbirth. She was a girl."

"Did she have a name?" I asked.

"My mother wanted to name her Mary." Faolan was quiet, then said, "My father never told us where she was buried."

I thought about how, the few times I'd met my father-in-law—once at our wedding, and once when he came to visit—he didn't seem much like a family man. The whole while he stayed here, the girls avoided being alone with their granddad, maybe because of that handy flask he kept inside his shirt pocket. I wanted to ask Faolan why his father wouldn't tell him where the infant was buried. But Faolan'd already turned to fumble for his rosary, and I knew I'd missed my chance. As Faolan whispered the rosary, I said my own prayer. *Please God, give me what I need to make it through this birth, and raising another little one.*

❧

With signs of winter in the air, things are slowing down for Faolan. The other day, he found a spare hour to come home for lunch. "Anybody home?" he called out, even though he could see me plain as day.

"You're back already?"

"Seems I'm all caught up."

"One of these years, you're going to find yourself with a boat froze in the water."

"And I won't have anyone to blame but myself," Faolan said, with a big grin. I noticed Faolan glancing at my growing belly. My one maternity frock was in rags, so I was wearing Faolan's shirt over one of my mother's woolen skirts; not fit for company, but at least I was comfortable.

"There's a thin layer of grey ice," Faolan said. "White lines on the water's surface, like God's lacework." I pictured God as an old lady doing lacework, and it gave me a smile.

"Remember," I said, "last December, you dragged me down to look at the lake. When I got there, it was so darned wet and cold, my eyelashes froze together. And you looked like Father Christmas, icicles hanging off your beard."

"Yuh, I remember. The wind blew all night, carving the snow up into swirls. It looked like a big wedding cake, with peaks of frosting. A big glass cake with snow icing."

"You sure you're a fisherman? You're sounding more like a poet."

"Maybe I'm both." Just then, Coreen ran into the kitchen and dove into her father's arms. "Coreen, how's my girl, eh? Where'd you get all those curls? You got more curls than a poodle! But I got a way to fix that." Coreen scrunched her nose up at her father. "If you comb your hair with the whiskers of a sturgeon, it'll straighten right up," he said.

"Daa-dy!"

"And if that doesn't work, we'll heat up your mother's iron and flatten them out."

"Don't listen to your father," I said. "Your curls are bonnie, like your Nana would say."

"I guess we'll leave her curls alone. So long as they don't misbehave," Faolan said.

"Hair can't misbehave, Daddy."

"Oh yes, it can. There's special schools just for children with misbehaved hair."

"And special schools for fathers who tease too much," I said.

"I'll tell you what, Coreen. You get your little sister ready and I'll take youse down to the lake. It's pretty as a picture down there. What about you, Prim, you coming?"

"You go on ahead. I'll get some sewing done." Once Faolan and the girls disappeared, I found my maternity frock and held it up to the window. It was the most catty-cornered dress you ever saw; threadbare under the armpits and the hemline coming undone. I needed to patch it up soon, but a weariness came over me and I couldn't so much as thread a needle. I let my head flop back against the chair and my dreams began to mix with my waking thoughts. *Maybe I'll wait until the bay turns into a sheet of lace, a thousand square yards of ice-lace. I'll go down to the fishing dock with my sewing scissors and cut a new maternity dress. I'll be the first fisherman's wife to wear a frock cut from Lake Superior. Won't that be just the thing to surprise the neighbours.* If only life were that simple: lace made of ice, babies that never cried, and sweaters spun and knitted by the elves.

CHAPTER EIGHT

The Truth About Thin Ice—Hurkett, Ontario, 1937
- ten months later

Faolan:

As I was heading home for lunch, I noticed two scruffy look-ing characters leaving our doorstep. I knew who they were, not by name, but I knew where they came from—from the throngs of men out of work. Since the early springtime, they've been jumping off at every junction, knocking on doors looking for work. We're facing some tough years ourselves. The pickerel run is late this year, and even if it goes well, it's not so easy to sell fish at a price that's worth our while. *Lucy* is pretty much the smallest fishing vessel in the bay, and I never did buy that second boat. At least I've got work. Those poor fellas riding the rails, they've got nothing to go on but the charity of others.

"Another week before the pickerel run," I said to Prim, stepping inside.

"Is it still all bottlenecked?" Primrose asked.

"Pretty much." During this year's thaw, the ice had worked its way up toward Lake Superior, creating a bit of a bottleneck.

I was about to explain to Primrose that Black Bay is long and thin, like a crooked finger pointing north, and literally shaped like a milk bottle, when I realized she probably knew the lay of the land and water. She grew up here, after all. This year, with the force of the ice having no place to go, sheets of ice got heaved onto shore, like a thousand panes of blue-tinted glass all piled up on top of each other. "Have you been down there at all?" I asked.

"Not since a week ago," Prim said. "Now it's got the look of broken egg shells. And ice cakes floating around. As soon as we can maneuver around the ice, we'll be dropping our gill nets. Fingers crossed, the ice doesn't work its way back into the bay, causing havoc with our poles."

"So long as it keeps melting, eh?" Primrose asked, as she put on an apron. For someone who didn't feel comfortable in a boat, Primrose took an interest in fishing. Maybe she thought if she knew something about it, it might ease her worry.

"That's right. Because if our flags go missing, which it can with the ice moving, then we've nothing to go on to locate our nets. And you can't leave them underwater, even if it means dragging the water with grapnel hooks. It's tricky business this time of year."

"Seems like you fishermen are pretty good to help each other out, anyways," Prim said.

"Or at least stay out of each others way. That's why we run cedar floats. To let each other know where we've dropped our nets."

"I guess you're looking for lunch?" Primrose asked.

"If there's anything left. I just saw a couple of fellas heading out." I wasn't sure how I felt about Primrose feeding every hard luck fellow who came knocking at our door.

Primrose can't say *no* to a hungry person. One tap at the door, and out comes the buttered bread, tea and sugar—even though sugar is scarce—and when there's soup or stew on the stove, the visitor gets a warm meal, too. I try not to complain. The Book of Hebrews does say, "Be not forgetful to entertain strangers, lest they be angels in disguise." And if we're to call ourselves Christians, we need to be generous, even when we feel the pinch.

"I gave them soup. It's the least I could do," Prim said.

"So, you saved the champagne and porterhouse steak for me?" I asked, teasing her.

"I saved you two boiled potatoes."

"Just as good, Mrs. Moore," I said, unlacing my boots, as I didn't want to track mud across the floor. "I just wonder, though, do you think it's safe letting in strangers while I'm out?"

"Don't worry. I've got my ways," she said, pointing to the cast iron kettle on the stove. "It's always there, in arms reach. And topped up from morning to night. Never boiled dry."

"A friendly cup of tea or a weapon? Well, you keep that kettle full," I said, "and I'll keep saying my prayers." I hung my coat on the hook by the door, sat down, and stretched my feet under the table. The dreary weather had put an ache in my hip joints.

"Don't forget them dogs. They'd come to the rescue if things got dicey," Primrose said.

"I ever tell you about them saving my life?"

"No."

"That time I picked up the loggers. We almost went through the ice, if it weren't for the dogs. As you know, it doesn't take long for hypothermia to set in once you're under. Maybe five minutes. If you've got a few extra pounds of fat, that might give you another minute or two. Yuh, that sure was a close call."

"You never said anything about it."

"You had enough on your plate that day," I said. As soon as the words were out of my mouth, I regretted it. Who was I to open up a wound after thirteen years of silence? The unhappy memory passed through me in a heartbeat, how I was absent that day, how I should've been with my wife, but instead was off doing a job. "How's our little Jerome?" I asked, looking to change the subject.

"I just got him settled. He squawked the whole time those men had their soup. I never saw anyone eat and run the way they did."

"You don't need a kettle to scare anyone off. Not when you've got Jerome."

"If he keeps this up, he'll be taming lions, just like that saint," Prim said. We both laughed.

"You had your morning coffee yet?" I asked, getting up to pour myself a cup.

"I'm in no rush," Prim said, heaping baked beans into the skillet. I was glad to see she was kidding about the two boiled potatoes. "Agnes is playing so good today. I made her a doll, if you can even call it a doll. It's an old sock I stuffed, and orange yarn for hair. Didn't even put buttons for eyes."

"No wonder. The last time buttons appeared on a doll, I gave you a hard time."

"I kept them, too. After all the stuffing came out of that doll, I kept them eyes."

"Really?"

"And sewed them back into your army coat."

"No kidding."

"Take a look if you don't believe me."

"Oh, I believe you. I'm just sorry I made a fuss in the first place." Prim probably thought I was sentimental about the coat and the few badges pinned to the lapel. The buttons belonged to my mother so they meant something to me, but the coat could evaporate along with the war.

"So, the dogs, eh? What about them saving your life?" Primrose asked, as she threw a chopped onion into the beans for frying. How could I tell Prim about that day without stirring up memories of Joseph's death? That would be like leaving out the giant when telling the story of Jack and the Beanstalk. She wasn't going to let me derail the story, though. "Where were you headed?" she asked, turning to face me with her nut-brown eyes.

"Across Hurkett Cove. We were going at a good clip, then all at once, the dogs slowed down and crouched low to the ice. And I knew we were in trouble."

"How long ago?"

"Long time now."

I saw Primrose freeze, then slowly push the skillet onto the backburner. She turned, holding the spatula in one hand, and placing her other hand on the top rail of a kitchen chair. "That's why you never made it home that night," she said in a whisper.

"The men were drunk; I was telling the truth about that. I was taking them across drunk or sober because I was anxious to get back to you. But we had to turn around with the thin ice, and by then it was getting dark."

Primrose let go of the chair. It seemed as if she wasn't standing on level ground anymore, like she was out on a raft, shifting her weight slightly to keep herself steady. "This is the first time you've told me this," she said.

"It's a tender subject," I said. Both of us were quiet. We had just walked to a precipice, like we were being herded by an invisible sheepdog toward a place neither of us wanted to go.

Primrose turned back to the stove and filled a plate with fried beans and onions. Setting the plate down in front of me, she said, "I never heard of anyone going through the ice in February."

"Your Uncle Freddy told me about Lake Superior's tides, but I thought it was an old wives' tale. I should've listened," I said, getting up to pour a cup of coffee for Primrose.

"You weren't a fisherman back then," Prim said, with a tinge of regret in her voice.

"And Freddy thought I'd be better off attaching a sail to my back and trying to fly than taking up fishing."

Primrose sat down across from me, cupping her freshly poured coffee with both hands. She slowly twirled her cup around, as if the cup were the world and it was up to her to keep it on a steady course. As she glanced up at me, in that split second, I saw the tears she never shed, but were fixed as a glossy film over her eyes. I read in her eyes a story never told of a young woman just out of girlhood, marrying a man who'd already seen the world; the story of a young mother forced to live in a shack, then a tent, then losing a baby and questioning why God would take a tender creature from her. She grew up too fast, and I played a big part in that. I pursued her; I knocked on her door every week with promises disguised as little gifts. I promised to protect her, but could any of us protect those we loved? We could try, and maybe in the trying, some good comes of it.

I thought if I could keep us talking about fishing, it might take her mind off things. "Henri used to get all in a knot every time I said *walleye*. He'd say, 'Around here, we call 'em pickerel. Get your fish names straight.' Everyone thought I was crazy picking up that boat. At the time, I figured there's nothing to fishing. I mean, any fool can read a compass or drop nets into the water, right?"

"What's a prairie man doing on the water? That's what most folks around here were thinking," Primrose said. "But you were born with water in your bones."

"I don't know about that. There's only one way to learn about fishing, and that's by doing it."

I thought about how, every season was different on the lake, and every year was different from the one before it. Some things stayed constant. The pickerel run was in the spring. The herring run always came late October and lasted until around December 1st. The old fishermen always kept a close eye on the shoreline: how it changed year to year, where it was boggy and where it was sandy, the depth of the water changing with the seasons and months. Henri, whose grandmother was Ojib-we, once pointed out a spot out on the point where there's a burial ground. He told me it might've been five hundred years old, or more. After that, I found myself noticing whenever a new piece of cloth was hanging from a tree, blowing in the breeze, telling me that someone had been there to visit the site. Over the years, that age-old cemetery had become a good reminder to me that, long before we built our homes, people lived here.

Sometimes, when I'm out in the boat at dusk and my eyes start playing tricks on me, I feel like I'm being watched by ghosts from the past. I can't help but wonder if we're all trespassing on the lake. Anyway, it doesn't hurt to appease the ghosts—if there are any—by offering up a prayer. And who knows, maybe they're keeping me from danger too, because I've had more than a few close calls.

"Henri and your Uncle Freddy did point the way. I'd be in trouble without them," I said to

Primrose, taking my last swish of coffee.

Prim abandoned her coffee cup and began folding laundry, making neat little piles at her

end of the table. I was glad to see her get her sea legs back, but something told me to not rush out just yet. Maybe I was hoping Jerome would wake up from his nap. Seeing his round face always gave us a lift.

"From what I can tell, you've got a sixth sense when it comes to Lake Superior," Primrose said, her eyes brightening.

"Maybe I get it from my mother. Not that it did her any good," I said. "It was more a curse than a blessing. Want a hand with that?" I offered, as Primrose stood to fold a bed sheet.

"Why a curse?"

"Ah, I don't know. Back where I grew up, the women didn't know what to make of her." As we stood across the room with the sheet between us, folding it this way, then that, shrinking it down to a manageable size, I nattered on about my mother. "Once I was over at a kid's house and this boy says to me, 'Your mom's a pagan.' I never knew what he meant, but I knew it wasn't a compliment. I went home and, well, you know how kids are. 'Mammy, what's a pagan? Peter called me a pagan.' My mother got quiet and said, 'I hope they're not treating you badly, the kids at school.' After that, she stopped telling me things, and she used to tell me everything when I was a youngster."

"Mothers get lonely, if there's no one around to talk to," Prim said, abandoning the laundry and pouring herself another coffee. She added a jot of cream to her cup, then another, and another.

"You making pudding or a cup of coffee?" I asked.

"Both," she said with a smile.

I was glad I'd given Primrose a smile. Maybe that was something I was good for, the odd bit of humour. "I used to follow my mother around the house like a puppy dog while she did her chores," I said. "And she'd chatter about this person or that person. You know? It's darn strange, but she knew things before anyone else."

"Sort of like them dogs knowing something's up."

"It's alright coming from dogs, but it's off-putting coming from a person. My mother knew the minister was carrying on with a married woman, she knew the Polish butcher—and this was a fellow who whistled from sunup to sundown—she knew he suffered from malaise. When he took his own life, everyone was shocked except for my mother. Once, when a girl headed up the aisle to marry her beau, my mother said, 'There's going to be trouble in that marriage before the cock crows three times.' And, sure enough, that marriage didn't last a year."

Just then, Jerome began to wail from the next room, breaking off my soliloquy and sending Primrose off to check on him. I was happy for the interruption. The rare time I spoke of Mary Moore, I felt uneasy. Was I embarrassed about her peculiar ways? Did I wonder if maybe she wasn't a true Christian, and that's why she befriended the Italian woman? And what about the mystery of her death, and the infant that died with her?

Primrose returned with our baby boy, and though I attempted to make him smile, he was only interested in one thing—mother's milk. As Primrose nursed him at the table, Agnes skipped into the kitchen, hanging onto her doll by its orange hair. The basket of clean laundry caught her attention and soon she was tossing the folded into a heap on the floor, including the sheet we'd just folded. "Now, Agnes," I said, "put them back in the basket. You don't want your mother having to wash these all over again, do you?"

"I can wash clothes," Agnes said.

"Not with the boiling water your mom uses."

"Yes, I can. I can wash clothes and I can skip to ten."

"Can you really? I'd like to see you skip to ten."

"When I get bigger."

"I'm sure you will, but in the meantime, you need to help your mother out. You've got a baby brother now."

"I don't like him." At Agnes's comment, Primrose glanced over at me as if to say, *I told you so.*

"How can you say you don't like little Jerome?" I asked.

"He smells," Agnes said.

"You used to smell, when we had to change your diapers. Maybe we need to give Jerome a bath in the creek," I suggested.

"No!"

"Why not?"

"It's too cold for a baby!"

"So, you *do* like your little brother, after all!" I said. Agnes didn't like being tricked into sticking up for Jerome, and gave me quite a scowl. "I'll tell you what," I said, "you help your mother with the baby, and I'll help you collect eggs from the chicken coop."

"Can we find ones with speckles?"

"What do you think, Prim?" I said, drawing my wife into the conversation. "If an egg shell's got speckles on it, when you crack it open, do the whites have speckles too?"

"All's I know is once we had a chicken with purple feathers, and her eggs came out purple," Prim said, winking at me. Agnes squinted her eyes at us, like she wasn't sure if she believed us.

"Well, then, as soon as I'm home from the lake, me and Agnes are off to collect speckled eggs," I announced to Primrose.

"Let's go now, Daddy."

"Don't you worry. I'll be back before dark." I took my last swig of coffee, and scooted out the door while laughter and brightness still lingered in the air.

⁓

A few days later, Primrose brought up my mother again. Obviously she'd been brooding about it. Either that, or she was just curious.

"What'd your father think?"

"About what?"

"What you were telling me the other day. Your mother and her predictions."

"Oh, he didn't like it one bit." As a boy, I noticed how my father's disapproval had its effect on my mother, and I couldn't figure out how to make her happy. In the spring, I'd pick her a bouquet of harebell or buffalo berry. She'd break out into a smile as wide as the prairie and I'd think she was cured. Ten minutes later, I'd see her leaning over the steaming laundry tub with that same woebegone look in her eyes.

When my father was blacked out from drink, my mother often sang to me—part Irish, part English. She fed my growing bones with music and the language of her childhood. My father forbade her to speak Irish in the house, but when he was three sheets to the wind, he wouldn't have known the difference between Irish and Russian. That's when she freely opened her vocal cords, filling me up with something I might need later on in life. Maybe she sensed her life would be cut short. And maybe she hoped that, if that day came, I'd have enough of her goodness and strength stored up inside me.

That's what a good mother does; she gives her children a cloak of encouragement. She doesn't take away your trials—nobody can do that—but she adds a layer of protection between you and the world. If she dies early, that little person has to find their cloak somewhere else, maybe a grandmother or older sibling if they're lucky. I didn't have anyone step in when my mother died. It was just me and my brothers. They were thick as thieves, those two, and I didn't fit in. Maybe, in the end, that was a good thing, as they left me alone with my books and schooling and tree forts. They stepped in when there was a threat of violence from my father—especially Thomas. Both of my brothers could pack a good punch, and my father knew it too.

My mother's songs and her ways never really left me. On the worst day of my life, as I lay on the ground, her songs were there. It started with the wind; how it carried more than one note, like a piano or violin, reminding me of my mother's language. It didn't take away the shock, and it didn't stop me from begging for mercy, but it pulled me to my feet and sent me back into the tent. I didn't only rifle through Charlie and Pat's tunics to find their personal belongings. That's only part of the story.

Once in the tent, I scrambled to locate a flannel shirt from my gear and began tearing at it where I knew the fabric would give way. The ripping of fabric isn't a sound a man often hears, but the odd time Primrose tears a piece of cotton, my senses are still jolted, after all these years. My intention was to cover the faces of my friends. The worst of it was their eyes. It didn't seem right that they had to go to the next life blinded. I first covered Charlie's face with the torn flannel, then pulled him up into an embrace. Then I did the same for Pat, wrapping my arms around him. I must've also removed their I.D. tags, though to this day, I've no recollection of doing that.

With their faces covered, I felt jolted into song in that old language of my mother's. I couldn't repeat those lyrics today, not if you put a fifty dollar-bill on the table and told me it was mine if I spoke three words of it. Yet there I was, following the tune and lyrics like it was the most natural thing in the world.

How did Primrose's simple question—*What did your father think?* —lead me so quickly to the war and its darker elements? I suddenly felt cooped up in the house and needed to get back outdoors.

"Good day to catch up on some jobs," I said to Primrose, eager to be on my way.

"You've hardly touched your lunch."

"That's okay. I'll eat it tonight."

I understood the outdoors. My area of expertise was the lake and sky and wind patterns. While some people recited Shakespeare, I memorized the ins and outs of Black Bay. Way out in Superior, with surface water alone in the neighbourhood of 100,000 square miles, the water froze over once in every hundred years. But here in Black Bay, it was the first point to freeze over, sometimes as early as mid-November—the first to freeze and the last to thaw. Getting a handle on fishing taught me that, if you didn't do things exactly right, you were finished.

Even so, as complicated and unpredictable the elements were, I still found it easier to understand than the heart of a woman.

That evening in the boat, I marked the stages of nautical dusk beginning with the sun vanishing behind the horizon. Then a dusky blue haze filled the sky, and I anticipated those few minutes where the lines became blurred between water and sky, when heaven and earth meld together. Though I normally make my way home with that bit of dusk in the sky, I decided to wait for the third stage of dusk. It was a full moon night, after all. With the sun setting and moon rising moments later, it was like the sun and moon were switching dance partners, spelling each other off on opposite sides of the hall. When I was a small fry, my mother taught me to take notice of that round ball of light. She'd point up to the sky and say, "You see up there, Faolan? As long as there's a moon in the sky to light your path, you'll never be lost."

A few weeks had passed. The waters were calm, and the ice cakes, I noticed, had become dark, a sign they were about to disappear. It felt strange to me that I was so far away from the prairies of my childhood, yet the memories were set in my mind like ice—not unlike the ice of Black Bay. Could memories melt the same way ice melts, changing shape and colour as the years go by? Or did memories remain frozen inside a perpetual winter?

On the morning of the day my mother died, I sat gobbling up a bowl of oatmeal when my mother stepped in through the front door, letting in a blast of cold air. Her eyes glazed past me like I wasn't in the room. Once her coat and boots were off, I noticed water dripping down her legs and pooling around her socked feet, and I couldn't figure out why she wasn't rushing to get the mop or a dish rag. Why was she staring at the wet floor?

And where did the water come from in the first place? "What is it, Mammy? Are you alright?" I asked.

"I don't usually walk so far. I must've worn myself out. Now, go find your brother, Thomas. Quick now!"

I ran as fast as my nine-year-old legs could carry me until I found Thomas out in the fields, attempting to poke holes in the still frozen ground. "Mammy needs you!" I called.

My brother abandoned his task and jogged over to the house. I hung around the yard, waiting to see what the fuss was about. When he bounced back outside, he began ordering me around. "Fill up the water pail! After that, get going to school."

"What for?"

"Because Mam's having a baby, that's what for."

"Does it have to be today?"

"We don't have a say about it. Don't you know anything?"

"I know lots."

"Then you know to keep out of everyone's hair."

"How long will it take?"

"As long as the highest beanstalk and then some. Now fetch the water and off to school with you."

"I don't feel like it. Not on a day Mammy's having a baby."

"Then make yourself scarce, cause if Da sees you—"

Thomas didn't have to finish the sentence. I knew how to make myself scarce. Didn't I disappear every time my father went on a binge? I had my favourite places: the creek, an old tree fort my brothers had made, even the wheat and corn fields in summer gave me a place of safety. I enjoyed secret places, out of sight places. This day, I decided to head to the creek where smooth, glossy ice clung to the edges, and water appeared and disappeared under the ice. There were a few places where the creek ran deep and, over the years, I'd caught bass and even walleye, but it was too early for fishing, too early for catching tadpoles, or pollywogs as my teacher called them, too early for anything but sitting on a rock and listening to the sound of the water rushing under and over the ice.

By now, I knew I'd get in more trouble by showing up to school two hours late, so I made my way back to the house. I got up my nerve to peek in through the kitchen window. My father sat at the table with an ashtray overflowing with smoldering butts, a shrine to the seriousness of things. When he got to his feet and headed to the front door, I bolted out behind the barn without him noticing, which was quite a feat considering the barn was more than a stone's throw away. Peeking out, I watched my father bundle up sunflower stalks into cats— fuel made of stalks—giving the job more force than what was needed. Even though we were set up with a coal-burning stove, my father insisted on using prairie fuel in the old drum stove, anything to save a few pennies to justify the betting he did on the weekends.

I passed the time poking around behind the barn until I heard a rattle of horses in the distance. Up the road, I was surprised to see Patrick, rather than Thomas, holding the reins. He had a passenger with him—a woman with a look on her face so stern, it could stop a freight train. Her arms were crossed over her bosom and her mouth puckered into a tight red knot. Patrick drove the buggy right up to our front door. As soon as she stepped down, I noticed the horses sigh with relief. With her carpet bag gripped at her side, the woman charged into the house. She didn't give a friendly tap at the door. No-sir-ee, it was all the spiders and cobwebs could do to scramble out of her way.

Approaching Patrick, I asked, "Is that the midwife lady?'"

"Never mind her. How come you're not in school?"

"Mammy's having a baby," I answered.

"I know that, you idiot." Patrick unhitched the horses and threw blankets over them, walking to cool them down. My father suddenly stepped outside and it was too late to hide myself.

"Get yourself to school!" he shouted.

"But there's only a half day of learning left."

"I don't care if there's a half hour left. And when you get home, find something to do. I don't care what. Just stay the hell out of the house until we call you in!"

At school, I told the boys that my mother was having a baby. They filled me with stories of birthing mothers, how the colour of their skin turned green, and their eyes rolled back in their sockets, and how their screams could be heard from here to the next township. As soon as school was out, I raced home, taking a short cut through Farmer Kempe's field even though I risked coming face to face with his half-coyote dog.

I circled our house two or three times, but didn't have the nerve to go in. By now, I was getting hungry. All I'd eaten that day was a few mouthfuls of oatmeal, and a jam sandwich my schoolmate, Ivan, had given me. His vittles had come with a condition—I had to promise to tell him everything I saw relating to the birth. He was planning, he said, to become a famous doctor and he needed all the gritty details. I told him I hated births and I especially hated the sight of a cow birthing. He plucked the sandwich out of my hand and told me I could eat it only if I reported back everything I saw or heard while my mother was in labour. I was torn. That sandwich, thick with his mother's famous strawberry jam, was calling out for me to bite into it. "Alright," I said, "but they're not going to let me into the room. They won't even let me in the house."

"That's where windows come in handy," Ivan said.

The minute I arrived home, I found an old block of wood and used it as a stool to peek inside my parents' bedroom, thinking I'd catch a glimpse. But the room was empty, and I was darned relieved. Next, I looked in through the kitchen window and found the same scene repeated from the morning, only this time, instead of my father hunched forward, I found him with his head tipped back, eyes closed, legs stretched out under the table, and a lit cigarette dangling between his yellowed fingers.

I gave up on my mission of scraping up a good story to tell Ivan, and wandered into the barn. My father had built the barn with windows on all four sides. He swore the horses had a slick coat because of the air circulation. He fussed with whether or not to open the windows, depending on the weather. At night, though, they had to be shut tight or there'd be hell to catch. When I stepped in, a cool current of air floated through, giving me a chill. I climbed up into the hay loft where I found the small window latched shut.

I pushed the window open wide, and leaned out almost far enough to touch the bare branches of the Manitoba maple, which grew next to the barn. From my perch, I couldn't hear much, other than the odd moan catching itself on the breeze. Clouds drifted by; a flock of red-breasted nuthatches swooped out of the tree branches and up into the open sky. After a while, I threw myself down onto the soft pile of hay. I wasn't there five minutes when I heard a gut-wrenching cry, the sound clamping onto me like a giant vice grip. I couldn't move, I couldn't react, I couldn't focus my thoughts, and when I finally mustered up the courage to return to the window, I saw the silhouette of someone moving around in the kitchen. By the shape, I knew it to be the woman with the carpetbag. She closed the curtains in the kitchen, then the sitting room, and on it went until the whole house was shut off from the world, and shut off from me.

After a while, I saw Thomas stumbling down the front steps of the house, and when the screen door screeched open, I heard a baby cry, but maybe it was just one of the barn cats. Thomas was carrying a basin and it looked to be full of bloodied sheets. Pictures were swimming around in my head: I saw a kitten in my mother's arms swaddled like a baby, my brother swimming in the creek with the icy water gone red, my mother floating up the chimney of our house and into the sky, her hair covered in soot. I saw all these things, and then I saw my own hands gripping the barn boards on both sides of the open window. Before long, smoke and sparks lit up the sky from the place where Thomas had disappeared behind our house. I wanted to go inside the house and ask what happened, but knew my father would have no qualms about going hard on the belt if I disobeyed him.

Not long after, I detected Patrick tearing down the road in the direction of our house. A man dressed in nicer clothes than anything we were used to seeing sat in the passenger seat, his back poker straight. I wouldn't go so far as to say the man's pants were pressed, but he had a polished look about him all the same. He wasn't a farmer, but I was pretty sure he wasn't a church minister either. I watched as he tipped his hat forward, trying to protect his face from the flying pebbles and slush. Before the horses came to a complete halt, the tidy-looking man vaulted off and dove into our house, carrying a black bag. My brother unhitched the horses and started the cooling down process for the second time that day. Those poor horses had been worked too hard, even I could see that. I climbed down from my post, and wandered over to Patrick to ask, "Who's that man?"

"The doc," he said, "come to help Mam."

"Why?"

"Why do you think? She needs help getting the baby out."

"But doctors are for broken legs and fevers, not birthing babies."

"They know something about birthing, too."

"They should've brought in Farmer Ferguson. He can birth anything."

"Animals aren't the same as humans."

"They birth the same."

"Horses are good for nothing now," Patrick said, changing

the subject. "Look at them panting."

"Sadler doesn't seem so bad."

"We'll see."

I followed Patrick around in a circle as he cooled the horses. "Why'd you work them so hard anyways?" I asked.

"I told you. Mam needs help."

"What about that lady with the sour face? Can't she help?"

"Mrs. Watts? They got a whole team in there, the midwife and that nutty Italian. For all I know, the baby's already born. Do you know?"

"I'm not supposed to go inside."

"Well, did you hear anything?"

"Like what?"

"Like a baby cry. Jesus, Faolan."

"You're not supposed to say *Jesus* unless you're praying."

"I am praying—praying my little brother will smarten up and say something useful."

"I didn't hear no baby cries. But I heard someone yelling."

"Well? Who was it? Mam?"

"I don't know."

"I got a bad feeling about this," Patrick said, more to himself than to me.

Patrick headed to the stables, while I returned to my post at the window. At least from there, I could see the comings and goings with no one to shoo me away. Nothing felt right. My surroundings were the same as always, but everything was topsy-turvy. My stomach was rumbling with hunger, the house was full of strangers, and my brothers were too much in their own world to pay attention to me. I slammed shut the barn window and, without a shred of a plan, made my way down the ladder. Twice, I circled the house looking for a crack in one of the house curtains, but there wasn't a sliver of an opening to be found. Next, I made my way to the chicken coop. As a kid, I talked to the chickens, but that day I charged across the chicken run, startling a few of the birds as they squawked and flapped their wings to bolt out of my way. Inside the coop, I collected two fresh eggs. Without rinsing them, I cracked them into the palm of my hand, and with one motion, swallowed them whole. It made me gag, but the eggs stayed put in my stomach.

My plan was to secretly get inside the house by climbing a set of outdoor steps, which led to the attic. The wobbly, half-rotting steps harkened back to the day when the garret was empty, fit only for mice and squirrels. As boys, we sometimes played pirates up there, pretending the stoop was our ship. Patrick and I had pissing competitions to see how far our urine could land out in the white snow. Once in a while he'd let me win, telling me that I had the makings of a true pirate, if only I'd stop hanging off my mother's apron strings. Eventually, my father built indoor steps leading up to the loft, and the outdoor steps were forgotten.

As I eyeballed the three-foot square platform at the top, I wondered if it would hold my weight. I worried the entire thing might be attached to the house by a few rusty nails and no more. Still, it was worth a try. Once safely on the stoop, I eyeballed the coal chute sized door that would provide me entry into the house. Crouching down low so as to not be seen, I stopped to reconsider. What if my father was up there? What if my mother was in the middle of having the baby? What if that woman with the big bosom was guarding the room, the same way our mutt guarded our house? With shaky hands, I pulled at the rusty latch, which gave way easily. Now I had no excuse but to step inside, or at the very least open the entryway a crack. I'd come this far, after all.

As I didn't want the late afternoon daylight pouring in from where I sat, I opened the trap door a crack. In the darkish haze of the room, I saw a round woman, who I assumed to be the midwife, sitting in the corner. She lightly swayed to and fro, and I heard her singing. As my eyes adjusted to the room, I saw that it wasn't Mrs. Watts at all, but the Italian woman. *What's she doing here? And what's that bundle in her arms? My baby sister? It must be. And look how the Italian lady's cooing and singing to her.*

Just as I was about to bolt into the room, I was stopped by the sight of my mother who lay flat on the bed. A white sheet was pulled up to her chest, with her arms on top of her body. I couldn't understand why no one had given her a blanket. She seemed smaller than normal, not only because the round mound that had hatched the baby had sunken down slightly, but also because her hands and fingers were so delicate looking. My eyes darted from her hands up to her face, and that's when it hit me: her pasty white face and her lips drained of colour told it all. She was dead, dead as stone.

I felt a rush of hatred for the new baby. How dare it cause my mother to die? *Stop being nice to the baby! My mother's dead! You don't sing with someone lying dead right beside you!* But I was just a boy. What did I know about these things? I inched my way back onto the landing, trying to remain undetected, and, once there, I heard men's voices at the front door of our house. Then I heard a horse trotting down the road. Even so, I didn't turn my head an inch to see who it was. Instead, I looked up to a sea of clouds, layers and layers of pink puffs near the horizon. The sky above reminded me of a winter blanket—the threadbare kind that never quite warm you from the cold.

Once things got quiet, I worked my way down the rickety steps. All the while, I didn't cry, not a tear. Crying would've made my mother's death true, and I didn't want it to be true. As I took a few steps toward our front door, a swarm of crows swooped overtop the roof, and I was reminded of the murder of crows we'd seen only months prior, including the albino crow. I soon found myself heading back to the safety of the barn. This time, I stole a horse blanket from the pile my brother kept handy, and dragged it up the ladder. Over the next few hours, I continued to hear voices and the sounds of horse hooves coming and going, but I stayed curled up in the hay, with that itchy blanket wrapped around me. Looking back, I wonder why they would send a boy out on his own the way they did. Not that I blame them; they were dealing with a birth and two deaths on the same day. No one was thinking logically.

With all the noises now faded away, I got up my courage to poke my head out the window one last time. Not a single star lit up the sky, yet strangely, a moon shone brightly. Our house had a couple of lanterns glowing—one in the kitchen and one in the upstairs bedroom where I pictured my mother's face, white and cold. Maybe my mother was truly gone, never to return. Gripping the blanket, I rubbed my face in it, not caring if it scratched me. In fact, scrape marks would be a sign of my allegiance to my mother, like a soldier with battle wounds. I thought of how she'd died in my bed and hoped nobody expected me to sleep there. I'd sleep on the dirt floor in the cold room, or back out in the barn, but I would not sleep in that bed of death.

I must've fallen asleep because there's no explanation for what happened next. A woman stood across from me, smiling. Other than her emerald green eyes, she was the spitting image of my mother. She wore a flowing dress that changed colours depending on where the shaft of moonlight hit the fabric. The gown was so long, the hem fell like little rivers into the hay. Could she be my mother's sister? But didn't they all die on the boat from Ireland?

The curious lady fished out the box of buttons I'd hidden under the hay in the barn rafters. I'd never told anyone about those buttons, never whispered the secret to a spider or a bird, but she knew exactly where to find them. She set the box down and motioned for me to come closer. I nestled in beside her, like a baby bird looking for protection from January winds. The green-eyed lady cupped her hand on top of my head so lightly it could've been a butterfly landing. That's when I noticed over in the far corner of the loft stood two gritty-faced fellas with toothless grins. One of them slipped a lit cigarette into the strings of his fiddle, and the smoke began to curl around him like a genie's lamp. The other held a drum and began playing a slow, pulsing, rolling sound. The fiddler kicked in with a lively tune, and for the next few hours as I curled up onto the woman's lap, the men performed their ditties. Eventually, the songs gave way to what my mother used to call laments—mournful songs that only the Irish could invent.

I woke to the sound of Thomas calling, "Faolan! Faolan, are you up there?"

I looked around. Daylight was streaking in through the cracks in the walls, lighting up the barn dust. The men were gone; the lady was gone, too, though the button box was sitting exactly where she'd set it down. The whole thing was a dream, of course. For a second, I wondered if my mother's death had also been a dream.

"Faolan? It's time to come down."

"I'm not coming until you tell me," I called down.

"Tell you what?"

"What happened to Mammy?"

"Just come down, will you?"

When I stepped into the kitchen, Patrick and my da were sitting at the table drinking coffee. Things looked the same as every morning, other than the fact that my mother wasn't at the stove cooking up our porridge. "Where'd you sleep? Up with the bats?" my brother Patrick asked me.

Before I had a chance to answer, my father barked at me, "Next time, tell somebody when you decide to spend a night in the barn. You hear me, lad?" My father's hair was matted with sweat and stuck to his forehead. His eyes were bloodshot, and he looked like he'd been wearing the same clothes for days.

"Yes, Da."

After my brothers broke the news to me, making sure not to sugar coat it, they started ordering me around. "You'll need to take a bath before the wake," Patrick said, "We all do."

"What wake?"

"The one for our mother. The neighbour ladies are coming today, to get things ready."

"They're putting a coffin in here?"

"Where else are we to have the wake? Out in the field?" my father shouted, his finger pointing out the window.

"I hate wakes," I whispered under my breath. I'd only ever been to one other wake, and it scared the wits out of me. It was a neighbour girl who'd died of pneumonia. At first, I didn't want to look inside the pine box, but then once I did, I couldn't pull my eyes away from her. Pearl was her name. Pearl in the casket looked an imposter of the real Pearl. And for some reason, they had her dressed all in white, which made the whole scene feel peculiar. Then my brother Patrick told me that, because I'd stared at Pearl for more than a minute, she was sure to come back and haunt me.

"It'll all be over before you know it," Thomas said. "Have some bread and jam. You look like you could use something to eat."

"I'm not hungry."

"Then get cleaned up," said Thomas. "I've boiled water for the bath. Mrs. Kelly will be fitting you up for a new pair of trousers."

"I don't want no one fitting me up but my own mother!"

"Well, your mother's gone now, isn't she?" snapped my father. "So, it's second best for all of us."

"Ease up on Faolan, will youse?" said Thomas. "The kid just found out ten minutes ago."

I wanted to tell my father and brothers that I saw the Italian lady cooing and jiggling the baby in her arms, and that I saw my mother too, sunken into the bed like a stick puppet. I wanted to tell them how Mammy sent me a green-eyed lady and two men to play tunes all night long. *Travelers*, I wanted to say, *from Ireland, just like Granddad!* But I didn't say a word. And in the cold light of day, nothing seemed real, not my mother's death, or the dirty-faced musicians, or the green-eyed lady in the loft.

My father kept sober through the wake, which was a shock to us all. Thomas brought home a catalogue of epitaphs and read them aloud, one after the other. Finally, my father moaned, "What the hell difference does it make? Nothing's going to bring her back, not the sweetest poem ever written. You pick one, son." And so my brother chose, "Sleeps in a valley so sweet/ But her spirit has taken flight/ Lo, her form is dust 'neath our feet/ While she is an angel of light." I wasn't fussy with the phrase "Lo, her form is dust 'neath our feet." How could my mother be dust? How could her singing under the open sky, be snuffed out forever? How could her cottony hands and soft eyes all be dust? It was a lie. So, I changed the words from "her form is *dust* neath our feet," to "her form is *just* near our feet." I recited it over and over at night when I couldn't sleep. I even set a simple tune to the epitaph, thinking my mother would like it better that way.

I'd gone through the story of my mother's death so many times, I didn't know if I was recounting the day of her passing or recounting a make-believe version of that day. Either way, it seemed to lead to the same questions. Where was my baby sister buried? Did anyone think to baptize her? How did my mother die? Was the infant stillborn? When would I discover the truth? Other things in life had been a puzzle, but I'd always managed to fit the pieces together. With this, there were too many missing pieces, and it would nag at me forever if I didn't solve it.

By the time I got home from the lake, everyone was asleep, including Primrose. Even though I was worn out, I began to compose a letter to my father. Over the years, I'd written him letters filled with questions, though they always found their way to the fire before they got mailed. After struggling with the first few sentences, I began to have second thoughts. I already knew what my Da would say about the matter; a few shots of whiskey and every hidden thought came out of his windpipe. It was Patrick or Thomas I needed to write a letter to. So, finding a fresh piece of paper, I started again, this time addressing the letter to my eldest brother. Thomas knew things. After all, I was stuck in the barn on that fateful day, while he and Patrick were mostly in the house. Once I was satisfied with the wording, I folded it up to put inside my tobacco tin for safekeeping until the morning when I would go to the post office and place it into the hands of the trusty postmaster.

CHAPTER NINE

Nautical Dusk—Hurkett, Ontario, 1941
- four years later

Jerome:

I see the moon and the moon sees me. The moon sees the somebody I'd like to see. God bless the moon and God bless me. God bless the somebody I'd like to see. Do you like that song when my sister Coreen sings it? I like it. And I like it when she tucks me in and says "Nightie night," and I pretend to close my eyes. As soon as she shuts the door, I take you out of my pocket so we can look out the window together. We see lots of things in the trees, don't we? Specially if Old Man Moon is shining up the world. Remember we saw a deer, his two eyes blinking at me, saying "Hi Jerome, I see you in the window!" Sometimes, I see a boy, but he doesn't never come inside and eat Mommy's pancakes. He only sits in the tree outside my window when it's nighttime. He's funny. One time, he wore an upside-down hat with sticks and flowers and things poking out of it.

You never see the boy? Maybe you're always sleeping under my pillow. I wish he would come back, 'cause I want to know his name, but it's hard to ask him when he's out there and I'm in here. One time, there was so much frost on the window and I couldn't hardly see out. I knew he was there, trying to visit me. I wanted to ask you what to do, but you were already asleep. So I took my sister's comb and tried to scrape the window. That didn't work so I found Dada's tool, the one he uses when he's taking fur off his face. I tried to shave the window with it. It kind of worked, but I cut my finger and then there was blood everywhere. I wrapped up my finger in my pajama shirt. Then I got so cold without a shirt. I was scared, too, because I knew I did something bad. But I didn't know how to fix it. So I started to cry and Brigid came up and when she saw the blood, she screamed. Then everybody came running upstairs and my mother sent them all away.

Mommy fixed my cut by wrapping it around and around with a rag. I wish I thought of that.

"What were you using Daddy's razor for?" Mommy asked me.

"I wanted to see out the window. Sorry, Mommy."

"Why did you want to see out the window? You're supposed to be in bed."

"Sorry." I started to cry because I wanted to tell her I was looking for the boy outside the window, but I knew she wouldn't believe me.

"Were you trying to see an owl? Or the moon? I know you love the moon."

I didn't say anything because then it would be a lie.

"Next time, you tell us and we'll scrape the frost off the window. Daddy's got the right tools for that. You want one of the girls to tuck you in?"

I said *yes*. Mommy sent in Brigid to sing to me. After that, I fell asleep. Since that day, I never see the boy anymore. I know he's out there, though. He's lonely in the woods all by himself. One day, I'll visit him where he lives and then he won't be lonely anymore.

Faolan:

It was January and I had lots to do, including bucking up a 50-foot birch tree that had come down in a wind storm. I dipped inside for a quick coffee before facing the cold again. The younger kids were at school, other than Jerome who was busy playing with his wooden blocks, turning the shapes into trees and foxes and whatever else his imagination might dream up.

"Faolan, they're looking for a new teacher at the school," Prim said, as she struggled to reach for something in the kitchen hutch.

"What do you need?"

"I'm after the sugar."

Leaning over my wife, I plucked the bag from the top shelf and handed it to her, saying,

"You sure you want to get me sweetened up?"

Primrose laughed, saying, "No such thing as too sweet when it comes to helping me around the kitchen."

"Helping in the kitchen! Aw, heck," I said, putting the sugar back up.

"I guess I'll be making cinnamon buns without sweetener."

"Cinnamon buns. Why didn't you say so?" I asked, handing her the sack of sugar. "Now what were you saying there? About the school?"

"Mr. Miller's planning to quit. He's moving to Regina where he's got an aunt."

"He might find a job there, you never know. Funny how folks went hungry for ten years. Now there's a war on, the money flows."

"I don't see money flowing out this way," Primrose said, snipping open the sugar bag and measuring it out into a bowl.

"Well, no. But there's money for arms and fighter planes," I said.

"He shouldn't teach. He's a jittery type, poor man. Brings up his breakfast before stepping in the classroom. Every morning he goes around to the back of the school and throws up."

"He's not drinking, is he?"

"Nerves. That's all it is. Mrs. Oivo's been spying on him for months, thinking he was up to

no good. But he was just having nervous problems."

"How come he boards at the Wychopens'? I know it's close to the school, but there's a perfectly good room up over the classroom."

"He can't cook an egg." By now, Primrose was busy filling jars with brown sugar. She knows that once a sugar sack is opened up, the mice find it quick. "Maybe Mr. Miller should find some other kind of work," she said, "Something he's more suited to."

"Like watch repair, or I don't know, maybe undertaker? That way he wouldn't have to talk to anyone," I said, half joking.

Primrose smiled, but lost her smile a second later. "I heard he's going to enlist."

"He's as meek as Moses, but you never know. Some of those timid guys turn out to be the most courageous." We were both quiet. I knew what my wife was thinking and I was thinking the same thing.

"We got a son almost eighteen," Primrose said quietly.

"The thought never leaves my head. Malcolm's going to have to register for service after his birthday. He's got no choice in the matter."

"I told him to go into the city next week and get signed up for first aid classes."

"What for?"

"If he's got training in first aid, they'll put him on an ambulance team."

"Prim, that's dangerous work!"

"If he's going to be in a war, risking his life, I want him saving lives, not taking lives,"

Primrose said, tossing on her coat and heading outdoors. I followed her, thinking I'd talk her out of her idea. But by the time I got my coat on, I began to consider her line of reasoning. War did do strange things to a man. Things that never should be accepted as a regular part of life—like weaponry and battle, and the wounds you can't see, but are hidden inside your soul—became normal. Maybe by saving lives, our Malcolm would see war through a different lens. Maybe it'd still be damaging, but not in the same way.

"So, you know about the meeting tonight?" Prim asked, handing me a basket full of stiff laundry. From her tone, I figured she was finished talking about war. It filled us both with dread, so why dwell on it?

"Primrose, can you help solve a mystery?"

"Maybe."

"When the kids were little, you said the cold sterilized the diapers. So now they're all out of diapers, and you're still hanging everything out in the cold to freeze. Even though I've rigged up a clothesline by the wood stove. Pully system and all."

"I've got my reasons, and if it doesn't bother me, it shouldn't bother you."

Once we were back inside, Primrose laid out the frozen laundry on every available surface in the house, like remnants of white sails, frozen in the wind. "So, do you think you'll go to the meeting?" she asked as she bustled around the room.

"I don't know," I said. "A cold day like today is perfect for splitting."

"We got six kids who've been through those school doors, and now Jerome's coming up to school age."

"When's this meeting start?"

"Seven. You could take Caroline with you. It's good for her to see how things get decided."

"You can manage without her?"

"You'll only be gone a few hours. I'll make soda biscuits for you to bring."

I looked around the room at all the places where Primrose had laid out the clothes. They were losing their frozen shapes and sinking into the surfaces. "Don't worry about baking," I said, "you've got enough to do."

I ended up going to the meeting and took Caroline with me, even though the mercury fell to minus twenty-five. The group of us spent the first half hour thawing out and reading through applications. Meanwhile, Caroline pulled her fur collar up around her ears, disappearing into the cavity of her coat. I thought about how, every year the township committee promised to install an oil stove in the school, and every year they put it off. And how, after all these years, the schoolhouse was still heated with a huge, wood stove. Finding a teacher to come to this neck of the woods wasn't easy, especially to work in a building that ate up wood faster than a prairie fire with a tail wind. Plus, the salary was pitiful, and rural boys did have a reputation for giving teachers a run for their money.

Most applicants, we found, weren't much older than the kids they'd be teaching. All of them were high school graduates, so there was no contest there. None of them had a certificate from Normal School, not that they needed one. The only one who had any experience was a Catholic girl and, even then, she'd only worked a few months at a Catholic orphanage.

"She's got experience, sure, but not in a public school," said Mrs. Kirkpatrick.

"I'd rather pick someone with no experience at all. That way, we'll have some influence," another person said.

"Don't chance it, hiring a Catholic. She might try and turn the kids into converts."

"What makes you so sure she's Catholic?"

"Says right here, she worked in a Catholic orphanage. And nuns aren't hiring Protestants, I can tell you that for sure."

"A Catholic girl should teach in a Catholic school."

And so, the conversation went around, with me not saying a word. One other person wasn't speaking up—Mrs. Toivonen, Jari's wife. Jari is my communist friend, which is no big surprise as Hurkett's earned the nickname "Tim Buck Road"— Tim Buck being the secretary of the red party. There are quite a few communist leaning people in this neck of the woods. It makes no difference to me; a good egg is a good egg. And even though Jari and I disagree on mostly everything, there's nothing I enjoy more than talking politics with him. I was surprised to see his wife turn up at the meeting as she's busy with ten or eleven children. Every time I ask Jari how many kids he's got, he comes up with a different number.

"What does Faolan have to say?" asked Jari's wife.

All eyes were on me. Everyone at that table knew I was Catholic, so they figured I'd fight to get the Catholic girl on. After taking a minute to collect my thoughts, I said, "Mrs. Toivonen, I think they're right."

"We shouldn't hire her?" Jari's wife asked.

"That's what I'm thinking."

"Why not?" she asked.

"Well, from the way I'm hearing the conversation go around this table, this committee wouldn't give her much of a welcome."

By now, I'd come down with a headache and needed to get outdoors for fresh air and a smoke. As I picked out a few constellations—Orion's Belt, the Big Dipper, the Northern Cross—I couldn't tear my mind away from the meeting. It wasn't anyone's business how that girl or any other applicant conversed with their Maker. Wasn't that why we soldiers risked our lives, to fight for our freedom? Despite that, put two people together in a room and neither one will agree on what the word *freedom* means. It just so happened that my form of freedom was to surrender to God. We all surrendered to something.

Maybe we surrendered to the bottle, or gambling, or maybe we surrendered to good things, too, like being neighbourly or fighting for workers rights, like Jari.

By the time I finished my smoke, the meeting had broken up, and Caroline joined me outside. On the way back, she gave me the news; the committee had decided to hire the Catholic girl, after all.

CHAPTER TEN

The Stranger & Other Riddles—Hurkett, Ontario, 1942-
one year later

Lotta:

When I first moved here, my chair sat at the opposite end of the bedroom, facing east. My view amounted to a farmer's field with a long trail of fencing, a few sheds, and a mountainous wood pile. I eventually pushed my unwieldy armchair over to the window facing west where I could enjoy the sunset as it sank into a chain of evergreens: white pine, jack pine, and spruce, as well as the occasional tamarack with its spindly, feather-like needles.

In my perfect reading nook, I read *Jane Eyre* twice through. Jane too looked after children in a one-room schoolhouse, and struggled with isolation. However, there was one major thing that set us apart—she had a suitor, and I did not. Now that I was in a place where you could count the men under the age of forty on one hand, the chances of meeting someone were as likely as a snowstorm in July. I found myself settling for novels and fanciful daydreams. In my minds eye, I usually created an improbable storyline, which ended with a well-heeled, handsome man offering me his hand in marriage. Charlotte Bronte, at the very least, created obstacles for her characters: the mad woman in the attic, the wedding ceremony foiled at the altar, the overly zealous suitor.

If it weren't for the cold, to this day, my evenings would be spent building castles in the air. I'm forced into reality, however, when the bedroom cools off, and I get up to feed the fire in my leprechaun wood stove. Fortunately, the parents in the township make sure that I never run out of firewood for both my bedroom stove and the monstrous, round stove in the classroom below. A daily supply of firewood is carried in and stacked up against the wall. Hotter burning fuel, such as birch, replaces the windfall once winter descends. I may feel lonely, but at least I'm warm.

When I first arrived, I thought I was equipped to handle anything, as I grew up in the wilds of Northern Ontario. I was in for a surprise, though, when I stood before the eyes of those thirty-nine children on that first day. I immediately felt intimidated by the boys in grade seven and eight. I noticed how they were taller than me, and refused to look me in the eye. One boy, Carl—a quiet, brooding fellow, occasionally showing up at school with a black eye, or a slight limp—was in grade eight for the third or fourth year in a row. I decided to confront him during my first month of teaching. "Carl, what's going on with this?" I asked, seeing bruises on his arms.

"Nothing," he answered.

"Did you get into a scuffle with someone? Or was it an accident?"

"Yeah."

"What do you mean, *yeah*?" I was determined to nip this issue in the bud. "I don't want your rough ways influencing the other pupils. Now what you do on your own time is your business, but fighting is not tolerated. You understand?"

"I'm not fighting anyone."

"Well, that's not the way it looks from this angle." Afterward, I was told by one of the parents that his own father was the culprit. It wasn't the best way to start off my year—misjudging one of the students. After that, I let things slide that I should've addressed, making teaching all the more difficult.

From the beginning, the parents made it known to me that, when in doubt, I should use the strap. I knew that most of the children got a cuff to the ear, or a belt across the behind in their own homes. Yet corporal punishment was the thing I dreaded most. It was on the lunch hour in mid-November that I was called to duty. The girls were clustered in groups playing clapping games, their hands stuffed inside their mittens as they gleefully thumped each other's hands. The boys had discovered a stash of cracked and broken hockey sticks behind the wood shed, and had taken to playing field hockey. They used frozen cow dung as their puck, and a couple of rotting fence posts to mark the goal posts. One minute, all was in order and, the next minute, two boys were using their fists on each other. Like bees drawn to the hive, every child flew out to the field.

I shouted, "Stop that boys! Stop now!" As I rushed over to the huddle, I noticed Brigid, the shyest of the Moore brood, keeping her distance from the crowd. As I drew closer, I saw that one of the troublemakers was none other than Ethan Moore, Brigid's older brother. By the time I reached the mess of spectators, my first concern was for the safety of the little ones, who were clinging onto the arms of their older siblings. Scolding the children, I demanded they return to the classroom. They ignored me, so I physically yanked children away from the knotted tangle. Realizing that it would take all morning to remove one child at a time, I hurried over to the water pump to fill a bucket, ran back to the scene, and promptly dumped the icy water onto the fighting boys.

"I'll see both of you in the school. Now! The rest of you will remain outside until you're called in."

As we crossed the field, Boris began to threaten Ethan, "When school's out—"

"—When school's out," I said, picking up the thread, "you will both be suspended for a week."

"No, Miss! Don't do that! My father will punish me," said Boris. Ah-hah! So, this was the way to get through to the rascals, by tattling to their parents.

"Maybe you should've thought of that before you raised your fists," I said.

As we entered the schoolhouse, the boys found their way to a joint plea. "Give us the strap. Five times on both hands," said Ethan bravely.

"Just don't tell our parents," said Boris.

I didn't know what to do. I hesitated to bring up an issue with parents, as it meant admission of my own inexperience. "If you follow my instructions," I said, "I won't tell your parents. But I don't know how you're going to explain that bruised arm, Ethan. Or your swollen eye, Boris."

"That's nothin'," said Boris.

"Your father's going to take one look at you, and know you got into fisticuffs," I said.

"He don't care about that," said Boris. "So long as we don't fight at school, we can wallop each other all day long. Eh, Ethan?"

"My dad says, if you're using your fists, you're not using your brains," said Ethan.

"Your father's right, and it's about time you both began using your heads." I suddenly noticed the boys were shivering. "Take off your wet clothes and wrap yourselves in blankets," I said, pointing to a shelf of emergency items.

"Can't we just dry off by the stove?" asked Ethan.

"You're not listening! Now, would you like me to involve

your parents or not?" The two boys snapped to attention. I went on to say, "While I turn my back, remove your garments and hang them on the rods to dry." On the perimeter of the wood stove, an enterprising father had rigged up metal rods for the children to hang their wet mittens and socks.

"Miss? What are *garments*?" Ethan asked.

"Clothes! Your jackets and trousers and shirts! And once you're wrapped in blankets, you will stand by my desk."

"Yes, Miss," they both chimed.

"You will receive the strap, five times on each hand and you will yelp," I continued, "as you've never yelped before." They both nodded, with confused looks. "Loud enough that every child outside hears you."

"They'll be watching, Miss Hirvi. Through the windows. They always watch when someone gets the strap."

"Well, not this time," I said, pulling the blinds closed.

Boris and Ethan lined up at my desk, blankets draped over their shoulders like monks. Pulling my arm back, I smacked down with all my strength, making a hard, snapping sound as the strap hit the side of my desk. I gave Boris a look, and he let out a loud, "Ow!" We continued the charade of five straps on each 'hand' until it was over. The desk had received twenty straps in total, and had held up quite well. "Now, return to your desks and don't make eye contact with each other, or with any other student. If I see so much as a wink—"

"We won't say nothing," said Ethan.

"You won't say *anything*," I corrected him. At that moment, I heard a cough from the back of the classroom. Whirling around, I discovered Carl slumped forward in his chair, eyes glued to a book. Had he been there all along? Surely, I would have noticed him entering the room. Why wasn't he outdoors playing hockey with the other boys? Perhaps he considered himself too old to be mixing it up with the younger students.

"Carl, what are you doing here?" I asked.

"I was just sitting here, Miss." Carl nervously tapped his fingers on his book.

"That's not an answer. Why are you here?"

"I was just catching up on my reading. Then you came in with Nathan and Boris."

"Why didn't you leave? This was none of your concern."

"I didn't want to bother anyone."

I turned to face Boris and Ethan, and asked, "Did you know he was here all along?" They both shrugged. "So, you did know."

"I've seen lots of kids get the strap," said Carl. "It's nothing to me. I didn't even watch."

"It may be nothing to you, but you must've seen me close the blinds. Didn't you?" I knew Carl hadn't deliberately undermined my authority, yet the whole incident unnerved me.

"I can leave now, Miss, if you want."

"No Carl, there's no point now."

"Miss Hirvi? When can we put on our clothes?" asked Boris, pulling my attention back to the matter at hand.

"When they're dry," I answered.

"The kids'll laugh at us for wearing blankets."

"I won't have you catching pneumonia, on top of everything else."

"Me and Ethan can sit up close to the stove," said Boris. "We won't cause no trouble."

"All right," I said. "Get dressed in the cloak room, but be quick about it."

By the time I called the students in, they were delirious with curiousity. I glanced to see if Boris was smirking, but he was as deadpan as a judge. Ethan was the same. "Ethan and Boris will be sitting up front," I announced. "Tatjana and Filip, take your books and swap desks, just for today."

That afternoon, we got more accomplished than the entire previous week. And, to my knowledge, no one gave away my secret.

Small and large challenges continue to present themselves to this day. The classroom with its white-washed walls and worn wooden floors seems small when filled up with pupils. But when four o'clock comes, and I'm left alone to mark papers at my desk, the space feels large and haunted with the problems of the day. I sense the past generations of teachers before me, and wonder—how many layers of chalk have been erased from the slate? What novels did the teachers of bygone days read? And most of all, how did they cope with loneliness? Perhaps, for the Hurkett teacher at S. S. Sterling, the only comfort from one day to the next was the view from the bedroom window facing west.

ॐ

"You must be looking forward to your holiday," Mr. Moore said one Sunday in early December.

From the beginning, I've felt welcomed into the Moore home, and have made a habit of visiting every Sunday. I wonder if their warm welcome has something to do with the fact that Mr. Moore mistakenly believes me to be a Catholic. My Italian grandmother did teach me a few Catholic prayers and hymns—her attempt to save me from the influences of my communist father—but the truth is, I'm no more Catholic than the cat that greets me on the Moore porch every Sunday afternoon.

"Oh, I am." I said. "The city's all lit up, and the Eaton's display windows are wonderful.

They dress mannequins in costumes from the 1800s, and pose them skating or carolling. And with the loudspeaker on the roof of *The Chronicle News* booming out Christmas carols, it's so festive. They still do all that, but Christmas doesn't feel the same as before the war."

"Nothing's the same," said Mrs. Moore as she set a towering plate of sandwiches onto the table.

"On the days there's a report of a causality, they halt the carols for the afternoon, as a sign of respect," I added, feeling uneasy that I'd shown too much enthusiasm for Christmas, during a time of strife in the county. By now, the children had swarmed in from various parts of the house, and all attention was focused on lunch.

"Hold your horses!" Mr. Moore said. "We have a guest. Let her pick first."

"Oh no, that's fine. I'm not hungry," I said.

"Later on, we'll take you out on the sleigh. The fresh air will give you an appetite," Mr. Moore said.

After the sandwiches were devoured, the Moore family gathered around the piano to sing. Mr. Moore took the lead on the first song with a voice as rich and smooth as chocolate pie. Following that, the family launched into a recital of old-time favourites. As was their habit, the eldest girl, Caroline, played violin, Brigid played mandolin, and the boys hammered away at the old piano, which sounded as if it hadn't been tuned in a dozen years. It was purchased from a traveling salesman who, according to Mr. Moore, could sell a fur coat to a beaver. I pictured a man wearing a fedora hat holding the reins of a horse-drawn cart full of pianos rattling along the dirt road; white keys glowing like seashells in the moonlight. However, Caroline piped in to say that the piano was delivered by train from a piano shop in Fort William, tossing cold water on my romantic vision.

As the music played, I thought of how Mr. Moore likely led a remarkable life, being a war veteran, a transplant from America, and a fine singer as well. Between songs, I asked him, "Mr. Moore, have you ever thought about telling your story?"

"You mean the story about Bobcat and his glass eye? Or the time Albert caught a sturgeon so big, it took two men to drag it in?" he answered, laughing.

"No," I said. "I was thinking of your own story."

"I'll let you in on a little secret, Miss Hirvi. I may be Irish, but I'm not one of those spin-a-yarn types. There's guys out there who could turn washing dishes into a story. That isn't me."

As the children moved from familiar songs to invented ditties, I was reminded of when my sisters and I were young, how my mother sang lullabies and simple songs. She sang while she cooked and cleaned, while she bathed us, and while she gardened. But, over the years, the singing stopped. Whether it ended abruptly or slowly dissolved over time, I couldn't be sure. The singalong at the Moores' made me long for those childhood years.

True to his word, that afternoon Mr. Moore hitched up the horse and, taking turns, we went out for a sleigh ride. He insisted I have the first ride, along with little Jerome, Brigid, and Coreen. As we glided across a blanketed field, Jerome said, "Tomorrow is St. Nicholas Day. When you go home, if you open your window and go to sleep, he'll put a candy in your shoe. Or a chocolate."

"Will he! Won't that be nice," I said. "Who told you that?"

Brigid answered, "We got a book from the library train. Mom says it's a made-up story and Dad says it's real."

"What do you think, Miss Hirvi?" asked Coreen.

"Well, I've heard of St. Nicholas, but I've never seen him," I answered, not wanting to take sides.

"He must be real," said Brigid, "because once a man left behind a tall hat in our porch, and inside the hat he put oranges and candy for us. And no one knew his name. He was probably St. Nicholas."

At school, Brigid was shy, and it was rare for me to hear her thoughts. When she spoke, her voice had a ring of kindness to it, even at her young age. There was something also mysterious about Brigid, though I couldn't pinpoint what it was.

"Can you tell us a story about St. Nicholas?" Jerome asked.

Coreen interrupted and said, "Miss Hirvi's not a teacher today, Jerome."

"She isn't?"

"Not on Sundays. Just like Mom and Dad rest on Sunday, so does Miss Hirvi."

"Then, if she's not a teacher on Sunday, what is she?"

Coreen looked at me, not knowing what to answer. It was a good question. If I wasn't a teacher, who was I? I hardly knew myself. As a woman, I had three or four choices in life: teaching, nursing, clerical work, and marriage. I'd chosen teaching mostly because my mother prodded me in that direction. If I'd met someone I loved, I probably would have gotten married. But things had become complicated with the war, and some girls my age did get married, only to find their husbands called overseas. It was a miserable business.

By now, we were entering the forest, taking a twisty turn down a gentle slope. The light suddenly changed as if filtered through a rose-stained cheesecloth, and the wind disappeared, giving our cheeks a reprieve from the cold. Jerome scrambled to the end of the sleigh, intently peering through the evergreen trees. Was he looking for St. Nicholas, I wondered? In the crisp winter air, Mr. Moore began to sing. I longed for it to never end—the singing, the enchantment of the woods, the cheerfulness of the children. But, of course, that wasn't possible. Soon I would find myself back in my cozy bedroom, sitting at my window, wondering if I'd made the best choice for my life.

❧

On December 21st, I lugged my suitcase onto the train, filled with gifts for my parents and sisters— watercolour paintings, Mrs. Delleff's famous raspberry jam, and sewing kits I'd stitched using a cheerful gingham print. I pictured myself sailing through the door to find my father reading the Finnish newspaper, my mother offering me a cup of her creamy hot cocoa, and my sister, Kaisu, showing me all her latest hats from her evening classes at millinery school. My youngest sister, Leena, would likely be on the phone giggling about a school boy. When I did step off the train, though, there was no one to meet me at the station, so I jumped on the streetcar with my suitcase in tow.

After a quick embrace at the door, my mother returned to her post at the kitchen table. I watched her work, noticing her strong arms from years of baking and gardening and kneading bread. All that hard work, though, hadn't robbed her of her looks. Her clear blue eyes, her oval face and soft features defied her age, and she took pains to keep her hair curled and swooped on top of her head.

"Want me to cream that for you?" I offered. For an answer, my mother tossed me an apron and slid the bowl of butter and sugar across the table. "I'll get going on the *joulutorttu*," she said. "It's a two-day job and I haven't started." As she banged around in the cupboards, locating a jar of prunes, I worked at softening the butter with my fork.

"Have you made any friends yet, out there in Hurkett?"

"Kind of. There's a family and they have me over for Sunday lunch."

"That's good."

"The children are really talented with music. Mom? Remember how you used to sing songs and lullabies when we were little?" I asked.

"It was the only way to get you to sleep," my mother said, as she dug through the fridge. My mother was one of the fortunate few who owned a refrigerator, and she made good use of it. Most people managed with an ice box, or neatly placed bottles of milk and packets of wrapped meats stored along drafty window ledges or back porches.

"When we got older, you stopped singing," I said, trying to pull my mother's attention away from her baking. "Why?"

"Who was I going to sing to? The trees? They do their own singing. Lotta, I thought we had more eggs. Can you run down to the shop?"

"There was one winter, when we were still in Lappe, you started to sing again," I said. "While Isä was away at work." During our growing up years, my father worked forty-four days in a row in the timber camp, then returned home for a week, then went back out again. As a girl, I counted the days when he was away. "Do you remember?"

"Honestly, Lotta, what difference does it make now? I need eggs!"

"Sure, Mom. I'll be right back," I said. As I skipped down the steps to the shop, my attention wasn't on the musky smell of the stairwell, or the heavy door at the bottom landing, or the whiff of spices and cheese as I entered the shop. Rather, I was drawn back to one particular night so many winters ago. That winter, I began bringing home riddle books from the library and testing my mother to see if she could solve them. She almost always did. "What do liars do after death?" I asked.

"They lie still," she answered.

"Who was the first whistler?"

"The wind," she answered. She wouldn't answer right away, and sometimes it took her a few days. Eventually she'd shout out the answer while taking the clothes down from the line, or feeding a log to the fire. There was one riddle she couldn't solve—*Though it be cold, I wear no clothes. The frost and snow I never fear. I value neither shoes nor hose, and yet I wander far and near.* For a whole week, my mother kept saying, "Don't tell me.

Give me another day."

When she finally gave up, and I told her that the answer was a fish, she said, "Oh, why didn't I figure it out?"

Something changed that night, not only because of the fish riddle, but because of what happened later on. During the night, I woke up for no reason. When I pulled open the bedroom curtains, I saw movement in the trees. At first, I thought it was a deer or an animal. But as I watched the creature move in the half light of the moon—or the *puolikuu*, as my father calls it—I realized it was a tall person. In the hazy light, I assumed it was my father, home a week early. My mother moved into the scene, wrapping her arms around my father to kiss him. Excited, I slipped on my woolen socks and hurried into the kitchen. Our dog, Charcoal, was asleep at the door. I gave him a nudge and said, "Isä's home! Want to see? Come on. Come on, old boy." Poor Charcoal was too old to get excited about anything, especially in the middle of the night.

I was just about to put on my coat and boots when my mother stepped inside, shooing Charcoal from his spot by the door. "Lotta! What are you doing up?"

"Where's Isä?" I asked.

"You answer me first."

"I just want to say hi to him."

"Well... you can't," she said, shaking the snow from her boots and setting them by the wood stove.

"Why not?"

"Because he's not here, is he?" My mother peeled off her coat, keeping her face to the fire.

"But I saw him out there. You were with him."

"Your imagination is playing tricks on you," she said, hanging her coat on a hook by the door. She then whirled around and said, "Now get back to bed."

I wasn't trying to act sassy, though it must have come across that way. "Why were you outside, if he's not here?" I asked.

"Don't you talk to me like that. I'm the mother. I ask the questions."

"Sorry, Mom."

"You were sleepwalking, that's all it was," she said in a gentler tone. "You used to sleepwalk when you were little."

"It didn't feel like a dream. It felt real."

"That's the thing about sleepwalking. It feels real, but it isn't. You know what helps? A cup of warm cocoa. I'll make some for you."

Any other night, I would've relished a cup of hot cocoa, but I declined and headed toward my bedroom.

"Lotta? I know you miss your father. He'll be home soon. One more week."

I couldn't sleep. Every hour, I opened the curtains a crack to see if the man—who I still believed to be my father—would reappear. When I did finally fall asleep, I dreamt that all of us, my mother, father and sisters, were living in the sauna house. It was positioned on top of a high cliff, and as it rained, the house slid a little closer to the edge of the cliff.

The next day, I asked my school teacher about sleepwalking. She said sometimes a sleepwalker might waltz right out into the snow in their bare feet and not even feel the cold. Yet I had certainly felt the cold of my bedroom floor, and I'd stopped to talk to Charcoal. So why did my mother not want me to see my father? Unless, perhaps it wasn't my father, but someone else. I thought maybe I could trick my mother into telling the truth by inventing riddles. "What's tall and is revealed in the moonlight?" or "What wraps its arms but can't be unwrapped?" But I didn't want to try her patience.

When my father did return home a week later, he looked thinner, and the skin on his face seemed tinged in blue. His fingers were also red and blistered with signs of early frostbite, and my mother scolded him for not taking better care of his hands. He told her that when his fingers turned black, she could worry; otherwise, he was fine. That night, when my sisters and I had all gone to bed, I heard my parents talking at the kitchen table. While my sisters slept, I pressed my ear up against the door. "I want the girls going to grammar school," my mother said.

"Education is waste of time. I got grade four, and what good did it do for me?" my father said with a chuckle. The truth is, my father is fluent in two languages, both Finnish and Swedish. As an immigrant, he worked entirely with Finnish men, making it difficult for him to learn English.

"You want them marrying the first lumberjack who shows up at our door?" she asked.

"Something wrong with lumberjack?" my father asked. The tone of his voice was no longer lighthearted.

"Of course not. But women can find jobs now. In the city. Not out here where nothing changes but the weather."

"You want to put moose in a cage? That's what city does to me."

"We'd get used to it."

"Why you want to move? You never said anything before." I heard my father scrape his chair back. I pictured him pouring himself a cup of coffee.

"The girls were young, and I wasn't thinking about their future," my mother said. "All three could go to the collegiate institute."

"We think about for one year. We don't go now."

"I think we should pick up and go. Soon. The boys are coming around Kaisu now that she's sixteen. I don't want her married so young."

"You sure this is only reason? For the girls?"

"Of course." After that, my mother and father went to the lake for a sauna.

A few nights later, my mother brought it up again while we were eating supper. "In town, you can attend Wobbly meetings, get more involved in the cause," she said to my father. *The cause* had to do with the union. Timber workers were taking action, holding secret meetings, and sending messages through the camp grapevine. "You risk your life every time you climb a tree. And do they care?" my mother went on to say. My father was a high-climber, which meant he climbed to the tops of trees and lopped off the limbs. "Not only that, how do they expect us to raised a family when you get paid only twice a year?"

"That's all bushworkers. Not just me."

"I'm happy when you're paid up in the spring, of course, but then it's Christmas before we see money again."

Leena, my younger sister, said, "The boss's kids eat chocolate like it's Christmas every day. And the parents drink fancy whiskey. Taina's mom said so."

"I don't know why Taina's mom is telling you those things," my mother said. "And how would she know what kind of whiskey the bosses are drinking?"

"Those Finnish women know what goes on," my father said.

"I did my part, don't forget," my mother said, as she collected up our dirty plates and stacked them on the counter. "I went to sewing circle for years. I don't know what it is, but lately I feel a cool breeze whenever I walk into a sewing meeting." It's true that my mother was very dedicated. While the women stitched and sewed, they were also organizing, writing letters to bring in speakers, and holding bake sales to raise money for the cause.

"Girls, what you think of move to city?" my father asked.

"Why are you asking them? We're the parents," my mother said.

"I want to know what they think."

My father's steel blue eyes landed on each of us, one at a time, like silver arrows. When he asked us a question, we knew to come up with an answer, not because of the threat of punishment, but because he demanded respect. Some of our friends had fathers who were to be avoided, especially when they were drinking. My father didn't drink, and perhaps that's the reason there was an intensity in his wiry, but strong body, and his eyes that carried a thousand untold stories.

Leena and Kaisu both said they wanted to move. I didn't know what to say. Whenever we visited our grandparents and cousins, it seemed so crowded. And our cousins, in my opinion, did bad things. My cousin had tried to entice me to smoke cigarettes. When I said "no," he called me a "country bumpkin." He said I should go back to Lappe and dance around in the snow naked because that's what bush Finnlanders did.

"Lotta, what about you?" my father asked.

"I'd rather stay. I can take courses in the mail, like Kaisu," I said.

"It's not easy, Lotta. Don't think it's easy," said Kaisu.

"Why?" my father asked me, ignoring Kaisu's comment.

"Because it's home. This is home," I said. I knew every corner of our land: where the Ghost Plant grew in the shadier parts of the bush, where the wild strawberries came up in the spring, where to find bottles buried in a mossy field—each bottle telling a story. I knew Lappe like I knew my own name.

My father nodded as my mother put out coffee and treats. She was trying to appear nonchalant, but when she set down the plate of sweet bread, her hands were trembling. And her hair, usually up in soft curls, was pulled back into a tight ponytail. "Just think," she said, "we'll see all the plays at the hall. I can picture your father on stage."

"Don't put me in front of people. I die of heart attack," my father said, not noticing that my mother was behaving differently. I thought again of the man in the snow on the night of my so-called sleepwalking. Did he, whoever he was, have something to do with my mother's wish to move? And why was she suddenly singing and humming to herself? I hadn't heard her sing in years.

"You could help build sets. I'll sew costumes. And maybe the girls will get involved," my mother went on to say.

"The last one was so good, remember?" said Kaisu.

"I fell asleep halfway," I said.

"—*Eramaiden Orjat*," my father said. "*Slaves of the Wilderness.*"

I could feel my father being pulled over to my mother's side. With my sisters excited about the move, I was outnumbered. "Where would we live, Mom?" I asked.

"We'll stay at your grandparents. They're lifting fifty-pound bags of flour and sugar, with my brothers off fighting. If we were there, I could help out."

"You want that? To lift heavy bags?" my father asked my mother.

"It's no different than out here. Chopping and hauling firewood."

"I don't like to take charity. Maybe we find rooming house," said my father.

"We can't live in a rooming house! With girls! We'll have to stay with my parents, at least off the start. And you can't get any closer to the Labour Temple than their shop."

There was no turning back. We were headed to the city, whether I liked it or not. Now here I was, ten years later, still questioning why we left Lappe in such a hurry. When I returned with the eggs from the shop, my mother was facing the stove, stewing up prunes.

"What took you so long?" she asked.

"I got talking to the customers," The truth was, I had walked around the block three times, agitated by this incident so long ago, and how it must've been the catalyst for our move into the city. I set the eggs onto the kitchen table and stood facing out the window. How many years had my mother taken in this view of a brick wall? "Mom? Do you sometimes wish you never had kids?" I blurted out.

"Lotta! Why would you say something like that?" she said, whirling around to face me.

"It's just, you're always saying that I should stay working, and you never encourage me to find a boyfriend, or get married."

"I want you to have more chances than I did. Is that so terrible?" She pointed the sticky wooden spoon in my direction. "I was still a girl when I started having children."

"I know, Mom."

"Fifteen. That's how old I was when I met your father," she began. "I was pulled out of school to help my parents run the shop. I don't blame them, with ten mouths to feed, they needed the help. Oh my God, some days were so slow, I'd rather count toothpicks. But that day was busy, people coming and going, ting-a-ling, ting-a-ling whenever anyone opened or closed the door. Then it got quiet and, of course, I thought I was alone."

By now, my mother had poured us both coffee and was sitting at the table, lighting up a cigarette. "I was counting up the dimes, pennies, nickels from the cash register. After a while, I felt someone's eyes on me. You know that feeling? I looked up and our eyes locked. Your poor father just grabbed the closest thing and raced up to pay for it. It was a box of baking soda. He didn't say a word, just paid for the soda and got out of that shop so quick."

My mother paused in her story, waiting for me to prompt her to continue. *How can she possibly tell me this tale of love, knowing full well what she did to my father?* She continued to stare at me, taking a long drag on her cigarette until I finally said, "And you didn't think you'd see him again."

"But he came back, oh, maybe an hour later. He walked up to the counter and, by now, I'm in another part of the shop, but I meet him at the cash register thinking he's going to buy something again. Instead, he puts tickets to a dance on the counter. He points to me, then points to himself, and it's obvious he's inviting me on a date. I'm so shocked. I don't know what to say, so I just take the tickets and then he's gone, out the door. If it weren't for the tickets, I'd think he was a ghost."

My mother continued with, "I told my parents I was going bowling at the Catholic church. I wasn't allowed to go to dances, and I couldn't say I was going out with a Finnish bushworker. My father was happy to do business with the Finns, but he didn't want me to marry a communist, did he? We danced every number, your father and me. He didn't know English, not even *please* or *thanks*. But we found our own language that night."

My mother had told the story a hundred times and each time, she changed the details slightly. One time my father bought baking soda, another time it was vinegar. No matter what, though, it always wrapped up with her saying that she and my father found their own language. When we were little, my sisters and I begged her to tell it, but I had no wish to hear it that day.

I got up and poured the rest of my coffee down the sink, as my mother went on to say: "I'm happy I married your father, don't get me wrong. But for you girls, it's going to be different. With your diploma, the world is wide open to you. Look at your sister, building planes over at the Can Car plant. The Hawker Hurricane. Did she tell you about that?"

"She wrote me," I answered.

"Three thousand women in that plant. Three thousand! You could fill every church downtown and it still wouldn't be that many people."

"Only because of the war," I snapped. "That's why those women have jobs."

"Yes, because of the war. But she's making a contribution,

isn't she? Just like your uncles who are over there fighting. If we were still in Lappe, she'd be married and tied down with kids."

"I wish the war would end," I said quietly. "If it keeps going, some of the older boys in my classroom will have to enlist."

"Oh, honey." My mother rarely called me honey, so when she did, I was a bit taken aback.

"The school children are all caught up with the war," I said. "They make models of warships out of scraps of wood. In their notebooks, I find drawings of aircraft or warships. If only they'd pay the same attention to their lessons."

My earlier agitation with my mother had waned. Given the backdrop of a war, it suddenly seemed wrong to talk about that man outside the window, or even think about it for that matter. My mother returned to her baking and, in the silence, I called to mind the younger Moore girls and how shocking the city would be for them. Their world consisted of fresh fallen snow, the whistle of trains during the night, and the intimacy of the forest. The three youngest girls had recently taken me for a stroll through the woods. After strapping on snowshoes, we followed each other single file through diamond-sparkled snow. When I asked where we were headed, Agnes answered, "To where our Dad met our Mommy."

"And where's that?" I asked.

"The community hall," answered eleven-year-old Brigid, with her usual quiet voice.

The children chattered merrily as we made our way, breaking trail on occasion and then looping back to a well-worn trail. At one point, while dipping in and around branches laden with snow and drooping low to the ground, Brigid suddenly stopped. I wondered if they'd lost their way, as all three stood motionless. With their soft, innocent features, it occurred to me that they were like china dolls. It was Brigid who spoke first. "That's where the baby is. Down there."

In that moment, I thought about a seemingly small thing Brigid's mother had told me—that Brigid was born with a caul. I'd never heard of such a thing, but according to Mrs. Moore, she came into the world with a thin veil over her face and head. Mrs. Moore told me that it was extremely rare, and that midwives often delivered babies all of their lives, and never saw a caul birth. She added that it was a sign of good luck and that the child would grow up to have a special gift.

"What baby?" I asked, quietly.

When Brigid didn't answer, Coreen said matter-of-factly, "The one who went to heaven. He only lived for a day."

How could I not grow attached to these children with their sensitive understandings of life? I felt a momentary urge to share this with my mother, to tell her about the infant buried in the woods, as well as the sleigh rides and piano playing. Still, as I watched her sifting the mixture of flour, salt, and baking soda for the pastries, I knew the moment had passed, just as the moment passed so many years ago when I first saw my mother with the unfamiliar man out my window.

Lotta: 1943

"Did I tell you how your father got a letter in the mail? He has to get fingerprinted," my mother said on New Year's Eve. Her apron was dusted in flour, and the kitchen looked chaotic. "For some reason, they got their eye on him."

"Why?"

"To tell you the truth, I'm surprised they haven't taken him in sooner. How many times has

he been at the hall or just leaving out the back door when

it gets raided? It's crazy because the RCMP wouldn't know the difference between political writing and a book of recipes."

"But it's not illegal anymore. To be a member of the Wobblies."

"The government can do anything they want during war time. Almost anything."

"He should just tell them he's got relatives over in France fighting. That's got to count for something. I can't believe you didn't mention this before."

"I don't like to sour Christmas."

"But it's okay to sour the new year?"

"How happy can the new year be, with a war going on?" my mother said, plopping the risen dough onto the table for a second kneading. As she found a rhythm with her kneading—press and push, push, pull and turn, press and push, pull and turn—I thought about a question I wanted to ask her. It had been nagging me for weeks. Just as I was about to speak, Italian voices could be heard outside. I looked out the window to see a group of men below, obviously in good cheer.

"They don't seem too worried about the war," I said.

"Well, they should be. They're classified as enemy aliens."

"All Italians? Even Nonna?"

"Nonna is old. It's the men they're keeping an eye on. The women are too busy with laundry and cooking to bother anyone. You know the man who owns the grocer down the street? They took him to jail for shooting off his mouth, saying how great Mussolini is."

"That wasn't smart."

"But why do you think he's sympathetic to fascism? Maybe because, in this country, he's treated like dirt. There's always a reason. Anyway, he had too much to drink, but he's harmless. Pretty soon they're going to round up every good Canadian."

"War just seems to divide people."

"Count your blessings. At least you don't have a soldier for a boyfriend."

"True enough. And I'll never meet anyone as long as I'm in Hurkett." In my year and a half of teaching, there was only one prospect—a widower who tried to woo me by showing up at the school with a bouquet of spindly looking wildflowers. As I politely declined, the school kids giggled and poked each other, and the silliness continued throughout the afternoon. I reminded myself that, for the most part, the students respected me and some even went beyond the call of duty. All winter, I took for granted the wood pile, neatly piled near the stove each and, on the coldest mornings, roaring with heat before I entered the classroom. One biting cold morning in January, I noticed Carl lighting a match to the stove. We were startled to see each other, as it was early yet.

"Oh my gosh! Is that you bringing in the wood and lighting the stove? I thought it was one of the fathers. You've been hauling wood all winter, haven't you?"

"It's only just from the woodpile to the porch."

"Why didn't you tell me it was you?"

"Didn't need to."

It occurred to me that, although Carl was inexperienced in worldly matters, there was an earnestness in his character, a quality rare in most grown men, let alone a boy of seventeen. Or was he eighteen? It was possible I was only one or two years his senior. I was suddenly flooded with shame for the way I'd treated him when I first began teaching—asking him about the bruises on his arms, and chastising him for not completing his homework. Perhaps, if I'd treated him differently, he would have kept up with his lessons. As it was, he rarely attended class.

"Carl, why is it you have time to keep us in firewood, but you haven't been in class for months? I'm not criticizing. But I'd rather you work on your studies than haul wood."

"I don't think you'd say that if your stove went cold," he

said with a smile. Then, embarrassed, he went on to say, "I won't be back for classes. My old man's been sick. I'm pretty much running the farm, me and my mother."

I always seemed to say the wrong thing with Carl. To make up for it, I offered to tutor him. He came once or twice after that, and I did my best to point him in the right direction. In the meantime, I assigned his desk to another student.

"You're a teacher, Lotta," my mother said, pulling me from my thoughts. "That's something to be proud of."

"Mom, you learned a whole new language when you married Isä. You know three languages! Going to school doesn't make you smart. Determination makes you smart." My mother braided the *pulla* bread as if it were a game of tug-of-war between her and the dough. My father often said he could tell my mother's mood by how tightly the *pulla* bread was braided.

"There are women in this neighbourhood, tied down with little ones who would trade their lives for yours, oh my God, including a war widow just across the street."

"I wouldn't wish that on anyone, but I am getting older. Before you know it, I'll be a spinster teacher!"

"When your head is covered in grey, then talk to me about *spinster*."

"When you were my age, you had three children. Three!"

"It's not a race, you know, to have children. And you think it was easy for me?"

"All I'm saying is a life of teaching can be lonely."

"Marriage can be lonely, too." As soon as my mother spoke those words, I saw regret flash across her face. "You see the crazy words you make me say?" she said. "Why do you have to push and push? You were always like that. Since you were a girl, every day a new riddle."

"You liked solving my riddles!"

"What mother has time for that?" My mother tapped her hands together, sending flour dust out into the air.

"I have a riddle I've been meaning to ask you," I said. My mother gave me a quizzical look, but said nothing. My heart was racing. I knew that if I wanted to bring up something serious with my mother, the best time was when she had flour up to her elbows and two pots simmering on the stove. I reminded myself, though, that conversation was a bit like mercury, it could start off in one round clump, and before you knew it, it was scrambling off in ten directions. *This is the time! If I'm ever going to say anything, it's now or never. But how do I bring up something that I've never talked about, or even mentioned before this moment?*

"Who was he?" I asked, my voice trembling.

"Who was who?"

At that point, I could've turned the ship around, and avoided the whole mess. But my time in Hurkett had given me an ounce independence from my mother. I pushed on to say, "That man at our place in Lappe. You and him, out in the dark." There it was. The words were finally out of my mouth.

My mother began digging through a kitchen drawer. "Where's a spatula when you need one? Ah, here it is," she said. "I'm wondering, Lotta, who should we invite for New Year's lunch? I usually ask over all your cousins, but I don't know why I bother. Half of them don't come, and the ones that do, drink too much and leave a big mess."

Clearly the topic was under lock and key. Nevertheless, there was no turning back, not after so many years of silence. "Mom, why won't you look at me?"

"I don't mind cleaning up after children, that's one thing, but grown men."

"Mom!"

She turned to face me, her eyes flaming. "Before you say one more word, Lotta, just remember, you're walking on thin ice."

"I wasn't sleepwalking. I know what I saw."

"You know nothing."

"I know...what I saw."

"You think you know. Do you know what it's like to be alone winter after winter taking care of babies, no one to talk to, no one to share a joke or cup of coffee, all the women for fifty miles around who don't speak English? I may's well've been in a foreign country out there. Do you know what it's like to run out of firewood, and your husband is working the bush camps and you've got one baby with croup, and the house is getting colder by the minute, and you have to go out in the dark with a lantern to split wood to keep your family from freezing? You know about that? And what about the miscarriage I had when the bleeding wouldn't stop and no one was around to help me. Lying in a pool of blood, too weak to get up and hold my crying toddler?"

I wasn't surprised by my mother's outburst. She often had a flare for drama. In a slow, steady voice, I said, "That sounds terrible, Mom. But I have problems too. I don't tell you everything."

"What are your problems, uh? The fact you haven't married a doctor yet? Twelve-year-old boys acting up in your classroom? And you think you're above me?"

"I don't think I'm above you, Mom. I'm just trying to understand."

"You're trying to judge is what you're trying to do."

"Mom, no! It's just, I love my Isä. And I don't know why you'd—"

"Because," she said, leaning in and planting her hands on the table, "plain and simple, I was losing my mind." When I didn't respond, she sat back down onto her chair and said, "He, this other man, saw the part of me that was gone away. He saw who I used to be, the girl who loved to sing and had friends and helped her parents run a shop. That girl was dead and he brought her back to me."

"Don't you love Isä, though?"

"Why do you think we moved to the city? It was the only way to end it. To start over again. Back to the place where I first met your father. Are you happy, now you've got your confession?"

"No, I'm not happy."

"Then you shouldn't ask so many questions, if you don't like the answers you get."

Now that I knew the truth, I felt wretched. I watched as my tears wet the flour-dusted surface of the tabletop. I wondered if anyone tasting the bread would also taste the bitterness in my heart.

My mother tried to console me with a fresh cup of coffee. I pushed it away. "You hate me," she said.

"No, Mom. I'm just confused. But one thing, if I'm ever lucky enough to find a husband, I would never sneak around in the dark."

"You don't know what you would or wouldn't do. You wait until you feel trapped. When that day comes, maybe you'll change your all-holy tune. Until then, we don't talk about this again."

"Are you afraid I'll tell Isä?"

"I don't have to be afraid. He already knows."

During the new year's festivities with all the cousins and aunts and Nonna, my mother played *You Always Hurt the One you Love* on the record player. My father's shy about dancing, but somehow, she got him up on his feet. I wasn't sure if she was trying to make a point, but either way, I was eager to get on the train and make my way back to Hurkett where life was sometimes lonely, but not so thorny and complicated.

Jerome:

I know you've seen lots of things already, like the war. That's where Dada found you. Dada says you saved his life when he couldn't walk because his legs were sore and swollened up. Some people are good and some people are brave, but it's hard to be both. You're brave and good, too. Ethan causes trouble sometimes. You never do. You're good in school and listen to everything I tell you. Even when I forget all about you, you stay quiet in my pocket. Just for that, I'm going to give you a bite of my apple because I know you love apples.

I'm sorry you have to stay in my pocket all day, but the teacher can't ever find out about you. I'm sorry I always tell you at school, "Stay in my pocket and don't come out." If you get found out, the teacher will take you away from me. She's nice and even comes to our house, but we're not supposed to have toys in our pockets. I know you're a real horse, but everyone thinks you're a toy. Even my sisters think you're a toy because you're so little.

So if the teacher finds you, she'll take you and put you in a dark drawer. She wouldn't keep you for a long time, but you'll be scared in one of her dark drawers. There's things you're not used to, like papers and wood rulers and some really sharp pencils. Teachers always have sharp pencils. Or she might put you inside the strap drawer. The strap smells like tears from all the bad children who got strapped. And it's black. It's a black strap in a dark drawer. You wouldn't like it. That's why I covered your ears that one time when the teacher took boys behind the wall where we hang out coats. I covered your ears because the strap makes a bad sound. It sounds like someone ripping the sky in half. It sounds like a rabbit frozen in the snow. I don't like the strap and you wouldn't like it neither. Even though you're brave and know all about the war, I don't want sad sounds going into your ears.

I'm not trying to scare you. I'm just saying, her drawer

isn't like my pocket, not one bit. My pocket has crumbs in it and soft balls. That's because when pockets get worn out, they pickle up into balls, and it makes it nice and warm for you in my pocket. And you'll never be lonely in there because you can hear me when I whisper things to you. I'm the only one who talks to you. My Dada's too busy to talk to you now. He's always on the boat or piling up big logs. But he talked to you a long time ago, before I was even born, didn't he? He told you all his sad secrets in the war.

Mommy has a sad secret too. It's in the bush. I saw her going to that place. I was with Coreen. Coreen wouldn't let me get close to Mommy, but I watched where Mommy walked to, and now I know where it is. It's close to a cranberry bush. But it's a tall bush, like a tree. Mommy never picks those cranberries. She never picks berries in the secret place.

Mommy's sadness is under some stones. And beside the stones are white flowers that turn into red berries in the Autumn time. That time we watched Mommy go there, me and Coreen hid behind trees and Mommy didn't know we were there because we were like the quietest little mouses. When Mommy came back from her secret place, her face changed. Usually her face is soft like a woolly doll face. But it changed into a jar face, with the lid screwed on very tight so no one can open it and see what's inside.

Secrets have to be kept hid in a safe place. That's so the tears in our heads don't come out too fast. It's better if they come out in little trickles. If the secrets stop being in their hiding places, there would be too many tears coming down and nothing could stop them. People would end up eating their own tears and that would give them a tummy ache. I'm going to find Mommy's place and look under the stones. I want to see what makes her sad. Maybe I can make her happy if I know what makes her sad. Do you want to come? When I go again to Mommy's secret place?

I don't have secrets, not even one, except maybe the time the moon turned orange and you were asleep under my pillow. It was an extra big moon that time, like one of Mommy's pumpkin pies. I wish I woke you up to see it. I was asleep and my other sister—because I have lots of sisters—my big sister, Brigid, she picked me up and brought me to the window and that's when I saw the orange moon. Brigid told me to make a wish and not to tell anybody, not even her. That's the only secret I have, not the moon but the wish I made when I saw the moon. We have to wait lots of years until the special moon comes again. I promise to wake you up when it comes. I'll be older by then and older boys remember things better. They remember how to make all their letters and numbers, and they remember to wake up every night and put a log on the fire so Mommy won't be cold in the morning.

Next time there's a big orange moon, I'll wake you up for sure. You don't care about the moon? Then why did you stop talking to me in the morning time? You were all huffy. Yes, you were, I remember. After breakfast, I gave you extra crumbs from my bread. When Mommy wasn't looking, I sprinkled sugar into my pocket, even though Mommy says sugar is a rash. Because there's a war in a faraway place and, when there's a war, they have to give all the sugar to the soldiers and there's not any left over for us. I gave you sugar and still you wouldn't eat the sugar and crumbs.

You were tired of talking that day? Oh. I get tired of talking too sometimes. There's lots of people who want to talk. They talk for the whole day and keep filling up the air with words. That's good because, when you and me don't have enough words, the air will never be empty. It will always have words floating in it, and it will never be lonely. I'm glad you weren't mad at me. I wasn't mad at you neither.

CHAPTER ELEVEN

The Milky Way—Hurkett, Ontario, 1943
- six months later

Lotta:

It was March and, as the weather had warmed up, I sent the students outdoors to eat their lunches. I was tired of the class-room smelling of boiled eggs and vegetable soup, and I also thought the fresh air would do them good. A number of the students were missing from class, and I wondered if there had been an outbreak of red measles or mumps. One by one, I watched the pupils shuffle through the door and, by the general mood, I sensed that something had happened during the lunch hour. Whatever the unhappy news was, it settled into the four walls of the classroom, like clouds gathering before a storm.

"What's wrong?" I asked, as the students removed their coats, and rescued their damp socks from the toes of boots. No one answered, not even little April, the chattiest of the bunch.

"Very well. Senior students, open your readers to page

twenty-six and grades one to three, we'll take up our number sentences from yesterday," I said, once the students had taken their seats. Moments later, Mrs. Oivo appeared at the door—her wide frame and serious look commanding our attention—like an actress making an entrance. She summoned me to the cloak room at the back of the classroom and, with her face framed in an embroidered blue velvet hat, she told me what happened. As she spoke, a warm dizziness overtook me and, a moment later, I awoke in Mrs. Oivo's arms. Twenty or more youngsters stared down at me, a sea of dead-pan faces and glassy eyes.

"Everyone, in your seats. This isn't the carnival!" Mrs. Oivo said, with more authority than I could muster up at the best of times. The children scuttled back to their desks and picked up their school books, pretending to read. I had been warned that rural children were more at risk than city children, but I never dreamed it would happen to one of mine. Did I not get on my knees each night and pray the Angelus for their safety, even though religion eluded me in every other way?

Mrs. Oivo whisked me into the kitchen, then brewed coffee. I welcomed the generous portion of cream and sugar she stirred into the cup. "Drink up," Mrs. Oivo commanded, bringing me back to the present moment. "Enjoy it, because you need to go back to teaching those children, at least until their parents get here."

"Do you think they'll be here soon?" I asked feebly.

"I think so. But Carl's here. I saw him outside and told him to stick around. If there's one or two children still here at the end of the day, he can walk them home."

As Mrs. Oivo took her leave, I resisted the urge to chase her down and beg her to stay. I needed to rally myself to the cause of teaching, so I slowly made my way to the book cupboard at the back of the classroom, thinking a story would keep the pupils occupied. I noticed Carl leaning up against the wall, watching me intently. I couldn't interpret the look on his face. Was it concern? Or distress? Was he annoyed that he'd been pulled away from his farm duties? Though I passed by him on my way, neither one of us looked at each other. Scanning the titles of the books, I selected Just So Stories by Rudyard Kipling. The stories, I hoped, would distract the children from the painful news. I returned to my desk by weaving my way in and around the rows of desks, rather than passing by Carl again.

From the head of the classroom, I began to read "The Elephant's Child" from the collection. As I read, I attempted to use expression, but there was a flatness to the narration. "'Then the Elephant's Child sat down most hard and sudden; but first, he was careful to say thank you to the Bi-Coloured-Python-rock-Snake.'"

Whenever I paused, even for a split second, I noticed Carl's gaze fixed on me. It struck me how much he'd changed since that day I'd given Boris and Ethan the phantom strap. If not for the shape of Carl's face and his greenish-blue eyes, one would hardly know he'd sprouted from the brooding boy of a year previous. He'd become a fine young man, exuding both shyness and strength. He seemed to be listening to the story, and strangely, this gave me the impetus to give voice to one more sentence.

As the story unfolded, a gloomy mood continued to circulate through the classroom. Whenever one child broke down in tears, it tipped off a half dozen more. A few of the boys also had their heads down on their desks, and some of the older girls had placed the younger girls on their laps. They soothed them by braiding their hair and whispering words of comfort into their small ears. I was afraid if I interrupted the narration, I also would burst into tears. Mrs. Oivo had promised me that the parents would arrive soon. Yet the minutes ticked by so slowly. The story concluded with a poem, "'But different folk have different views: I know a person small, She keeps ten million serving men, Who get no rest at all! She sends 'em abroad on her own affairs, From the second she opens her eyes—One million Hows, two million Wheres, and seven million Whys!'"

"Children, what do you think the story's about?" I asked. No one raised their hand. "It's about curiosity," I said, answering my own question. I was about to continue with, 'and what things are you curious about?' but on this day, such a question could open a Pandora's box.

I dared not glance up at the clock as the more often I looked, the slower it seemed to move. Desperate to coax the clock forward, I instructed the children to tidy up their desks. By now, clusters of mothers had appeared at the door, with their bosoms large enough to gather two or three children into their arms at once. I felt overcome with gratitude for these Hurkett women. Even though many of them had large families of their own, not to mention the gaggle of neighbour children piling in and out of their homes daily, their warmth never seemed to expire.

With the last child out the door, I collapsed into my desk chair and covered my face, expressing the emotions that I had kept so tightly controlled.

"Miss?"

I looked up. There before me stood Carl. *Is there no private place for me? Am I to be watched, every step of my day?* "Carl, why are you here?"

"I just... I thought maybe you need someone around. In case you faint again."

"I'm not going to faint."

"You're sure?"

"I'm sure."

"Maybe you need help with something? I never got around to filling the woodbox."

"That can wait. But thank you, Carl."

"Miss? You don't look so good. Maybe you should eat something."

"Maybe."

"You shouldn't let yourself get too thin."

"Carl? I'm sorry for not helping you more with your schooling, and for treating you like you were just a boy. I didn't know anything when I first came here." Blushing, I whirled around to clean the blackboard behind my desk.

"I'll put the class back in order, Miss," Carl said. Then, without waiting for my approval, he straightened the desks, brought in firewood, and opened a window a crack. As he worked, I returned to my desk and attempted to prepare my lessons, knowing that I wouldn't see another day of teaching until after the funeral. Not able to concentrate, I looked over at Carl, who was now sweeping the floor. *What is the reality of this boy's life? It's common knowledge his father's a hard drinker and has health problems, which means the son works twice as hard on the farm. And yet, he finds time to help me.*

When Carl had completed all the tasks and could find no other work to undertake, he made his way over to my desk. Without a word, he took me by the arm and gently brought me to my feet. I was content to have him lead me wherever his fancy took him—to the top of a hill or the bottom of a cliff, it made no difference to me. As it was, his destination was to my kitchen.

As we walked, Carl wrapped his arm securely around my waist. I floated my head onto his sturdy shoulder, feeling like a giddy schoolgirl. Once in the kitchen, he turned me to face him. We gazed at each other without either of us moving, like two osprey hovering in the air, waiting for the opportune moment to dive-bomb into the waters below. Time slowed, but this time, I welcomed the frozen clock. With his forefinger, he lightly traced the shape of my face, his hand a pencil and my face a line drawing. His fingers traveled down the centre of my forehead, under my right eye, then circled over to my left eye, and down the ridge of my nose, until finally his fingers grazed my lips and stopped there.

How long would he have stayed frozen, had I not moved closer to him? Only a scientist of the heart could answer such a question. A moment later, I realized, if anyone discovered my indiscretion, I could be let go. And the worst of it? It wasn't him who leaned in to kiss me, but the other way around. And even then, he seemed reluctant.

"I know you can be trusted, Carl. Because this can't go any further than this room." I was sure that even a single kiss was enough to have fired from my job. The schoolhouse was not the place for uncomely behavior.

"Don't worry, Miss."

"Lotta. Call me Lotta."

"I won't tell anyone. Should I leave now, Miss? I can stay or go." His look was of genuine concern for me.

I wavered between inviting him to stay, or asking him to quickly leave before anything more happened. With reluctance, I said, "You should probably go."

"Don't forget to eat something."

"I won't."

Afterward, in my bedroom, I curled up in my chair and gazed across the rough-hewn walls of my room—a spacious, narrow loft with angled walls and eight-paned windows at each end. Reaching for my jar of water and pallet of paints, I brushed water along the top half of the page with long, sweeping strokes. I dribbled a mixture of *Phthalo Blue* and *Indigo* with a whisper of *Geranium Lake* onto the page, and watched as the colours spread, like wings growing wider and wider, stretching to the outer corners of the wet surface. While the wash dried, I undressed, changing into my nightgown and a warm sweater. I threw open the curtain and allowed the hazy light of dusk to gently fall through the window. The sensation of Carl's fingers on my face lingered and, for the first time in a long while, I didn't feel so alone.

Once my page dried, I painted a silhouette of treetops along the horizon, using my darkest green and a smidgen of *Cadmium Orange*. On the bottom half of the page, still void of colour, I painted a window with four panes. I completed the image with a silhouette figure of a girl looking out of the window. I knew she was a memory of me from long ago, peering out of my bedroom window into the darkness of the night, and seeing my mother embrace a man. I had returned to that scene many times, but never before with such vividness. Never did I imagine that, in a place such as Hurkett, I could feel so alive and so shattered in the same breath.

Jerome:

They don't know we're gone, but we'll go back in a minute. See? It's close to here because there's the cranberry tree. Oh, I forgot you're in my pocket! But if I show you, don't tell anyone, okay? There it is. There! Where I'm pointing. At least I think it's the cranberry tree. It's only March so the tree can't have berries until later. First, it has little white flowers that smell nice, then the flowers change to green berries, then the berries turn to red. Mommy never picks them here. She goes walking and picks other things, but she never takes even one little cranberry from this tree. She wants the birds to come and eat them. She likes when the birds are making chirps.

I hear my sisters calling. Do you hear them too? No, I'm not answering. Because I need to see my Mommy's secret place and look under the stones. I'm putting you back in my pocket now because you're making too many words and how can I look at Mommy's place when you're talking so much? Just stay quiet for a little while, okay? But where's the tree now? I can't see it anymore. It was right here but now I see a different tree—a dogwood. I know all about dogwood because I went cutting sticks with Ethan and they have red branches and bend easy for making baskets. But where's the cranberry tree? Is it that way? Should I go this or that way? Why won't you answer me? Tell me what way to go! Why won't you talk?

The cranberry tree is gone and my sisters stopped calling my name! We're in the stranger woods. The trees are stranger trees. And the slippery snow is stranger snow. And the birds are stranger birds. I never saw them before and they never saw me. Maybe I'm lost. I'm not supposed to be lost. I'm supposed to be at my mother's secret place listening to her secrets under the stones, and my sisters are supposed to be on the path. I want to go home. Do you remember the way back?

I'll take you out of my pocket because it's too dark in there. Now do you know what way? That way? This way? What way? Home, I need to go home! I need to find my sisters because they always know the way home. You can help me. I know you can, because you took my Dada to a house and that's where he got his life saved! So you have to take me home, too. You didn't save my Dada's life? Then who did? A bigger horse? A real horse? But you are real! Dada named you Millie and he said you came all the way from France and I have to take good care of you. So if Dada says so, then you're really, really, real and you have to help me find my sisters!

My hands are cold. And my cheeks sting. Boys get cold easier than horses because we're not all covered in hair like you. I want Caroline and Brigid to find me and, if I stay here, they won't never find me. Sometimes they take me to a little creek. Maybe we should go there! Maybe if we go there, they'll find me. The creek's that way, I think. I don't know, I don't know, I don't know. You're not even the real Millie horse. You're just a fake Millie who didn't save my Dada. I'm sorry. Don't be mad at me. You're still my best horse. You can still sleep under my pillow tonight. Don't be mad. I'm just scared. You're my very best friend and... you're scared, too? What should we do? Maybe we should run. If we walk, it might take a long time to find my sisters and after lots of hours, it might get dark. If we run, we'll find them faster. I'll run if you run. Okay? I'm running. Are you running? We'll run together.

✑

Where are you Millie? Where'd you go? Under the snow? Under the ice? Where is everyone? I got a dizzy head now, sharp air, ice hands. My brave is gone. Millie! Are you here? Are you brave? Help me! I have no brave. It's all gone now. Dada! Mommy! Why won't you come? Mommy! Mommy! Mooooooooommy!

Primrose:

The dishes were washed up, the girls were in bed, and it was a clear night. *This is the best part of the day, when the kids are home safe and it's getting too dark to do anything but put my feet up.* From upstairs, I heard the girls giggling in their beds. They're a bit cramped up, being that there's four of them. It's a small house. It has to be, otherwise we'd run short of firewood trying to heat up a big space, and there's no sense in that. Me and Faolan sleep in a room off the kitchen and, when the kids were babies, I kept them in our bedroom until their first birthday, except for Jerome. I couldn't get him to sleep upstairs until he was over two, and even then, he used to come down in the middle of the night to crawl in with Faolan and me.

After ten minutes of pure laziness, I told myself I should light the lantern and do some sewing. I was thinking of using up the few yards of broadcloth I'd picked up from the general store. My plan was to dye it a pale blue. I was picturing how to get two skirts out of it for the girls, maybe three if I cut the waistband from a remnant. I could keep sitting in the rocker like an old grandma, or go on a hunt for the fabric. But who was I fooling? I was too worn out from a day of hustle-bustle to start up a new project.

I knew if Faolan didn't come in soon, I'd nod off in the chair. I thought about how Faolan liked open spaces, the lake and the sky. He often pointed out the constellations to me and the kids, but I could never figure out the difference between Cassiopeia and the Plough. Besides, I didn't mind being crowded up inside a warm house. After spending that first winter in a shack, and then a tent, our house always felt like a castle.

It was late when Faolan wandered in. "You sitting in the dark?" he asked.

"There's a trickle of light from the moon." The rag rug, especially the yellow and cream threads, caught the moonlight. Also, above the kitchen door, Faolan's crucifix glinted in the darkness.

"Too dark for me," he said. "I'll be tripping over my own feet." When I followed Faolan into the bedroom, with him holding a lantern out for both of us, I figured the next day would be the same as any other day.

First thing in the morning, while the kids were doing their morning chores, I got busy with dyeing the cotton. It came out a nice sky blue. With the kids off to school, I went out to the porch, feeding laundry through the wringer, taking care to fold the buttons and snaps inside the fabric so they wouldn't pop off going through the rollers. Didn't matter how many times I pushed up the sleeves of my coat, they kept creeping back down and getting wet in the wash water. In the end, I took my coat off and flung it over the porch rails. It felt good to have the sun on my arms, even though the air was cool. When a shadow came over the porch, I looked up from the steaming water and there stood Caroline and Coreen, both trembling. I noticed Caroline wasn't wearing her coat. She said, "Mom? You better come."

Oh my God, oh my God, don't let it be so. "Take my coat!" I shouted to Caroline. The girls led the way down the path, all of us running like wings were on our boots. The only sound was our feet landing on the mushy snow. It's a wonder we didn't slip and break a leg. Even though I wasn't wearing a coat, I didn't feel the March air as the sun was breaking through the trees.

The girls slowed down and then stopped. Caroline reached over to take Coreen's hand. In the distance, I saw Jerome beside the brook, face down and turned away from us. Caroline's wool coat was tucked under him and folded over his legs. He must've wandered off on their way to school. Maybe something caught his attention, like a deer or a rabbit and he chased after it. Or maybe the ice caught his curiosity, how underneath, the water bubbled. It's a trickling brook that dries up mid-summer, too small to be named anything and only eight inches at most. No one ever thought it could be dangerous. But for a frightened boy who maybe tripped and fell. I thought of all these things at the same time. They say you can only have one thought at once, but that's not true. We have layers and layers of thoughts, like sheets of snow in winter.

I ran to Jerome, knelt down and pulled him up into my arms. They say when a person's gone, they're heavier than normal, but my boy was as light as new-fallen snow. I couldn't hear a sound: no birds, no wind, no snapping of twigs. By now, my lungs were on fire, and the burning spread from my lungs into my heart. The girls didn't come any closer. I shouted, "Go find your father!" I couldn't bring myself to standing, let alone walking, my legs were quivering that bad. I found out later that when Caroline and Coreen ran to the boathouse, Faolan didn't scold them for letting Jerome wander off, or say anything to make them feel bad. He just asked of our whereabouts and ran as fast as his legs could carry him.

Once the girls were out of sight, I began to think there was a chance in a thousand Jerome could be revived. My mother delivered a baby once that wouldn't take its first breath. She thumped his back and rubbed his limbs, she drew mucus out from his mouth and nose, but still he didn't breathe. When there was nothing more to be done, she bundled the infant and laid it on the mother's chest. The mother stroked the baby, talking to him all the while, even though he was gone. A half hour went by, and then the infant started to move. My mother thought it was just nerves dying off, causing little tremors. But the mother snuggled the baby closer to her breast, and before long, it was suckling. My mother wasn't one to believe in miracles, but she always said, "We *cannae* explain everything."

I touched Jerome's chest, but couldn't feel his breath. His eyes were closed, his lips blue, his eyelids spotted with tiny red spots. His skin was ivory white. My hands were shaking too much to feel for a pulse, but if there was the smallest bit of life in him, he first needed warming up. I laid him back down onto Caroline's coat and, tearing off my old sweater, I tucked it under him. All's I could think about was getting his wet clothes off. It wasn't easy undressing him with his buttons and button-holes half frozen together. I yanked off his beige wool coat, and gave it a toss. It landed on a low branch of a spruce tree and hung there, like a ghost. I tugged open his shirt, ripping the little wooden buttons off. His trousers came last.

Opening my house dress, I placed him next to my skin. I closed up the front of my dress around him and put my sweater over top both of us. I wasn't one to sing, but I sang him his favourite song, *I've Been Workin' on the Railroad*. He used to do a funny little dance whenever the kids sang it, and Ethan was teaching him how to play spoons. Jerome never got the hang of it, but he had fun trying.

When Faolan arrived, he threw his coat over my shoulders, and we ran like we were carrying a picnic basket filled with the finest china in all of England. I wish it'd been bone china, and not our sweet boy. The whole journey, Faolan tried to keep his hand on my back, while I hugged Jerome tightly to my chest. If it'd been a week later, the snow would've been too soft to hold our weight. But that day, it was well packed with only an inch of slush on the surface. Faolan sunk down now and then. Somehow, he managed to keep up with me, though I'm sure his boots were filled to the brim with snow.

Word travels fast and, by the time we got home, I was surprised to see Esther standing in our sitting room. She's not too popular around here, mostly because she's known for taking men into her bed—and some of those men happen to be married. Since a few of the husbands came down with Scotch fiddle, they're behaving better. Everyone likes to blame Esther, but it takes two. Anyways, I've always had a soft spot for Esther. When she was barely fourteen, her parents died in a train accident, and she was left to raise up her brothers and sisters.

There stood Esther, strong as a stag and saying, "I know something about putting the breath back into a person. Maybe there's a chance for your boy."

"Where should we put him?" Faolan asked.

"I got a spot ready," she said, pointing to the floor where she'd spread out a blanket near the wood stove. The girls were scared so Faolan took them outside to play with the dogs. While I knelt beside my little boy, Esther put her mouth over his nose and mouth, giving him rabbit breaths, knowing his lungs were small. I watched his chest move up and down, and I started to breathe at the exact same time that his lungs filled and emptied, and filled up again. Twenty minutes later, that good woman gave up her efforts. "He's gone, Mrs. Moore. I'm real sorry."

Esther set two cups on the table and filled them with

strong tea. I picked Jerome up, blanket and all, and sat at the table beside Esther. All the while, I wailed and cried, feeling that never in a lifetime would I let him go. Biscuits were out from the morning, biscuits I'd made while my little boy was still with us. *Time is mean. Time is very mean. It marches on and it doesn't let us go back and change a thing. We can't make one single change, not dot an i, or cross a t, or add a hair clip to our hair, or stir a teaspoon of sugar into a cup of tea already drank. If only I'd known how important every word is, every chore, every thought, because it's never coming back round. Life gets chiseled into a giant stone. The chisel's done its work and it can't be undone.*

Once I was able to find my voice, I told Esther, "He's the sweetest boy you'll ever know. There's none sweeter." Esther draped her arm over my shoulder. It was too late for our Jerome, but her trying to save him meant the world to me—not that day as I was too distraught, but in days to come.

When Faolan walked through the door, Esther said, "I couldn't bring him back." Faolan opened his arms, wanting me to pass Jerome over to him, but I wasn't ready. So Faolan went through the house closing all the curtains, then called the kids inside. By now, we were all together—Caroline, Ethan, Malcolm, Brigid, Coreen, and Agnes. When they saw me holding Jerome, limp in my arms, they all broke down, all but Caroline. She stood gazing out the window, as if waiting for someone to come along and fix our broken family.

Once the first wave of tears let up, Faolan and the kids went on their knees to say the rosary. As it was Thursday, it was the Joyful Mysteries: The Annunciation, the Visitation, the Birth of Our Lord, the Presentation, and Finding the Boy Jesus in the Temple. I thought it strange to hear them saying the Joyful Mysteries, on that day of all days. At least they weren't reciting the Sorrowful beads. The kids barely whispered, "Holy Mary Mother of God, pray for us sinners, now and at the hour of our death. Amen." That word *death*, every time it came up, their voices disappeared. Fifty times they skipped over that word.

After rosary, Ethan and Malcolm headed outdoors with Faolan while I carried Jerome upstairs. This time, he felt heavy, as if his body had taken on the full weight of our sorrow. Once upstairs, I needed to see my boy one more time under his own covers. Meanwhile, our girls stood in the doorway, looking in on me. For some reason, I cracked the window a few inches, and turned Jerome's head to face the glass. He used to stare out the bedroom window, almost like he was expecting a visitor. Maybe St. Nicholas? Near Christmas, the girls'd taken out a library book on the saint. After hearing the story, Jerome had a hundred questions to ask. "How long is St. Nicholas's beard? Does he speak a funny language? Does he give to poor children? Mommy, are we poor? Is St. Nicholas friends with the other saints, like St. Brigid and St. Peter? Why don't all the saints bring candy? Why's he the only one?" On the questions went until finally I said, "Hush, it's only just a story." Then Faolan piped up and said that St. Nicholas was real.

As I sat by Jerome's bed, the girls headed downstairs one at a time. Brigid was the last to leave. Through the open window, I heard the sounds of the saw, followed by the tapping of a hammer, driving the nails with more force than usual. The odd time, I heard someone step inside to rummage around in the cupboards, then slam the door as they rushed back out. A while later, I could tell by the sounds of furniture being moved around that the boys had brought in the casket they'd built.

Our neighbour, Maureen McDonald, came over to help wash and prepare the body. Maureen sent the girls off doing little jobs, like boiling water for the sponge bath, picking sprigs of cedar, and locating clean clothes. It was late in the afternoon, and we were racing with time to get everything done before the sky got dark. By evening, I sent Ethan to see Maureen home safe.

We laid Jerome out in the corner of the sitting room for the wake. At the bottom of his box, we first pressed down a flattened pillow. Because it was old and stained, we robbed a wool blanket from Ethan's bed, folded it, and laid it on top of the pillow, then laid Jerome on top. One white feather'd come loose from the pillow and found its way into Jerome's curly hair. The casket had leather hinges along one side so's we could open and close it easily. I didn't want to frighten the younger ones by leaving it open, but I needed to see Jerome's face, touch him, let him know I was close by.

Maureen'd done her best to make Jerome presentable, but I cringed at the condition of his shirt. It was the best of the lot, but too worn for my liking. I decided I needed to make him a new shirt, right then and there. I could use the broad cloth I'd dyed that morning, as it was hanging up over the wood stove, and probably dry. The girls would just have to wait for their new skirts. It took me late into the night and I didn't have time to do a proper job— no back on the shirt, just the front with buttons, a collar, and sleeves without cuffs. Sewing by lantern light wasn't easy on my eyes, but the shirt did look handsome on his little frame.

When all of the kids were finally in bed, me and Faolan went back to sitting with Jerome.

"Faolan, do you think the wool blanket might irritate his skin? It used to make him itchy," I said.

"Let's change it up then."

"But all our blankets are wool."

"We can give him our quilt," Faolan suggested.

Faolan lifted Jerome up a few inches while I pulled away the blanket. I fussed with the pillow, then folded our quilt at least four times to fit on top. When Faolan gently placed Jerome back down, I noticed the feather was still tangled up in his soft curls. With the white feather and star-patterned quilt, I imagined him going back up to the sky, back to wherever he came from. He belonged in the sky, not the swampy earth. I suddenly felt like Jerome was saying to me, "No! Don't let them bury me there."

"I won't have him buried in the Hurkett cemetery," I finally said.

"But...why not?" Faolan asked.

"Every time they dig a hole for a burial, that hole gets filled up with water even before they lower the coffin. How many times've you and the men been called to bail out water from a dug grave? My boy drowned! I won't have him buried in muskeg."

Faolan didn't say anything right away. "Alright, Primrose, I'll see what can be done."

Throughout the night, we took turns keeping at Jerome's side. Faolan put his head down for maybe an hour or two, then I did the same, not that either of us slept a wink. Faolan headed out the door at first light. All morning, I wandered around the house not knowing what to do with myself. I walked into one room, then another, and then back into the first room, half expecting our Jerome to pop out from the upstairs closet with that imp grin on his face, and say, "Mommy? Can you make *cimmamum* buns?"

Every hour that Faolan was gone was another hour of fretting. Would they send up a doctor for the death certificate? Did Faolan get a hold of the priest? What day would the funeral be set for? People kept coming and going like passing ships. Most brought food, and thank goodness for that as the kids would've starved otherwise. Mrs. Oivo brought over a fish stew, and Mrs. Stenlund brought over her Grevé cheese. I thought it odd how closely Grevé sounded like *grieve*. When the neighbours talked to me, I didn't really hear their voices. I was still back at that creek, holding my boy next to my chest, hoping and praying he would fight the odds and survive.

Finally, when the house cleared of visitors, Ethan borrowed Jari's horse and took the kids for a sleigh ride. Ethan told me he'd be careful not to overwork the horses as the snow was heavy and wet. As soon as the door closed, I dug out my sewing scissors and snipped a patch of hair from the back of Jerome's head. It smelled like fresh hay and maple syrup. *How can he be gone but the smell of him is still here?* I hid the sprig of hair inside my apron pocket. With the house to myself, I went three more times to his side and, each time, I snipped. I didn't cut willy-nilly, and I tried to make sure he still looked tidy. I needed a part of him to be in every corner of the house: my dresser, my apron pockets, inside my hope chest along with the swaddling blanket and robin's egg. Wherever my hands took me for the rest of my living days, I needed to find a piece of Jerome there too.

When Faolan came home late in the day, he took my hand and asked, "Have you eaten anything?"

"Neighbours've been dropping by all morning. There's fresh bread and cheese if you need a sandwich."

"I'm alright. It's you I'm worried about."

"I'll eat when I'm hungry."

"I've gotten the word out and every one's been notified. The priest too." Faolan pulled his chair up close to mine and said, "This'll surprise you. You know the Thomlinson farm? About two miles west of here?"

"By the main road?"

"That's the one. He's got a field on high ground. He said we could bury our boy up on that hill."

"But it's private land. There's laws about that."

"I've been all over talking with this person and that higher-up, down at the post office sending telegrams to Ottawa. We got the go-ahead."

"But how'll we pay for it?"

"It won't cost a dime. Thomlinson's donating the land. For Jerome. And for our peace of mind."

"So, it's a cemetery now?"

"It is. Jerome will be first, but he won't be alone. In time, there'll be others. Thomlinson said the field was a nuisance to plow, nothing but field stones, is what he told me, but I don't think that's true. It's a perfectly good field, to my eye."

During the wake, neighbours kept dropping in, bringing preserves, soups and baking. My good husband took on answering the door, and receiving sympathies. Some came in for a visit, but most stayed at the door. Miss Hirvi came by, but I barely said two words to her. That night—the night the teacher was here—a thunderstorm came up. Faolan thought Miss Hirvi should borrow Ethan's rubber boots and cross the field to spend the night with the MacDonalds', but I didn't think Mr. MacDonald could be trusted on a Saturday night. He'd be as drunk as a broom.

The skies cleared for the funeral on Sunday. It was attended by over a hundred people, not counting us. Pretty well everyone in the village came, including Esther. My mother and father and sisters and brothers came up from Dorion. I had my girls dressed in their Sunday best, and Caroline did my hair up nice. There were prayers out on the Thomlinson hill after the church service, but I didn't hear the priest. It was too soon seeing Jerome put into that cold ground. I had things to say to him, clothes to make for him, picnics to pack with his favourite foods, afternoons of berry-picking, a thousand nights of tucking him into bed.

I couldn't sleep for weeks. When I did sleep, I had nightmares of Jerome running through the bush, his little foot breaking through the thin ice. The water wasn't deep, but he didn't know how to save himself. How could he, a boy of only six? Faolan and me drew strength from different wells. His was the well of Catholicism, and mine was the well of Scottish grit. What other choice did we have with the spring equinox around the corner? It was time to germinate seeds for the garden. The hens had gone off-lay for the winter and were starting to lay again. The ones that quit laying altogether were ready for the stew pot, and our Jersey cow was close to calving out. With spring break-up, Faolan needed to get busy repairing nets for fishing season. In the middle of all this, our barn cat gave birth to a litter of four. Brigid fussed over the runt, a calico cat with green eyes. She named the kitten Melody, and asked if she could bring the kitten into her bed that night. I reminded her that I didn't like house cats, never did, but later when I went out to the barn and heard the girls giggling with delight, I told them to bring Melody inside. How could I refuse?

When the blossoms came out, I went out to pick flowers. The field was in full bloom with black-eyed Susans, daisies, purple clover, and blazing star. As I picked a bouquet for Jerome's grave, hundreds of white butterflies, each one no bigger than the tip of my thumb, fluttered from flower to flower. *These little creatures aren't heavyhearted. They're light as air.* I sunk down in the field, hidden by the wildflowers and cried bitter tears. It wasn't long before I heard, "Mommy! Is that you, Mommy?" It was Agnes looking for me. Before I headed back to the house, I asked Jerome to forgive me for not visiting him more often.

CHAPTER TWELVE

The Unopened Letter—Hurkett, Ontario, 1943

Lotta:

On Friday, not a single child attended school. I spent the day doing odd chores, my thoughts seesawing between Jerome and Carl. Early Saturday morning, I found myself descending the stairs, still dressed in my nightgown and wrapped in a shawl. Stepping into the orderly classroom, I walked up and down the rows, tapping the lid of each desktop as I passed it by. When I got to Jerome's desk, I sank into his child-sized chair, my knees pushing up against his desk. Slowly, I peeked inside, as if searching for a clue as to why this tragedy took place. Remembering how he'd always hidden a tiny horse either in his pocket or in the desk, I scrambled through his books and papers to see if I could find it. It wasn't there. Of course, it wouldn't be, since he took the little toy with him wherever he went.

The chilly kitchen was my next destination. Opening the cupboard door, I touched each teacup, searching for nicks and chips in the chinaware, and deliberately choosing a cup with a hairline crack. *What happened to me is only a tempest in a teapot.*

Sitting with my coffee, I stared down at the tabletop and, for the first time, noticed initials carved into it—*P* and *R. Patrick and Rachel? Penelope and Pasquale? Hope and Hilary?* On the wall, mounted above the icebox, was a photograph of a woman dressed in white surrounded by at least a dozen children, likely a teacher of bygone days. While she taught here, I wondered, did she also face a loss?

I thought about how, only a short while ago, I had enjoyed a skate along Morrow Creek with the Moore family. The creek, bordered by evergreens, was about 30 feet wide, the perfect size for an ice rink. As we made our way through a snowy path with skates slung over our shoulders, we agreed that this would be the last glide of the season, given that creeks can be unpredictable during spring thaw. We sat along a fallen tree where we hurried up the job of lacing up our skates. Caroline helped the younger ones while the boys shoveled snow to reveal a gleaming surface of ice.

The sky was clear and Coreen pointed out The Milky Way. She told me that her father called it The Great Fence of the Stars. I thought about how all around the world, stars have different names. I asked the children what they would name The Milky Way, if there wasn't yet a name for it.

"Mm. How about Star Soup!" said Coreen.

"I'd name it Angel Lanterns," said Brigid, getting into the game.

"What would you call it?" I asked Jerome. He took this question very seriously, and at first said, "I don't know." But later, he tapped me on the shoulder and said, "Mother's Tears."

"What made you think of that?" I asked him.

He shrugged and said, "It just looks sad to me."

"But your own mother isn't sad, is she?" The moment the question had left my lips, I felt embarrassed as Mrs. Moore was within earshot.

"Everybody is sometimes," Jerome said truthfully.

"Yes, of course. Everyone is."

Before we stepped out onto the ice, Mr. Moore tested the rink, darting here and there, and if I didn't know him better, I would've thought he was showing off. Once Mrs. Moore was satisfied that every inch was safe, we trickled onto the makeshift rink and, with our skates we carved circular and moon-shaped lines into the ice. At some point, we all held hands, forming a snake-like line with Ethan taking the lead, and the rest of us fish-tailing behind him. Ethan dipped this way and that, occasionally coming to an abrupt stop as we arched around him, like the seconds hand of an immense clock. Being that Jerome was on the tail end, the more momentum we built up, the more he sailed around us like a top, laughing gaily. Little Jerome, that sweet fellow of only six years of age, with eyes of blue sapphires and a smile that lit up the darkest room, was gone. No longer would his hair be tussled in the wind or his laughter travel along invisible breezes. No longer would he look up into the night sky to see Mother's Tears.

Taking a generous gulp of my coffee, I scurried back up to my bedroom, impulsively deciding to visit the Moore family. Perhaps I could help in some small way. As I walked along the dirt road, I hugged a tin of sweets close to my chest. A few weeks earlier, my mother had mailed me a package filled with tasty items from the shop: Brach's chocolate cherries, figs, cookies, and her famous cherry cordial. Since our disagreement at Christmas, my mother had been sending packages with more frequency that usual. I was eager to share some of my sweets with the Moore family.

Thinking about my mother, I considered how excited she would be about starting up seeds for her garden. With her window panes leaning against the shop, and her rows of seedlings on her window ledges, she attempted to outwit the short growing season every year, and I was sure this spring would be no different from the last. The moment the weather warmed, and the days lengthened like leather in a shoe stretcher—a fraction of an inch each day—she began to think about her garden. And why not? All winter long most of us live like bears, dwelling in our dens until we forget how remarkable it is to feel the sun on our naked heads.

Though the trek to the Moore home was familiar, each time I traveled the distance, I noticed something new. That day, the sky was a powdery blue, spotted with clouds lazily changing shape above me. Far to the west, darker clouds were gathering close to the horizon, and I wondered if we were in for rain. Dried grasses floated out from the snow like frozen ribbons. Off in the distance, a lone raven sat in the skeleton of a jack-pine. Everything was tinged with both sorrow and beauty. *Yes, this world is bittersweet, like the jams my mother makes each year.* As children, when we cleaned fresh-picked blueberries, my mother insisted that we keep a few of the green berries in with the ripened ones. "It's good to mix bitter with sweet, just like life," she'd say. "Nothing is all sweet."

I stepped onto the porch of the Moore home, my hand hovering over the door knob. In Hurkett, visitors usually gave one tap and let themselves in, calling out *hello* as they entered. But on this day, I would knock and wait for an answer. Mr. Moore opened the door. "Come in, Miss Hirvi. Nice to see you," he said, ushering me inside. Mr. Moore's voice sounded strained, like a guitar that had been strung too tightly. He pulled up a chair and motioned for me to sit. Before I had the chance to unlace my footwear, the children emerged from the shadows of the house—first Caroline, and then the three girls, trailing behind her like lost sheep. The boys were nowhere in sight. The girls took turns saying hello with the formality of a classroom. "How are you, Miss?" and "Good afternoon, Miss," they chimed.

"I have something to go with your tea," I said, opening up the tin and offering it around, beginning with the youngest girl, Agnes. She shook her head, and I was immediately sorry I hadn't first spoken some charitable words, rather than popping open the tin, like a silly jack-in-the-box.

"Agnes, thank your teacher," Mr. Moore said. Almost against her will, Agnes chose a cookie from the tin and whispered a barely audible 'thank you'. She took a nibble, though a grasshopper would've managed a larger bite. I continued to pass around the canister as each girl politely chose a cookie or chocolate. No one touched the figs. In retrospect, they probably didn't know what they were.

I glanced over at Mr. Moore, who had taken a seat at the kitchen table. With his wide frame collapsed, almost as if someone had punched him in the chest, I didn't have to guess where his thoughts were. "I'm sorry, Mr. Moore. So very sorry for all you've been through," I said. Mr. Moore acknowledged my poorly expressed sympathy with a slight nod.

Coreen said, "He's over there, Miss, if you want to see him." I followed her finger to a corner of the room where a plain wooden box sat balanced between a piano bench and a kitchen chair. It never occurred to me that Jerome would be a few feet away from us. But of course. Where else would they place him? Lit candles glinted on the narrow shelf just behind the casket. There was an imprint on the wall where the crucifix usually hung, and the cross now lay flat on top of the closed casket.

"We're waiting for the priest. He'll say the funeral tomorrow afternoon," Mr. Moore said.

I wondered how many times he'd relayed that piece of information, and how difficult it must have been each time.

"If I can do anything at all," I offered.

He gestured for me to take a chair before asking, "Do you know any hymns?"

"A few, yes."

"Which ones?"

I paused before saying, "*Love Divine* and a few verses of *Amazing Grace*. I also know *Immaculate Mary*." This was the one hymn my grandmother insisted we learn as children.

"Could you sing *Immaculate Mary* for us?" Mr. Moore asked.

"Now? Or at the funeral service?"

"Now, if it's no trouble." If Mr. Moore knew of my behavior only two days past, would he be inviting me to sing praise songs? I doubted it.

"Would you like that? A song?" Mr. Moore asked his girls.

"Yes, Miss Hirvi. You sing so pretty," said Brigid.

Then Agnes said, "Could you sing the one we learned in school, about the frog?"

"I think for today we'll stick with hymns," Mr. Moore said kindly, "until Jerome's funeral service. After that, we'll go back to all your favourites."

"It's okay, Daddy," Agnes answered. "I like hymns too."

For the first time since my arrival, the girls' eyes brightened. No one offered to play piano so

I sang *a cappella* at the kitchen table with the faces of the children surrounding me, like sunflowers reaching for sunlight. Having all four of them together made me marvel at their similarities; all had round faces and button noses. Of course, I noticed the differences, as well. All but Agnes had chocolate brown eyes. Brigid was small for her age and had a serene quality. Agnes's features were more delicate than the others, and Caroline had the looks of a young Mary Pickford, the movie star. She was clearly a second mother to the girls, though it may not have been a role she chose for herself. Once I had finished all four verses of *Immaculate Mary*, inventing the odd word when I tripped over the lyrics, Agnes called out, "Sing it again, Miss. I especially like the hearts-on-fire part."

Before I completed the song a second time, I segued into *All Through the Night*. Mr. Moore surprised me by chiming in with his deep voice. As the song ended, he began to sing *Amazing Grace*. I wasn't familiar with all of the verses, so I hummed along, adding harmony. It was as if, through the music, we were all being transported to a softer, kinder place. As we sang, the girls floated through the small house, picking up a doll or folding laundry or putting a log on the fire, but they always returned to the kitchen table, like kittens returning to their mother for milk. Agnes worked her way onto her father's knee, even though she was on the cusp of being too old for a father's lap. He patted her head and continued to sing. He eventually broke his hymns-only rule and sang *Shenandoah*. Agnes took me by the hand and led me to Jerome's rustic, but solidly built casket. Coreen and Brigid followed until we stood in a semi-circle around the casket, all but Mr. Moore who hardly seemed to notice our absence.

"You can open it, Miss," said Coreen, tapping on the lid.

"Oh no, I couldn't!"

"Mrs. Lalonde did."

"So did Mrs. Toivonen," added Brigid. I was mortified at the thought. I'd never viewed a deceased person up close and certainly never a child. Yet the girls looked at me as if they were about to show me a new baby lamb.

"Mom made him a shirt. It's not sewn all the way to the back. Just sleeves and a front part," said Brigid.

"He's facing up, anyways. He don't need the back of a shirt," said Coreen. I stopped my impulse to correct her grammar.

"And there's special buttons on it, too," said Brigid. "Remember Coreen? How they were the eye buttons on your doll?"

As the girls chattered, I glanced back at Mr. Moore. He had come to the end of *Shenandoah* and now sat, eyes closed, the purple glass beads laced between his fingers.

"To open it, just do like this," Coreen said, popping open

the lid as she spoke. I gasped. Jerome seemed so small, and younger than his six years. Without the smile that so often animated his face, he looked more like a porcelain doll than a real person.

"He looks nice, eh Miss?" said Agnes.

"He looks like an angel," I answered.

"He *is* an angel now," said Agnes.

"He's in heaven, but he's here, too," added Brigid.

"No, he's in heaven. This is just his shell," said Coreen.

"It's not his shell," said Agnes. "He's not a turtle. He's a little boy and boys don't have shells."

"Let's sing to him," I said, nipping the disagreement in the bud.

"That's all we ever do," said Agnes. "Why can't we tell him a story? Miss, you tell good stories."

"Yes, tell him a story!" the other two girls chimed in.

"Well, I'm not sure if—"

"We need to close it," ordered Caroline, charging her way through the cluster of girls. "Mom'll be getting up soon and she doesn't want it open all the time."

"Caroline's right," I said, gently closing the lid. At that moment, as if in synchronicity, the light from the windows darkened, and a pattering of rain could be heard. I placed the crucifix, which had slipped onto the floor, back in its place. Jerome was now sealed inside the coffin, like a pearl inside a dark shell.

"Can we still tell him a story?" Agnes asked again, not seeming to notice the sudden change in weather.

"What story, do you think?" I asked the girls, though my mind was in two places. As long as the children wanted to hear stories and songs, I wanted to be with them. A part of me, though, was worried that I hadn't properly dressed for the weather. Rain in March was never a good thing. The ground would be slick and dangerous to travel, even short distances. It could also change in a blink from rain to sleet or hail.

"'Billy Goat's Gruff'," suggested Coreen.

"It's got trolls," said Caroline. "We can't be telling troll stories to a boy in heaven."

"What about 'The Selfish Giant'?" I asked. They all looked at me with blank faces. "You've never heard of the 'The Selfish Giant'?" The girls shook their heads. "It was written by Oscar Wilde. He was Irish, just like you girls."

"Mom's from Scotland," said Agnes.

"I guess that makes you half Irish, half Scottish, and half girl," I said.

"Three halves don't add up."

"I was only teasing you, Agnes."

"We never met our grandmother, but she talked Irish," said Brigid, proudly.

"I've never heard Irish. What's it sound like?" I asked.

"Dad says it's like singing a melody with oats stuck in your throat," said Brigid. All the girls giggled at this. Caroline glanced worriedly at her father, but he was lost in his own world.

"I can't tell the story in Irish, but I can tell it in English. Would you like that?" Three of the four girls smiled encouragingly.

As I turned my attention to recalling the story, I tried to quash my concerns about the weather. At the very least, I would finish the story before setting out to make my way home. "The Selfish Giant" was the perfect story to tell the children. The little boy crawls into a frozen winter garden and melts the heart of the giant. The garden blooms again after countless years of winter's frost. I thought of the Moore family and hoped that their garden wouldn't always be encased by winter's grief.

Moments after the story ended, Mrs. Moore appeared. Normally, she looked hardly a day over thirty with her round and cheerful face. That day, though, her eyes were puffy, her soft shoulders were hunched forward like an old woman's, and her mouth hung open slightly, as if she didn't have the energy to close it. She was a short lady, but seemed to have shrunken even more. Her hair hung loose and for the first time, I noticed that she had silver strands mixed in with the brown.

"Girls, it's getting late. I need help getting supper on," Mrs. Moore said, looking vacantly in our direction, her eyes avoiding the corner of the room where Jerome lay. The girls quickly made their way to the kitchen, and began peeling potatoes and tidying up. Mr. and Mrs. Moore shared a few quiet words before Mr. Moore made his way outdoors. The grief-stricken mother sat at the kitchen table and began twirling her fingers as though she were coiling imaginary wool. I found myself gazing at my own hands—hands that had never buried a loved one, hands that knew so little of true loss.

"Mrs. Moore, is there anything I can do to help?" I asked.

"Miss Hirvi! I didn't hear you come in," she said, noticing me for the first time.

"I'll be heading back soon, but if there's anything you need me to take care of first."

Mrs. Moore turned to face the window. "It's only getting worse out there..." she said.

"Maybe Malcolm can bridle up the horse and bring you back," said Brigid, trying to be helpful.

"Malcolm's taken the horse," whispered Caroline. "Mrs. Lalonde needed help setting up, so

Dad sent Malcolm."

"I can make my own way back," I said. I immediately regretted visiting the family so soon

after the tragedy. I couldn't possibly ease their grief, not even if I sang a thousand hymns. I turned to Caroline and said, "If I could just borrow a raincoat, and a lamp, if you have one to spare." Caroline scooted away to locate the items I needed. As I waited, Mrs. Moore absentmindedly swept crumbs from the tabletop into a little hill in front of her with the same reverence as if she were building a shrine. I wasn't sure if I should interrupt her thoughts by collecting my purse, which hung on the kitchen chair where she sat. Caroline returned with the lantern and raincoat, and I had no choice but to retrieve my purse.

"It's not letting up," Mrs. Moore said, without lifting her eyes from the table. "Brigid, see if you can find your father." Mrs. Moore looked directly at me for the first time. I could see that every decision was agony for her: what to say to the intruding guest, what to warm up for supper, what to do with herself for the next minute or hour. She began to speak, then stopped herself. I noticed her staring at my shawl. Why had I worn the most tattered thing in my closet? Was I trying to cloak myself with my grandmother's fortitude, perhaps?

"I'm sorry I wore this old thing," I said. My grandmother had given me the shawl all cleaned up, smelling of lavender, and wrapped in tissue. She said she didn't expect me to wear it out, as it was coming undone on every corner, but that I should have it as a keepsake.

"It's hand-woven," Mrs. Moore said, as her fingers floated along the worn threads. She then sighed deeply, and returned to building her hill of crumbs. I stood awkwardly holding the raincoat and lamp, as I thought I should wait for Brigid's return which, thankfully, didn't take long.

"Dad's coming," Brigid said breathlessly, addressing her mother. A moment later, Mr. Moore stepped inside, but not before taking off his wet jacket and giving it a good shake in the porch. "You're going to have to spend the night, Miss Hirvi. Malcolm's back, but it's too slick out there. Either that, or I could walk you over to the MacDonalds'. I'm sure they wouldn't mind taking you in for the night."

Mr. Moore must've seen the look of panic on my face at the mention of the MacDonalds', but for reasons other than he thought. I dreaded being under the same roof with a heavy drinker, but even more terrifying to me was the prospect of spending a night in the same house with the drinker's son—Carl. "Never mind, stay here," he said, noticing my distress. "Coreen, you can sleep on the floor on some blankets, and Miss Hirvi can take your side of the bed." The girls turned their faces toward me. They didn't dare speak, but their faces said, 'please stay!'

"Well...whatever's best for you Mr. Moore," I said. "but, if I do stay, I'll sleep on the floor. I don't want anyone to fuss."

By now, Mr. Moore had turned his attention toward his wife, gently coaxing the grieving mother to her feet in the same way one might come to the aid of an elderly person. "We'll sit in the porch for a while, and listen to the rain," he said to her. Taking Mrs. Moore's coat from the hook by the door, he threaded her arms through her coat sleeves, first one, then the other. I handed him the lantern that Brigid had fetched for me, as I no longer had need of it.

Before following her husband out the door, Mrs. Moore stopped to say, "Don't leave Jerome with no one to keep him company." With that request, the mother of seven, now a mother of six, let herself out the door.

There was general confusion as the girls fluttered around, locating every spare blanket and quilt they could find. Caroline remained downstairs, near to Jerome's casket. Once in the bedroom, I insisted on taking the spot on the floor between the two beds. Letting down my guard as teacher, I invited the girls to call me by my first name, though they mostly slipped back into the habitual 'Miss Hirvi.' As we lay in the dark, the girls riddled me with questions. "Miss Lotta, have you ever had a beau?" Corine asked. I was stung with shame at the mention of the word *beau*. What if the girls somehow discovered I had kissed Carl—until recently, their schoolmate. What kind of hypocrite was I?

"No, I don't, but maybe one day I will," I said.

"Do you have any sisters?" Agnes asked.

"I have one older and one younger. They're prettier. Everyone says, so it must be true." The girls protested, saying I was very pretty. I mentioned that my older sister had inherited thick, dark hair from my mother, and my younger sister's hair was whitish blonde. They both had fine features, with perfect shaped noses and heart shaped faces. "When they stand together, they look like Rose Red and Snow White," I said.

"Who do you look like, Miss Hirvi, your mom or dad?" asked Brigid.

"No more questions. Let Miss Hirvi get some sleep," ordered Caroline, upon entering the room. "We all have to be up early. We need to look nice for the funeral."

"That's true," I said. "We should all try and get some sleep."

Just as things quietened down, Agnes began to sob. "We're all up here and Jerome's alone downstairs," she said. I crawled out from my cocoon of blankets to sit on the side of the bed nearest Agnes.

"Mom and Dad are with him," said Caroline, softly. "He's not alone."

"But they're too sad. Maybe he wants to be with us."

Caroline's eyes gleamed at me in the darkness, as if to say, *You talk sense to her.*

"Agnes," I said, taking her hand, "I know you're worried about Jerome feeling left out. But when we're all together, maybe he hears us. Maybe he doesn't feel left out at all."

"He's too far away. How can he hear?"

If only she were to ask me the names of the nine planets, or what causes volcanoes to erupt, or a list of British poets, then I might be of some use. "I can't explain it," I said. "Nobody can. But maybe Jerome hears us, after all." Agnes continued to whimper under the covers. She hungered for a plausible explanation, but I had none to give her. I limped along with answers that felt like rain at the finish of an already damp week.

Eventually, the girls quieted down and fell asleep. I lay awake for some time, listening to the occasional sigh or sniffle from the four misses. There were other sounds, too—the front door opening and closing followed by the heavy footsteps of the boys making their way to their beds, a light tapping of rain on the roof, the rumbling of a train. Later, I heard Mrs. Moore crying, and I found myself thinking of my own mother. She must've been lonely in Lappe where everyone, including the dogs, spoke Finn. Maybe loneliness really could drive a person mad. If I hadn't felt so isolated, would I have kissed Carl? And did my one mistake obliterate any good I'd done in Hurkett? Suddenly, the grudge I'd held against my mother seemed so trivial, so pointless.

As I pondered these things in the darkness, I heard someone choking back tears into the blankets. The voice said, "I won't marry and have children. Never!" It was Caroline. She had waited until she supposed we were all asleep before allowing a single tear to fall. Eventually, I too fell asleep, though it was a fitful slumber.

๛

A dream woke me, the fragments of the dream vanishing before I opened my eyes. Feeling chilled, I fumbled for my shawl, which had found its way to my knees. The wooden floor pressed against my bones, and I found myself turning this way and that, trying to make myself comfortable. Finally, I sacrificed my pillow and shoved it under the makeshift mattress of blankets, hoping it would soften my ribs against the floor. Nothing helped. Perhaps fresh air was what I needed.

With the girls all asleep, I slipped out of the room, and descended the steps slowly in the darkness. Remembering that I'd placed my boots on the braided rug by the door, I hoped they would be easy to find. At the foot of the stairs, I noticed a figure slumped over the casket, surrounded by a half dozen candles. It was Mr. Moore, singing a melodious tune in a foreign language. I instinctively crouched down into the shadows of the stairwell, not wanting to be discovered. I felt the music—imbued with both sadness and beauty—enter my body, giving nourishment to my bones. Every part of me hungered to hear more as Mr. Moore's voice gently wavered and danced and rose and fell. I grew up in a shop where customers spoke many languages, but never before had a foreign language moved me so.

Mr. Moore suddenly grew silent. The notion of fumbling for my boots now seemed out of the question. When I turned to go back up the stairs, Mr. Moore said, "Miss Hirvi? Is that you?"

"I'm sorry. I didn't mean to disturb you," I whispered.

"Not at all. Take a seat, why don't you?"

Not knowing what else to do, I sunk into a soft chair a few feet behind the mourning father.

"The song you were singing is so beautiful," I said.

"*The Parting Glass*," Mr. Moore said, more to himself than to me. He then asked, "Have you ever lost someone?"

"No. I've been fortunate."

"Even though he's here beside me, it's still not real. Maybe singing helps to make it real, I

don't know." We sat in silence for some time before Mr. Moore spoke again. "And the teaching? It's going well?"

I was surprised to hear Mr. Moore make small talk in the midst of a tragedy. "I've nothing to complain about," I answered.

"I'm sure Thursday wasn't easy. I guess the kids were upset, eh?"

"Everyone's sad. But don't worry about the school kids. They have each other."

As Mr. Moore made conversation, he kept his face toward Jerome. "Wasn't Jerome the youngest of the bunch?" he asked.

"The McIntosh girl is a few months younger."

"That's right. I forgot about Julie. She was born in the city."

"They were friends, but she's too young to understand

what's happened."

I was about to excuse myself when the kind man spoke again. "Lotta...you don't mind me calling you Lotta, do you?"

"No, of course not."

"Thanks for staying the night. It's a help to the girls."

"It's not much."

"Come by as often as you can. The kettle's always on, as my wife would say."

Mr. Moore obviously thought highly of me, yet I'd done nothing to deserve his respect. I felt suddenly felt like an impostor. "Mr. Moore? I don't think I should stay on here."

"You can't go now. The rain's let up, but it's darker than the Earl of Hell's waistcoat."

"I mean, teaching. I'll be putting in my resignation soon. I'm sorry. I shouldn't be bringing this up now."

"You just said you were making out fine," he said, turning to face me. The candlelight glowed behind him, creating a halo around his head.

I'd opened a can of worms and didn't know how to catch the little creatures as they wriggled away from me. "I can't explain. I just need a change."

"Do you have a sweetheart overseas?"

"No, thank God. I do have two uncles in the war, though."

I was hoping he would let things go, but he kept on. "Lotta, if there's something you're not happy with on the job, you can tell me. I was on the hiring committee."

"You have true sorrow, Mr. Moore, true problems! I don't deserve to—"

"—Everyone deserves an ear."

"Not tonight. And it's nothing."

"It's nothing, but enough that you're thinking of leaving us."

"I should never have brought it up. Not today of all days."

Mr. Moore fell back in his chair, and sighed deeply. "There's one thing hard for people to understand," he said. "When we're talking like this, for a minute, I can put my mind someplace else. Because the sting is always here," he said, pointing to his heart. "It's not going any place. It's good to talk about every-day things, you know? Even if we're just pretending things are normal."

"I just don't think I should trouble you," I whispered. And then I did the one thing I swore I would never do, which was to burden Mr. Moore with my own trivialities. "It's one of the boys here in Hurkett. It's Carl," I blurted out.

"He's giving you grief? I thought he was starting to show some sense, that kid."

"He's hardly been in class this year. But he delivers fire-wood, so he's around. And on the day we heard the news, the children were upset, like you say. I was distraught and he, Carl, was kind. It was a moment of weakness. He didn't do anything wrong, nothing at all. It was me."

Mr. Moore paused, trying to understand. A part of me wanted him to chastise me while another part ached for his approval. His response was not what I expected. "I guess that boy is not so much a boy anymore, is he?" A look of embar-rassment was my only answer. "Maybe I'm over my head here," he continued, "but if it's woman's trouble, you should talk to one of the farmer's wives."

"Oh no, it's nothing so serious as that! It was a kiss. That's all it was. I don't mean to say *that's all*. I know I crossed a line."

"Miss Hirvi," Mr. Moore said, turning in his chair to meet my eyes head on, "feelings happen between folks. Feelings you don't expect."

In that moment, I knew that my motivation for the visit was mixed. As much as I wanted to offer my help, another part of me craved Mr. Moore's fatherly company. I had approached a man who'd been given the worst news of his life only a few days prior, and why? Was I looking for absolution for my improper behaviour? "It was a mistake, Mr. Moore. I know that now."

"You should keep on here. You might bump into him, but that's not a crime, is it?"

"It's just that, he's still keen to keep up his studies. And it'll be my fault if his education comes to a complete halt."

"How's that your fault?"

"I'm still helping him out. I give him lessons to take home, that sort of thing. And he comes by when he gets stuck on something."

"Wait and see. I bet he'll keep coming around for your help."

"And if he doesn't?" In answer to my own question, I went on to say, "Maybe I should write him a note. Just a simple note encouraging him to not give up. But how would I get it to him without drawing attention to myself?"

"Then I wouldn't send a note. But if you want, I could talk to Carl."

"Oh no! I couldn't ask that of you."

"Look, I buy chicks from the McDonalds every other spring and I'm heading over there

anyways. Not for another week, of course. I'm just saying, don't leave Hurkett. You've done too much good to throw it all away over—"

"—poor judgment. Very poor judgment."

"Yes, well, from what I gather, it's not enough to banish you to the hills," he said, turning his eyes to rest again on his son's casket. With his back to me, he added, "And if it makes you feel any better, this isn't the first time something like this happened around here."

But a teacher? Someone who is supposed to know better? I was about to make my way upstairs when Mr. Moore stopped me by saying, "You know, there's a reason you're here tonight. The way you sang to the girls and…I'm wondering, is it too much to ask one more favour?"

"Not at all."

"See that?" he said, pointing to a coffee table close to where he sat, "I guess it's pretty hard to see anything in the dark."

"Looks like an envelope?"

"You won't believe how long I've had that letter. Five years. And not once did I feel tempted—well that's not true—I did feel tempted, but not enough to open it. Until tonight. I've been staring at it for the past hour, but I can't bring myself to do it."

"If you think it's bad news, maybe you shouldn't—"

"It's not bad news. But it could tell me something I've been curious about for a long time."

"Do you want me to open it for you?"

"And read it to me, if you don't mind."

I tentatively tore open the envelope and pulled out a few pages of handwriting. As I did so,

Mr. Moore lit a lantern and handed it to me, saying, "You'll need this, unless you've got the eyes of an owl."

The letter was dated and Mr. Moore hadn't exaggerated. It had remained unopened for close to five years. *"Dear brother,"* I read aloud, *"You'll be glad to hear we're all doing well. I surprised everyone and got married last year to a local girl named Katherine. I guess twins run in the family. Or maybe they run in Katherine's family, but either way, we got more than we bargained for with twin girls.*

"I was shocked to read your letter and I must say you're like a dog with a bone.

I thought about it a fair deal and at first, I couldn't understand why you needed to dredge up the past. But I came to the conclusion that it must be something to do with you being so religious. If things were done proper, according to the Catholic Church, the baby should have been buried with Mam. But she wasn't. That's what you want to know, right? Where the infant was put to rest? I'll write it all down the best I remember, but don't ask me to write about it again, or talk about it. And burn this letter once you read it.

"We hadn't planned on losing Mam that night, let alone the infant too, so we weren't prepared for anything. Me and Patrick and Da were all downstairs in the kitchen. There was lots going on, and then things got quiet. Too quiet. Da went upstairs. He told us to wait in the kitchen. He didn't know it, but I followed him up and stood outside the bedroom door where I heard it all. Da was shouting, 'Bring Mary back! God Almighty, I'll give up the bottle if only You'll bring her back to me!' Then the Scottish midwife told him promises wouldn't bring her back, and either way, Da would do well to give up the drink. 'She's with God now,' said the midwife, 'as is the baby.'

"I could hear Da moaning and crying and I wasn't doing much better. But for whatever reason, I wanted to hear what was going on in there, so I kept quiet. I remember Mrs. Watts saying, 'The baby's left us. But if you want to see her, she's there in the Italian's arms.' I have to tell you the honest truth, Faolan, I didn't really care about the baby. If Mam didn't make it, I couldn't see us boys raising up a baby. Later on, I felt bad. She would've been the first girl in our family. A sister for us boys.

"Da said something like, 'I never want to see that baby. Put it up in a tree with the ravens, for all I care.' He was all in a rage, saying all kinds of things, accusing Mam of taking other men to bed, saying the baby wasn't his. When I heard him ranting, I never wanted to fight someone more than I did that day. I had to grip the stair banister to keep myself from going in there and laying him flat. I couldn't believe he'd go so far as to accuse a dead woman, his own wife. I hate to even tell you what he said, but you're the one who wants to bring up the past. So don't blame me if it troubles you to hear it.

"Da turned on the Italian too, and yes, she was there the whole time. 'You put my Mary under some kind of spell,' he said. 'You covered her tracks, I'm sure of it!'

"The Italian lady wasn't keeping quiet. And you know how she

talked, 'I no do nothing. Only make the tea to help with the stomach problem. Morning sick. You wife, she no go to other man.' But Da kept accusing her of hiding Mam so Mam could meet up with this phantom lover. He was just losing all reason. But you can't totally blame him for being suspicious. Remember how Mam disappeared for a week? Did she really think he would take that sitting down? I'm not saying it was Mam's fault, but she could've saved herself a lot of grief if she didn't befriend that batty Italian lady. Finally, things got quiet behind that closed door. When I heard Da rattle the door knob, I flew down the steps, faster than you ever saw anyone move. I knew if we saw each other, fists would fly.

"The next thing I knew, I was taking Fiorella home with the horse and buggy in the dark, and she had the infant in her arms. The baby wasn't breathing, that's a fact, but she looked so content under the lamplight, like maybe she didn't want to be born into this crazy world in the first place. When I dropped the Italian off, I asked her some questions. It seemed damned strange to me that my baby sister, dead or not, was being taken away. I've always been angry about how things went. But I guess it was something decided by the midwife and Da, and we can't argue with fate, can we?

"I dropped Fiorella off at the path leading up to her place. The Italian wasn't in the mood for talking, but I did manage to tell her Mam had a name picked out. Maybe I thought she'd make some kind of plaque or something for the baby. I don't know. Anyway, I told her the baby's name was Mary Violet, because that was the name Mam picked."

The pages fell onto my lap, as I struggled to make sense of the letter. The night had already been strange and now this too. Everything I thought to be true was put into question in that pinhole of a moment. I glanced over at Mr. Moore. Who was this man that I sat in a room with in the middle of the night? Why had I thrown myself into the centre of this tragedy? Why did I feel as if nothing solid was beneath me? The floor, the chair I sat on, the very house that enclosed us seemed weightless. Was this how Dorothy felt when her house got lifted by a tornado?

"It's all right, Miss Hirvi. You don't have to finish. I've heard everything I need to know," Mr. Moore said, both us of reaching to pick the letter up from the floor where it had dropped. As I passed the letter to him, Mr. Moore tapped me on the hand saying, "Remember what I said. There's a reason you're here."

As I slowly climbed the stairs to return to the girls' bedroom, I heard Mr. Moore opening up the wood stove and closing it again. I pictured the letter going up in flames. I cursed myself for dropping those pages, as those final words might have revealed what I felt in my heart to be true.

As I settled back under the covers, I tried to recall the details of the letter. It told the story of a stillborn infant—Mr. Moore's sibling—being shuttled away by an Italian woman in the dead of night. Though the letter did not specify the woman's age, I pictured an elderly *nonna* hunched over with a kerchief wrapped around her wrinkled face. Why would Mr. Moore choose to read such a letter—or have it read to him—on a night already filled with misfortune? It was strange enough, but stranger still was the name of the baby. Mary Violet was so close to my own mother's name—Maria Violetta. And when I thought of my mother, it did seem odd that, she had so little regard for her own Italian background. She married a Finnish man and, in almost every way, molded herself into a Finnish woman. Why? Was it because she never *felt* Italian?

In the morning, after less than four hours of sleep, I heard the sound of a distant rooster. Peering through the curtains, I noticed touches of pink grazing the horizon, a sign that night was beginning its journey into day. Still wearing my clothes, I slipped out of the bedroom, not wanting to disturb the girls. As I descended the stairs, I noticed a single candle flickering by Jerome's side, and Mrs. Moore asleep in a chair nearby.

As I was putting on my shoes, a soft voice from the kitchen called out, "Miss?" Sweet Brigid emerged from around the corner.

"Brigid! I didn't even hear you get out of bed! What are you doing up so early?"

"I was hungry," she said. "I ate the last cookie. I hope you're not mad at me."

"Someone had to eat it. And better you than the mice."

"The huge raisins? I ate them, too."

"Figs. They're called figs. Did you like them?"

"Yes, but the seeds are sticking to my teeth," she said, holding out the empty tin and the ribbon I had used to wrap the treats.

"You keep the ribbon. Maybe you can put it in your hair."

"It's not my birthday."

"It doesn't have to be a birthday to receive a gift."

"It's long enough to cut and give to my sisters." Brigid draped the ribbon over her wrist and again held out the tin.

"As far as that goes, keep the tin too," I said. "For your Mom. She'll find some use for it."

As I collected up my hat and coat in the dim light, Brigid asked, "Miss Hirvi? Did you bake the cookies?"

"I wish. They're my mother's invention. She sells them in our shop."

"What makes them that pretty colour?"

It occurred to me that Brigid was riddling me with questions, not because she cared about the colour of the cookies, but because she didn't want me to leave. "If you can keep a secret, I'll tell you," I said. "My mother mashes blueberries through cheesecloth and uses the juice to colour the batter. She calls them *Violettas.*"

"I've never heard of a cookie with a lady's name."

"Give something a name and people will pay an extra five cents for it. I could say, 'Would you like a cookie?' or I could say, 'Would you like a *Violetta*?'"

"My mother and aunties are all named after flowers."

"Really?"

I pulled up a chair to lace up my boots, while Brigid launched into a litany of names, "Auntie

Iris, Auntie Marigold, Auntie Aster, Auntie Clover, Auntie Posy, Auntie Violet, Auntie Flora—"

"My goodness, how many aunts do you have?"

"Ten aunties and two uncles. But there's more. Some of them moved away."

"Brigid, I'm so sorry, but I have to slip out."

"Yes, Miss Hirvi," she said sadly. I hated to leave Brigid alone, overcome with grief, and no one to comfort her. But I couldn't stay. I needed to get home to clean up and iron my clothes for the funeral.

"Are you coming to the funeral?" she asked.

"Yes, yes of course! I just need to change out of these old clothes, but I'll see you at the church. Now why don't you go back to bed. It's a big day today and you'll need your sleep. Bye Brigid."

With her one free hand, Brigid motioned a goodbye and shuffled up the stairs, her head bowed. I had to trust that time would soften her pain, in the same way that Lake Superior polishes stones into perfect rounds along the shoreline. I waited until I heard the creak of the bedroom door open and close before I slipped outdoors.

Daylight had begun to seep into the sky, like cotton slowly absorbing colour from a stick of dye. For the first leg of the journey, my mind felt wrapped in a cocoon of confusion: the letter, the coincidence of my mother's name, the confusion I felt in my role as a teacher. As I walked, and the sky became open and clear, so too did my thoughts. Why not stay another year? Why slink away? The only person who knew of the incident other than Carl was Mr. Moore, and he could be trusted to be discreet. How could I abandon the Moore children now?

Jerome's passing brought an unbearable sorrow to his family. Yet, for me, it broke open the frozen ice and allowed the waters to flow again. Just as spring breakup was filled with violent groaning and cracking sounds that ricocheted across the bay, so too did grief release itself with tremendous force. Twice I felt that tremor: once when I heard Mr. Moore singing in Irish by Jerome's casket, and again when I read the letter aloud. Both times I felt grief forcing open a pathway, perhaps not yet for the immediate family—that might wait another generation—but in me, something extraordinary took place. *Life's path is indeed filled with toils and snares. And it is also lit by a thousand stars.*

CHAPTER THIRTEEN

The Long-Awaited Night—Hurkett, Ontario, 1943

Primrose:

The other night, I accidentally set a plate for Jerome. It wasn't until we said grace that I noticed. We ate our supper with the empty plate staring back at us, no one saying a word about it. Even after supper, when Brigid cleared the table, she was nervous about picking up the clean plate and putting it away. I think I was feeling unsettled about my wedding dress. Earlier in the day, I'd fished it out of the back of the wardrobe and had taken scissors to it. My idea was to make bloomers for the girls.

Silk makes for a nice undergarment. It keeps you cool in the summer and warm in the winter. But it's daylight robbery to buy it, so you won't find too many of us with silk under our skirts. I was about to figure out a pattern for the bloomers when an idea popped into my head. I knew I had some indigo dye hidden away, so I went on a hunt for it. It wasn't in my sewing basket where it should've been, or on the high shelf in our wardrobe where I tended to keep things away from the little ones. Finally, I found the dye in the kitchen, with my spices of all places.

The wedding dress was in good condition, other than some slight tearing at the underarm seams. It was a floor-length dress with no frills or lace. I did once have a lace veil, but that went to the mice decades ago. I first prepared the dress with tannic acid and, while it was soaking, I went out to pick some chicken-of-the-woods mushroom and wild leek. By the time the kids came home, I'd already dyed it and had it hanging with the laundry. I kept checking to see if it'd dried as I didn't want Faolan to see what I'd done to my wedding dress. He and Malcolm got home just before supper and, by then, I'd tucked it away.

"How was your day, Prim?" Faolan asked. I noticed how Faolan's colouring was ruddy and his whiskers were coming in white.

"As good as yesterday."

"Well, then, how was yesterday?"

"Fine," I said. It was more or less the same thing we said every night. I couldn't tell him the truth. I couldn't say that I worried from sunup to sundown about him being out on the lake with Malcolm. If a little brook could take the life of a boy, what could that enormous lake do? It could snap Faolan's boat in two like it was a toothpick, or toss it into the rocks. My mind ran straight to the worst thing. Why wouldn't it, when the worst thing already happened?

Later that evening, Faolan pulled a tiny wooden horse out from his trouser pocket and said, "I found something. Do you recognize it?" Of course, I did. Jerome was always trying to hide it from the other kids. I guess he thought they'd take it from him.

"Where'd you find it?" I asked. *Jerome must've lost it on the day he died.*

"Just down the path a way," he said.

I got up from the table to dry up some dishes and put on

the tea. *Was little Jerome looking for his toy horse? Is that why he wandered from his sisters?* When the tea was steeped, I offered Faolan a cup. He shook his head *no*. "If you're tired, go off to bed. Don't wait for me," I suggested.

"You're coming soon?" he asked.

"Right after my tea."

"What should I do with this?" he asked, holding out the horse.

"You keep it," I said, "since you're the one who gave it to him."

Faolan headed to the bedroom, but not before leaning down to kiss the top of my head. The next morning, with the kids off to school, I got back to working on the dress. I slit open the side seams and widened the ribcage by using fabric from the hem. The dye took beautifully, the colour of a night sky on a starless night. I tried on the dress, pulling the curtain closed in our bedroom, even though the chances of being seen were near impossible with the closest neighbour a half mile away. As I hadn't bothered putting on a slip, the dress felt cold against my skin.

Looking in the oval mirror, a ghostly woman looked back at me; her lips without colour, bare-legged and quivering. No wonder I shivered, with my naked feet on a cold floor, and barely enough embers in the fire to heat up two square feet; not to mention the dress fell to my knees because of all the trimming and cutting I'd done. I tore the dress off, rolled it into a tight ball, and shoved it into the back of our wardrobe. I hurried to put on two layers of woolen stockings, my house dress, and one of Faolan's heavy woolen sweaters, but for the rest of the day, I felt chilled.

Over the next few days, whenever I was alone, I pulled out the dress and added something to it. I snipped croqueted roses from an old doily and stitched them below the waistband where the fabric gathered. The roses were too heavy to be added to silk, but I fought with it until I got it right. The next day, I threaded dried rosehips, until I had ten inches strung together. Some of the rosehips were so brittle that when I drove the needle into them, they snapped in two. With persistence, though, I managed to attach the string of rosehips to the neckline of the dress.

"Mom, what are you doing?" My youngest, Agnes, was home, sick from school, and she'd wandered downstairs.

"Do you need something, Agnes? Maybe a bite to eat?"

"I had a bad dream."

"Dreams aren't real. They're just leftover thoughts from the day." Agnes dove into my arms. "It's okay, Agnes. Here, let me feel your forehead."

Agnes didn't seem to be running a fever, though she did feel clammy. "Do you want a bucket of hot ash for your room?" I asked her. She shook her head. "Then sit here by the fire."

As I scooped up the dress from the back of the chair, it caught her eye. "What are you making, Mommy?" she asked. "Is it a dress?"

"It's a surprise," I said, disappearing into our bedroom with the dress.

The garment, with each added thing, was getting harder to hide. I couldn't roll it up into a ball and stuff it somewhere. If I jostled it around too much, the rosehips might break into bits. For now, I laid it out on the bed until I could figure out where to keep it away from curious eyes. When I returned empty-handed, there stood Agnes, peering into the bedroom with her blue-grey eyes. Then she said something I'll never forget. "Where's my other Mommy?" she asked.

I wondered if Agnes was running a fever, after all. Maybe she was delirious. "I'm right here. Come. I'll fix us up some bread and jam," I said, patting the cushion on the chair next to the fire. When I returned with the toast and jam, she took one nibble and asked again, "Where is she?"

"Who?"

"My other mother."

"I'm right here."

"But where's the mother I used to have? She looks like you but she's not the same."

"Agnes, you only have one mother."

"No, no, no! She went away when Jerome died. He took her away and I want her to come back!" By now, my girl was sobbing and there was no talking sense to her. I knew it was the dress that'd scared her. I needed to put it away where she wouldn't see it again.

While Agnes napped, I picked open a few inches on the waistband with a razor, and inserted a pocket big enough to hold a silver dollar. Before pushing it to the back of the wardrobe, I slipped the robin's eggshell—the one I'd stored inside my chest years before—into the pocket. I couldn't see anything more to be added or changed. It was an odd-looking thing with no practical use, now pushed out of sight.

For a few weeks, I never gave the dress a second thought. Then one night I couldn't sleep, and Faolan was snoring to beat the band. I crawled out of bed and fumbled for the dress, slipping it on over my nightie. Once outside, I felt soothed by the low hanging, soft-edged moon and a few stars that lit up the darkness. I wandered down our familiar path, taking heed as the shadows of the moon altered the look of everything. As I stepped, I noticed mushrooms glowing on the forest floor, and shadows that may not've been shadows at all, but dense arms of a jack pine. I felt relieved when I got to the moss-covered section of the path, though not long after, the ground became a carpet of twigs and tree roots again.

I kept on until I came to the familiar open field. The moon's edges had become clearer and a few more stars glittered. By now my feet were cold, as the soles of my shoes were worn thin, but I kept my gaze up to the night sky. Maybe Jerome was up there—maybe one of the stars that glinted brighter than the rest. Jesus had his own star, so why not our Jerome? Then the thought crossed my mind that Faolan might wake up to find me gone. Would he set off with a lantern, calling my name? Would he wake up the boys? What reason would I give for wandering alone in the night?

The minute I slipped back into the house, I slid the dress from my shoulders and folded it over my arm. Faolan was still asleep when I crawled back into bed. When morning came, I felt Faolan's eyes on me as I bustled around in the kitchen making porridge and coffee. "Don't fuss, Primrose. I can make my own coffee," Faolan said. "Sit down while it perks. Take a load off."

I don't want to take a load off. The load I carry is our son, Jerome. Why would I want to unload the sorrow I feel for our own son? Doesn't Jerome deserve a mother's sorrow? "I'm better off keeping busy," I said.

"Well, I've got lots on my plate, too, so I better get rolling," said Faolan, placing his hand gently on my back. The house wasn't big enough for us anymore. Strange, that our Jerome took up more space in the house now that he was dead than he did when he was alive.

With the last one out the door for school, I pulled out the dress. It'd absorbed moisture from the night air, so I laid it over a chair up close to the fire. I no sooner turned around to tidy up when Faolan came rushing back in, saying he'd forgotten something. He was headed to the bedroom, probably to look for his rosary lost in the bedsheets, when his eye caught the dress. Did he recognize it as my wedding dress? I felt myself shrink, as if I'd been caught in a lie.

"What did you forget?" I asked, trying to turn his attention away from the wedding dress, but it was too late. I could see in his eyes that I'd hurt him; not deliberately, but I'd hurt him all the same. We stood, looking at each other, neither of us saying a word until finally he said, "It's cold for a morning in May."

"You can't control the weather," I said.

"You're right there. And there's no point in trying, is there? Well, I better get back to the boathouse. Malcolm will wonder where I am."

After Faolan left, I held the dress up to the window's light. Seeing it with fresh eyes—with *his* eyes—I realized how ridiculous it must've looked to Faolan with its rosehip neckline and chopped hemline. The indigo was so dark that it was almost sinister, like something an old crone might wear to cast a spell in a fairy tale book. What came over me to alter it in the first place? It'd lost all its charm. I'd ruined it.

Eager to be rid of the dress, I wondered what I should do. Burn it? Hide it? Silk was rare, even silk that had been darkened with grief. Because that's what it was, wasn't it? Not just the dress, but every part of my life was now tinged with a dark sorrow. The young woman who'd walked up the aisle in a white dress wasn't the same person anymore. I wrapped the dress in paper and string, but couldn't find any place suitable to hide it. I was about to put it under the bed, but wondered if it might give me nightmares, being so close to where I slept. Finally, I opened the trap door on the floor of our kitchen, and went down into the cramped dugout below. Any time over the years that I'd asked Faolan to get something for me in the cellar, he always said he'd rather face Lake Superior's waves than fumble around in a hole in the ground. At least down there, I thought, I wouldn't have to worry about Faolan coming across it.

Once I got down to the cold room, I set the package on a bottom shelf, behind some jars of honey. No one would bother with it, as I was pretty much the only one who went down there, other than the kitty who liked to hunt mice. Maybe in a hundred years, once the house had rotted out, someone might find the dress. If they did, they would probably say, "This is what a mother's grief looks like."

Faolan:

Ever since Jerome's passing, most folks are nervous around me. They don't look me in the eye, and the men stop their kidding around as soon as I'm within earshot. It's as if Jerome's death brought every one's heartbreak to the surface, like a shipwreck that gets dragged to shore, and every crusty barnacle on that ship has a tale of woe. All but Carl, who treats me the same as he always did. Because his father's got health problems, Carl's been saddled with running the farm. Mrs. McDonald has a shelf full of medicines for her husband, but if he'd just lay off the bottle, I'm sure it'd cure his ailments. He'll have one foot in the grave and still be crying for his whiskey.

Yesterday, I showed up to lend a hand to Carl for a few hours. Mrs. McDonald invited me in for a cup of tea. "Drink it while it's hot. And here's some cake just out of the oven." As I was stirring sugar into my tea, I noticed Mr. McDonald in the corner, slumped over in his chair, passed out. I was just as happy to not converse with him as, whenever he's had a few drinks, his Scottish accent gets all the stronger and I can't make out a word he's saying. He raves about the communists, and the cost of feed; if he could, he'd complain about the air he breathes. Mrs. McDonald, on the other hand, is always cordial and kind.

"Your son's not stopping for a cup?" I asked.

"Oh, he'll be here. Don't you worry."

Just then, the door swung open and Carl stepped in. "Sarge, did you see how that weed's taken over? I never seen it before. Don't know what it is." For some reason, Carl's taken to calling me Sarge, ever since I told him I fought in the Great War.

"I'll take a sample home to Primrose. She can identify anything," I offered.

"Don't worry, I got a book on it somewhere," Carl said. And, with that, he walked over to the hosier, and yanked out a pile of heavy books. Smashing them down onto the table, upsetting my tea, he said, "Sorry about that, Sarge. I keep forgetting how heavy these things are." He went right to the task of looking up information. I glanced over at his mother and saw her eyes beaming with pride.

"Here it is," Carl said. "See this? 'Invasive plant species'. It's got to be in this chapter."

"You could start up a library with all these books," I said.

"That's where I got them from, the library."

"So, you read all these?"

"Have to. Only get them for a month, then you got to return them when the train car rolls in again."

I suddenly remembered the promise I'd made to Miss Hirvi, to talk to Carl about his education. "So, Carl, you planning on sticking with your studies?"

"I got to keep this farm going, but I started taking courses by mail. You can do that, you know. You can do all your learning by mail."

"Well, you keep going, Carl. It doesn't look like anything's going to stop you."

I couldn't help but wonder if Carl was doing all this to impress Miss Hirvi. I thought about the eve of Jerome's burial when Miss Hirvi read out my brother's letter. I wondered why I'd asked her, of all people and of all nights, to recite something so personal. I hadn't even told Primrose about it. I burned it the next morning, as my mother's death was all knotted up with my father's jealousy. Maybe the infant died and maybe the Italian buried her, like my brother wrote. The one nagging question, though, was why the infant wasn't baptized, like she should've been. And who knows what pagan prayers the Italian woman said, because there's no doubt in my mind Fiorella dabbled in magic. Why else would she have had those symbols painted on her floor?

Who was I to trust: my own memory, or my brother's version of events? As a kid, I did hear a baby cry, though it could've been a barn cat. But I also saw a baby in Fiorella's arms. What if she secretly raised my baby sister? But no, she couldn't have. The townspeople would've known about it. Either way, I had to burn my brother's letter to erase his version of events, and separate his story from mine. I knew it wasn't logical, but death was never logical. Right after Jerome's death, I walked the train tracks daily. Whenever I heard an approaching train, I hid behind a tree, and with the deafening sound of the whistle, I screamed with all my might. Was that logical? No, but it was what I needed to do, much like an injured animal that goes off alone to lick their wounds.

"Sarge? You okay?"

I looked up to see Carl and his mother looking at me. I was clutching the teacup and, any tighter of a grip, I might've cracked the cup in two. "Yeah, I'm okay. Just didn't get enough sleep last night," I said.

"You don't have to come around to help. We're managing fine," said Carl's mother.

"But where else would I get cake as good as this, Mrs. McDonald?"

"Oh, go on with you. I'm sure Primrose makes cakes as good as the rest of us... when she's up to it again."

"Do you think we'll ever be up to it? Do you think that's possible?" I could hear the anger in my voice, but it wasn't Mrs. McDonald I was angry with. I'd seen a lot of horrible things in my life, things that haunted me still, but losing an innocent boy whose heart was so light it could've been a bird's, just didn't add up. Why did God take him from us?

"Faolan," Mrs. McDonald said, "What are you doing here when Primrose needs you at home?"

"Mom," Carl whispered. He didn't like his mother's line of questioning, yet it needed to be said.

"What you say is true, Mrs. McDonald. But every time I look at Primrose, I feel guilty. It's not logical, but I feel like it's my fault. She may not be thinking it, but I am."

"It coulda happened to anyone," Carl said.

"God brings comfort to those who mourn. It says so in the Beatitudes," said Mrs. McDonald.

"I believe that's true, but now's not the time to tell that to my wife."

Just then, Mr. McDonald woke up from his stupor to say, "Where the hell's my breakfast?"

Mrs. McDonald rolled her eyes, and said, "Maybe if you didn't sleep the whole day, you'd know."

"I see what you're doing, woman. Putting out fancy cakes for the neighbours. I'm your goddamn husband, aren't I? That counts for something!"

"Do you need me to stay?" I asked Mrs. McDonald, as I was worried her husband might become more aggressive.

"He won't lay a hand on my mother so long as I'm here," said Carl. And he meant it.

"I'll be on my way then," I said.

As I headed home, I thought about that poor woman's burden, being married to a drunk. Even so, Mrs. McDonald was able to think of others. I took her words to heart. It was time to pay more attention to my wife. Primrose had lost some weight and it didn't take a doctor to see her colouring wasn't good. I reminded myself, minute to minute, that Jerome was with God and the angels, but I didn't feel free to say this out loud to Primrose. Anything I said about Jerome could be cause for hurt.

It was around suppertime after coming in from a day of fishing that the kids told me they couldn't find their mother. I told them not to worry. It was a sunny day, and I figured she was out looking for wild strawberries. When the clock read seven and we'd all had our supper, I got wondering where she'd gone.

Hitching up the horse and wagon, I headed out to ask the nearby neighbours. No one knew of her whereabouts. It was Mrs. Oivo who mentioned that it was exactly three months from the day of Jerome's passing. Maybe Primrose had taken a notion to visit the new cemetery, she suggested. I thought that was likely where she'd gone and decided to walk there.

When I got to the cemetery, a low mist hung in the air. A field full of men stood silent as statues. I could see Lucas and Szymon and Henri—who was now older than the hills—and Jari, and Grampa Lanktreee, andBirch Bark Al. Even Carl and his father were there. Also, a few women stood in a cluster—Mrs. Delleff, Mrs. Oivo, Miss Hirvi, and Lucy Manitowabi. Esther, the woman who'd tried to revive Jerome, crossed the field to join the others. I'd misjudged these people. I'd thought they were avoiding me because of their own grief, but I could see now, that wasn't true. If they had avoided me, they had done so as a gesture of kindness, that I might have my privacy. These neighbours—more than neighbours, these comrades—were ready to go to battle for each other, and, in this instance, for me. I thought I'd seen courage on the battlefield, but this was a different kind of quiet, persevering, tough courage.

Though it wasn't yet dusk, mostly everyone in the field held lanterns. As if directed by a conductor, they all turned their faces toward me. Why was everyone gathered here? What had happened? Finally, Henri broke free of the frozen picture and said, "You want to know why we're here?" Without waiting for an answer, he said, "We know you're looking for Primrose. We've organized a search party." I was grateful to the lot of them, but also troubled. If Primrose wasn't at Jerome's resting place, where was she?

"Have you got any idea where she might be?" asked Mrs. Delleff.

"I thought she'd be visiting one of you ladies."

"Does she have a favourite spot? Down by the lake? Or out walking?"

"She goes walking in the bush, but never for long." My mind was racing with worry about bears, and about Prim losing her sense of direction, even though she'd never lost her way before. I wanted to ask the good people of Hurkett to pray with me, but how could I with half of them communists and the other half a sprinkling of different faiths? I wanted to call for a priest, borrow a truck, and make my way to Nipigon, but by then the sky would be dark. As I scanned their faces, for the first time I noticed my own sons were among them. The two boys, Malcolm and Ethan, looked fierce with their jaws tight and their shoulders back, as if about to go into battle.

I fumbled in my pocket and took hold of my rosary. Stumbling over to Jerome's gravestone, I fell on one knee and tried to pray. I found myself calling on my mother, and the Italian woman as well, whispering, "If either of you can help us find Primrose, please, we need you now." I immediately filled up with shame that I hadn't directly addressed our loving Father.

Not often, every now and then, I have felt my mother's presence. Once, I breathed in a whiff of her pipe smoke. I was out on the water with my son, and we were having one heck of a time steering the boat. In bad weather, I shouldn't have given the wheel to my son, but I wanted him to feel the force of Lake Superior, as it was the only way to make him understand the power of that lake. The waves were beating on every side of the boat, and we were soaked to the bone, my boy and me.

Between me barking orders at Malcolm and the sky looking more menacing by the minute, I breathed in a trace of sweet-smelling tobacco smoke—the same smoke that lingered in our porch as a kid where my mother lit up her pipe. I'm not saying she came to me as a ghost that day. I don't believe in ghosts, except for the Holy Ghost. I'm just saying I felt my mother's protection out in that storm, and I could almost hear her saying, "Are you trying to drown yourself? For heaven's sake, take over the wheel and guide that boat to shore!" So, I did, and it's a good thing, too.

It made sense, didn't it, that out in that graveyard, I would call on my mother. She would know the pain of losing a child. But then again, maybe she died before the infant was born, or maybe they left this world together, one cradled in the arms of the other. I'd never know for sure. If only I'd gone to talk to Fiorella before I enlisted. She might've been able to help me separate the truth from the lies. Certainly, my brother's letter didn't help to clear things up. Maybe that's why I found myself calling on both my mother's help and Fiorella's out in that cemetery with its one lone tombstone. Maybe, those two women could help me from the other side.

When I stood up, the neighbours had the look of race horses about to bolt from the gate, eyes burning and lanterns lit.Birch Bark Al—who knew the bush better than anyone after decades of trapping and prospecting—shouted to the small crowd, "We have maybe an hour before dark. Good thing it's long days in June. We got that on our side. Spread out in pairs. Search starts here and moves in the direction of the lake. You bunch," he said, pointing to the group furthest away, "walk toward Hurkett Cove. The rest of us, we'll walk southeast to Cranberry Bay. Make sure you get out of the bush before dark. We'll meet at the railway station in one hour."

The group fanned out far and wide, as if they'd done this a hundred times before. Henri turned to me and said, "Maybe you should head home, in case she shows up there."

"I can't just sit. I've got to help."

I started toward my sons when I sensed someone rushing up behind me. "Dad, wait!" shouted Caroline.

"Go home, Caroline. No use all of us combing the bush."

"I've an idea where Mom might be," Caroline said, out of breath.

"Where?" I asked.

"I've seen her go to this place. I think it's the place where my baby brother is buried."

"How do you know about that?"

"Mom used to go there while I watched the kids."

The odd time Primrose disappeared for an hour, I often wondered if she was making her way to Joseph's resting place. "Boys, you keep on the search. Me and Caroline will check out this place she's talking about." With a nod to their heads, Malcolm and his brother were off, but not before handing me a lantern.

Taking the road by foot, me and Caroline first stopped by the creek where we lost Jerome. The ferns were unfurled, the Labrador plants seemed to have populated, and the place looked very different with the snow gone. We pushed on to Joseph's resting place, which wasn't that far off from where Jerome died. Sure enough, we discovered Primrose sitting on a fallen log, her head bent forward, and her arms wrapped around herself. I'd never seen her looking so forlorn. *This poor woman. This poor broken woman.* Not wanting to startle her, I gently called her name.

"Faolan! Caroline! What are you doing here?" she asked, looking confused.

"Mom, we've been looking all over for you," said Caroline.

"Why?" she asked. I realized Primrose didn't understand the seriousness of the situation. By now we were close enough that I could see she was trembling. Caroline took off her scarf and wrapped it around her mother's shoulders. "Let's go home, Mom."

"You go on with your father. I'll catch up with youse later," Primrose said.

Caroline looked to me for guidance, but I was at a loss. "You've been here for hours," I said.

"I have?" Primrose asked.

"The sun's setting."

"Getting close to the longest day of the year," Prim said wistfully.

I whispered to Caroline to call off the search. I also told her to send one of the boys to bring us blankets. I warned Caroline to stay on the main road or the railway tracks, even though it meant a longer route.

I removed my jacket and draped it over Primrose. Sitting beside her, I took her limp hand and put it in mine. Her fingers were cold and thick and worn. My mind flashed back to the day I'd come into the house looking for an extra pair of socks only to find that she'd done something strange to her wedding dress. She'd turned it black, and the worst of it was, it didn't occur to her how bizarre this was. And now this—my wife wandering away in the night and not telling anyone where she was headed.

After waiting for what felt like an hour, but was likely only ten minutes, Prim said, "Here it is, June, and we still have turnips. That's a first."

"Is that right, eh?"

I was worried about Prim's mental state, but also worried she'd catch a chill. "Prim, are you cold?"

"Not really."

"Hungry?"

Just then, I saw lanterns in the distance, dancing through the trees. I called out, "Everything's fine. I've found her."

"Found who?" Prim asked.

I couldn't bring myself to tell her a search party had been organized. "Ah...Mr. McDonald's cow broke out."

"Again? That cow's more nuisance than what she's worth."

The lanterns continued to make their way forward, so I shouted, "Go on back! Tell the others!" The lights then disappeared into the thick bush, like fireflies in the night.

"It's too early for strawberries," Prim said, "but they're in blossom.

"We'll need some warmer weather to bring them out."

"They were his favourite. He used to go picking with me. None of the other kids had the patience. You pick all morning and all you get is a handful."

"But the taste, eh?"

"He used to call them 'star berries'," she said. Primrose began to cry.

The darkness was closing in around us by now. A glance up to the sky told me we had fifteen or twenty minutes at most to get out of the bush. Thankfully, Malcolm had quietly dropped off the blankets, and, being the good kid that he is, he also brought us a jug of hot tea. It's too bad he didn't think to spike it. After wrapping a blanket around Primrose, and encouraging her to take a few swigs of tea from the jar, I got up to cut balsam fir bows with my pocket knife. My military training didn't hurt me that night. I hadn't roughed it for some time, but I wasn't put off by the idea of a night in the bush. I set the boughs under a nearby pine, layering them in one direction, then the other. Primrose watched me, like I was doing something perfectly ordinary, like this was something we did all the time. Finally, she said again, "Faolan, you go on home. I'll catch up later."

"I'd like to stay. It'll be an adventure, like we used to have when we were first married. Remember that pitiful house we lived in?" I asked. Prim gave a hint of a smile. Or I thought she did, but how could I know in the twilight whether she was smiling or not?

"I'd better start a fire," she said. Primrose could no more start a fire than she could swim the ocean, but I wanted her to move around and get her blood flowing, so I let her collect up twigs.

Anytime there's a fallen tree in and around the area, I buck it up for firewood. In the winter, I go around with the sled and collect it all. I had it in my head that there was a pile of firewood not far off, but I needed to get to it soon. "I won't be long," I said, and bolted in the direction of where I expected the woodpile to be. I kicked myself for not bringing along a saw. With a saw, I could've chopped down a standing dead spruce for firewood. In the end I found a small pile, but I'd run out of daylight, so I made my way back to light a fire with my one armload.

We sat side by side, blankets around us, the stars appearing one at a time, as if to encourage us, as if to say, "Wait, more light will come. It might take a long time, but it'll come." Eventually, Primrose fell asleep on my shoulder. With the night fully upon us, I half picked her up and carried her to the tree boughs. I used the blanket to cover us both. With Primrose now asleep in my arms, I thought back to the cemetery, and how fierce the people of Hurkett were—how determined they were to rise above this tragedy. Jerome's death was like a Lake Superior tempest ripping through the hearts of everyone who lived here, yes. Yet when hardship came, they reached out their arms to share the burden. That's just the way they were. With the death of our little boy, with the floorboards opened up wide, we surely would have fallen through, if not for the good people of Hurkett.

Primrose:

I woke up with the crisp air biting my face, and the weight of Faolan's body pressed up to my side. For a second, I thought I was back at home, and Faolan'd forgotten to stoke up the fire. Then I realized where I was—outdoors—in the place where Joseph was buried. "Cold morning, eh?" I said.

"Let's go home. It'll be warmer there," Faolan said.

As we walked along the trail, I tried to unravel the day before. Malcolm'd brought home a male grouse. This time of year, you can hear them drumming in the bush looking for a mate, so they're easy to spot. Anyways, nothing suits roasted partridge like cranberry sauce. I must've been foggy-headed that day because I went out in search of highbush cranberries. Only when I saw the blossoms did it dawn on me that I'd come two months early. It rattled me, but I kept on walking until I found myself at the place where Joseph was laid to rest. Over the years, I'd been there dozens of times, but not since Jerome's death. I began to talk to Joseph, telling him all about his brother, how Jerome had dimples on his round, rosy cheeks, how he loved chickens and barn cats, and loved to sing. Then I told Joseph every detail about how we lost Jerome, right down to Esther trying to revive him. I knew I was acting peculiar, saying all these things out loud. But, at the time, it felt normal.

After doing all that talking, my heart began to ache. It wasn't the kind of ache you hear about in poetry, all flowery words and such. It was an actual throbbing pain in the centre of my chest. I wore a woolen sweater under my coat, but my feet were tingling from the cold, and I didn't have matches in my pocket to start up a fire—all warning signs to get to a warm, safe house. Even so, I couldn't leave.

When I was a girl, my favourite thing to do was climb up into our treehouse. Everything looked different from up high. Mum's laundry flapping in the wind reminded me of the Great Blue Herons that migrated in the springtime, and our house seemed so small that I wondered how we all fit inside. The treetops were so alive, like a million green butterflies fluttering. I felt like, if I jumped, the leaves would turn into a magic carpet and carry me across the sky. That's what was happening out there in the woods that day; I was making myself big enough to hold the sorrow I felt. My own body was too small; it couldn't contain it. If I grew as high as the trees, though, if I let myself have the wing span of a blue heron, then maybe I could carry the sorrow. I couldn't go back home, no matter how cold or miserable it was. Because at home, I'd have to push that sorrow down, make myself small again.

Faolan found me. Or maybe it was Caroline who found me first. Originally, I couldn't figure out why they were there. I wasn't ready to leave, so Faolan stayed the night. Thanks God. He got a small fire going and kept me from getting a bad chill, or worse. It was the next morning before we walked home. When the house came in sight, Faolan only said a few words, but those words I'll never forget. "Now we can be sad together, or we can be happy together. It doesn't matter which, as long as we're together," he said.

Inside, Faolan had me sit by the wood stove. He perked up some coffee, though I hardly took a sip. It was early yet, so the youngsters were asleep, and the boys were out doing barn chores. Caroline was up, and she got it in her head to run a bath for me. It was probably the first time the bath was used by only one person. What little energy I had seemed to drain into that tub. I could barely towel myself off, and didn't bother to comb my hair. I just twirled it tight and pinned it on top of my head.

I slept the whole day, through the night, and the day after that too. On and off, Faolan brought me tea, soup, and fresh bread, made by our Caroline. He read to me from a book of poems by Emily Dickinson. I was so tired, not only in my bones, but every part of me. Most of the poems washed over me, except one. *Hope is the thing with feathers/ that perches in the soul/ and sings the tune without the words/ and never stops at all.*

CHAPTER FOURTEEN

No Stone Unturned—Port Arthur, Ontario, 1943

Carmela:

My granddaughter, Lotta, the one I gave my shawl to, she comes to visit whenever she's in town. The last time she dropped by, she was asking me questions about her mother's adoption. Funny, my own daughter, Maria Violetta, has never asked me a thing. But Lotta's the curious one, probably because she's a school teacher. She wanted to know who her mother's real parents were. I said, "We're her parents, me and Nonno. We raised her, didn't we? Doesn't that make us her real parents?" Lotta kept on with her questions. "Why did you adopt my mother?" she asked.

"Because we get along."

"I do try. But Nonna wanted children. That's usually the way it goes."

"Yes, but look how many times you gave birth."

"We didn't have ten children when we adopted. For two years we tried to conceive. Funny thing is, your mother was only six months old when I found out I was carrying. I guess

I just needed a baby in my arms to kick start the whole thing."

"So…who was my mother's real mother?"

Nobody, not even my own daughter, Maria Violetta, has ever asked me the name of her real mother. Once, when Maria Violetta was about nine or ten, she asked me why her mother gave her up. I told her that her mother was too poor to buy her clothes, or feed her properly, and that her First Holy Communion dress wouldn't even have a crinoline. That seemed to do the trick. She never asked again.

"Do you know anything about my mom's natural mother?" Lotta asked.

"I don't like that way of putting it," I said. "It's like saying the mother who did all the rearing
wasn't natural about it."

"That's not what it means."

"I know what it means. I just don't like it."

Lotta knew enough to back off. She asked me how I was getting along without Nonno. I told her it was an adjustment. I told her I missed him, but I also have my grandchildren—twenty-seven to be exact—and that keeps me busy. Lotta told me that she remembers how, when she moved in from Lappe, she didn't adjust to the city as easily as her sisters, but I always found treats to give her when no one was looking—*amaretti* and candies. The more she talked, the more I felt I should just tell her the truth. What harm could it do? "Okay, if I tell you something," I said, "just remember, I kept it quiet all these years for your Nonno's sake."

Renzo thought the world would cave in if people put it together that my crazy mother, Fiorella Bellettini, was Maria Violetta's birth mother, and the father unknown. It was the unknown father that was the most troubling to him. So fine, I kept it quiet that I was raising my half-sister. But Renzo died last year from a heart attack. So, I think when someone dies, that changes things.

"And you'll be telling your mother? Because once the cat's out of the bag, there's no putting it back in."

"Maybe not. We don't always see eye to eye, me and my mom."

"You should try and, didn't you have trouble with your own mother?"

"That's different. My mother was...you know."

"No."

"Put it this way. People called her a witch. And she lived on land that wasn't her own. We were poor, oh my God. After my father died, it was better I moved to the city with my *zia* and *zio*."

"Why did they call her a witch?"

"She had superstitions and potions from the old country. That's fine in southern Italy, but you can't expect people to understand that kind of thing here."

"I wish I'd met her."

I went into the kitchen and put some biscotti on a plate and made fresh coffee. As I fussed, I thought back to the adoption. The whole thing started with a photograph and some money I'd put in the mail for my mother. I thought she'd buy a goat, or sheep, something practical, order in seeds, for God's sake. I never expected her to buy a train ticket and land on my doorstep out of the blue, after me not seeing her for ten years. But here's the real surprise; she stood there, looking about a hundred years old, a dark kerchief tied under her chin, and a baby in her arms. A baby so small she fit inside my mother's picnic basket. How did they let my mother onto the train, an old Nonna in rags carrying a baby in a basket?

I hugged my mother. What else was I supposed to do? Mamma started to cry, tears spouting from her eyes. "*Mia figlia!*" she kept saying, kissing my cheeks and every inch of my face.

"Don't cry, Mamma. Come. Come inside." Looking to get

her off the sidewalk before the neighbours started talking, I added, "I'll make coffee. Remember how you used to read our coffee grounds when we were little?"

"Everything, I remember. Everything! Look. You so grown up," my mother said. By now, the tears were dried and we were sitting inside with our coffee and ginger cake. The way my mother was gawking at me, you'd think I was some sort of movie star. She looked dreadful; her crinkled hair a lot more salt than pepper, her face puffy, and her clothes —her clothes covered her body, but that's the only good thing you could say about them. If I'd known she was coming, and that she'd be looking like a starved cat, I wouldn't have done my hair up, or worn my pretty blue dress with pearl buttons all the way from the neckline to the hem. And I definitely wouldn't have put on lipstick.

So, there we were, staring at each other, too embarrassed to talk about the past or future. God, it was awful. All I could think about was how I hadn't invited my own mother to my wedding. At the time, I thought it was the right decision; that is, until the day of my wedding. All of a sudden, I felt like the worst daughter. But even so, did I invite her to visit us? No. Did I go and visit her in Aspen Bluff? No. Did I mail her a photograph? Yes. It took me a year to put a stamp on it, and another year to get the damn thing into the letter box. Who knows if I ever would've mailed it, except for my brother noticing it tucked inside the doorframe and offering to post it? That letter was what got my mother on the train and to my doorstep. Still, never in a thousand years, did I imagine she'd arrive with a baby in her arms. "Were you all night on the train?" I asked my mother.

"*Si, che viaggio!* Ma Maria Violetta sleep good on train. All that shuga-shuga is good for baby."

The afternoon sun poured in through our front window. I was glad my mother hadn't shown up on a gloomy day. She stood up and took a spin around the room, holding the baby in one arm. She touched my curtains, rubbing the fabric between her fingers. One thing about Mamma, she was poor, but she knew quality when it came to fabric. Then she stopped to look at the pictures on the wall, first the little seashell picture, then the print of a cottage in the woods, then finally the Assumption of Mary—a dozen cherubs hovering at the Madonna's feet, lifting her up into heaven.

When I was a girl, my mother had Italian prayer cards tacked everywhere. We had Our Lady of Perpetual Help, where baby Jesus's sandal is falling off, *Santa Maria di Angeli* with stars circling Mary's head, Our Lady of the Seven Sorrows with swords piercing her heart, and those were just the ones I remembered.

My mother said a Hail Mary while staring at the Assumption picture. Then she sat, looked down and said, "Is nice rug. You make?"

"It's made by a Finnish lady. They're good weavers."

"What is Finnish?"

"You know, people from Finland.

"Next time, I make for you. You no spend money for rug."

"They buy from our shop, and it's good to buy from them, too. You know, I scratch your back, you scratch mine."

"Never hear like this."

The emperor was wearing no clothes, but I wasn't going to be the one to say so. Sooner or later, my mother would have to tell me where the baby came from.

"You feed Maria?" my mother offered.

"That's her name?"

"Maria Violetta."

"Big name for a little girl."

"You want feed baby?" she asked, pulling a bottle out from her pocket. Even though I didn't have a baby of my own at the time, I knew what a baby bottle was supposed to look like, and this did not look normal. It had a long black nipple on it. She was using a goat feeding bottle!

"Maybe later. She's not used to me. But I'll warm it up for you."

"Wait," my mother said, twisting off the cap to take a whiff. "Is sour. You have milk from goat?"

"Why not regular milk?"

"She no have before. It give for her the gas."

"I don't have goat milk."

"Is okay, I make *latte di mandorla*."

"I can make almond milk," I offered, "but that might give her gas too."

"Is no problem. You have the cloth? Cheesecloth? To take away lump."

"Yes," I said, working my way into the kitchen.

The baby's fussing got more agitated, while my mother shouted orders at me. "And made little bit sweet! No too much!"

"Yes, I know how to make it. You forget we had it as kids," I called out from the kitchen.

"Make fast. She hungry. And make boil water for nipple."

"Yes, Mamma!"

Five minutes later, I handed the bottle to my mother, and she squirted a few drops onto her wrist to test the temperature. "*Ha un buon appetito*," my mother said, popping the giant black nipple into the baby's mouth.

"I can see that."

"*Hai capito ancora italiana?*" my mother said, asking if I still understood Italian. I did more or less. Not that we ever spoke it in the house. But I was used to hearing it from shop customers, so I kept my ears tuned to the language.

"I understand. Most of the time."

"Maria Violetta, she no trouble in this house. Madonna Maria close by, make piccolo bambina happy," my mother said. The Madonna picture was the thing that made my mother feel at home; not the pink and rose floral curtains, not the doilies under every lamp, not all my efforts to keep the place neat as a pin. Only the Madonna counted for something.

"Where is you brother?" my mother asked, moving the baby onto her shoulder for a burp. This was the first time my brother was mentioned.

"Wasn't he up to see you?" I asked.

"I no see Nuccio long time. At you papà's funeral," Mamma said.

I'd heard it from my brother's own lips that he'd been up to see her. So why would she say otherwise? "Everything good with you brother?" she asked.

"Yes, it's just...didn't you know? He's a priest now."

"A priest!" Mamma said. My mother started thumping the baby's back with a little too much punch.

"I'm sorry no one told you," I said. "He took Holy Orders a year before I got married." I

closed the curtains, hoping it might help the baby—and my mother—stay calm.

"What church he go?"

"He's in Upsala. It's a few hours west. I could get a message to him."

"No! No message!" my mother said.

"Okay, but you don't have to snap at me," I said. Then I felt bad because I could see my Mamma was upset. She laid the baby on the sofa and dug in her skirt pocket for something to dab her nose with. I found a hanky for her. "Mamma, I'm sorry we never got up to see you."

"I talka to you every day. Every day, I sit in chair and tell you all the thing."

"Really?"

"Is true."

"That's funny, because a few times I swore I heard your voice." I wasn't telling a lie. For years after I left Aspen Bluff, I heard my mother's voice, usually just as I was falling asleep. It only happened maybe once or twice a year, and I always told myself it was a dream.

Mamma was going to say something else about it, but just then, Renzo walked through the door. He took one look at us, and waved me into the kitchen. "Your mother?"

"Who else would it be? It's too early for *Old Befana!*"

"She's got a lot of nerve showing up on our doorstep. And what's the story with the baby?" he hissed, like a mean old cat. "Did it come with your mother?"

"Not *it! She!* She's not even two months old. So sweet."

"Carmela, to you every baby is sweet." That was a low blow, and he knew it. "Aw heck," he said, "I'm sorry. I shouldn't a said that. You know what the doc said. We just have to give it more time."

"I'm the only one, Renzo, the only one of the girls I grew up with, who doesn't have a baby. I'm in my twenties already."

"What about Carol?"

"She's a nun! I don't want to talk about this. Can we please just visit with my mother?"

"The same mother you didn't want anything to do with, uh?"

"I feel bad we didn't invite her to the wedding. Father Bellettini even talked to me—"

"Call him *Nuccio*. It's crazy how you call him *Father.*"

"Don't you know anything about respect?"

"Just because your brother's a goddamn priest, that don't mean he gets my respect."

"Not so loud!"

Renzo had something against Nuccio. Maybe it was because I insisted my brother marry us. Renzo wanted an old priest with one foot in the grave to do the wedding mass. I guess he was a friend of the family, but I put my foot down. After that, we could never agree when it came to my brother.

"My brother studies the Bible," I went on to say. "He knows things, okay?"

"I know things, too."

"He quotes the Bible. Can you quote? I don't think so."

"I say the *Our Father*."

"Stand on Pearl Street in front of the Madame's brothel, anyone coming or going can recite the Lord's Prayer. What does the Bible have to say about forgiveness? Tell me that," I said.

"Turn the other cheek which, if you ask me, is stupid. Some asshole wallops me in the face and I'm going to give him the other side of my face to make a mess of it, too?"

"Turning the other cheek, that's a symbol for something. A symbol, Renzo."

I swung around to put on a fresh pot of coffee for my mother, but one thing about Renzo was he always had to have the last word. "So, what's the symbol mean, uh? Tell me that, Sister-Carmela-know-it-all."

By now, Renzo was almost breathing down my neck. I slowly turned to face him, saying, "How should I know? That's why you ask a priest."

"Funny how your brother, who quotes the Bible sunup to sundown, how many times has he been to see your mother? Uh? How many times has he turned his cheek? Not too damn many."

"He went to see her last year. But you know what's funny? Mamma doesn't remember."

"Because he didn't go, is why. So, what happened to seven times seventy-seven?"

"He did mail my letter, though."

"What letter?"

"The letter I wrote her. I sent Mamma a wedding photo, and a bit of money."

"That's it! That's why she's here! She's after our money."

"Don't be ridiculous. It was the card that brought her here," I said. "And anyway, I've been thinking about going up to see her."

"Oh yeah? When were you planning on telling me?" Renzo asked, lazily leaning back on the

kitchen counter like he was the cat that swallowed the canary. What makes short Italian men so damn sure of themselves?

"I said thinking about it. Do I have to tell you every thought? And that's not the point, anyway. The point is she's here! Sitting in our living-room!"

"With a baby! I'll bet ten dollars she took it from a farm woman who was running around and got herself pregnant."

"Not so loud! Can we please join her? Is that going to kill you?" I opened the kitchen door, wanting to end our spat.

"Maybe," Renzo said. "It might. I'll check my pulse after ten minutes to make sure I'm still alive."

"Very funny," I said, slipping by him with the pot of fresh coffee.

My husband's nose was out of joint, but he did sit with us. By the time we were all together, including the baby asleep on the chesterfield, I was wishing I'd spiked the coffee, just to lighten up the atmosphere. "Mamma, the shop downstairs where Renzo works? One day, his zio says we can buy it from him."

"Questo appartamento? This belong to you zio, too?"

"Yeah, it's in the family," said Renzo, saying his first two words to my mother. "But I got no say where the money goes. You know what I'm saying? It's not like we got a mouth full of gold teeth."

I shot Renzo a look. I knew what he was alluding to, but it seemed to breeze right by my mother. "What part of Italy you come from?" my mother asked Renzo, just as friendly as can be.

"I'm not Calabrese, if that's what you're asking."

"You have problem with Calabrese?"

"I wouldn't be married to this one here if I did," he said, pointing to me. I stuck my tongue out at him. It was very childish of me, I know, but sometimes with Renzo, I couldn't help myself.

"Why you no speak Italian?" my mother asked. "You too, Carmela. Why you no speak?"

"We're Canadians," Renzo said.

"You no speak, you forget," Mamma said.

I could see where this was going. My husband and mother weren't going to agree on anything. "You like my curtains, Mamma? I made them myself."

"Is good. I'm happy to see my girla make nice thing."

"So, what'd you do? Take the overnight train?" Renzo asked Mamma. Was Renzo trying to pick a fight, or being polite? I wasn't sure.

"*Si, si.*"

"Sleep much?" Renzo asked my mother.

"Maybe two hour, maybe three."

"You should go for a rest," Renzo said.

"Yes, Mamma," I said. "I'll watch the baby. You must be tired."

"If she cry, give the bottle."

"Don't worry about anything," I said, lifted the sleeping baby into my arms for the first time.

"She's cute as a button. Look, Renzo!"

"All babies are the same. Curled up like snails, but they make a whole lot more noise."

"Go, go, Mamma. Take a nap. The bedroom's just down the hall."

"*Seconda porta a sinistra,*" Renzo added. When Renzo spoke Italian to my mother, I knew he'd softened up.

"You see? You speak good Italian," Mamma said, before

heading down the hall.

The baby did start to fuss. I gave her more almond milk from the strange bottle and she took it, no problem. *I guess, to a baby, milk is milk. What does it matter what the nipple looks like?* After the baby fed, she began to complain again. I didn't want the crying to wake up my mother, so I decided to take the her outside. But first I had to find proper baby clothes, not the pilled woolen dress—probably made from an old sweater—that she was wearing.

I sent Renzo out to get goat's milk, as I knew the Italian butcher sometimes carried it. As soon as Renzo disappeared, I dug out a box from the hall closet where I'd been saving baby things: blankets, sweaters, diapers. The doctor had told me I just needed to relax about it, find other interests, but I couldn't. Every time my monthlies came, I cried my eyes out. So, if I happened to have a box of baby clothes hidden for that hopeful day, what was the harm?

For Maria Violetta, I chose a flowered cotton dress and a rose blanket. Once I got her changed and dressed, I took her out the back steps where I wasn't likely to run into anyone. The last thing I wanted was a bunch of nosy-bodies asking me questions. If there's one thing I've learned over the years from running a shop, people love gossip more than blueberry pie. The baby stayed awake while Mamma slept, but to keep her happy, I had to walk up and down the back lane about a hundred times. Renzo came back with the quart of milk and kept me company for a while in the back lane. It was an excuse for him to have three cigarettes in a row, but I didn't mind. After maybe an hour, I glanced up at the window to see Mamma waving at us.

"I no stay long," my mother told us. We were inside now, sipping glasses of sherry. Maria-

Violetta was asleep in my mother's arms.

"But Mamma, you just got here. Stay for a week, at least," I said.

Renzo cleared his throat as if to say, "Not over my dead body." I ignored him. He picked up a newspaper and buried his head in it.

"Carmella, you get for me *un ago e filo*?" she asked, making sewing motions with her hands.

"What colour thread?"

"*Nero, blu, viola.* All colour is good."

I traded off a needle and thread for the sleeping baby. I watched my mother stitch three buttons onto the corners of her old shawl. *It's going to take more than buttons to perk up that old shawl*, I thought. It was the strangest shawl I'd ever seen with its odd long shape and erratic pattern.

"The colours are beautiful," I said, thinking I should say something nice.

"My friend, her name Maria, she weave."

"I'll be down in the shop, if anyone needs me," Renzo blurted out. "The shelves don't get stocked by themselves." Renzo never worked on a Sunday, but I wasn't about to argue with him.

I knew, once Renzo left, this could be my one chance to ask about the baby. I tipped back my last drop of sherry, and blurted out, "Mamma, how are you going to raise a baby? You can barely take care of yourself."

"Maybe we talk," Mamma whispered, even though Renzo was long gone.

"First, you have to tell me, whose baby is it?" I hated to put her on the spot, but I didn't know when we'd be alone together again.

"Okay, I tella you."

When my mother finished her story, I said, "I need to talk to Renzo."

A minute later, I sailed down the two flights of stairs, finding Renzo in the stock room sitting on a sack of oats, smoking. "I need to talk to you about the baby," I said.

"You mean the one up there in our apartment? The one no one knows who the mother is?

Or the father, for that matter."

"It's my mother's baby," I said, deciding not to beat around the bush.

"Come on."

"A trapper spent a few nights with her, and she never saw him again." I thought I'd tell Renzo the whole thing, rather than spoon feed it in bits and pieces.

"That's what she told you? She's *pazzo*. No way she's the mother."

"Look how attached she is to the baby! Of course, she is."

"How old is she?"

"Not even two months."

"Not the baby, your Mamma!"

"Forty-eight, maybe forty-nine. It can happen."

"No, no, no, no. That story 's got more holes than swiss cheese. First of all, if it is her baby, which I doubt, that trapper spent more than a few nights with her. Maybe a month. Or two months. Maybe all winter long."

"Think what you want, but that's what she told me."

"I don't believe it's hers."

"She's not an *it*!"

"I just hope your mother doesn't think she's moving in with us."

I guess Renzo was afraid my penniless mother would invade our neat-as-a-pin apartment and upset our neat-as-a-pin lives. I wanted to scratch his eyes out for being so selfish. But if I didn't want to ruin my chances, I needed to play my cards just right. "That tiny baby, that's my half sister," I said, trying to coax him into an ounce of sympathy.

"*If* she's telling the truth."

"Look at all the things we do for your mamma!"

"But my mother's normal. This person, is she even your mother?"

"Oh my God! I know my own mother! What do you take me for?"

"Look, Carmela, we're married what? Not even two years. I'm not dying to inherit your mother *and* a baby."

"I inherited your family! I chose all your sisters for my bridesmaids, even Isabella, who bossed me around that whole day. 'Your veil's crooked. Who did your hair? Why aren't you wearing earrings?' On and on and on. But did I complain to you? Say what you want, my Mamma's welcome to stay for two days or two weeks or two months!" Not waiting for Renzo to argue back, I charged up to the apartment. When I stepped through the door, I saw the baby sleeping on our stuffed chair, like a tiny pearl wrapped up inside her blue blanket. And my mother was singing a lullaby.

"Mamma?" I whispered, "I was thinking, maybe, you don't have to answer now. But if I can get Renzo on my side, I'd like to raise up my sister. You're getting older now and—"

"*Madonna Maria. Jesu Christo!*"

I wasn't sure if she was happy or upset with me. "So... it's okay or not okay?"

"Carmela, you make you Mamma so happy," Mamma said, throwing her arms around me.

"Wait, wait, wait. Don't get too excited. I have to get Renzo to agree. He's in a mood right now."

"Renzo, he's no problem. He say yes. Maybe no today. Maybe no tomorrow. But before moon is full, he take baby. I make prayer when moon is big," she said. "Strong prayer on big moon."

It brought a smile to my face that my mother was still hanging onto old superstitions. "Remember on the new moon, how you sang that song and put pennies in our hands? And didn't you put dried bean shells all around our beds to keep away bad spirits?"

"No, no, is no for bad spirit. Why you think for that?"

"What's it for then?"

"To keep away beetle bug."

"So, the beans have nothing to do with the moon?"

"No, is different thing. Inside bean shell, is soft, yes? *Ma*, is like sword for bug. Bug crawl in shell and cut, cut, cut. In Canada, when trouble with bedbug, I give bean shell. All the lady, they grow my bean after that."

I knew Renzo was going to burst through that door any minute. "Mamma, we should talk," I said, "about the baby."

"You take Maria Violetta. All the thing is good."

"Even if Renzo says it's okay, it's complicated. Have you registered the birth?"

"No!" she shouted, "I no make government paper! They try put me to jail again!"

Mamma hated anything to do with the government, or filling out forms, or anyone in a uniform. I tried to explain to her that it wasn't a crime to have a baby, and that I'd take care of the paperwork, but she kept carrying on. "Mamma, listen to me! Listen! We have to register the birth. I can't pretend I found a baby on my doorstep."

"*Sì, sì*! You say you found! *Una buona 'idea*!"

"I can't. They'll take the baby and put her in an orphanage. They'll give her to some other couple."

"I no give to stranger!" Mamma said, making the sign of the cross, and shaking her head, like she'd just heard somebody died.

"Calm down, Mamma. We'll tell them you had a baby out of wedlock."

"What is?"

"It means you don't have a husband."

"I do! You papà! Salvatore!"

"Yes, but Mamma, you don't have a living husband." My mother still thought of my papà as her husband, even though he'd been gone almost ten years. She lost everything the day of Papà's funeral, including her husband and children. No wonder she allowed a bush worker into her bed, and got herself into this boat.

I was glad she'd told me the truth. In truth, I had no idea if they'd let me adopt. Maybe they'd take my mother and put her in a mental asylum. Or maybe they'd remove the baby from our custody. But we had to register the birth, that much I knew, because if it was left up to my mother, that little baby would've been hidden away like Rapunzel all her life.

"Oh my God, oh my God. You promise they no put me to jail?"

"I promise. But you have to register the birth. It's the one thing you have to do," I said.

Mamma was beginning to trust me. "What she call you? When she grow up and talka?" my mother asked. "*Mamma*, yes? She call me *Nonna*, and you *Mamma*?"

"Of course. What did you think? That I'd tell her the truth? It would be so confusing."

That evening, I emptied out my sweater drawer, lined it with a soft blanket, and turned it into a baby bed. My heart was cracking open like a big walnut. I hadn't said a rosary in a long time, probably not since my First Communion. But that night, alone in the unlit kitchen, I prayed the rosary to *Santa Maria Assunta*. Mother Mary would have to help us. Look how many times my mamma went down on her knees to pray Hail Marys. Okay, maybe my mother was superstitious, but if it came down to chanting to the moon or praying to Mother Mary, Mary would win out every time.

I waited for three days before mentioning anything more to Renzo. He was the one who brought it up. "When's your mother planning to take the train back?" he asked.

"Well, she can't raise that baby alone, can she?" was my response. That got us talking about adoption. The thing that bothered Renzo most was the idea of people finding out I was raising my mother's baby. He thought the gossip might get around and that people might start crossing the street to buy their eggs and cheese. I told him, "Fine, we'll say we adopted her. I'm sure everyone knows I'm a barren woman. The whole damn world knows by now." Renzo came around, on the condition that my mother didn't move in with us. But Mamma was set on going back to Aspen Bluff, as she thought the police would take the baby away from us if she stuck around.

The city clerks were nincompoops. They tried to sniff out details about the father and about how old Mamma was. I guess their lives were as dull as pea soup. I wanted to say, "If you want a juicy story, try reading Captain Billy's Whiz Bang. Leave my mother alone!" Finally, the papers were signed, and Maria Violetta became our first child. The next day, Mamma took the train home. I gave her a carpet bag stuffed full of dried beans and seeds, dates, almonds, and packaged flower seeds. She left behind her woven shawl, maybe on purpose or maybe by accident. I was planning to throw it out, it was so ratty, but I couldn't do it. I washed it by hand and put it away in the closet. That's where it stayed until I gave it to my granddaughter, Lotta, just before she took that teaching job.

I told Lotta everything. I explained how my mother was actually her grandmother and not her great-grandmother. "So Nonna, I'm confused. You're my aunt?" she asked.

"I raised up my sister, so that makes me your aunt. But you should still call me *Nonna*."

Lotta was very quiet, then said, "Nonna, I don't mean to be rude, but it doesn't add up." I couldn't believe my ears. Finally, after decades of stuffing the secret inside, I told someone. And she didn't believe me.

"What part doesn't add up?"

"Well, for one thing, how old would your Mamma have been? Wouldn't she be too old to have a baby?"

"She was in her late forties. It can happen."

And then Lotta said the craziest thing. She said, "Did you ever think, Nonna, that maybe your mother was hiding something from you? That maybe it was never her baby?"

"Why would she hide that from her own daughter?" I asked.

"Maybe there were people who shouldn't know, who might hurt the baby if they knew."

"Lotta! You read too many books. It's simple. My mother had an illegitimate baby and couldn't raise her. I'm not saying we should all go around having babies with strangers, but it happens! Okay? It happened to your *Bisnonna.*"

"But my great-grandfather was the love of her life. You always said he was."

"Yes, but he died young. And people get lonely, especially all alone in the tree bluffs." Those were my words, but inside my heart, that old question came up about why Mamma, with all her difficulties and too poor to raise a baby, why would she let this happen? While I was thinking this in my head, Lotta started to tell me about a family she'd met in Hurkett where she was teaching—how close she felt to them. There was a strange letter that the one brother wrote to the other telling about a baby who supposedly died, an Irish baby.

"And the baby's name is Mary Violet!" Lotta said, finishing up her story.

"So," I said.

"That's my mother's name!"

"No, it isn't."

"Close enough."

"Mary Violet and Maria Violetta are two different names," I said. "Mary Violet is English and Maria Violetta is Italian. English baby, Irish baby, not the same thing."

What Lotta said next, I couldn't shrug off. "Nonna, I did some searching around, and more than just the names are the same. They were born on the same day, in the same year!" While Lotta was talking, my chest was buzzing like there were a hundred bees inside me.

"Where?" I snapped. "Fishing around where?" When I went to take a sip of coffee, I spilled some cold coffee onto my lap. Lotta could see I was rattled.

"Maybe you're right, Nonna. Maybe it's just all a big coincidence. I didn't mean to upset

you," she said, running to fetch a cloth to wipe up the spill.

Lotta felt badly, but it was too late. I felt that seed of doubt going deep inside of me. "You can believe what you want, Lotta," I said, "but be careful who you talk to. You know what a Pandora's box is? Well, that's what this is."

"I won't say anything to anyone," Lotta said, "especially not my mother. I owe her an apology anyway, so now's not the time."

I've had a few weeks now to stew over this business. I don't know if Lotta is right or wrong about this Irish baby with the same birth date, and part of me never wants to know, but it's a worrisome thought. At night now, before I go to sleep, I can almost hear Renzo laughing at me from the other side, saying, "I never did believe that crazy story of the lumberjack and your mother, not for a minute. I knew she was hiding something!" My Renzo, he always did try and get the last word.

CHAPTER FIFTEEN

Beyond the Veil

Fiorella:

"Carmela, you old now, older than me when I come visit with little *bambina*. Now you talka to me. So many year, you no talka. Now you say, when you all alone and the tear come, 'Mamma,' you say, 'tell me what really happen. I need to know.' Okay, so I tell you. But maybe in morning, when sun is come up, you think, *Mamma is dead. She can no talka to me. Justa dream*. But is no dream. Is you Mamma talka to you. For long time, I have to put lock on secret. Now the lock broke and secret come out.

"When Maria Violetta come born. I right away give the medicine. My heart, it go fast like bird. Is no easy to do, but I have to do. Everything I have ready. I give three drop, drop I make with the tea, *il latte di Papàvero*. When you give, it go to blood fast and no pain. What if I give too strong, the drop? What if I give too weak? I know is danger, *il latte di Papàvero*. I know because wife of farmer give to bambini. Is for to help *bambini* sleep when time come to pick up the crop. What you call when all the people work hard for this? Harvest. When big harvest, everybody go out to work long day in field. The mother, they take rag and wet with milk of poppy. They put close to baby's face, so when baby wake up and cry, they suck on rag. Put back to sleep. Sometime, those *bambini* sleep two day, maybe three day.

"Every time harvest come, the wife of farmer ask for me to make. Justa you soak and crush seed of poppy and it come like milk. I tell to the Mamma never, never, never to give to *neonato*, new baby. This tea very danger. No big danger for baby three-month, six-month, eight-month, but for *neonata*, is very danger. I know already about this medicine from *vecchia rugosa*—old lady from *Jugoslavia*. She show me all the thing, how to make. But when Maria Violetta come born, this time, I play with big danger. The clock, it no go all around the circle, not even one time. But I promise to take *la piccola bambina* to my house. No leave *bambina* with husband of Maria. How else I can do this?

"After I give the drop, I tell midwife lady sad thing. '*Il neonato è morto*,' I say. She no believe. She listen for baby heart with funny thing that look like horn. Midwife look different now, no the same. She no like me, she never like me, but she look different for me. After, she tell doctor how baby come stillborn. He sign paper. Doctor no argue. Nobody like to make fight with Signora Watts. I say to that midwife lady, 'I take *bambina* to my house. Okay? Put in little box and make to bury. Is better.' She say is okay I do this. Husband, he no care. He no want to look at *bambina*. The midwife, she go to tell Maria's boy, the big boy, to take me home right away fast.

"Still, is big problem for me. All the family think *bambina* is dead. I put *bambina* in deep sleep, same kind of sleep like story. You know how girla get finger prick from *filarello*? '*La Bella Addormentata*' is how you say in Italian. You know, she no wake up until prince come. But no prince coming to wake up Maria's baby. I think maybe she never wake up, maybe I make *il latte di papàvero* too strong, maybe little baby go with angel now. All the thing I think when Maria's boy take me home. He drive like crazy-man. Stone, mud, all go fly from wheel. I think, *Mio Dio! Now we all die on road.*

"When Maria's boy stoppa the horse, I want to go fast on path. But that boy, he talka to me.

He say his Mamma have name pick out. Maria Violetta he tell me. He no say like that, he say *Inglese* name—Mary Violet. Is dark sky and light from moon make boy look heartbreak, like all his trouble now paint on face. I feel sorry. He lose Mamma and baby sister too. He say, 'Why you take my sister?' I say, 'Sorry, big sorry for you and you brothers.' But he ask more time why I take baby. I tell him, 'You Papà, he have to bury Mamma. Too much sad to put baby in ground.'

"I run. Is good to have moon in sky. Is no full but is coming to full. I get home and make match for lamp. On table, I see letter. Never I go to post office in ten year, but on table, I see letter. I no think about letter. I have medicine ready and quick open. It make strong smell, *chiodi di garofano*, ammonia too. I put under nose of baby Maria Violetta, but she no wake up. I wait. I no see baby chest move, I no see breath come in, breath out. What I can do? I try three more time, then she cry. So happy. My heart, it go from heavy brick to feather.

"*Bambina*, she is awake, but I have to feed something now. She white like snow. I scared maybe she no live. I have the goat milk and try give. Nipple too big, baby cry, hungry too. So, I put milk in dropper, and drop on lip of baby. Oh! Good taste! Now she stoppa the tear. I give more drop, but is still big problem. *Bambina*, she is weak. What I can give to make *bambina* strong? Only one thing—foremilk. Is like gold, this milk. Better than gold because you can no drink gold. But where I find this? I have to go to farmer who raise the goat. Is good time for this, in March. Always the farmer mate doe in fall time. After five month, baby goat is coming.

"When new kid in barn, that is only place to find gold milk. But farmer, he no give to me. No, no, no. He no give to anyone. And if farmer see baby, he tell wife, wife tell more wife, now everybody know how Fiorella have baby. Then husband of Maria come to take Maria Violetta away. And promise to Maria broke.

"I take sheet off bed, break in two. One part I wrap *bambina, vicino al mio corpo*. I put big winter coat so baby no get cold. I put molasses in jar. I take dry hare meat for pocket. Lantern. Now I have all the thing to go to farmer place in dark sky. I go. I no think about me, I only think about *bambina*. I have to put on the snowshoe. Some part is okay, snow flat and I go fast. Other part take for me all the strength. I open coat and look to see *bambina*. She sleep good.

"When I come to *granaio del contadino* after long mile, I scared. *What if farmer dog bark? Try to bite? Wake up farmer?* I put meat in hand and wait. If dog come, I try make friend with dog. I wait. I no breathe, justa wait, see if dog come. Nothing. Justa quiet. I open door of barn, *gli animali* make little bit noise. 'Who come here? Who open door?' *gli animali* say. I find nail to put lantern. Ah, now I see all the thing in the barn. Right away, I find goat. Two goat, ma, no baby kid. Then I see in corner, baby goat. Is good luck, no? My heart, it go ticka, ticka, ticka, fast.

"All my life I have goat. Goat *eccitabile*. What you call in English? Excite. That good word for nanny goat. So, I talka nice to goat to make *tranquillo*. I find bucket, justa small bucket of feed, mix up with molasses from jar. Make very tasty, lot of flavour. Now I shut harness. The goat, she want to eat black molasses. Now I have to work fast. Bottom of pail fill with yellow milk. I no take chance. I make only five ounce, maybe six. Is okay because Maria Violetta have little stomach, justa like one fat grape.

"I go home. Is dark now. Moon go away behind cloud.

Bambina cry. She hungry now. I get home, and right away put gold milk in bottle. *Bambina* no like nipple. I have to put gold milk on finger and she suck finger. I do again. When she happy, I pop bottle in mouth and sit with baby in arm. Rocking, rocking. She sleep, I sleep, she wake up, I wake up, give more milk. She get heavy in arm, *ma* I no put down. She sleep long hour but still I no put down. When light come in window, I think about letter. I open. Surprise! Picture of you, Carmela, in wedding dress. I cry to see picture. You send money too.

"After Maria Violetta drink all the gold milk, I milka my goat. I have already this goat more than one year. All the time when I go to barn, I tell goat in nice voice, 'You no dry off. Okay? You have to make milk for *bambina* now.' That goat, she listen. Now all the day is good with *bambina*. *Una picolla rosa*. She want always I hold her. Is okay because I like. I make *culla* for her. I think you call *cradle* in English. I take off from rocking chair, and put wood box on that bend wood. Oh, that baby, she love to rock. I do all the thing for her. Justa cook little bit every day, make some soup, bread. Make cheese from goat milk. And rock Maria Violetta.

"I think maybe Maria Violetta afraid with no Mamma, so I sing. Oh, she love the song. Nobody hear baby cry, only justa bird and gopher and me. But what happen if somebody find Maria Violetta? They take away, put for me to jail, call me *kidnapper*. I have to find new place for baby before she get too big. I think about all the time. I have bad dream somebody come and take away Maria Violetta.

"Every day, I say to God, 'Where I can take Maria Violetta?' One day, He answer to me. That day, *bambina* have six-week-old. I do all the thing God tell me to do. I pick up picnic basket in shed. This one have wood top. Is good for baby to sleep, no? I pack some good thing to eat, goat milk for baby. I'm putting button in pocket, same button Maria give me first time she come to visit. I'm putting rosary in pocket, *bambina* in basket, shawl to keep warm. I walka to *la stazione ferroviaria* when sky is coming to dark. Ticket man, he say, 'What you have in basket?' I say, 'Old cat. She no like people.' He say, 'Cat have name?' I think fast what is good name for cat and tell him 'Cinder'. He say, 'Why I no surprise you have black cat?'

"When I get on train, I look here, look there, but no one get on from Aspenna Bluffa. Only one family already on train, lot of children. They no care about old lady with new baby. Then I get off in Winnipeg. I have letter in pocket from you, Carmela, with name of city. They give for me ticket to Port Arthur. On train, a big man is coming to look at ticket, he see baby. He say, 'That you granddaughter?' I say 'Yes.' He tell me he put milk in cold place so it no go sour. When baby get hungry, he can bring. Justa to call him when baby cry. Then after maybe two hour, I call. He come right away with jar. Inside is warm milk. That good man.

"When I come to Port Arthur, I feel scare. How I'm coming to you house, Carmella? Only one time before I see city, when I come from Italy. That time I have bambino too. You, Carmela, you justa *neonata*! You no born in Italy. You no born in Canada. You born on ship — you and Nuccio. When *bambina* born on ship, is no like other *bambini*. This baby you have to rocka all the time, rocka, rocka, justa like ship. For one year, I tie string to *la culla* and all night I pull string so you and you brother no cry. Is very tired for me.

"Okay, so again, I go to city. Again, I have *bambina*. Again, I feel scare. If big wind come, it blow me and *bambina* away. I have to hold feet strong on ground. Lot of horses pushing cart, going here, going there. Machine too—*la machina*. Not too many I see. It go zip around fast, take off toes if step on road. I pick up letter from pocket and I'm justa looking, not thinking what I can do, justa looking. Then someone calling to me—*uno sconosciuto*. 'Hey lady! he calling to me. Pretty girla with man so I think is okay to talka to him. 'I go this way?

That way?' I say. 'Wait here,' he say. He come with *la machina* right away. I go in back with baby. When he drive, road is like dance floor, is smooth. I like. Then he show off, big man have to drive fast. I scream. That pretty girla in seat beside man, she laugh. I justa hold Maria Violetta close and say to Mary, '*Ave Maria. Pieno di grazie.*' All the way to you house, I pray.

"Carmella, I know is shock when you see me. Still, you nice. You make the coffee, give for me bed to sleep. I want to tell you all the thing. I think it come out of mouth, like big waterfall. But you husband, when he come up the stair and make sour face to me, I think, *He make trouble if I tell true.* If I tell to you, *Baby come from Irish lady who die*, maybe Renzo, he no want baby. If I tell to you, *Baby is you sister*, okay that make different kind of story. Maybe you husband, he no make big fight about this. I go this way, I go that way. True story? Falsa? The Bible say to tell true. What is true, uh? I mix together true and falsa. You forgive you Mamma for this, no?

"Maria Violetta, she come from Irish lady, but she go to you. You make good Mamma to Maria Violetta. Now you know all the thing, Carmella. And Lotta, she know too. She smart girla. She put puzzle here, puzzle there, and all the picture come out. Is good to have true picture to keep in you heart."

Mary:

Once, when I was a girl, my aunt took me to the circus. She told me that, if it weren't for me charming the customs man, we'd both be back in Ireland. After a year of penny pinching, she'd saved up enough and we took the train to Winnipeg. I didn't see any dancing bears like my granddad talked about, but we did eat candy as airy and light as a cloud, every colour of the rainbow too. My favourite thing was the flying trapeze act, the girls wearing white sequined outfits and wings of red feathers. They looked so free, as if nothing could ever colour their world dark. Maybe they had a cruel ringmaster or any number of trials, but once a day, they climbed up a ladder and took to flying through the air, as graceful and strong as God's own angels.

Every night while we sleep, we're after making friends with death. And every day as we go about our chores and chatter—whether we're circus girls or ordinary people—we sense the veil lifting, if only for a split second. It happens more often than we think; quick as a firefly and our hearts are lifted. Then darkness returns, and we begin to doubt if we ever did feel that spark of joy. We shillyshally between shadows and light, too often settling into a place of shadow.

For me, I latched onto motherhood as my place of goodness and, for my children, I'd do it all again. I'd board the boat from Ireland infested with typhus, I'd hold the hands of my dying mother and father and sisters and brothers, and I'd do my best to please my dour aunt who smiled as often as lightning strikes the North Pole. And, though it be shocking to some, I'd fall in love with James all over again. In our courting days, he had the look of adventure to capture a maid's fancy. Whenever he came within a mile of any horse, his eyes lit up much like my own father's.

Some said of me, "She burnt her coal, and didn't warm herself." Had I the pluck to leave James, where would I've gone without kin, and my only friend as poor as a church mouse? It would've been easier to draw in the tide than make my way alone in the world. And though we had four children together, James only counted three. He was all for denying the existence of Mary Violet, and forbade my sons to speak of *the bastard child*. He cried out to God, saying, "My Mary was a good wife, until she went off to befriend the Italian widow. And to think my Mary's gone and the witch lives! What did I do to deserve this?"

When I first arrived in Aspen Bluff, I felt no urge to meet the Italian lady. It was only when I got spooked by our cow, Cattail, who nearly died, that I felt drawn up her path. Oh, how I treasured our visits, scarce as they were. Sometimes I wonder, why did I cotton on to Fiorella so? Was it because she also knew of the sting of heartbreak, as familiar to her as the frigid winds that crept through the walls of her rickety shack? Yet she didn't dwell on her woes. Sitting at her table, I heard about her days of sunshine; how when her children were still under foot, she made her famous *biscotti* for the church bazaars, kept her garden of healing herbs, and loved her Salvatore so.

I wasn't able to see Fiorella as often as I liked, but each time I darkened her door, I reminded her of the promise she'd made me. Come birthing time, I was never so glad to see her face. I said to myself, "I'll face whatever God puts before me. If the midwife tries to come between us, she'll have as much influence as a feather in the wind." All the same, Mrs. Watts did have a good heart. When I died, she cried out, "Dear God! I fear it's too late. She's gone and there's nothing to be done."

The midwife pulled the soiled sheets out from under me. She cleaned me up with a basin of warm water, and floated a clean sheet over me. She tucked it all around me, like an Egyptian mummy, with only my face showing. All the while, Fiorella sat, holding the infant with a cold stare that had come into her eyes. Mrs. Watts didn't seem to notice. As if she'd saved up words since the day she was born, she began rattling on about a girl named Farrah. 'Twas hard to tell if she was talking to herself or to God or to Fiorella.

"I've seen this very thing before," the midwife whispered. "Only once, years ago now, and by God I hoped it was the last. It was a girl from Nipigon. Farrah was her name. Weren't we all surprised to see Farrah floating up the aisle in a wedding dress far too tight around the middle? And it wasn't from eating too many cakes, I'll promise you that. Everyone was there, all up and down the ladder. Her father was a timber lord. You know how it is, everyone hates the rich, but offer a sandwich and a cup of tea in fancy china, and all is forgiven. Four months later, I was called in to deliver Farrah's *bairn*. I can't say why they didn't call up a doctor from the city. They had enough money for ten doctors. Of course, there's nothing a doctor could've done for her. The hindwater had gotten into her blood. There she was—married and buried inside of a year."

Fiorella didn't understand half of what the midwife was saying. Either way, she was paying little attention, as she had her own job to do. Fiorella pulled out from her pocket a glass vial and, with a quivering hand, she tipped the tiny vessel onto the lips of my baby. Stopping to make the sign of the cross, she dribbled one last drop onto my child's tongue.

All the while, Mrs. Watts kept on with her story. "Once Farrah went unconscious, it was quick. Just like our Mary here." The midwife paused to dig inside her skirt pocket for a few pennies, which she then placed over my eyes, saying, "Not a penny of hope."

"*Una tragedia.*" Fiorella said, talking for the first time.

"For once, I understand you."

"*Piove sul bagnato,*" Fiorella said. "First Mamma, now *bambina.*"

Until that moment, the midwife had been so busy fluttering over me like a moth at the light, she hadn't turned her eyes to the infant. Mrs. Watts shouted, "No! Not the infant too!"

"She stoppa the breathe."

"Did you suck the mucous from her?"

"What you think? I try everything."

"Give her to me!" The midwife wrenched my baby from Fiorella and began jostling her up and down, like she was churning butter. When that didn't help, she unswaddled Mary Violet and began rubbing her tiny spine. "Why didn't you say anything sooner?" she shouted at Fiorella, as if she were King

Solomon himself passing down judgment. "You let me rattle on about Farrah and her wedding dress...good God, and all this on the same day! In the same hour!"

"You try keep Mamma alive. I try keep *bambina* alive. You give baby to me, yes?"

Fiorella carried my slip of a girl to the bed where I lay, pulled back the sheet, and placed the tiny creature on my breast. Mrs. Watts was after picking up my baby, but Fiorella said, "No touch! Mamma and *bambina* together. Give for them a chance."

"What chance?" said the midwife. "What was the point in sending for the doctor? He'll only arrive to find them both gone. Dear God in heaven, who's going to give the news to Mr. Moore? Your English is dreadful. I suppose the wretched job lands on my shoulders. We have to put the infant in the bassinet, though. It'll be enough of a shock without seeing mother and child, one on top of the other. Where you foreigners get your morbid ideas is beyond me!" Mrs. Watts swished from the room, but not before reaching up to stop the hands of the mantle clock.

Fiorella picked up my baby, wrapped her in a cotton square, and placed her in the cradle. Just then, James burst into the room with Mrs. Watts close enough behind to be his shadow. When he saw my lifeless body, he turned on Fiorella, blaming her for my death. Once James took to the stairs, Fiorella offered to take the infant home and bury her. "There are rules about these things," Mrs. Watts said. "Don't you immigrants know anything? We'll need to examine the infant, for one thing."

"Signora Watts, no touch. Her and Mamma with the saint. Is no good to put off blanket, put on blanket."

"It's either I examine the baby, or ask the doctor when he arrives. Is that him now?" Mrs.

Watts said, swishing over to the window. "Yes, it's him."

Fiorella placed the baby in Mrs. Watts's arms, saying, "Do

now. Before doctor come."

The midwife placed a wooden horn on my infant's chest to listen for a heartbeat. In a flicker, her face changed expression. The midwife and Fiorella locked eyes for over a minute, neither of them speaking. The Scottish midwife held all the cards, while Fiorella's promise to me hung in the balance. Finally, Mrs. Watts spoke, with a voice heard only by Fiorella and the angels above, "So you'll take care of things from here?" Fiorella answered with a nod. Mrs. Watts went on to say. "Before you go anywhere, the doctor will need to issue a death certificate."

"You ask doctor for this?"

"It should be Mr. Moore to take care of it, but Lord knows, he's in a state. I suppose I'll do it."

"I go. *In quattro e quattr'otto!*"

"I'll have one of the boys take you home, you and the infant. I've never had a day like this, and pray to God, never will again."

As Mrs. Watts turned to leave, Fiorella called after her, "You try. You try everything."

"But all the effort in the world can't bring back the dead, can it?"

Now alone in the room, Fiorella wrapped my tiny baby in her shawl. 'Twas the shawl I'd woven with my own hands. On the night, months before, when I sat at Fiorella's loom with a rainbow of yarns twisting around my fingers, Mary Violet's destiny was settled. As if I knew then of her future, I spun song into the loom. If she learned to sing through her troubles, she'd be spared the curse of despair. If she learned to sing, she'd be shielded from the dark shadows dancing over the surface of the earth. *Keep singing, my sweet child*, my fingers told the loom, *keep singing*.

Once my baby was wrapped snugly in the warmth of the shawl, I thought Fiorella would dash out the door with the baby limp in her arms. I expected her to hurry down the road before night stole the daylight. But no, she went back to the chair and there she sat, baby in arms. She sang a lullaby song in her own language with a voice almost as deep as a man's, and not a sour note to be heard. If tenderness be gold, Fiorella was just then the richest woman alive.

My husband James, the true father of the infant, assumed that on that fateful night, Fiorella took the lifeless baby to her cabin in the bluffs. To be sure, he pictured how, in the murky light of dusk, *The Italian* dug a hole deep in the ground to keep away the coyotes, then placed our infant girl into the cold ground. Did he think to send Patrick or Thomas over to help bury the child? He didn't. If he had, the infant would've been discovered as alive, landing Fiorella in a prison cell.

James never once cast eyes on his daughter, Mary Violet, either by accident or by design —not on the day of her birth, or in the years to come. He knew nothing of her upbringing, how every morning, the child sang like a lark for an hour or more before hunger got the better of her. Even then, she waffled between fussing and singing, as if it broke her heart to be torn away from the pleasure of song. She was as Irish as a four-leaf clover, a clover amidst an olive grove.

Mary Violet, or Maria Violetta as the Italians named her, grew up with the smells of drying red peppers and simmering tomato sauce in the air. Sweet peas and snapdragons danced at her ankles in the garden. She was an orphan girl, cut off as she was from her brothers Thomas, Patrick and Faolan, but she didn't know it. Instead, Mary Violet was given an Italian garden of ten sisters and brothers.

Fiorella never breathed a word of the true story, that my infant girl was rescued from a father who drowned himself in a sea of whiskey. She spun a clever story with threads of copper and gold, and not the wisest woman from the mountaintops of Caherconree would know which threads were fine and which were false.

Mary Violet hardly brushed the doorstep of maidenhood when she gave birth to a child of her own. It's no surprise she passed on the joy of song to her daughters, especially Lotta. And it's well known where Lotta's voice took her—into the kitchen of her Uncle Faolan and her Auntie Primrose and all her cousins around her like a grand quilting frame, stitching together layers of the family quilt. It happened over time, a stitch here and a stitch there. Then, on that night, when Lotta listened to Faolan as he sang by Jerome's casket, Lotta knew. With a heart as open as the four winds and almost as fierce, Lotta found her kin that day. All the compasses in the world, all the books and learning, all the reasoning of the Greek philosophers couldn't have taken her there. It was her own true heart that took her. It is near impossible to grasp meaning with our minds. Our minds and all the meandering pathways we travel often times lead us nowhere.

Where I live, there are no secrets—only messages and messengers. There are no crevices where shadows hide. In time, all hole-in-the-corner secrets are brought into the light. If ever you find yourself moved by a song, or by a shift in wind, or by a stranger's words, you would do well to remember it is possibly a loved one from long ago—a mother, brother, aunt, grandmother, child—come to pay you a visit. Some say it be *draiocht*—magic. But if it be magic, only magicians would sense it. When it is your birthright, it is yours to see, touch, and claim as your very own.

Jerome:

Millie and me, we found the creek. We were running fast to see if my sisters were there. But I slipped. I slipped on something hard, maybe a rock and that's when Millie fell out of my hand. After that, I went into a dream and Millie wasn't with me anymore. The creek took me under the ice and showed me things. I saw fish and rainbow light and ice windows and Jack Frost patterns. I didn't have any frozen tingles. I wasn't even cold. And everything looked like a faerie tale. Except I didn't see any faeries.

At first, I was happy under the ice with all the pretty things. Then I wondered where Millie was. I tried to stand up, but my legs were wobbly like baby legs. Maybe a little boy or girl would be walking in the woods and they might find Millie. Maybe her hoof would be sticking out of the ground, or her head hiding behind a leaf and they'd pick her up and say, "You're a little horse. Want to come to my house and play?" But maybe they wouldn't know what to feed her. She likes apples the best, and crumbs. Maybe they'd try feeding her hay. Only I know, she chokes on hay. That made me scared, thinking about Millie and how I couldn't go looking for her because my legs wouldn't move. The ice wanted to show me more things, but I didn't care about ice windows anymore. I just wanted to find my Millie and go home to my Mommy.

After that, a boy came to help me, the same boy who sat in the trees. He told me not to be afraid and that it was somebody else's turn to look after Millie. He told me how he's my brother, but I kind of already knew. Now we go lots of places, Joseph and me. He likes to tease me and ruffle up my hair. He even brought me to see my mother's sad place. I found out it isn't sad. Everyone just thinks it is. But really, it's happy because that's where my brother Joseph first went to sleep when he was a baby. When he was born, he lived two hours, and that's what made Mommy sad.

I don't know why Mommy thought this was a sad place, because Joseph is funny and likes to make jokes. But maybe she never heard him. It's hard sometimes for people to hear things. Dogs hear better than people and so do deer and owls. People don't hear very well, except for my grandma who always hears me. Her name is Mary and she comes and sings songs to me in a different language. I never learned that language, but still I know what she's singing.

Joseph plays with me every day and says I can grow up one day, if I want to. I climb up onto Joseph's shoulders and hold berries from the cranberry tree for the birds to eat from my hands. Sometimes they poke a bit with their beaks, but it doesn't hurt. Sparrows especially come and sometimes chickadees. I like to be up on Joseph's shoulders. Up high, I see swallows flapping their wings, a thousand snowflakes dancing in the air, and at night time, I see Mother's Tears. A long time ago, the teacher lady said I could name the Milky Way whatever I wanted to, so I named it Mother's Tears.

One time, two ladies visited the cemetery place. One of the ladies had long dark hair and the other lady had light curly hair. They sang a song and talked to me. Later, they walked with their arms linked together, reading all the names of people who were written on the white and grey stones. Then a big thunderstorm came. They opened up an umbrella and watched the thunderstorm. Joseph said they would come back. Joseph said they were making a special thing for both of us, and that it takes a long time to make special things.

When the snow melted, the ladies did come back and lots of other people came, too. A white stone was put close to my stone. It has Joseph's name on it because he never had a stone with his name on it before. Our names are together now, Joseph and me. Joseph says the wind blows lighter now, and the wild rose bushes have more blossoms than before, and the sky has more stars. I guess that's because two brothers finally found each other. And because my mother's secret place isn't secret any more.

Postscript:

If you happen to visit the United Church Hurkett cemetery, you may see a plot with a headstone and a footstone, with the names Jerome Morrow and Joseph Morrow. These two brothers, my mother's siblings, have inspired this tale of woe and joy.

ACKNOWLEDGEMENTS

Writing this novel was a journey into many worlds, and those worlds were accessed only through the generousity of many people who were willing to share their time, knowledge, and expertise at every turn. I never would have put pen to paper had it not been for my dear friend, Alanna Marohnic. I will always be grateful to her for her initial suggestion, her spiritual clarity, and her ongoing encouragement. My husband, Gary McMahon, my children—Wade, Rose, and Connor—and my amazing siblings—Philip, Monica, Mary, Andrea, Sean, and Sheena—have been a constant and unwavering support to me. I truly could not have spent the hours, days, and weeks developing this story without the underpinning of family to carry me through.

As this story was inspired by and based on my maternal heritage, I would like to acknowledge my grandparents—my grandmother "Lilly" and my grandfather "Jay"—who raised their large family in the community of Hurkett. I was fortunate enough to also draw on the oral histories of my relatives, whose memories of Hurkett were imperative to the storytelling in this novel. This includes my Uncle Walter Morrow, my late Aunt Irene Morrow, my Aunt Bernice and Uncle Bernard and my own mother, Geraldine Albanese. Also, thanks to Roger Delany and Karen O'Gorman who captured the history of my great-grandmother's role as midwife in their publication, "Natural Helpers in the North." In the writing of this novel, I also drew deeply on my Italian heritage. My vivid memories of my Italian grandparents, and the many connections I continue to have with the Italian community in Thunder Bay have fed my imagination and my storytelling throughout my life, and most certainly in this project. Fiorella Latimer has assisted me on many projects, including this novel, as a translator.

A number of writers and friends including Tony and Wilma Kempe, Monica Storozuk, Holly Haggarty, Alanna Marohnic, Mary Jane Safronyck, Nancy Ewachow, Betty Carpick, and Anne McCourt read drafts and offered their helpful feedback. Expertise has been offered in many areas include Barbara Kemeny (midwifery), Fritz Fischer (Lake Superior fishing), Sita Holland (equestrian), Lieutenant-Colonel David Ratz, CD, PhD (military history), Dr. Michel S. Beaulieu, (military history and the labour movement in Northern Ontario), the many helpful people and historians at the US Army War College Library, Kirsten Spence and Albert Holder (Hurkett history), Mary Frost (Irish culture), Fiorella Latimer (Calabrese culture), the late Jean Morrison (labour movement in Northern Ontario) and Elder Esther Lachinette (Anishinaabe culture). I would also like to acknowledge, in addition to the research already mentioned, the Hurkett United Church Cemetery, the Thunder Bay Museum, and the Carnegie Regional Library in Grafton, North Dakota. Others that have provided their support in a variety of ways include Sonja Obljubek, Mary Veltri, Paula Thiessen, and Jennifer Tett.

Last but not least, my many thanks go out to Latitude 46 Publishing, who embraced the story from the beginning and provided resources to me, most importantly, my editor, Kim

Fahner. Kim offered invaluable feedback and support in the development of the story, in her knowledge of Irish traditions and culture, and in her keen observations that led to a stronger work.